Conscience Point

A novel

by

Tade Reen

"Come on honey

let's get lost

In the long nights, old cars

Backroads and the boneyards

You dropped the pedal like a holy roller

Sheriff of hell couldn't pull you over

Tough girl from the bad town

Brought up not to stay down

Sweet tea, white lightning

Breaking hearts and not minding

Come on in it's so good to see ya

It's been so long I know I know I…

Let's see where the night takes us

Let's see where the night goes…"

Josh Ritter – "Where the Night Goes"

1) Dogfish

Walter would never be able to stop calling a dogfish a dogfish. When he was eight his dad had scoffed at him when he brought home a whopper dogfish in a little igloo cooler.

"Son, that's a toadfish! Doesn't it look like a toad to you? What fool told you that was a dogfish? One of those city boys down at the dock? Dogfish's a shark Walter. That's no shark. It'll bite 'ya though. That's sure." And it did look like a toad. Toadfish have blotchy, pale brown bodies, slimy skin that's covered in mucus and warts, a plump belly, massive flat head, rounded nose, and a tremendous mouth with large, sharp teeth.

Nostalgia dictated that Walter stuck with dogfish.

He knew when you catch a dogfish it's nearly impossible to unhook your line. If a dogfish takes your bait you have three choices, cut the line and let it swim back where it came from, try to rip your hook from deep within the fish knowing you risk a nasty bite as thanks for your mercy, or kill the fish by blunt force, slamming it on the dock. His parents had taught him to value all forms of life, and he did, truly. But when faced with a fat-faced, spike-toothed dogfish at the end of his line, he usually took the third option. Trying to save the ugly thing would end in blood, likely his own, and he couldn't let the fish swim off with his gear. He needed it.

It had been several hours since they'd first baited their hooks, and they had yet to catch a thing. His son sat next to him, legs crossed, quietly humming a Beatles song he must have picked up while hanging around his mother's kitchen. This spring, this was their Saturday morning ritual. After morning workout, they would grab a five-gallon pail filled with water and the killies they'd caught behind their house the night before, grab their fishing poles from the shed, and hop in his pickup truck to make the mile and a half drive down the road to Southampton Shores. They'd stop at the Country Deli, just across from the entrance to "The Shores", and get egg, bacon and cheese sandwiches on hard rolls and a banana for each of them. They'd park in the empty parking lot of the small marina, the crunch of their feet on the pebbles and shells of the parking surface echoing across the empty neighborhood. Seven weekends in a row they'd done this.

Walter had gotten his son a real fishing pole, it was a child's size pole, but still it was big for him. He did well when it came to reeling in a catch, but Walter had to help him cast out. So far, there hadn't been a Saturday where they'd walked away empty handed; they'd caught something, snappers, baby bluefish. But today didn't seem to be their day. They'd leave soon to head over to his mother's house.

Walter looked out across Wooley Pond. It was waiting.

There were only two boats parked at the dock with room for two dozen, and one other moored further out in the center of the small man-made lake off

Peconic Bay. The dock sat just to the left of a celebrity's cottage. To their right was a small private beach, empty now except for the marks left by a gaggle of Canada Geese. Right now, all was silent. The early morning landscapers, had come and gone, their spring cleanup done, the lawns of their clientele mown and the hedges trimmed. Walter could see out to the bay through the mouth of the pond. There were small whitecaps out there, the wind had picked up over the course of the morning. In a few weeks Walter knew the pond would be packed with small boats, kids on paddleboards and clandestine clammers from the neighborhood. Walter understood the "circle of life" in the Hamptons better than most. He was a local with a family who was at the epicenter of daily lives of the summer people.

Each year, on Labor Day the "residents" of Southampton Shores stacked the dining chairs on the table tops, hung sheets on the chandeliers and draped them across the upholstered surfaces, stowed away their outdoor furniture, pulled up the moorings, and packed up their SUV's, heading home to the city, only to return on Memorial Day weekend of the following year. If they weren't having the floors of their beach homes refinished, or a new dishwasher installed, there was no reason to disturb the dust covers until next season. Walter remembered when their SUV's had been station wagons, and the outdoor furniture had been made of that skinny vinyl tubing that had left red marks on the backs of his legs after he and his friends had taken a popsicle break on a lounger. He had been fishing off this dock since he was only a bit older than his son. He'd fished here in every season.

When he was a kid, he'd often show up at the dock in the spring and fall, certain that one of his summer friends would be around. He'd convince himself that their parents had gotten bored with the city, or that his friends' begging to come to "The Shores" to play with him would result in an unexpected fall or winter reunion. It never happened. Disappointed he'd sit with his feet dangling from the dock wondering why he lived in a place where others just spent the summer. Why wouldn't they want to live here all year? What could they be doing in the city? There was no fishing, no swimming, no animals to track, not even any chores to do. His friends told him they lived in apartments with no lawns to mow, fences to paint or chickens to feed. What did they do when they weren't at school? He couldn't imagine it.

Walter wasn't an official resident of The Shores, he lived outside the boundaries of the private community, but he was its foremost expert. A-buzz in the summer with activity and gossip – the houses in "The Shores" were set so close together that every outdoor conversation held above a whisper was a public proclamation – Walter found himself completely alone in the off-season – he explored each one of the two hundred and twenty backyards until he knew every hole, shed, and tree. On lonely off-season weekends, he'd run from swing set to swing set pulling himself up the ropes and chains of the swings and flipping over the cross pieces, sitting on the rooftops of treehouses belonging to his absent playmates. He used the entire neighborhood as his personal obstacle course, doing daring tricks the mothers would never have allowed had they been there to see him.

After blizzards, he loved silently trudging through the snowy yards leaving his footprints in the fresh deep snow, as if he were the lone explorer of a distant planet, or the only person left on earth post-apocalypse. In the early spring, he'd shoot ducks from the backyards of the homes on Turtle Cove and Wooley Pond and bring them home for his mother to cook for dinner.

The spring he turned eleven he worked for months building a fort in the crawlspace underneath the pavilion at the beach. In secret, he dug a wide tunnel that began in a small clearing in the middle of a patch of bushes about twenty yards away from the pavilion, and came up just under its trellised undercarriage. Every day, before and after school, he dug the hole and access tunnel. Once he broke through, he furnished the hideout with milk carton chairs pushed through the tunnel and some boat cushions he'd found in the dumpster at the Peconic Marina. Fort Walter. He was so excited to share it with his friends on Memorial Day weekend that for the two weeks leading up to their arrival he was nauseous. His mother had made him drink a disgusting morning and evening tonic of ginger and lemon water.

That summer he had the best gang. There was Patrick Regan from Manhasset, Jim and Eric Murray from Garden City, and the Spinelli kids, three boys and two girls from Pelham. Walter would arrive in the morning to fish with his friends and then play all day around the community. In the afternoon, they'd either play at the beach, or have games of kickball or basketball at the sports field. As soon as the sun went down, they'd get a big game of "kick the can" going around the pavilion, which was epic fun and usually involved at least twenty kids from around the community. While they played with almost all of the kids in The Shores the secret clubhouse under the pavilion was just for his gang. After "kick the can" they'd pretend to go home, calling "goodbye," and "seeya tomorrow", and then shimmying through the tunnel to crouch together and listen to the teenagers who used the pavilion as a place to gossip, smoke cigarettes and flirt.

It lasted about three weeks. The fun came to a dramatic end when Walter's big brother Tim and his friends were sneaking a few beers in the pavilion one night in early June, and Walter couldn't resist temptation. He crept directly below his brother's high-top Reebok, placing himself at a hole between the floorboards. He shot off a fog horn he'd been hiding in the fort, scaring the crap out of his brother and his friends. Tim, pulled himself through the tunnel and dragged his brother out by his bare feet. He carried him down the beach, kicking and screaming, and tossed him in the water. Once they'd forcibly removed the rest of the gang from underneath the pavilion Tim's friends collapsed the tunnel.

Walter hadn't seen or thought of those Spinelli kids in years. By the time high school rolled around they'd drifted apart. Walter had to work during the summer, and the kids from The Shores weren't always around, even on summer weekends. They had sports camps, girlfriends and boyfriends, and trips to Europe that their parents wanted to take them on before they lost them to college. He would occasionally run into some of his old friends while he was working, or at Flying Point Beach, or the Country Deli. But the connection was lost, the local boy seemed to stay exactly that, while his friends felt their lives expand beyond Southampton and beyond The Shores. He wondered about them while he sat on the dock next to his young son. Things were different now. Kids were under the microscope, even at the beach, their parents terrified they would be hurt or pushed off the path they'd set for them. He doubted his son would find his own little gang here.

Something tugged on his line and he pulled up sharp, feeling the hook find purchase. "Quick, quick, grab the net," he said to his son, who fumbled the net that was too large for him, then thrust it out over the water. "Careful, back up a bit, this is a big one, I don't want you to fall in the water."

He reeled and the fish cleared the surface. Walter knew immediately what it was. A dogfish. And a big one. It was fourteen inches of unhappy. His pole pulled one way and then the other as the wart-covered fish curled itself into a terrible ring of gelatinous brown wrath. He motioned to his son to step back with his foot, it was the only thing that was free.

"Step back my boy, step back, these guys bite. This guy really wants to bite *us,*" he laughed. His son backed up to the other side of the dock, carefully checking that he wasn't going to back right off it. Walter reached out over the water and grabbed the dogfish at the base of the tail, careful to avoid the fins he knew could slice his hand. The fish's underbelly and teeth were facing him and he could see that his hook was in good. He sighed on the inside and then he turned his back to his son and slammed it against the deck of the dock with a brute force many men would hesitate to use. In a moment, the fish's muscles unclenched and it laid prone on the dock.

His son crept forward. "Daddy, it's killded," he said in awe.

"Yes, my boy," he smiled kindly down at his son, "I guess it's a dogfish day today."

"Can I touch it?"

"Sure! Go ahead."

The little boy touched the fish's belly and an involuntary shiver shot through his small body. "Hmmm. Uck," he stood up wiping his hands on his sweatshirt, "Why did you kill-ded it Daddy? You said we should be kind to the animals, honor the birds and fishes and skunks." He looked down at his hand, unable to get the feeling of the dogfish off.

"That's true my boy. But dogfish are tough. They're a little different."

"Well, since he's kill-ded, can we make some soup from him?"

Walter knew that dogfish soup would taste more or less like dog shit soup. But he said, "Sure, let's go make a tasty dogfish stew. Yummy," knowing that after one bite his good-hearted boy would decide that dogfish soup was disgusting. Walter believed that children learn best through experience, and that there were important lessons to be learned from dogfish.

Walter saw certain events in life as "Dogfish" moments. Moments when a man came face to face with a creature that was not only without use, but a danger. There were times when kindness and empathy should rule a man's actions. Most times were those kinds of times. But there were also "Dogfish" moments.

Walter had seen and committed violence, many times. But he had only had one true "Dogfish" moment.

2: The Man Who Was Late With the Vegetables

Rachel Jones stood facing a cool, strong summer wind that had just begun to cut across Peconic Bay. With her eyes closed against the sinking sun she took one deep breath, momentarily rooting herself to the shifting deck beneath her. It was nearly over, and it had been faultless. Frank Sinatra's voice crooned on the speakers positioned on the back of the yacht shuttling her guests from Robins Island to Peconic Marina in Wooley Pond, located in North Sea on Long Island's South Fork. Rachel lithely headed up the steps to the flybridge to thank the captain. Another half an hour, a few more conversations and she would be out of her "casual" cocktail dress, the biggest day of her work year successfully behind her. She longed to shed the dress and strappy sandals she'd put on for dinner and put her dark hair in a ponytail.

Rachel was the Head of Investor Relations & Marketing for Tallmadge Capital, one of the largest hedge funds in the world. Once a year, the weekend before Memorial Day, Tallmadge gathered its biggest investors for a day of entertainment on Robins Island, a private island located in the center of Peconic Bay. The bay, formed by the two long land fingers at the eastern end of Long Island, is easily accessible from the small towns of the "East End". Convenient. Convenient too that Robins Island was owned by Burnham Tallmadge, the founder and president of Tallmadge Capital. Tallmadge normally kept the island as a sanctuary for native plants and animals, preferring their company when he took his respite there, to the company of his fellow East Enders. But once a year he opened up his luxury hermitage to his clients, and it was part of Rachel's job to make certain the event was at once impressive and enjoyable for the elite group who was included.

The guest list was composed of a few representatives from Pension Funds, Family Offices that managed the assets of some high net worth families, Government owned Investment Funds, University Endowments, and Charitable Trusts. The remainder were impressively affluent individuals. Always top secret, the invite list never totaled more than one hundred guests. Those invited never missed the event. It was engineered to be unlike any other they might attend and legendary amongst the small circle who had attended in the past. Rachel had organized it and served as hostess for the past 3 years and she was proud that its cachet had grown during that time. There were other events for lesser investors to attend during the year, but this was *the* event.

As Rachel descended to the main deck, she smiled to herself. Elizabeth Warren in her signature red suit invaded her mind - the Senator was lying in a coffin doing monkey rolls after having been confronted with the scope of the party Rachel had just given. Rachel chuckled. This was her job and she was good at it.

This year, the group was flown from Teterboro Airport in New Jersey to the airport in nearby Easthampton on private jets. They had been shuttled to

Peconic Marina in a series of rare antique and vintage cars, each one matched to the passengers who would appreciate it the most. From there they boarded four mid-sized yachts, much larger than what the marina normally accommodated, for Tallmadge's Island.

The major event today had been a foxhunt, complete with a master, hounds and a fox flown in from Scotland. The entourage had come with a full set of "kits", the traditional riding clothes worn for fox hunts, in every size so that the guests could dress up. "Glamping" tents had been set up and fully staged for changing and pre-hunt cocktails, and as she had suspected, a majority of the guests chose to take part in the charade. It *was* truly a charade because the hounds and fox were a trained team. They had been raised together and trained to create the illusion of a hunt, but they stopped short of the traditional gory ending. Rachel had been a big fan of "The Fox and The Hound" as a kid, plus some of the guests were big animal rights donors. No one really wanted to see a gorgeous fox ripped apart by a pack of hound dogs. But dressing up, riding and making pretend was a complete novelty. Tallmadge had a beautiful stable of horses on the island and guides were available to help guests who hadn't grown up riding take part in the masquerade.

The weather had been perfect, cool enough for the riding clothes with a small breeze throughout the day. Victorian shade tents and elaborately tasseled beach chairs had been set up at good vantage points for the guests who weren't particularly "horsey", and a celebrity chef from the Hamptons, the famous Carlos Duke and his staff, served meals. Guests had been called to the lavish cocktail hour by a bagpiper who placed himself romantically on a rock formation at the tip of the island. They ate fresh clams, oysters and lobster from raw bars carved into the bases of ice sculptures of a fox, hounds and horses, and passed h'ors douvres were served by double-take stunning waiters in kits. Later, one of the entertainments had been a very convincing young Elvis impersonator doing "Hound Dog". Rachel liked to make sure there was something for everyone.

The guests had been ecstatic with the novelty of dressing up, experiencing the horses and the hunt, and enjoying the beauty of the island in the casual setting that had been so carefully crafted for them. Rachel was pretty sure they had all imagined themselves in an episode of "Downton Abbey", the few boats that had been out on the bay had slowed down to wave and wonder.

The day was long and exhausting for Rachel. While a third-party event marketing firm did much of the heavy lifting, planning and transporting, Rachel had to be 'in the zone' all day long with the coveted investors. Rachel was the go-to for each investor, a point of contact for everything. The goal of the event was not simply client appreciation, a chance to give their clients a good time, its purpose was to ensure that they both continued to invest with Tallmadge and to convince them to increase that investment.

Rachel spent the day tracking down some guests to make sure she had connected with each one, while others sought her out early and came with heavy questions. Over the course of the day Rachel had discussed the performance of the underlying securities in the various investment vehicles offered by Tallmadge, future outlooks for those investments, how Fed policy might affect them, macroeconomic trends, the effects of new governmental regulation on the markets, so many times her jaw was exhausted. Rachel knew each of the guests personally, she probably knew far more about each of them than they realized; it was part of her job. She had a talent for couching her sales tactics (a term she *hated*) in genuine conversation about her clients' families, their hobbies and their history.

"How is your favorite grandchild Sofia? She just turned two isn't that right? Did your daughter buy that house in Sausalito?"

"Now you guys just hired Jimmy O'Donnell from Moorton Capital as your Event Driven EM PM. Good hire. Really nice guy too. He knows his stuff. His gamble on the Bimbo '19s is legend. I thought he was completely crazy given the spreads."

"Yes. I did get your message about your grandson Emmett. We can make some calls, but I'm sure he will get an internship somewhere. Goldman might be a stretch. I'm pretty sure you have to be a rising senior. How is he doing at Princeton?"

Rachel was known in her small industry circle for her hallmark friend-giving-good-advice act which always ended with a spectacular finale in which she "closed the deal". It wasn't difficult for Rachel, she genuinely liked most of her clients, she wasn't faking it. She was ninety percent sure she'd manage to procure an internship at Goldman Sachs for Emmett the grandson, and she'd really enjoyed seeing all of them dressed up today, doing their best impressions of British Royalty.

The end of the day was near as the boats pulled into Wooley Pond, the man-made harbor off Peconic Bay that's home to Peconic Marina. The plan from here was to get the guests onto luxury busses and efficiently off to the Airport. Rachel and her team of ten had rented a large house within walking distance just on the other side of Noyac Road. They were going to stay for the weekend, relax, and do a little team building. They planned to begin their celebration of a job well done at The Coast Grill, the restaurant above the marina, just as soon as the busses pulled away. As they neared the marina, Rachel just had to check in with one final client. Stewart Campbell was still on her to-do list. She'd saved the most difficult for last.

Stewart was terribly awkward. He was a nice person, but talking with him was like talking to an android with the demeanor of an in-session therapist; he said next to nothing but seemed to be waiting for you to let something slip that would reveal one of the mysteries of the universe to him. He used those revelations to build software. Stewart had built and sold over fifteen successful software companies in the past twenty-five years. This inventiveness, productivity and entrepreneurial success was even more impressive when you took his odd personality into account. Stewart had asked Rachel out the last time she'd seen him, which added a new element of difficulty in making chit-chat with him. She'd been to his office to discuss some changes Tallmadge had made that might affect his investment, and he'd awkwardly asked her to attend a fundraising event with him the following month. Rachel didn't date clients; it was absolute career suicide. It had been easy for her to decline the few inappropriate invites she'd gotten over the years. In general clients understood that if they asked, she would have to say no, it wasn't appropriate. Not Stewart. The fact that he had invited her to an event so far in the future made her extra uncomfortable. She knew he almost always attended those events on his own. He was good looking, but in an odd way that allowed him to disappear into the woodwork. When he was at a social gathering, he made almost no impression. He'd show up early, have a few robot-shrink conversations with people, watch the festivities from the sidelines, and leave early. She thought the impetus to ask her on a date must have come from a place of real regard for her, maybe even something beyond regard, and that was a no-go for Rachel. She had politely declined as she always did, but she was concerned that she may have genuinely hurt his feelings. It was so difficult to tell with him, and he was an important client. This morning she'd said a quick hello as he'd boarded the yacht and walked away wondering how, if at all, he would participate in the day's events. She could not see him getting on a horse. She *could* see him spending a few hours staring into a horse's eyes searching for an epiphany. She really hoped he'd find something less odd to occupy him.

In the end, Burnham Tallmadge had saved the day. He had noticed Stewart uncomfortably milling around the changing tents and examining a few of the native grasses that grew in the area where the tents had been placed, and he seized the opportunity. Tallmadge wasn't much of a host, he preferred to have the island to himself. Rachel had expected him to spend the day trying to have as little interaction with people as possible, without leaving the impression that he was indeed having as *little interaction with people as possible*. This was Tallmadge's true talent. People were always left with an impression of a kind, intelligent man who was generous with his home. Only his upper-level staff understood that this day was a chore for him and that he would have preferred to spend it silently birdwatching while they carried on running the business he'd spent his youth building. He was, however, an enthusiastic amateur botanist, and when he noticed Stewart's interest in the plants, he saw an opportunity to help out with a challenging client while enjoying the party himself. He took Stewart under his wing, brought him inside and got him outfitted with waders, binoculars, a magnifying glass and a fishing hat and they'd spent the day together exploring the plants on the shores of the island. Rachel had seen them at a distance several times throughout the day talking easily to one another while they examined leaves beneath a magnifying glass. Rachel was grateful. Not only had Tallmadge made the day enjoyable for Stewart, he'd sent him home with a box full of specimens that had occupied Stewarts attention on the short ride back to the marina. They'd give her something to discuss with him. Perhaps their conversation would not be too awkward. She needn't have worried.

"Stewart, how are you?"

"Good, good, I'm good." He was a bit more animated than usual, but it was still like wading through conversational sludge. Rachel dove in.

"I see you brought back some specimens from the island."

She bent over the box to see if there was anything amidst the random blades of grass and bits of leaves that she could actually use as a conversation starter. Aha! There was something in there that looked like a small hard black apple.

"What is that one there Stewart? I don't think I've ever seen those before."

"Oh!", said Stewart with more enthusiasm than she'd ever seen him display. "That's one of last year's black walnuts! It's a bit rotted, that's why it's black. When they're fresh they are the same green as the leaves, that's this leaf here."

Rachel picked up the leaf to examine it. It was a leaf.

"Black walnuts are actually quite rare now, very valuable. In colonial times they were used to make furniture, still are when they can be found, but there just aren't many left. Tallmadge has 6 growing on the island…"

Stewart was cut off by a loud screech coming from the rear of the boat. Rachel looked up and around, she was sure the sound had come from a person, but couldn't see who it was that had made the noise, or what the problem was. But she knew it had not been a screech of delight, that was for sure.

"Excuse me Stewart, I'd better go see if anything is the matter. I'm so glad you enjoyed your day, it was really nice to see you here."

As Rachel headed to the rear of the boat she saw Lauren coming at her moving fast while attempting to appear calm, cool and collected. Lauren was a junior member of the team, and the one she trusted most and relied on to be almost an extension of herself.

"Rachel, we have a problem. Swizzle Hooper was showing her watch to someone, she took it off, the boat jerked a bit as it docked and she lost it over the side," Lauren said as she tried to catch her breath.

"Fantastic!" Rachel said, a bit of sarcasm rippling the surface of her refined but game demeanor. "Valuable?", she asked.

Lauren shrugged, "Well she's upset, so I assume." Rachel made her way to the front of the boat with Lauren behind her, both of them wearing their best party faces.

While most of the guests where now disembarking and heading towards the busses, about a dozen people were tending to Swizzle Hooper. Swizzle was a pleasant but excitable southern woman in her mid-sixties, whose husband Charles "Cooper" Hooper had made his money by developing much of suburban Charlotte, North Carolina. He was also the owner of the NFL's Carolina Panthers. The Hooper family office had more than one hundred million dollars invested in Tallmadge. Swizzle was one of those bird-like, tan ladies of a certain age, whose petal pink nails and stacks of gold bangle bracelets seemed to be all over the place, in constant motion. They were certainly taking up a lot of real estate at the moment. Swizzle had been so taken with her riding outfit she'd asked if she could keep the black Victorian riding hat that was trimmed with a jaunty (and very mobile) feather in the front, and a long black veil off the back. She was wearing it now with the bangles and her brightly colored cocktail dress. Rachel couldn't help but think to herself, "Well…she looks insane…"

"I'm so stupid for taking it off. What was I thinking? That watch was a wedding gift from my Grandma to my Momma. Oh lordy...this isn't good," Swizzle said as her arms waved about, bracelets clinking, black veil dancing in the wind.

Her husband Cooper was a little worse for scotch and annoyed that Swizzle had taken off her watch.

"Ya think?" He said too loudly. Then, he glanced at the hat unsteadily, rolled his eyes, and rubbing his face as if to clear his head. "It's almost dark, you've been drinking, and you are on a boat for the love of Pete!" Rachel had to do something to try to diffuse the situation, it was uncommon for Cooper to be impatient with his wife, and at the moment he was being outright rude and embarrassing her in public. He was also making the other guests, who had remained to help, feel uncomfortable. She just wasn't sure what she could do.

"Swizzle I'm so sorry. I'm sure the water is deep here, and I don't know that there's anything we can do. Let me run inside and see if I can find someone and see what they suggest."

Rachel nodded to Lauren and threw her eyes in Cooper's direction to let Lauren know she would need to be on him while Rachel tried to find a solution. Then she grabbed her phone from the spot she'd stashed it, and made her way onto the dock. She was helped ashore by Stewart of all people, who was looking a little traumatized by the strife between Swizzle and Cooper. He took her hand as she stepped off the boat and then gave it the commiserative pat of an octogenarian grandpa. Good *lord* he was strange.

Rachel had been at the marina last weekend at about the same time of night to solidify the plans for today. She thought there might be a chance the manager would be in the garage, but she found the double barn doors padlocked shut and a note on the door that read "upstairs @ Bar" in green magic marker. Rachel began to move a little faster, there was a time to maintain your image, and there was a time to get things done. This was the latter.

The business of raising money for hedge funds is brutally competitive, and she knew her rivals would use any means that presented themselves to pry the Hooper fortune away from Tallmadge. She could envision Sheldon Kimbal, the short, obnoxious former Ivy League soccer player who held her position at Goldman Sachs Asset Management, and was incidentally one of her least favorite people on the planet, working Cooper Hooper into a rage about the treatment of his wife and her watch at the Tallmadge event.

Cooper Hooper could be touchy. Rachel had capitalized on his famous temper when she successfully diverted the Hooper's money away from a rival fund, Arrow Capital, five years before. Rachel had been courting the Hoopers for some time with no success when she learned from an ex-Goldman colleague that Arrow had invited several of their very high net worth clients to a game at AT&T Stadium, the home of the Dallas Cowboys – competitors of Hooper's Team, the Carolina Panthers. Not only had Arrow not invited Cooper, they had asked their guests not to mention the outing if they happened to speak with Cooper. Cooper was not just the owner of the Panthers, he was their number one fan. Loyalty to the Panthers equaled loyalty to Cooper himself in his eyes.

Rachel had called the family office portfolio manager George. She'd spoken to him at least a half dozen times in the past year, and while he had always been nice, and they'd had some pleasant chats, she'd never gotten anywhere. She knew this time she had a real opening.

"Hi George…I know we spoke just last month and you said that you and Mr. Hooper were all set, but I thought there was a chance Mr. Hooper's loyalty might have shifted with that whole Cowboys gaffe they made last week…" The following month, the Hoopers redeemed their money from Arrow and invested in Tallmadge.

While the Hoopers were now long-time clients, and had been happy with Tallmadge, Rachel couldn't help but be nervous as she rounded the corner to the restaurant at the maximum speed her heels, which were sinking into the grassy lawn surrounding the restaurant, would allow. It had taken her a long time to get where she was: an entry level position in Goldman Sachs analyst program, the move up to High Yield Credit Sales, a Masters at Harvard Business School, then fighting her way up the ladder at Tallmadge. She'd given up a social life that went beyond colleagues, hobbies, sleep, and the moral high ground. Losing a client like the Hoopers would be disastrous for her career. She really hoped someone inside The Coast Grill would have a clue how to retrieve an antique watch from the murky bottom of Wooley Pond.

It was Happy Hour and there were a half a dozen people at one end of the rounded bar. The restaurant was largely empty, seven thirty is on the early side for dinner in the Hamptons and this was pre-season. Several women around Swizzle's age were finishing up happy hour drinks. Rachel had met the trio the weekend before when she and Lauren had been there. They'd chatted with them about their grandchildren and what type of margaritas they preferred. On the other end of the bar, a man with a mustache sat by himself drinking a martini. Through the window that overlooked the marina, Rachel could see Swizzle Hooper and Kurt, a new recruit to her team, chasing that darn hat across the bow of the boat. It must have blown off in the wind. Lauren was handing Cooper a fresh glass of scotch and pointing out the now blooming sunset. Rachel turned back towards the bar and was relieved to see the bartender who'd been there last weekend come through the swinging door to the kitchen with a cutting board of lemons. They'd met the weekend before and Rachel remembered his name was Mark, a local teacher, coach and father, who had worked at The Coast Grill for years as a second job. She thanked *whatever* for her ability to recall personal details after meeting someone so briefly.

Mark noticed her immediately. Her ability to get noticed quickly by the opposite sex was also something that served Rachel well. "Well Hi there. It's Rachel isn't it?"

"Yes, hi Mark, good to see you again, I'm so glad to see you're working tonight, I'm in a bit of a jam…" She explained the situation succinctly and without dramatics. "Do you think there is anything we can do?" she asked.

"I doubt it. They dredged the marina two years ago. It's high tide and now almost twenty feet deep I'm sorry to say." The ladies at the bar took up the cause, "Perhaps there's some type of underwater metal detecting device that could be used. Quickly, because once the tide goes back out, who knows where it will drift." Rachel smiled at them and lifted her phone to look up "underwater metal detector rental hamptons," when the screen door at the front of the Coast Grill swung open and slammed shut. A tall man in work clothes that included a light blue zip-up hoodie which read "North Sea" walked in, carrying a large crate, piled high with vegetables.

Mark saw him, "Did you take the ferry to Connecticut to get that stuff? Next week why don't you wait until nine to drop off the 'locally grown' stuff for God's sake? Take that in to Put-Put, he's getting creative in the kitchen." Instead of taking the crate to the kitchen the man pointedly placed it on the bar, his surfer style curly hair partially obscuring his face as he impishly pushed the crate across the bar to Mark.

"Save it, compadre. My Mom was arguing with my sister and I wasn't headed in there to grab this stuff until that was over. Apparently, my sister wants to hire her friend's daughter from the city this summer to work the cash register, and my mother says the work should go to a local kid who *needs* it." He walked behind the bar, opened a beer, grabbed the remote control and switched the music from a 70's classic rock station to country. He was obviously a regular.

"You should start a TV show. 'As the Farm Turns," Mark said. "Hey there Rachel," Rachel looked up from her phone which wasn't giving her any good news.

"Tell this freak, who just wandered in late with tonight's vegetables, as in the vegetables we need for the people eating here, your problem. If anyone on planet Earth can help, it's this guy," Mark said as he grabbed the crate of vegetables and headed back to the kitchen.

Rachel looked at the tardy vegetable guy and smiled. They stared at each other for a brief moment, wondering who would speak first.

"So what about you, Betty Lou? What's a sweetheart like you doing in a dump like this?" he asked with a wink, trying to annoy Mark who'd just come back through the swinging door to a chorus of "Hurra" in a Spanish accent.

"Easy there chief," Mark warned.

"My colleagues and I just had an event over on Robins Island, and as we were getting off the boat, one of our guests dropped an extremely valuable and sentimentally significant watch off the side. She is a very important guest. I'm not sure how you would be able to help? You wouldn't happen to have an underwater metal detector, would you?" Rachel smiled helplessly at him.

"I can find the watch. But if I do find this watch, you have to buy me, and a friend over there a drink. And you have to hang out with us. Sound good?" he asked as he took a swig from his Anchor Steam. His friend with the mustache at the bar waved at Rachel.

"Sure...how exactly are you going to retrieve the watch?"

"Grab the lady who dropped the watch and meet me on the boat in five minutes," he said as he walked out the door.

Three minutes later, Rachel had Swizzle and Cooper Hooper on the boat, and the other guests and team members were gathered on the dock and bulkhead. The man who was late with the vegetables walked down the dock wearing only a bathing suit and a large pair of diving goggles that looked like they'd been "Macgyvered" across his forehead. There was some sort of light bulb on the front of them, and there were different shaped antennae coming out of both sides. Despite his height and slim build he had a distinct muscularity. This was particularly striking because the muscles of his arms and some of his back were covered in elaborate tattoos. He looked like a carnival freak with a particularly nice body. Rachel pointedly realized her mouth had fallen open a bit and pointedly closed it. "What am I doing?" she thought. She looked at the dock lined with her guests and was thankful that Tallmadge had stayed on the island. She'd just invited a deranged looking tattooed-townie-farmer to salvage her luxury outing for billionaires. He however looked completely confident as he easily hoisted himself from the dock onto the boat, and looked at the trio.

"I hear you lost your watch, darling. Tell me exactly where you were standing when you dropped it, exactly where your arm was, and roughly what time it was," he instructed.

Swizzle answered these questions, and then the man who was late with the vegetables pulled the absurd goggles down over his eyes, hit a small switch on their side, which activated a headlight, and dove into the freezing cold water.

Cooper looked at Rachel accusingly and she looked away into the water. Bubbles came up from where the man had gone under, as the light from his goggles rapidly dimmed.

A minute went by. Then two minutes. The guests on the dock craned their necks attempting to see what was happening. "Who *is that man?*" floated up to Rachel from the dock. "The angel of death come to escort my career to the beyond," thought Rachel. She glanced over at Lauren. Her unflappable assistant's eyes had bulged to roughly the size of limes and were darting back and forth frantically searching the water.

"She's probably composing her resume bullet points in her head," Rachel thought.

Three minutes became five and a panic rose up through Rachel's core that had nothing to do with her career. Where *was* this guy? Had she just sent someone to his death over a watch? She got ready to push the emergency call button on her phone.

Five minutes and forty-five seconds after he'd gone under, Swizzle spotted the light. The first thing to break the surface was a heavily tattooed arm holding an antique watch. The crowd applauded and Swizzle was bent over gasping with laughter, repeatedly hitting her knees with her hands as her bangles danced.

"Oh my! Amazing! How amazing! Cooper, did you see that? Rachel that was amazing!"

The man pulled himself onto the dock, handed the watch to Rachel, who returned it to the overjoyed Swizzle who hugged and squeezed her, oscillating from side to side, giving her a long, loud kiss on the cheek. Rachel was dizzy with relief. She turned to say thank you and stopped short. The man who was late with the vegetables was smiling down at Swizzle and Cooper who were now kissing one another in that way that couples who have been together for decades and still have genuine affection for one another do when something lovely happens. He was silhouetted against a pink and orange sunset, hands reaching up to remove his goggles. He didn't look ridiculous anymore. He looked like he belonged there. He belonged there in a way that no one else on the dock, in the restaurant, or perhaps even the neighborhood did. She took a deep breath and he looked at her. Who *was this man?* He raised his eyebrows.

"I'm going to shower behind the marina, then I'll see you at the bar. You owe me a drink," he said and walked past her down the dock.

Swizzle grabbed her arm, "Who is that *man*, and how long can he stay underwater for?"

"I don't know who he is, or how he can stay underwater for five minutes," Rachel said. They turned together to watch him at the end of the dock where he casually stopped to talk to an employee of the marina, seemingly oblivious to the cold and the fact that a crowd of influential billionaires were marveling at what he'd just done.

3: The 1979 National League MVP

Ten minutes later, Rachel sat at the bar surrounded by members of her team. The buses had gone, and Rachel had her cell phone next to her so that she could see the texts from Raj and Patty, who had escorted the guests back to the planes. She was reasonably confident that nothing else of consequence would happen to the guests before they were safely delivered home. They were corralled on a bus. The novelty of riding a *bus* ought to keep them glued to their seats. She'd ordered a Ketel One martini straight up with olives.

Kendra, a willowy girl with strawberry blond hair who Rachel had hired a few months ago put her tequila on the rocks down with as much force as a person who had grace to spare could do.

"That guy was *amazing, AMAZING!* Is he just some local guy who runs around saving the day? Do they have a small-town superhero at every dock out here? I spent summers on Cape Cod growing up and that is NOT what was hanging around the docks. That was wild!"

She bent over laughing and the sunglasses she'd perched on her head came tumbling off onto the floor. Rachel took a big sip of her martini and a looked at her phone to cover an eyeroll while Kendra retrieved her glasses. Rachel had been unsure about Kendra's place on her team. She didn't like her much. She said *amazing* far too often, and she was one of those women who had the ability to get other people keyed up, leading them to enthusiasm or outrage with a slight gesture or a single sentence. Unpredictable. She might be great at the job. Clients would love the combination of her aristocratic beauty, grace, and slightly less than perfect manners, and be easily infected by her enthusiasm. Or she'd cause a riot. At the moment, in a small bar full of people, she was about to cause a scene. Rachel was regretting the hire. Kendra could easily lead the charge that would have the team making fools of themselves with the mystery of the man who was late with the vegetables as fodder for the lowest kind of girl talk. Mindful of her own reputation and the reputation of Tallmadge, she didn't want them acting like idiots in public.

"Kendra, will you come check the dock with me to make sure no guests left anything behind? They didn't leave under normal circumstances and I just realized something might have been left."

She let Kendra step in front of her as she headed for the door and then turned to catch Lauren's eye. She put her index finger to her lips and shook her head "no". Lauren nodded back, and as always took the cue.

"Hey guys, did you see that Netflix just released the final season of <u>Bloodline?</u> We should binge the whole thing tonight. You've all seen it right?" Thank god for Lauren.

As Rachel caught the screen door at the entry as it swung back towards her behind Kendra, it sprang from her hand as the hero of the evening pulled the handle to come in. His hair was still wet from the outdoor shower behind the marina and he was wearing a fresh hooded sweatshirt half zipped, shorts and flip flops. Rachel was startled enough to exclaim "Oh! It's you!". She didn't like being caught off guard. She'd already composed a "thank you" speech in her head while she'd listened to the sounds of her martini being shaken. But now that she was staring directly into the zipper of his hoodie because he was looming a good two feet above her it seemed formal and inappropriate.

She scooted around him and they turned in an awkward circle so that they were both standing outside on the lantern-lit walkway to the Grill. It was nearly dark outside, and the landscaping that flanked the path was draped with twinkle lights. They seemed a bit too twinkly to Rachel and she realized that the martini was hitting her a little harder than she'd thought it would. She really hadn't eaten much all day, she'd been too busy. Just for a fraction of a second she reached out and grabbed the man's arm to steady herself. She immediately pulled it back a bit embarrassed. Realizing she was being watched she straightened up and turned to Kendra.

"Go ahead without me and let me know if you find anything. Thanks Kendra," she said, her composure returned now that she had assumed her usual role. She then turned back to the man.

"I just wanted to thank you," she said and put her hand out with a practiced formality that she felt would establish a professional relationship with him. He shook her hand firmly.

"No problem sister. You owe me and my man in there a drink!" He smiled and turned her around by the shoulders and pointed her back inside. He walked her up to the man with mustache who'd been at the other side of the bar.

"Rachel, this is Keith Hernandez. Keith, this is Rachel. She owes us a drink!"

"Hello there," Hernandez said as he reached out his hand. "You owe me and Aquaman a drink? That's great news."

Rachel recognized Keith Hernandez before he was introduced. The deep diving man was friends with Keith Hernandez? Keith Hernandez of the Mets? Keith Hernandez of Seinfeld? This night was becoming a *bit much*. Keith had invaded far too many summer evenings during her childhood. Her father had commandeered the family room television in order to watch his beloved Cubs play the Cardinals and the Mets, Hernandez was the first baseman for both Cub rivals and Rachel had vivid memories of her dad shouting profanity at his onscreen image. She also had vivid memories of pathetically trying to bond with her father over the games. Her dad had showed far more enthusiasm rooting against Hernandez's on-field exploits than he ever did for anything Rachel or her sister did. An endless string of academic awards, soccer goals and dance solos were greeted with ambivalence. The rare botched first base play by Keith Hernandez got Rachel a high five on her way back from refilling her father's stiff Manhattan. On those nights there was no chance Rachel would get to watch a summertime rerun of "Dawson's Creek", but she did get the chance to spend a few hours with her dad.

Rachel held out her hand, "Hi Mr. Hernandez, it's so nice to meet you, I'm Rachel Jones. My Dad was a Cub fan and you used to get him very riled up."

"Ha!", he said. "Call me Keith please."

"Sure. And I have to circle back, because although you quite possibly just saved my career, and I'm going to buy you as many drinks as you want tonight, I never got your name," Rachel swiveled toward the man who was late with the vegetables and smiled. The bar area was loud and crowded, the restaurant was packed, and she couldn't find a place to put her body where she didn't feel like her nose was poking into the vegetable guy's sweatshirt zipper. It was disconcerting, because it was a *sweatshirt zipper* and because she thought the last time she'd been in such close proximity to a man wearing one was her junior year in college, *and* because she was actually finding it charming. There was something at once youthful and incredibly adult about this guy. As she motioned to Mark to bring the three of them a round of drinks, she realized the last time she felt this eager to impress someone this dressed down was in middle school when a group of high school boys had come to watch her play soccer. "Rachel," she thought "what is your deal tonight? You don't need to relive all your girlhood fantasies. Just have a drink and get back to your team."

"Allow me," Hernandez said. "Something tells me this might be an introduction for the ages. Rachel Jones," he winked at Rachel, and then made a Vanna White motion as he continued, "meet *Scallop* Kozlowski."

Hernandez paused for dramatic effect so that he could let the name "Scallop" fully land on Rachel.

"Scallop Kozlowski; meet the lovely and talented Rachel Jones."

"Scallop?" Rachel asked. Why would anyone name someone who looked like this man after a gelatinous mollusk? Or name their child that? Obviously, Scallop was not his real name.

"Rachel?" Scallop shot back, mocking her tone.

Hernandez snorted with laughter. "Thanks for the martini Rachel," he handed the other two their drinks. "I'll be back. There are a few ladies over there who must have no idea that the 1979 National League MVP standeth here in their midst," Keith said as he clinked glasses with Rachel. They watched him walk over to one of the dining tables filled with five young women. He pulled up a chair and confidently began talking to them. Scallop rolled his eyes and raised his beer to Keith.

"Character," he said to Rachel.

"I'd say so," she turned back to him. "Is your name really Scallop?"

"Yes."

"Scallop is on your birth certificate?" [SEP]

"I had another name, but I forgot what it was a long time ago. Too much water in the ears."

"I see. What do you do, Scallop?"

"Oh, I am an investment broker," he said, obviously putting her on.

"Is that so? And where do you work?"

"JP Stanley Morgan Bank," Scallop said as he took a dramatic swig of his beer.

"Ahh yes," said Rachel, playing along, "JPSMB. A good shop. And what precisely do you do there?"

"Rachel, now you're just being silly. *Investment brokering.* I broker investments of course! What do you do, Rachel? Party planner for the rich and clumsy?" Rachel laughed out loud.

"Sadly no. I only do that once a year. Hence the bang-up job that brought you to my attention. I'm the head of Investor Relations & Marketing for a hedge fund. Those exhausted looking millennials over there are my 'team members', that's the latest PC term for underlings, just so you know, maybe you call them something different at JPSMB. And we just had our biggest client schmooze of the year. Which went perfectly until the watch incident. Really that would have been a complete disaster if you didn't have super human lungs." [SEP]

"Yes, well, I think you'll find I'm multi-talented. I'm also a brain surgeon. I do surgery on brains. It's fun."

"It must be," Rachel giggled. Flirting was not something Rachel usually indulged in or enjoyed all that much. She felt it weakened her position, whatever the situation she was in. But there was something about batting trivialities back and forth with Scallop that was not only fun but somehow grounding. Scallop wasn't offering her anything about who he was, but standing next to him there was one thing she understood. Scallop Kozlowski knew exactly who he was, despite his joking. He wore his silly sweatshirt because it was comfortable, not to advertise the location of his second home. He wasn't wearing play clothes after a week in a suit. This was a man utterly unconcerned with what people thought of him. Rachel spent her life constantly looking for angles of advantage. She couldn't imagine what it would be like to feel that way about yourself. But she did know that it was nice to be standing in a crowded bar pressed a little too close to it.

Keith Hernandez leaned in between them and handed Rachel martini number three. "Whew," she said as she feigned a feint against the bar. She was joking; but she was pretty sure she'd passed tipsy on martini number one. As she leaned there, she could see her team at the other end of the bar. Kendra and two others were looking directly at her, when she caught their eyes they quickly turned away. "Oh wonderful," she thought, "it's not Kendra who's making a fool of us over this guy. It's me. I *am* like a fifteen-year-old talking to the captain of the football team." She sighed to herself, set her drink on the bar, and drew herself up straight.

"I see you two are getting to know one another. Did Scallop tell you he taught me to surf, how to hunt for ducks and other such fowl in local creeks, how to make a proper bonfire, and, let's see…how to open a beer bottle with my teeth. He also made my dock for me. Scallop is a man of many talents. The last of which he won't let me tell you about," Hernandez said as Scallop motioned for him to stop speaking.

"Now if you two will excuse me, I'm going to talk to Rachel's team over yonder. There are a few young ladies that look like they could use a healthy dose of Hernandez," Keith said as he took a sip of his martini and walked away.

"Don't worry about him. He's joking, and happily married. He'll entertain your underlings though," Scallop said. They both watched as Keith sidled over to the team, blocking Kendra and her cohort from their view and them from theirs.

"Kurt might give him a run for his money. He likes a well-aged mustache," she joked. "I'm still getting over the fact that I just met him. My Dad hated that guy as a Cubs fan. Anyhow, where are you from, Scallop?"

"Across the street. My family has run North Sea Farms for four generations now. I'm also a carpenter. Sort of. But not really. Where do you live?"

"Tribeca. Do you live right there at the farm now?" Rachel asked. She'd never set foot on a farm. The only thing that came to her mind when she thought, "farm," was an image of a hand pulling a carrot out of the ground by its stems set to some cheerful background music. She was fairly sure it had come from a Sesame Street montage.

"No. I live in the neighborhood behind us, sort of, on the beach on the bay. My parents and my sister live at the farm. Where you from, Rachel from Tribeca?"

"I grew up in Winnetka, outside Chicago. But I went to high school at Lawrenceville in New Jersey," she answered.

"Your parents still live in New Jersey?"

"No, my parents still live in Winnetka. Lawrenceville is a boarding school. I don't go back to Winnetka much. My sister lives in California now and Winnetka is, well, there are lots of better places to spend your time than Winnetka. Like here." Rachel was surprised at herself. She rarely said anything even remotely negative about her life. It wasn't part of the happy persona she cultivated for professional purposes. Her dearest friends and her sister knew she'd rather suck on dirty socks than spend time in Winnetka, but she didn't usually share that with strangers.

"Here *is* nice," he said gently as he squeezed her upper arm. As she looked up at his face, she saw an unexpected deep sympathy. She had told him next to nothing, but somehow it seemed he must know about her father's distance, her mother's focus on all the little things and none of the big ones and her sister's escape. Her head swam. She sat down heavily on a bar stool and took a sip of the mudslide that had found its way into her hand again. Open-faced kindness was not something Rachel Jones encountered every day, and not something she particularly trusted.

There was a pungent musty smell in the bar as Van Morrison's "Caravan" could be heard over the din of the restaurant, the same smell that emanates from a summer cottage when it's first opened for the season. It should have been unpleasant, but it was comforting, reminding of the carpet in her bedroom at her grandparent's camp on the lake when she'd been little, where she and her sister had spent hours battling one another in "Uno" tournaments. She looked down at the tiny ice chunks in her drink and she could see Scallop's feet through her glass. Flip-flops. She'd been flirting with the only man in the place wearing flip-flops. Scallop cleared his throat and when she looked up at him he lifted his foot, wiggled his toes, and smiled at her. He's seen her staring at the flip-flops.

"So…what do you do on the farm?" Rachel asked.

"I'm a farmer at the farm," Scallop said. "I do all the things that farmers do. And a bunch of other things farmers shouldn't have to do. But that's another story. What do you do at your job?"

"I raise money, and then I handle the relationships with the people and organizations who give us money. That woman whose watch you recovered, she is a big investor."

"In that case, I tell you what; if you swing by the farm tomorrow, I'll set you up with whatever you want. Peaches, milk, blueberries, chicken...whatever you want, we can charge you double for it." Rachel laughed.

"You said you are also a carpenter? You're a farmer, diver who is also a carpenter?..."

"Yes ma'am. I specialize in docks. Some decks, but mostly docks, rafts and a few small footbridges from time to time but not often. All these things are part-time. I am a full-time surfer, free diver, paddle boarder, hunter, and fisherman. That's what I do. I do something on the water every day. Tomorrow at dawn I'll be out there. Should be a good one."

"Ah, so the hammer and the spade are just a means to an end? We've all rented a house right down the street. Tomorrow we're planning…"

Rachel was cut off by a sound of screeching tires and a grinding crash that sounded as though it had come from feet beyond the grill's front door. Everyone at the bar jumped, or ducked, in shock. Scallop hit the floor, pulling Rachel and two others with him. She looked up and people were streaming out the screen door to see what had happened. She looked around for Scallop, he wasn't anywhere in the crowd that she could see. He was taller than anyone who had been standing at the bar that night, she should have been able to pick him out easily. She looked down at her ruined dress and saw to her surprise the flip-flops laying on the floor. Wherever he'd gone, he was barefoot.

4: The texter from Bronxville

He made a right at the fork in North Sea Road onto Noyac Road, again. Earlier, he'd stopped at Schmidt's Market and picked up fresh oysters, clams, and some other provisions for the weekend. It was getting late, it was getting dark, and it had been a long day. He'd worked a full day in Midtown, then he'd made the commute home on Metro-North to Bronxville. He'd changed, watched the final three innings of his eight-year-old son's baseball game, and then loaded him into the car to get on the road to their summer home in North Haven. Being out in North Haven for the weekend was great. Getting to the house on a Friday night was an absolute slog that he accepted with limited grace. They'd listened to the Yankees game on the radio for a while until his son had asked to turn it off so he could go to sleep. This was fine. It would be great if both his children were asleep by the time he arrived at the house.

He was looking forward to a drink on the deck with his wife when he realized he'd forgotten to stop into North Sea Liquors next door to Schmidt's to pick up the case of wine his wife had asked him to get. His wife and daughter had come out earlier in the day to open up the house, let the must out and the fresh air in, remove dustcovers, put out the patio furniture and make beds. His wife was probably exhausted and he didn't want to let her down by showing up without the rosé she'd be counting on.

Annoyed at himself, he'd turned back. He caught a break and the liquor store hadn't closed yet. Now, twenty minutes later after having left his sleeping son in the car in the dark to run in for the wine, something he hated to do, he was back at the intersection.

The texter had just passed the Country Deli and North Sea Farms when his phone vibrated with a new text message, "Don't forget the wine please ☺." He smiled as he began texting back "Already done!", glad he'd decided to turn back for it. He glanced up from his phone and panic streaked through every nerve, he had drifted into the left lane and an oncoming pickup truck's bumper was just twelve feet off his grille. Instinctually he cranked the wheel to the right hard, as far as it would go, and pushed past the urge to screw his eyes shut and wait to see how it turned out. The car jackknifed off towards the roadside trees and his eyes flew wide, there was the sound of smashing glass and crunching, scraping metal, and an accompanying ripping in his chest, then nothing.

5) North Sea Volunteer Fire Department

Scallop flew through the screen door of the restaurant, Mark quick on his heels. The rear of the Mercedes was visible at the head of the slope on the other side of the road. As Scallop ran across the road he could see the car was on a steep incline and wedged tightly between two trees so that the front doors were pinned in. There was no fire. He leaned across the trunk so he could see into the interior in the dark. The airbags had deployed and the one in the backseat was deflating to reveal a child. Scallop ran around and pulled the rear door open, half climbing into the car to jimmy himself between the child and the airbag. The little boy was unconscious. Scallop placed fingers on his neck, immediately finding a slow and steady pulse. Odds were good he had only been knocked unconscious when the airbag had connected with him. It would be best not to move him until the ambulance came, but when he pushed aside the airbag to discern the state of things in the front seat he decided that the boy needed to be moved before he came to. He checked the pulse of the driver, reaching with difficulty through the branches of the tree that had punctured the windshield and the airbag. The pulse was weak and irregular. Navigating the bristly pine branches that had invaded the cab was difficult. He snaked his arm through them and carefully scanned the man's upper body with his hands, trying to avoid jostling the branches that were scratching at him and snagging his hair, for fear that disturbing them could do the man further damage. His right hand came to an abrupt stop when he found what he'd feared. The man's chest had been stabbed on the left side just below the clavicle and a few inches off the shoulder by a branch about three and a half inches in diameter. Scallop quickly turned back and unbuckled the boy, pulling him out of the car in a single, smooth movement while cradling him, taking great care to stabilize his head. Mark was there.

"Scallop, how can I help?" Mark yelled.

"Come over there and help me lay him down flat on the ground."

Mark steadied the boy's head as they laid him on a flat area out of sight of the car, in a spot where there was some light spilling from a telephone pole. Scallop didn't want the boy and Mark getting hit by Campbell when he pulled the ambulance up to the scene. There was a crowd of people who had been in the restaurant gathering across the street. "If he regains consciousness make sure he doesn't move. Keep him calm and laying still until the guys get here. Distract him from the car. When they come tell them that the airbag deployed."

Scallop took off running back across the street to the parking lot. He ran over to a red four door pickup truck that had seen better days.

SCALLOP KOZLOWSKI DOCKS
NORTH SEA FARMS
631-283-9517

The lettering was barely visible on a dirt streaked magnetic decal on the side. He reached through the open passenger side window and grabbed his surfing socks, pulled them on and launched himself into the bed, wrenched open a newer looking toolbox that spanned the width of it, and pulled out an axe which he quickly put down, followed by a chainsaw, and then a flashlight. He gathered the tools and jumped out of the bed and ran back across Noyac Road shouting "We need the ambulance" to the crowd. He was going to have to take down the tree that was prohibiting him from opening the driver's door.

Scallop reached around the maple tree and through the driver's side window which had been smashed by a pine branch from the inside, and then balanced the flashlight on the misshapen dashboard. He pointed it right where flesh met pine, and then positioned himself where he could both see and get a good angle on the maple's trunk. It was about an inch and a half away from the door and about two feet wide. He took up the ax and took a light swing at the tree keeping his eyes on the spot illuminated by the flashlight. The force of the strike did not disturb the pine branch jutting from the man's chest and he was free to use fast force.

He dropped the ax on the ground and started the chainsaw. He reached under the car and cut down with the best angle he could achieve while still keeping the notch below the level of the door, "Had to have the s-class didn't you?" he thought, "not something less sexy like a Toyota 4-runner. Much too much ground clearance there." He brought the chainsaw around to the left side of the tree and starting almost at the ground he cut upwards toward his first cut. The moment the two cuts met he quickly stood and rammed his right elbow between the tree and the car to and used his full body weight as a fulcrum to ensure that the tree slid down his cut away from the car, instead of falling on top of it. The tree toppled and he put the chainsaw down about fifteen feet off the car, the ambulance to the side of the road even with the wreck, and he could see the lights from one of the firetrucks right behind, he didn't want his chainsaw tripping anyone. His old friend Jenna, who he'd been on duty with every Wednesday night for the past few years, was the first EMT to make it over to the car. Jenna looked like she'd been pulled away from taking a shower, her short blond hair sticking up in spikes as though she hadn't had time to wash the soap out. And she was not wearing any makeup. Blue eyeshadow had been Jenna's thing since high school. She shined her flashlight where Scallop had pointed his. She looked quickly up at Scallop.

"The bleeding's not too bad, at least not on the outside. You think bolt cutters? A saw will vibrate too much." Scallop nodded.

"We'll have to try not to move that branch, and as soon as he's free we've got to move." The EMT on the squad was just arriving with the stretcher and a blanket. "Run back for another blanket and bring bolt cutters. They don't need hoses."

She grabbed the folded blanket off the stretcher and ran around the car to the passenger side. In the headlights she could see that the ancient lichen encrusted pine had skewered the windshield as the car came down the slope. She pointed her flashlight at Scallop so she could see his face.

"What do you think? This looks like the best angle to cut from. Steady the tree so it won't pull if we don't cut through on the first try. I don't think that will happen, there's more than that branch holding it in place on the hood. You and Jason can be ready to get him on the stretcher."

"Yes," was all he needed to say. Jenna took the blanket and used it to push the tiny bits of glass that were on the hood of the car off to the side, most of the glass had gone into the cab, and then laid the blanket out across her side of the hood so she could reach through the branches with the bolt cutters. The other members of the rescue squad were there by then, and Scallop handed her the bolt cutters. He'd filled the others in, who were poised under the tree to catch its weight if it shifted. Jenna reached in and cut the branch easily with the cutters. Scallop had his eyes glued to the remainder of the branch sticking out of the driver's chest, and when she cut it the branch shifted enough to open up pathways for the blood that it had been previously holding in. It was coming fast and heavy and just moving him meant that Scallop's sweatshirt wasn't going to get much further use. Exactly what he'd feared, heavy bleeding meant they would have to remove the stick in the ambulance. Scallop climbed into the ambulance with the rest of the team and the ambulance pulled away from the scene.

Rachel watched a bloody Scallop Koslowski jump into the ambulance and close the doors just before it pulled away. She was shaken by what she'd just witnessed. It was a brutal display of bravery, quick, clear thinking, strength, skill and some kind of training. The man who was late with the vegetables had saved the day again, this time for a father, a son, and their family, forever. Hazily she wondered at the trust the first responders had shown him, and that he had left with the ambulance. Did he know the victims? She didn't think he had mentioned "fireman" as one of his many part-time employments, but at this point she was in no condition to remember every word of their conversation, all of which now seemed inexcusably silly. One of the fireman was telling the crowd that the man and his son would be taken to Southampton Hospital, and that for the next few hours police and cleanup would be on the scene, if they wanted to head out without having difficulty navigating emergency vehicles, *now* would be a good time to do it.

Rachel turned to Lauren. "We should call the drivers." Lauren was just hanging up her phone. "All set Boss." Lauren said with a sympathetic smile. "That was pretty intense. I think we could all use a change of venue. We can have a nightcap at the house, we're all stocked up. I'll just run in and settle the tab."

"Guys, the cars are on the way, let's just stand on the edge of the back lawn there out of the way of the driveway and the emergency vehicles." Rachel waived her team over to the edge of the parking lot, near Scallop's truck. She stared at the bumper stickers and decals on it, "Local", "NS", and another one that was two shotguns forming a cross. She couldn't believe she was doing it but she stealthily peaked into the truck. In the backseat was a net bag full of child's beach toys and a paddle and in the front seat there was a canteen and one or two scattered CD's. Nothing that told her anything beyond what she'd learned talking with him. She leaned her back against the dirty bed of the truck. The front of her dress was already covered in wine, the back might as well be covered in dirt. Kurt walked over and silently offered her a cigarette. She hadn't had one since one of the drunken nights at the end of her senior year in undergrad. She took it.

Two SUVs pulled up and the team climbed in. Rachel was the last and was ducking her head to climb in when she felt someone grab her shoulder. Keith Hernandez stood behind her holding a martini.

"Rachel. I'm leaving. It was a pleasure to meet you. Life is weird. Enjoy the ride and have a great rest of the evening. Trust your gut. Stay with it. Don't judge it. See where it takes you. You might like it. The 1979 National League MVP is calling it a night," Hernandez said as he popped a Marlboro Red in his mouth and walked out onto the road heading off into the night carrying his martini.

Rachel's mind drifted on the short ride home. She'd excuse herself as soon as they got back to the house. She was done for the night.

6) Flying Point

Six AM, and the new agey spa music Rachel had set on her phone to serve as her alarm was keening in her ear. It was a long running personal joke she had with herself. The goofy tuneless music kept her from being too pissed off every morning when she had to wake up and then launch full throttle into the day. This little part of her routine made her feel relaxed. It was a ritual she'd started in her early twenties when she was getting up at four-thirty to hit the gym and be the first at her desk at Goldman. But it wasn't working today. She vaguely recalled setting the alarm to wake her before the rest of her team when she'd come in last night. She'd noticed her bag had been delivered by the party planning team as she'd pulled off her dress and climbed into bed. She wanted to be the first up this morning for a couple of reasons. She had the master bedroom in the rental house, but she didn't want to be caught wandering around in dishabille. Also, she wanted everyone to enjoy the rest of the weekend, but she felt like it was always important for her to maintain a slight separation between herself and her team, she was the boss. She planned on getting out and going for a run on the beach before they all crawled out of bed, which she expected would be fairly late. She was sure they'd stayed up after she'd said a hasty good night and thank you the night before.

She turned down the spa alarm but left the music on and slowly sat up. She'd felt better. How had she managed to go from total triumph to a confused boozy mess who was watching the man she'd spent the evening flirting with wielding an axe by the light of flashers?

She looked around at the large ultra-modern room and out through the three gigantic floor to ceiling windows that revealed a picture perfect view of the bay. Everything in the room was the same shade of bright white, but heavily textured. The only thing that was the wrong color was her camel leather weekender bag which was sitting on a molded wool chair in the corner. "Womb chair," Rachel thought automatically. Her mother was an interior designer, a particularly well-known one, although not as well-known as she thought she was. Her mother's constant chatter about furniture and finishes had given Rachel the ability to recognize designer pieces on site from the time she was thirteen. Rachel resented this involuntary recognition. It was a complete waste of her brain space and a constant reminder of her mother's focus on form over substance in all things. She plodded over to her bag, taking note as she went that her pedicure also did not match the décor, and pulled out her running clothes. She still ran in soccer shorts. Drafty polyester and a sporty stripe made her feel like herself. She unlocked the huge sliding door and carefully pushed the giant piece of glass sideways. She was greeted by a light sea breeze that cleared a bit of the fuzzy feeling from her head.

Summer. Even though Rachel's weekly routine altered very little with the seasons these days, she still loved summer and the feeling of freedom that came with inhaling warm, damp air. Thrice weekly yoga classes had made Rachel a big believer in taking a deep breath in just about any situation. A run would clear out the rest of the booze sludge she could feel coursing through her system. She thought some time alone on the beach would also banish the images of "Scallop" grimacing, wild, and blood spattered as he closed the doors to the ambulance last night. It was playing on repeat in her brain interspersed with the image of yesterday's guests playing dress up in Victorian riding clothes.

When she stepped out into the hallway she had a bird's eye view of the common spaces downstairs. As she'd hoped, no one else was stirring. She rolled her eyes. White. Everything white. Not her taste at all. She'd let someone else handle the rental house. It was walking distance to The Coast Grill, large enough for the whole team, on the water, and it had a pool, but she preferred something more traditional and comforting. "Honestly, Rachel, it really doesn't matter for the purposes of this weekend," she told herself.

She was relieved to see that her car had also been delivered to the driveway as she'd requested. She drove down the street headed towards a deli she'd noticed when they'd been there the weekend before. While Rachel had spent lots of time in the Hamptons she wasn't terribly familiar with this area. Her ex-boyfriend Tucker's family had a large house in Amagansett and she'd spent many summer weekends there. She passed what she assumed was North Sea Farms on her way. The only signage was a painted plywood cutout of a chicken. Decades ago it had probably been bright hues of red, mustard and green, but faded from years of exposure to the sea air, it was now barely legible in shades of shabby chic grey. Despite herself she checked the sandy parking lot for Scallop's truck. Not there. He was probably recovering from the previous night, not picking strawberries. Was it time to pick strawberries? She had some vague idea that it *might* be.

She pulled into the small parking lot of the Country Deli. It was a small, neat Cape Cod style building on the side of the road amidst small side roads and driveways that lead to summer homes. While she was the only customer at the moment, the little deli still felt cramped. As packed as any Bodega in Queens, bags of chips, packages of cookies, and single items of miscellanea were stacked nearly to the ceiling. A tall blonde woman in her early twenties was behind the counter.

"Can you tell me how to get to Flying Point Beach?" Rachel asked after she ordered her coffee and fruit salad. The woman gave her directions in a Russian accent and rang her up. Somehow coffee, a little salad and a Wall Street Journal had come to fourteen dollars. Rachel thought she was perhaps in the wrong business. At least the coffee was good.

When she stepped out of the car at the beach she inhaled deeply a familiar heady floral scent and was choked by a sudden wave of sadness. It was sudden, but not shocking. Last weekend she'd had such an easy time being here, she'd thought she would be fine going forward. Apparently she'd been wrong. What she was smelling was the omnipresent little white flowers that grow over every unmanicured inch of roadside in the Hamptons. Her early morning summer runs in Amagansett had always been accompanied by them. Rachel thought they were some type of rose, but she really didn't know anything about flowers. Whatever they were they smelled wonderful; like summer, fertility, sex, and innocence all at once. The warmer and sunnier it got the more their scent filled the air. They weren't in full bloom, it was too early, but she could smell their beginnings.

It had been two years since her sudden, painful and embarrassing breakup with her ex-boyfriend Tucker. Since then, she hadn't spent much time at the beach, devoting herself to work instead. When friends from college took summer Friday's off and planned their lives around their vacation time, Rachel worked. She'd all but stopped dating. Dating was time consuming, and when the end-result was a lot of time invested in a man who at best she would have happily traded for a good glass of wine and a good book, it just didn't seem worth it. Most men she met were either clients, which of course was a no-go, or otherwise connected to her career. She didn't want to date in the industry. Keeping herself to herself was one of the ways she'd gotten as far as she had. She felt like letting her guard down now might jinx her. If her success faltered, so would she, and so would the success of her firm and her clients. She felt responsible for the people she worked with and the clients. She was making nearly four million dollars a year, and was recognized around the industry as one of the best, if not *the* best, in the business. It was what she had worked for with single minded purpose since she left college. Sometimes she wondered at people who had some grand plan that was incongruous with their careers. She didn't understand working at a career in finance so that you could one day be a painter or an organic farmer. She worked as hard as she could because being good at her job and being respected was her only end-game. She was self-aware enough to understand that that was not necessarily a normal way to be.

It was part of her job to travel to meet with investors at least two weeks out of every month, which was both grueling and tough for anyone she might date. Tucker had been around as she had risen through the ranks. He'd seemed not to mind her traveling, her focus on work, or her disinclination to build fanciful castles in the sky around their future. She'd thought it was because they had such a solid relationship. Tucker was the champ of listening to a blow-by-blow of her work day, and making helpful suggestions. He had an intelligence that spanned disciplines. His family money came from food manufacturing and while he chose not to participate directly in the business, he managed the family fortune himself. But he did it in a quiet way, as if it took no effort. On a daily basis he was an art dealer. He could have been managing a fund, but he wasn't interested. He'd shared his instincts with Rachel. She hated to admit it now but Tucker's family connections had helped her a bit here and there in her career. Before their breakup she never doubted that the progress she'd made in her career was due entirely to her own merits. But their breakup had made her doubt a lot of the things she'd been sure about before.

She crossed 'The Highway', the main access road to all the villages in the Hamptons. She'd taken this road so many times on the way to Amagansett with Tucker. She'd taken it the last time she'd been there and had avoided it since, burying her head in her laptop when her driver had brought her out for last summer's investor event. She'd decided to bring her own car this year, drive "The Highway" and just *move on*.

She'd met Tucker Pennington during her first semester at Harvard Business School. He'd slid unnoticed into a bar where she and some friends were having a study break via tequila. He'd known one of her friends from Bowdoin undergrad and was able to talk shop as though he'd just sat through their Financial Reporting course with them. But it turned out that he was studying Anthropology and Archeology. Tucker was almost too handsome, one of those guys it was difficult to look away from once you started. Tall and wiry with green eyes and dark hair, cut in a conservative, almost old-fashioned style, and without any styling products. His clothes were one hundred percent tucked-in, well-worn Brooks Brothers, as though despite his good breeding he didn't really care how he looked, but like someone who loved him did, and it was they who periodically made sure he had the wardrobe he needed. Rachel learned later that this was, in fact, a look Tucker carefully cultivated. It was the one thing that she'd found annoying about him when they were together. He was charming, interested in what other people had to say, and in things that Rachel didn't bother to spend any time on. Within three months of that night in the bar they were dating, juggling grad classes, his business, weekend trips to Amagansett in the summer, and museums and gallery openings on the other weekends. Everything with Tucker was easy.

The one thing Rachel *did* imagine was that they would always be doing just what they were doing. Tucker talked about marriage and kids, he'd started talking about it three months in. Rachel found his complete certainty that they would one day be raising children and hosting backyard barbeques comforting. When they were together at the beach house she could see how easily that could come to be. She'd always felt comfortable in the grand cedar-shaked beach side "cottage" that was always filled with a rotating crowd of Tucker's family and friends. She could see herself sitting by the pool handing out goldfish crackers to wet little people wrapped in bright beach towels, a sleeping small head pressing against her chest while she read a book under an umbrella. Never mind that in all her weekends at that house she'd never sat still long enough to read under an umbrella.

In their three years together Tucker never pressured her to get on with it and he never officially proposed. Pregnancy wasn't something Rachel was eager for. She'd seen it derail the careers of superiors at Goldman Sachs. A big wedding wasn't all that savory a thought either. Her mother would make the planning and the day a horror show for her, and with Tucker's family and the sphere of people who were important to them, elopement wasn't not an option. When they were done at Harvard they'd moved into a large shared apartment on the Upper West Side. Rachel had felt like she truly "made it". Now Tucker was married to someone else and had six-month-old twins.

The sun was low in the sky just above the horizon, the day was definitely going to be warmer than yesterday. There was almost no one on the beach. Just a few people letting their dogs play in the surf despite the "No Pets" signs in the parking lot. The waves were high and powerful enough to have cut away the base of the beach to create a three-and-a-half-foot cliff where the beach met the water. A Black Lab and a Doberman were taking turns hurling themselves over the cliff in pursuit of their sticks. Rachel loved watching dogs. She'd never had a pet. She remembered once when she was about six or seven, watching her mother attack a cat-owning guest with a lint roller before the unlucky woman had a chance to sit down on her mother's hand felted wool sofa in their den. She never dared to ask her parents for a dog, she knew it was futile. Rachel turned to run backwards a few times not wanting to miss out on any joyful canine acrobatics. After a mile and a half, Rachel slowed a bit, running with the water on her right was making her left ankle fatigue. She had an old injury there that she tried not to overstress. On this end of the beach there were a few surfers out on the water. They were staying fairly far out from shore, and their distant grace was just as pleasant to watch as the dogs. She *was* feeling much better. The sound of the surf had married with the hangover buzz in her head and carried it away in the wind. Someone, probably one of the surfers had driven a pickup truck out onto the beach. A small boy was climbing up onto the tailgate and jumping off into hole a large hole that had been filled with sea water. There was a woman sitting on a blanket trying not to get sprayed with sandy water each time the boy splashed down. As Rachel closed the distance between herself and the truck she was shocked to see "Scallop Kozlowski Docks" emblazoned on the side. It was Scallop's truck. Could that crazy man really be out there surfing right now? He'd had cuts all over him and gone through a physical and emotional ordeal last night. Not to mention it was unlikely he'd gotten home before 2 or 3 in the morning. It was barely 7am.

The little boy was digging in the sand, shoring up the edges of his personal pool with a shovel, as Rachel took off her headphones to approach the pair he shielded his eyes with his shovel to look out at the surfers. Rachel walked up to the woman.

"Hi there! Good morning. I met the man who owns this truck last night briefly and I just wanted to make sure he was ok after the accident last night, are you here with him?" Rachel sheepishly asked.

"Yes, he's fine. Fine enough that he's out there surfing. He had a few cuts and most people would have gotten some stiches, but he is fine and, more importantly, the driver and his son are fine. They were very lucky," the woman said. "I'm his sister, Lucy."

Lucy looked exactly like Rachel would have imagined a sister of Scallop Kozlowski would look. She had long blond curly hair that was parted a bit to the side and loosely braided. She had the type of muscular build that Rachel envied in good yoga instructors, although Rachel doubted that Lucy spent too much time in a bikram studio. Her long neck and legs and the air of belonging to that beach that she carried made her plain red tank bathing suit and the white men's oxford she was wearing as a cover-up look positively fashionable. Rachel was glad she'd met her while she was in her low-key running gear instead of one of the fussy bikinis she'd spent more hours than she wanted to admit shopping for.

"Hi, I'm Rachel. Nice to meet you."

"Likewise," Lucy replied as she sipped her coffee and squinted as she took a drink. "Oh, Rachel?! Are you the girl who had the difficulty with the tipsy billionaire's wife and a watch last night?"

Rachel nodded and Lucy rolled her eyes and then looked more closely at Rachel's face. "He mentioned you. Do you think he showboated down there when he was finding that watch? I'll bet he did. He probably found it in 30 seconds and stayed under for 20 minutes to cause a spectacle." She smiled as though she would have done the same if she'd had the chance.

Rachel laughed. "I don't know. But he absolutely saved the day, so he's maybe entitled to show off a little."

"He also mentioned that he'd been startled at the sound of the accident and that he took you down with him. He was afraid he might have hurt or scared you."

"It wasn't a big deal," Rachel brushed it off. "The sound was terrifying and weird. I didn't understand at first what it was. He could have thought we were under attack or some drunk idiot was driving right into the restaurant."

"Yeah," said Lucy. "But Scallop was a Navy Seal in Afghanistan. He knows how to throw his weight around.... Do you want to sit down for a few minutes? We've been here a while and they might come in soon. I bet he'd like to see you're unblemished." A Navy Seal, Rachel thought to herself. That explained quite a bit.

To her own surprise Rachel said, "Sure." And sat down next to Lucy on the red plaid blanket that looked as though it had been making trips to the beach since around 1974. Something about Lucy made Rachel feel comfortable, "It must be a family trait.", Rachel thought. "Do you surf?" Rachel asked.

Lucy scoffed. "Not any more. I used to, every day. Scallop and I used to get up at the crack of dawn, do our chores at home and then ride our bikes over here. He was in elementary school! If there were waves we'd surf until the last minute, change in the bushes where we kept our boards, and bike to school. This place wasn't crawling with people back then. We just left our boards there from April until October. Sometimes I can't believe that no one gave us a hard time about it. Scallop was pretty young to be out surfing with just his big sister. But we never had a close call, and no one ever said 'boo.' We had a good time. I could probably still do it, but I have two daughters who need me to be in good condition. I feel like doing anything risky is a poor parenting choice. Maybe that's just my excuse, and I've really become a wuss in my old age!" Rachel laughed, Lucy did not strike her as a wuss.

The little boy walked up to Rachel, "Look. I have a shovel and I dug a hole."

"I see that you did. That is a big shovel and the hole is great," Rachel said back with enthusiasm. He was striking looking. He had very dark skin, blue eyes, and long blonde hair.

"My name's Kosumi," the boy said.

"Hello Kosumi. My name is Rachel."

"Kosumi was up late last night. Weren't you Kosumi?" said Lucy.

"I stayed up late with Grampa. I watched baseball and I had ice cream. And I slept in the bed with Grandma and Grandpa," Kosumi said. Rachel guessed he was three and a half or four. He was very well spoken for his age, no baby talk or missing sounds, he spoke clearly and with excitement.

"Yes, you did! And that is going to make you very tired today Kosumi. You need a nap today big boy," Lucy said.

"OK!" Kosumi shouted as he jumped into the hole and sprayed Lucy with water. Lucy shrugged good-naturedly at Rachel.

"Are you here for the weekend or for longer?", Lucy asked.

"Oh, just for the weekend. I had that work event last night and we rented a house for my team for the weekend. The event takes a lot of work, so it's nice to give them a break and a chance to celebrate a bit before we launch back in on Monday. I used to come out here every weekend though during the summers, but not the last few. I travel a lot for work. It would be nice to spend a little time at the beach though this summer. I'd forgotten how much I like it, especially at this time of day."

"Euff," said Lucy, "I travel across the lawn for work, and that's how I like it."

"You work at the farm?"

"Yup, I basically run the business side of things at this point. My mom still does a lot of work with the crops and in the store, but she really needed to be released from the accounting and supply management, so I do that now. My dad isn't in condition to work much anymore. I live right at the farm so that I can be there for them."

"You know," said Rachel, "I'm a little embarrassed to say I've never set foot on a working farm. I've been to an animal sanctuary benefit where they paraded around a couple of sheep but that's the closest I've come. I don't really think that's the same thing…"

"Well, it's thrilling, let me tell you," Lucy said with a sarcasm that had no ill-will behind it. "Why don't you stop by later today? It's the end of the strawberry season and you don't want to miss them. The waves are so good, I think we could all be sitting here waiting for Scallop to come in until lunch! Come by and he can apologize for putting you in the dirt." Rachel could tell that this was a genuine invitation, not a sales pitch for the farm's strawberries.

"Sure," she said. "I bet the team would love some strawberry shortcake if I could figure out the shortcake part. I'm not much of a cook."

"Shortcake!" Shouted Kosumi as he leapt, limbs flailing into his hole.

Lucy laughed, "I think we can help you there too."

"Ok, well, I'll come by later then. You'll be there?"

"Absolutely, there's not a Saturday afternoon in the summer where you'll find me anywhere else."

"Alright, I'll see you later then."

"It was nice to meet you, Rachel."

"It was really nice to meet you too. Bye Kosumi!"

"Bye bye Rachel. I want you to stay!" Kosumi ran over and hugged Rachel's leg. "Wait, I have a present for you!" He ran around his hole and began sifting through a beach pail. He ran back over with a clam shell. "Here! This is for you. You can use them to drink soup like the native people did! It tastes the best."

"Thanks Kosumi. I love soup! This is the perfect present for me."

"Bye!" Yelled Kosumi as he jumped again.

Rachel smiled at Lucy and then set off running the way she'd come. She held onto the clam shell, pressing her thumb into the inside of it as she ran. She knew she should probably toss it aside once she was out of sight of Kosumi, it might make her car smell terrible. But she wanted to hang onto it.

Rachel ran back down the beach toward Flying Point with renewed energy. She knew she should head back to the house but kept going all the way past Coopers Beach and back as her iPhone cranked to her running mix. Peter Gabriel's "Solsbury Hill" played.

"So I live from day to day, though my life is in a rut…"

She pressed the shell into her hand harder. Rachel hadn't felt like she was in a rut when she'd gotten here this weekend. For the last few months she'd actually been seeing herself as a survivor. She'd survived and escaped her uninspired childhood. She'd survived the trap of being pigeonholed as a "pretty girl who was not much more than that", that she'd seen other young women in her industry become ensnared in. She'd survived her relationship with Tucker ending.

Once riding in the car with Tucker they'd listened to a Ted Talk on the radio in which a psychologist spoke on how the human brain works. Her theory was that the person that you are is just as much about the story of your life that you tell yourself in your head, as it is about your genetics, and what we traditionally think of as our "personality". While she ran, Rachel considered that perhaps she'd been telling herself a lie. Was she really happy? Or did the fact that she didn't have a vision for her own future, beyond doing a good job and making a certain amount of money, mean that she was afraid of something? Maybe she just had a hangover, but as she watched the waves cut into the beach she realized she was actually *looking* at her surroundings and *listening* to people in a way that she hadn't since she'd been in grad school. Being a survivor wasn't much. It probably wasn't enough.

7) Turtle Pond Road

When Rachel walked into the living room of the rental house it was looking far less stark then when she'd left two hours before. There were coffee cups and half eaten muffins on the coffee table, Raj and Trevor, still in their pajamas, were lounging on the couches reading and colorful beach towels were stacked in a pile by the door out to the pool. Trevor, the one member of her team who was older than her, stood when he saw her come in. Trevor had been at Tallmadge for over twenty years. His husband owned a successful gallery downtown, and Trevor was the dominant parent of their four year old daughter. While other men might be embarrassed to be on a team with a bunch of kids twenty years his junior, Trevor was just fine. He did a great job for Rachel and he was a perfectly contented guy.

"Rachel, there's breakfast in the dining room, can I get something for you?"

"No, it's alright Trevor, I can get my own breakfast." She smiled at him. "Anything good in there?"

He raised his eyebrows and followed her into the dining room. Breakfast was spread out across the table. Quiche, bagels with all the fixings, salad, muffins, coffee carafes and juices had all been delivered by the party planning company while Rachel was out. Someone had set up a well-stocked Bloody Mary and mimosa bar. Waving her fingers in a circle over the bottles of champagne jutting out of an ice bucket she asked, "Who put *this* together?"

"Who do you think?" asked Trevor. They smiled at each other. They had a good natured joke about Lauren being the *perfect* next Rachel. "My Lady?" he asked as he held up a Champaign bottle.

"Well, I've had your Bloody Mary's before, why don't you mix me up a *small* one?" Through the window she could see the pool. Kurt was sprawled out on a pool float in a speedo, which Rachel was sure he'd brought as a joke, drinking a Corona. Kendra floated into view doing the same. Rachel was relieved to see she was *not* wearing a speedo. She wouldn't put it past Kendra to be out there floating topless while her coworkers looked on. Rachel looked down at her soccer shorts. She'd been hoping to sneak in and change into something that was better than this, but she realized that right now, she didn't care if her team saw her in her soccer shorts.

"Well," Rachel chuckled to herself, "The ship has sailed on the teambuilding exercises I was planning." She turned back to the table and cut herself a generous slice of quiche and filled her plate with salad. She'd been planning on working with the team doing some new team building exercises she'd just read about in one of her books on good management. But, really if she was honest with herself she thought that some slightly buzzed poolside bonding would accomplish the same thing. She'd been a little infected by the Hamptons vibe, and she hadn't expected to be. It was warmer than it normally was this early in the season, and she really just wanted to sit with her feet in the pool and read the paper, she decided.

"You know Trevor, I don't think we're going to do what I thought we were going to do today. I know John and little Bella are probably at your house in Sag Harbor, if you want to go home and be with them it would be perfectly fine. You shouldn't feel obligated to stay."

Trevor rolled his eyes. "Are you kidding? *This* is the most debauchery I've seen in years. AND Kurt's wearing a speedo!" He winked at her. "You know what's happening in Sag Harbor right now? A wrestling match over putting on spf 75 sunscreen. I told them I was required to stay here the whole weekend and that's the story I'm sticking with."

"I gotcha. Thank you sir!" She said as he handed her a bloody Mary that wasn't small by anyone's standards. She headed out the giant slider to the deck. Lauren was arranged on a Danish modern chaise under an umbrella, both white of course. She had on a perfectly fitting navy blue one piece and a hat to match which suited her red hair and freckles. She had a small table next to her stacked with today's papers and some magazines. Rachel kicked off her sneakers and pulled up another chaise. She put her copy of The Wall Street Journal on top of Lauren's and pointedly put the bloody Mary down next to it.

"You?" she asked Lauren. Lauren smiled with the confidence of a friend who knew she really couldn't do any wrong in Rachel's eyes. Rachel pursed her lips, "Were you trying to make sure that no one had the ability to do any work today?"

"Please," Lauren said and took a sip from her huge bottle of Poland Spring water, "These people need a little something after last night. After you went to bed everyone was on their weirdest behavior. Kurt and Trevor were dancing to Corey Hart, Kendra was telling everyone about her college boyfriend who hit her *and* is now a transvestite, I'm taking *that* with a grain of salt, and two people who shall remain nameless were making out. I'm not telling you who because I am one hundred percent positive that it will never, ever happen again. Something about the day plus seeing that accident got people weird."

"Oh god," Rachel said. She looked at Lauren. "Were *you* one of the people who needs to remain nameless?"

"I was *not*. I was just the watcher. I don't think anyone did anything they can't take back, but it was good that we came back here instead of being out in public when people were in that kind of mood. And Kendra…when we go out later one of us needs to be on her. *The mouth.* How's the quiche?"

"Yes, you're right about Kendra, we'll stay on her. And the stinking quiche is *too* good."

They both picked up their papers. Lauren said wryly, "Start on page 3." Rachel opened to an article about Alec Baldwin berating a Starbucks Barista over Twitter. After Lauren was sure she'd finished the article she said quietly,

"Even *you* got a little weird last night. How was your chat with North Sea sweatshirt guy? Informative, enlightening, deeply intellectual?"

"Don't be a snob. I don't think he fits the stereotype." She said a bit more firmly than she meant to. "I actually met his sister at the beach this morning out of the blue. She was really nice."

"Hmph, well, they're everywhere," said Lauren and put her head back in her paper.

Rachel wasn't surprised by Lauren's attitude towards Scallop. She wasn't surprised because if it had been Lauren flirting with him the night before Rachel would have pulled her out of the situation. She decided she wouldn't take anyone with her when she went to the farm later on. She was certainly going to go.

8: A Small Farm With A Little Bit Of Everything

Rachel pulled into the sandy gravel parking lot and parked beneath the sign that said: "North Sea Farms: A small farm with a little bit of everything." It was now mid-afternoon, and she'd just left the rental house to cheers. She'd gotten herself dressed in something presentable and announced with fanfare that she was heading out to get supplies to make them all strawberry shortcake.

When they'd taken a vote that morning the majority had wanted to stay at the house and the pool for the afternoon rather than go to the beach. They'd all eaten their way through the breakfast leftovers hours ago. Since then they had just been full-on "cocktailing".

Years ago, after a painful learning curve, Rachel had come to understand that in the Hamptons "cocktailing" is both a verb and a major pastime. Eating on the other hand, was purely optional. Her first summer out with Tucker they'd been invited to party after party where she'd expected to be fed dinner. She'd seen enough episodes of "The Barefoot Contessa" while on the treadmill at the gym to believe that beautiful salads made of fresh local fruits and vegetables and carefully considered main courses were always going to be on the menu when you were invited to someone's beach house out here. Instead she'd found the reality to be a seemingly never-ending geyser of booze and wine accompanied by the occasional pitiful piece of dry grilled chicken. She'd gotten used to it. Now she automatically dropped into "cocktailing" mode as soon as she drove through Manorville, everyone's landmark for being "almost there" as they drove out to the Hamptons from New York City. But many of her team were not veterans of the East End summer, and after hours of marinating in the sun and eighty proof beverages they needed food. Rachel had stopped at the Bloody Mary, and was really the only one in any condition to go anywhere at the moment, which gave her the excuse she needed to visit the farm alone. Lauren had offered to come help her but she'd told her she should stay and supervise the others. Rachel, despite herself, was still a little annoyed about the comment that Lauren had made this morning about Scallop. Now that she was at the farm she felt awkward about marching in and asking for Scallop.

There were several wagons lined up outside the store filled with watermelons, flowers, strawberries, blueberries and raspberries. She was parked in front of the red outbuilding that served as the farm stand. It was a neatly painted two car garage with the doors rolled open. Rachel could see inside from where she sat in her car. It was painted white and was well lit, neat and tidy. A couple teenage girls in t-shirts were leaning on a simple counter made of rough-sawn boards topped with a concrete, waiting for something to happen. When she'd gone past the farm earlier it had been busy, but now hers was the only car in the parking lot. Scallop was nowhere in sight and neither was Lucy, which meant she'd have to ask for them.

On the way there she'd managed to convince herself that she really was coming only to reiterate her thanks to Scallop and buy some strawberries. But now, as she stared blankly at the little raised areas of the leather on her steering wheel, feeling trepidation at the thought of buying some fruit, she had to admit to herself that she'd come for more than that. She'd come because Scallop was compelling. She was more excited by the thought of trading small talk with Scallop in the midst of a pigpen than she had been about all the dates she'd been on since Tucker combined. And what was the point of being excited about this? Was she going to have a wild quarter of an hour with him in the hay loft of the barn? Because constructing an actual relationship with him seemed preposterous. Despite his looks, she couldn't imagine bringing him to a charity event in the city, and she actually needed someone to go with her to these things. Also, it had dawned on her that with the never-ending parade of beauty he encountered between the beach, the bar, and the farm, it was a safe bet he had enough women lined up for a roll in the hay to take him through the winter. How would he squeeze her in?

Looking in her rearview mirror she could see the clapboard farmhouse, its solid squareness calling out the frivolity of her carefully chosen sundress and turquoise encrusted flip flops. Some shabbily utilitarian kitchen chairs sat on the porch on either side of a wooden crate that functioned as a side table holding books and a recently abandoned newspaper. "Rachel, just go in and buy the damn berries," she told herself as she pulled off her favorite Gucci sunglasses, discarding them next to her as being just too much, and got out of her car.

The farm smelled. She could smell the fruit in the wagon lightly cooking under the sun. She smelled dirt, something sweet and rotting, and the clean, calming scent of hay. Rachel had forgotten that she loved the smell of hay. Sometimes it was spread along on the edges of the suburban soccer fields of her childhood as a mulch. She remembered how she used to sit down next to it to tie her cleats, taking a momentary break from the endless chatter of her teammates. She'd had a ritual that helped her concentrate on the game, to focus her mind and relax her joints. She pretended that her cleats needed re-tying and fell behind her teammates as they jogged the field to warm up. She sat down on the side of the field and tied her shoes slow enough that her teammates would be done just as they lapped her and she could rejoin the group. The smell of the hay, when there was some, had always helped her drop into the place where she could play the game without self-examination. She wondered if hay had the same effect on everyone. Maybe that's why everyone romanticized farming?

She walked over to the wagons, intent on searching out the most perfect looking quarts of strawberries. Something tapped lightly on her outer thigh. She jumped back about a foot and turned to find Kosumi smiling up at her. He was wearing an adult sized apron that had been folded up on his chest so it wouldn't drag on the floor. His hair had streaks of something greasy in it, and his face and arms were decorated with smudges of flour. He looked like a little cake making Indian brave. He was holding up a plate of biscuits.

"Rachel! We made the shortcakes. Me and Aunt Lucy made the shortcakes for you and your friends."

He was so excited he seemed about to take flight. His heels were going up and down as he repressed the urge to jump for joy. His little arms were wrapped all the way around the plate like a bumper protecting the stacked biscuits from falling off while he wiggled.

"Oh my goodness! Are you sure those are for me?" She figured he must be confused. She hoped he hadn't stolen the biscuits off the kitchen table, she didn't want him to be embarrassed when it turned out they weren't for her.

"Yes, these are for you. Aunt Lucy said we should make you nice ones and I should help because you were coming back to Grandpa's to get strawberries and you don't know how to make the biscuits. But I do! I made them for you!"

"Oh, Kosumi, thank you. These look like perfect biscuits. You did a great job. Did you get some in your hair?" She picked up a strand of the blond hair that was particularly caked with dough as she took the plate from him. He reached up and pulled the strand of his blond hair out over his face so he could look up at it. He gave it an incredulous look, shrugged and let it fall across his forehead having deposited several fresh pills of flour into it from his fingers.

"Where is your Aunt Lucy?" Rachel was impressed that Lucy had taken their casual small talk to heart and taken the time to bake something for her. When she'd said that they could help her with the shortcake at the farm, Rachel had assumed Lucy meant that there was something available at the farm stand that would do, not that she was going to personally embark on a mess making extravaganza with a four-year-old. Judging from the state of Kosumi the kitchen must have been covered in flour. She couldn't believe that anyone would spend their Saturday making baked goods for a complete stranger.

"She's inside. She said for me to tell you to go into the farm stand and she will come. She's cleaning, then she's coming out to see you." He grabbed her hand and pulled her into the farm stand, dragging her towards the counter. The girls at the counter smiled as they approached. "Inga, can you put my biscuits into a bag? They're for Rachel."

"Hi," said Rachel, taking both of the girls in. They were somewhere between fifteen and seventeen and both of them obviously belonged to Lucy, long legs, long curly hair pulled up in quick buns and an aura of peace and good humor about them.

"Kosumi, did you make these yourself? They look really good." Inga came around the counter and picked Kosumi up with a small grunt, giving him a hug and parking him on her hip. "You must be Rachel." She looked Rachel right in the eyes as though she were used to being on the level with adults.

Rachel didn't spend a lot of time with teenage girls, and really hadn't since she'd been one. But, when she did encounter them she usually found them to be completely incapable of carrying on a conversation with an adult. Something happened between twelve and nineteen that struck them dumb. Inga seemed like she'd escaped the usual affliction.

"Yes, hi. I am Rachel. Rachel Jones. Are you Lucy's daughters? I met your Mom this morning on the beach with Kosumi. It's so nice of her to go to the trouble of making me biscuits."

"She put aside a flat of strawberries for you too. I picked them this morning. I'm Veronica." Veronica reached over the counter and shook her hand. "I'll be right back." She said as she went through a doorway behind the counter to a darker room in the back where there were cardboard boxes filled with vegetables and fruits. She winked at her sister, much the same way Scallop had winked at Rachel the night before as she went. Either this farm had the best customer service on the planet or something was going on that Rachel didn't quite understand.

"Mom said that you and Uncle Scallop met last night," Inga said with a clear twinkle in her eye that wasn't pure teasing, the twinkle was laced with something else.

"That's it!" Rachel thought, "They're matchmaking!"

She was sure she was right. Her perception of people's motives was usually bullseye accurate. Lucy had made sure that she came to the farm this afternoon so she'd talk with Scallop again. Most of her day had revolved around the preparations. But that meant that something about her read on Scallop was off. Either he didn't get around much, and Lucy was snatching the opportunity to put him together with someone, or he got around so much that Lucy was trying to steer him towards someone who seemed appropriate. The first scenario just didn't seem plausible. Hadn't she just been imagining him with a jam-packed schedule of hayloft trysts? Veronica came back carrying a squat, open cardboard box piled to the breaking point with strawberries.

"Uncle Scallop should be out back fixing the fence by the pig shed. If he isn't there he's moving the turkeys. Just walk around the side of the red barn and you should see him," she pointed eagerly. They were all in on it.

Rachel walked out laughing. She didn't think she'd been party to such an obvious setup since middle school. She followed a gravel path around the corner of a two-story red barn. Judging from the smell it was where they stored the hay. So this would be where the hayloft was located, whether it was being used frequently for anything other than dead grass storage, or not. She looked inside the barn as she walked by. It was dark inside, constructed of old posts with chinks in them. There were stalls that were filled with neatly organized supplies and tools and obviously not used by animals anymore. But the hand-painted names of horses long gone remained centered over each stall. This must have been the original barn for the farm. It looked about the same age as the house.

As Rachel came around the far corner of the barn she almost tripped over a peacock. It let out an unearthly loud call, somewhere between a crying cat and a giant parrot, and stalked off towards a half dozen tractors in a small field behind the barn. Some of the machines were old, surrounded by too many weeds to have been used recently, and some were newer with fresh shining oil peppered with bits of plants stuck to the tillers. They all seemed to have been placed there for curious visitors to try out. There was something solidly comforting about them. Rachel had never been interested in driving things that weren't cars: go carts, four wheelers, snow mobiles, boats, she'd never been tempted. But there was something about the fact that these vehicles did work, important work, that was appealing to her. She could see why people would want to climb in and see how it felt to be a farmer.

She spotted Scallop working on the fence next a shed with an open front. This must be the pig shed, it smelled like a pig shed for sure, although she didn't see any pigs at the moment. He was crouched in a catcher's position, attaching a section of metal fencing with big open squares to a fence post by wrapping a piece of wire around the post and twisting it through the fencing. He was wearing worn jeans, a t-shirt and a baseball hat both baring the farm's name. His high lace up work boots were encrusted with muck and some hay and he was concentrated on wrapping the ends of the wire so that they weren't sticking out. She passed working men in the city every day. Men dressed like Scallop, working on road crews, delivering food, coming out of the service exits of office buildings and residential skyscrapers. She didn't really look at them. She certainly didn't look at them twice. No one really looks at each other on the street in New York City. They let their eyes relax into a soft focus so they see the shapes of other people, but not the details. If you were to engage with everyone you passed walking twenty city blocks you would have nothing left for the day. Scallop stood to cut another wire and stopped for a moment to look off into the woods at the edge of the field, leaning on the post he'd been working on. Her feet crunched against the gravel path but he didn't look up.

She cleared her throat. "Hi there. Rachel ... we met last night." He turned quickly, looking a bit dazed, as if he'd been shaken from sleep. His forehead was pinched together and Rachel got the feeling that he had not been admiring the beauty of the woods, but thinking of something far less pleasant. He gave her a peremptory smile and then looked down while he took off his pair of well-worn leather gloves.

"Hello hello hello! Look what the cat dragged in. Did someone drop a watch or a necklace in the water? How are you Rachel?" He smiled charmingly now and took a swig of water from a canteen he had leaning against the base of the post.

"I'm well, thank you. No emergencies today. But, I thought I'd stop by to see if you were okay after last night. I heard the passengers were okay. I met your sister this morning on the beach. How are you? You were bleeding pretty badly when you got in the ambulance."

"Nonsense my lady. I've been worse. That was mostly their blood I had on me. The father was lucky. That tree branch hit him in the top of the shoulder, just missed his neck. The boy has a concussion but is looking good. I stopped in today and saw them. Everyone is recovering. You and the crew having a good day?"

"Yes. We are. We're just relaxing before dinner tonight."

"Okie dokey doggie daddy. You want a tour of our little piece of paradise here?" She did. She found that she didn't care that she was part of an obvious plot. She didn't care that this man had just referred to her as "what the cat dragged in" and said, "Okie dokey doggie daddy," in almost the same breath. Unbelievably, she wanted to see his farm. With him.

"Meet the pigs," Scallop said as he walked around the far side of the shed and rattled the bottom of the fence with his boot. A split second later four pigs shot out around the other side of the shed. They'd been wedged between its back and the fence, and now they were on the run. They weren't piglets but they weren't the big giant pigs she'd seen at a country fair either. They were about the size of a medium dog. When they ran they seemed to teeter totter front to back without their spines flexing, and their little ears flapped up and down as they shot across the pen. Rachel laughed. "They're cute!" she said.

"Yes, the biggest one there, that's Carter. To her left, the one that just sat in the muck, that's Nixon." He winked. "Behind her over there, that's Clinton. And the smallest one, that's Reagan."

She leaned on the fence and dangled her hand towards the pigs. They looked at her but didn't come near. "Do they like to be petted?"

"Ha, no. They're too big for that. Piglets will let you hold and pet them, but as they grow they get meaner and meaner. Think of these guys as ten-year olds. They like to run. Right now they love this game. Run as fast as you can to the end of the pen and then wait a few seconds and run back the other way."

She looked at him. He was serious. "Okaaayyyy." She said and ran to the end of the pen which was a little challenging wearing flip flops on the gravel. "I am an idiot." She thought. Three of the pigs took a few lolloping trots in her direction.

"Go back fast," He called. She did and this time all four pigs turned and met her at the end of the pen. "Again." Called Scallop. The pigs ran along the fence edge directly behind her. When she stopped they came to a screeching halt, starring at her to gauge her next move. She ran back again and they ran with her. She did it three more times laughing as she watched her four piggy shadows run behind her.

"That's hysterical," she said, a little breathless.

"Yup, you came at the right time. Right now they'll do that all day. In a month they won't be interested, they'll only do it if you're running carrying a pail of delicious peelings. You're a natural farm kid." She felt like this was genuine praise.

The they walked the grounds of the farm with Scallop pointing out the chicken coop, the goat and cow pen, the different areas of the acres wide field where the vegetables were grown. He showed her beans, squash, onions, potatoes, and tomatoes.

"Back over there, that's my garage for my carpentry business. Either I'm in there, out here, or at a job making something. You went past the barn right? Site of my early romantic conquests? That's it Rachel. This is my whole childhood, family history and work world, you can see it all from the front porch of my parent's house."

"Early conquests huh?" said Rachel. She was so good at figuring people out, and there was something that just didn't add up here. Why did Scallop's family seem so eager to please, for that matter, why was he?

"How long has your family had this farm for?"

"My family is one of the original Polish families who lived out here and never left. My ancestors all worked on the farms around town since the early-1800s. My great grandfather worked this farm for a wealthy family, the Swabs, who lived in town back in the day. When my Grandfather came home from World War II, the Swabs and he made an arrangement for him to buy the place. My father grew up here, my Dad and his siblings worked it growing up, and when he came home from Vietnam he took over. I grew up there in that old white house, and my sister Lucy, who you met, lives there now. My brother lives on that street just past the corn field, which is named after my Grandma," Scallop said pointing past the cornfield. "Here, do you want to see the greenhouses?"

They walked further away from the house passing the new corn plants and towards two long, low plastic greenhouses. From out of corn came a small voice.

"IT'S DADDY!!"

From a second gravel path Kosumi came flying at them and launched himself into Scallop's arms which swooped down like a tattooed cradle, perfectly timed to catch the enthusiastic leap.

"My…boy! Who's the best? How was the town with Aunty?" Scallop asked as he kissed him several times on the forehead.

"We got flour to make biscuits for Rachel. You should see my biscuits Daddy!"

"I think I see some of them in your hair. Can I try?" Scallop pretended to pick a bit of dough from Kosumi's hair and give it a taste test.

"Hm! Not bad! Quite good in fact!"

Rachel felt absolutely blindsided. How had she not put this together? Now Scallop's availability and his family's well-intentioned match making made sense. Her heart was racing. She could hear it in her ears, the same thing she'd heard the last time she'd seen Tucker. It was probably rushing blood or spinal fluid, but to her it was the sound of her sixth sense failing her. The one that protected her from awkward positions just like this, the one that made her so good at her job. How had it not been shouting, "Gorgeous, kind, interesting guy! What happened with his wife, or girlfriend, or *baby mama*? Something! There ought to be one!" in her ear since every moment she'd spent with Scallop? She took a deep breath.

"Yes, they made some beautiful shortcake biscuits for me to take to my crew. I can't believe that they went to all that trouble. Your sister seems like a really a special person Scallop."

He took a deep breath of his own and crossed his arms. "Yeah, she's special alright," he said wryly, "Kosumi, would you go and ask Inga for a flower for Rachel? Okay?" Kosumi sprinted back down the path.

He looked down at his feet and then straight at Rachel, "And that's my son, Kosumi," he smiled at her, and the faintest glimmer of defeat crossed his face.

She suddenly had a headache. The truth was that she actually believed, for about twelve hours, that the prince charming, rustic, Zen farmer, surfer man had no history. He'd been in suspended animation awaiting her grand return to the Hamptons, the next chapter in her story, a blank slate waiting for her. She felt like a total jackass.

"I see that. He's beautiful. He's really out of this world. I actually didn't realize that he was your son." Rachel uttered as she tussled her hair trying to cover her thoughts; something she hated when other women did.

"He is beautiful, but he had a bit of an advantage over you and I. He's a mixture of quite a few ethnicities. His mother was half Shinnecock Indian. As the story goes, in the 1800's just about a whole generation of Shinnecock men were killed in a storm when they were out whaling, and many of the woman took up with the newly freed slaves who were new to the area after the Civil War. So Kosumi here is a Polish, Shinnecock and African American mix. I knew his grandfather pretty well. This guy Jonas Rodgers. He looked like a black guy not a Native American, and he was like their main man on the reservation. A great guy…anyways, where is this dinner tonight?" Scallop asked, sharply changing the conversation.

"The Bell and Anchor," Rachel managed to get out as she digested the information she just received.

"I've got an idea, Rachel. Why don't you all swing by my house for a drink before you go there and we can watch the sunset. It'll be great. I live right on the beach. After all, I owe you a drink from last night. Come on…join Kosumi and me for a drink, see the natives in their habitat. What do you say?"

"Let me go back and see if the team is ok with that, and I can text you? Does that work?"

"I don't have a cell phone. You can show up, or not. 11 East Shore

Drive. It would be great to have you guys over. The sunset should be wonderful tonight," Scallop tipped his hat and walked away.

Rachel came back around the corner of the barn and saw Lucy carrying a bucket of water towards her. Lucy lifted her hand in a wave. Rachel hurried towards her, "Lucy, thank you so much for going to all that trouble and making those biscuits. I can't believe you did that!"

"Well, Kosumi likes to help me in the kitchen, and I thought Scallop could use a break from his shadow after last night. It was a good activity. Besides, I thought you might be one of those people who made strawberry shortcake with pound cake instead of biscuits, and that's just unacceptable," she joked. Rachel laughed with her.

"Scallop invited me to bring everyone over for drinks at his house tonight before we go out." Rachel told her. Lucy's eyebrows shot straight up.

"Wow, well *that* will be an experience for you all." Then she paused, "Yup, that's actually all I have to say about that. I've got to get this water to the turkeys, but listen, next time you're out here I'd love it if we could go out and have a glass of wine. You work in finance right? I'm exploring some ways to increase the farm's profitability and I know you're not a farm person, but I would really appreciate it if I could pick your brain a little. Sometimes the Kozlowski's talk each other in circles and I just need to bounce some things off a trustworthy outsider."

"Of course, I'd be happy to." Rachel was flattered that Lucy trusted her enough to discuss personal business with her. Plus, she'd be a fun drinks date. She'd make a point to come back out again in the next couple weeks.

"It's a plan then," said Lucy. "Enjoy the shortcake and we'll meet up soon, just call the farm stand when you're around."

9: Peconic Sunset

Rachel was a little concerned that the van behind her carrying her team wouldn't be able to navigate the narrow dirt road. She was carefully driving a one lane packed sand road bordered by ten-foot-high reeds so close to the car that she could have stuck her hand out and grabbed one. It was enchanting, but it wasn't really a road that cars should be driving on, it was more like the path to a boat launch than a residential street. When they'd pulled off Noyac Road down the street from the Coast Grill she'd assumed that 11 East Shore Drive would be one of the quaint cottages from the 1920's that made up the neighborhood. They were clearly the area's original homes; split rail fences separated yards where bikes and balls had been haphazardly abandoned by children. They'd probably found something more fun to do! The small cottages with their screen porches and their windows with working shutters were so different from the eight thousand square foot "cottage" Tucker's family had owned. They were lovely and loved, carefully kept relics of a simpler time, and Rachel knew from looking at local Real Estate listings, all worth more than a million dollars. But about half a mile back they'd turned onto this dirt road that felt like it was going to descend into the marshes at every bend – East Shore Drive - and the neighborhood here, was not as well kept.

She'd announced to her team that they were all going to go together to Scallop's house to have drinks and watch the sunset before they went out. Everyone had been game. They were all full of strawberry shortcake, and no one was in any particular hurry to get to dinner. Dinner in the city was rarely before nine for any of them, and watching the sunset on a private beach sounded swanky. She knew some of their enthusiasm was motivated by the chance to talk to Scallop again. Having a fully fleshed tale to tell about the Aquaman of the Hampton's at cocktail parties was worth more than anyone outside their industry would understand.

But as they headed down this reedy path Rachel wondered if she was making a misstep. She hadn't expected Scallop to live anywhere grand, but the two cottages she'd just passed on this road had looked almost derelict. All she'd been able to see of number 9 East Shore Drive was an old sign tacked to a makeshift easel by the road, and an unevenly sloping roof jutting from the reeds.

She came around the next bend and the natural tunnel gave way to a flat open meadow with a beautiful view of the bay. The beauty was marred by what Rachel knew immediately to be Scallop's house. She slowed nearly to a halt to take it in. It was a contemporary of the charming cottages she'd passed moments before, but the most apt name for this structure was a "shack". The cedar shake siding was painted an awful shade of light brown. There were places where the shakes had come off and beneath there were patches of bright white in some spots, and black in others. The house was raised on lumber supports to keep it above flood levels in rough weather, but no attempt had been made to camouflage the starkly naked undercarriage. The weather worn wooden windows were opened to different heights, and in various states of decay. Rachel pulled off the road and onto the patchy front lawn. There was no obvious driveway. Scallop's truck was parked closer to the house, next to a boat that looked like it might float, on a good day.

As she pulled her keys out of the ignition Rachel started to laugh. What was her team going to think of the hillbilly haven she'd brought them to for cocktails? It was anything but swanky! She whooped and put her head down on the steering wheel, grabbing her stomach just to feel herself losing control. It was a good feeling. The truth was she didn't care what her team thought. She was resolved to have a good time. She stepped out of the door as Trevor stepped down the steps of the small Mercedes bus that was carrying her team.

"Well, this is it!" she said with unjaded enthusiasm.

"Yes, this *is* it," said Trevor slowly raising his eyebrows as he hesitantly let go of the bus railing. She waited while the rest of her team got off the bus, smiling at each one in turn.

On the side of the house was a stack of firewood that was an eight-foot-high stack of wood. Kosumi ran from behind it and along the row of pine trees that bordered one edge of the property. He was still in the bathing suit he'd been wearing when she'd seen him earlier.

"There she is! Hi Rachel! Follow this way!"

Rachel looked down at her clothes, a flowing cream silk dress with a plunging bodice and heeled sandals that were sinking into the sandy yard with every step. They looked absurd she knew, showing up here wearing designer "going out" outfits. This was a cutoff and t-shirt kind of place. Behind her she could hear Lauren and Kendra grumbling about their own shoes sinking while they leaned against one another to steady themselves. As she walked she reached down and pulled off her heels, letting the girls catch up with her to give them a smile. She let just a bit of smugness into it. They followed Kosumi to the front of the house, which faced the beach. When she turned the corner, Bob Marley's "No Woman No Cry" was playing.

The back door opened and there was Scallop; showered, wearing a light V-neck sweater, shorts and flip-flops. "Now *that's* how someone cleans up!", she thought as she took a sideways glance at the girls. Her thoughts were reflected in their faces. Gone was the farmer covered in mud. He looked clean, neat, casual and comfortable.

"Hello, hello, hello Rachel. I see Kosumi is being a good host." He smelled good too. Earlier that day, he could have smelled better. "Maybe he *could* do fund raisers...", Rachel thought.

"Welcome everyone! I'm so glad you all came to share the sunset with me and Kosumi. It should be a great one. There are drinks over here, help yourselves." He turned to Rachel, "What can I get you?"

They walked over to a rustic outdoor table with ice filled buckets of beer and wine. Scallop poured Rachel a white wine in one of the glasses he'd set out. Rachel looked around. This side of the house gave a distinctly different impression than the side they'd parked on. Fifty yards from the back door were the waters of Peconic Bay and a view of Robin's Island and the North Fork, this was maybe the nicest view in North Sea. While the house was small and modest from this angle it was well maintained, and the yard was something special. Despite its simple, rustic, beachy style, it was perfect. Anyone could tell that this was someone's oasis, a little piece of paradise. There were Caribbean style lights hanging in several trees. Old anchors and beautiful pieces of driftwood were meticulously placed around the small area, some for decorative purposes, some as seating. There was a hammock tied between two trees that looked handmade. Kendra and Kurt had already found a ring game nailed to the outside wall of the house - the type you'd find in a bar - and were drinking a beer and betting dinner on the winner. There were two bamboo standup paddleboards and a wind surfer lying neatly by a path to the water. The music mix was exclusively Bob Marley, early Jimmy Buffett and the Zac Brown Band, none of which Rachel particularly liked, but it fit perfectly here. This was an outdoorsman's man-cave.

Within minutes the team had made themselves comfortable around the firepit and down by the water. Trevor looked a bit unsettled perched gingerly on one of the hunks of driftwood by the fire. He'd taken a couple of napkins from the drinks table and spread them out where his pants were touching the wood. But he was chatting and in good spirits. Lauren on the other hand was standing a ways off, arms crossed, looking out towards the water. She turned back to the group at a break in the conversation.

"So, *Scallop,* how did you come to own this slice of paradise?" she asked with an edge that Rachel hoped Scallop did not catch.

"Once Kosumi was with me full time things got a little crowded at my family's farm. So we moved down here. It's an interesting story actually. I always loved this spot. In high school this house was abandoned except for one weekend of the year when this old man would come out with his fishing buddies. The same weekend every year. So my friends and I used it as a clubhouse and called it 'The Shack'. We always cleaned it up right before he came for his one weekend. I guess he knew we were doing it, but he got here and there wasn't any dust inside, there weren't raccoons living in there, and the path to the water was cleared for him. He probably thought it was a win-win. Anyway, he left it to me in his will. I was overseas and I got a letter from an attorney saying it was mine. I was blown away at the time. Turned out he knew what we were doing all along. He didn't have any family and he wanted the place to go to someone who would enjoy it the same way he did, not knock it down and build a modern monstrosity. So, I keep it the way I think he would have liked it."

"I'd have a hard time restraining myself from HGTV-ing it," Raj joked.

"I think we all would.", said Lauren unkindly as she turned back towards the water.

Rachel was shocked. She hadn't realized that Lauren was such a snob. She'd never known her to be rude. But when she thought about it she realized she'd never been around Lauren with anyone who wasn't fairly wealthy.

"So where exactly is the property line?" Rachel asked to change the subject.

"Along that tree line there. Kosumi was very anxious for you to see inside. Why don't I give you a quick tour." He led her away from the firepit to the side of the house. As they walked away Rachel glanced back at Lauren in time to catch a quick exchange between her and Trevor. Trevor shook his head at her in reprimand, and she shrugged self-righteously as if to say, "How can I help it?", rolled her eyes and rummaged through her purse in search of her cell phone, signaling that she was done with their conversation.

Rachel felt terrible. She'd taken her team where they didn't belong and didn't feel comfortable. This hadn't been what any of them had expected to be doing this weekend, and while she didn't think it would hurt them to be reminded that there were plenty of people who didn't spend their weekends being catered to by hedge fund employees who were only slightly less privileged than they were, she was aware that bringing them here hadn't been entirely fair. At the same time, she was appalled that Lauren had been so pointedly rude to Scallop. He had extended his hospitality to all of them. She felt responsible for his generosity being met with insult.

"Over here is the outdoor shower, which I use three hundred and sixty-five days a year." Scallop pointed at an open boarded square attached to the side of the house, floored by a single flat rock. He didn't seem insulted, in fact the insult seemed to have increased his pride in the humbleness of his home. Kosumi ran up and grabbed his father's hand. Rachel felt a flash of anger. If anyone made Kosumi feel that his home was not a utopia she would fire them tonight, right in front of everyone else.

"Now if you follow me up here, I'll show you my kitchen, last updated in 1955 if you were wondering. Behind you here, that's the living room. To your right, that's Kosumi's room," Kosumi ran into his room and jumped on the bed, as happy as could be. Obviously, his feelings had not been hurt.

"And to your left, that's my room. And over there, towards the back behind Kosumi's room, that's the bathroom in case you need to use it. And right there, next to the door, that's the wood-burning stove. Outside you might have seen a great big pile of firewood. That's to keep this sucker running from Columbus Day to Cinco de Mayo muchacha." He said hugging Kosumi as though muchacha was a pet name, "That's the only source of heat we need in here and we do just fine. Excuse us for one second, Rachel, while I get this little hermit crab of a boy into his pajamas," Scallop chased his son into his room, tickling him as they ran in laughing.

Scallop could have given her the full tour right without leaving the living room. Everything in the cottage was visible from that one central point. Rachel looked around and marveled at the simplicity of their setup. There were toys, but not too many of them, all neatly tucked away for the night. There were pictures of father, son and extended family. The walls and floor were knotty pine, which in any setting other would have seemed dated, but here they created a feeling of warmth and hominess. On the walls were some impressive pieces of folk art. There was a tapestry of a mountain scene whose origin Rachel couldn't guess at. On another wall was a series of five masks that looked like they had all come from a different culture, and on the floor in front of the woodstove there was a huge, deep sheepskin rug of three different natural colors, sewn together in a repeating seagull pattern. The furniture was beyond simple. There were two chunky wooden chairs with turned arms and legs and cushions made from well-aged Moroccan rugs, a pile of floor pillows in one corner, and lined up neatly underneath the front windows, were four gigantic matching beanbags, the type that can be molded into different shapes according to need.

Rachel was enchanted. Of course, she'd been in homes where every item had been carefully chosen for aesthetic reasons, or to impress; with her mother being who she was she'd been in too many. But she'd never been in a home where every item had been carefully chosen purely for comfort and utility. It was humble and at the same time completely serene.

She wandered into the adjacent dining room. A huge ornately painted Japanese lantern hung over a large dining table with a top of wood inlaid with some kind of shell in a geometric pattern that made Rachel think of an intricately woven basket. On either side were benches with bases of made of driftwood painted a rich red to match the lantern above. On low shelves under the windows that wrapped the dining room were stacks of plates and bowls and cups, all made of pottery with a variety of glazes. Rachel got the distinct impression that everything she was seeing had been given to Scallop as a gift or somehow had a sentimental significance for him and Kosumi.

Back in the living room she perused the large bookcase. It was jammed with children's books, novels, some philosophy and religion books, and some biographies. Covering a large area of the bookcase was a large framed quote, set on a background of a photograph of a local marsh. It was a passage from Pat Conroy's "The Prince of Tides".

"To describe our growing up in the low country of South Carolina, I would have to take you to the marsh on a spring day, flush the great blue heron from its silent occupation, scatter marsh hens as we sink to our knees in mud, open you an oyster with a pocketknife and feed it to you from the shell and say, 'There. That taste. That's the taste of my childhood.' I would say, "Breathe

deeply," and you would breathe and remember that smell for the rest of your life, the bold, fecund aroma of the tidal marsh, exquisite and sensual, the smell of the South in heat, a smell like new milk, semen, and spilled wine, all perfumed with seawater. My soul grazes like a lamb on the beauty of indrawn tides."

Scallop came up behind Rachel. "That's my favorite passage by my favorite author. That was given to me by my family when I got out of high school," Scallop said as Kosumi ran by him and out the door. "It was the only book I read in high school. I thought it was about me, living in the water and creeks that I knew growing up, right here. I remember actually looking forward to going home at night and reading that book."

"It's beautiful."

"It is. I always thought that was describing exactly me, and my youth, even though he is talking about South Carolina. I went down there a few times and the marshes look just like the ones we have here. As a kid I spent all my time crabbing, clamming, duck hunting. All of it."

She wandered to the dining room windows. "This must have been a great place to grow up. There's so much beauty."

Outside she could see her team, all very involved in what they were doing and saying. Were any of them really paying attention to where they were? "I don't know if everyone who gets the chance to be out here appreciates how incredible it is. What a great place to call home. Is that a local painting? It looks like it could be your yard," Rachel said as she eyed a painting above the chairs. A group of Native Americans cooked fish on an open fire sitting on pieces of driftwood arranged like those outside. The details were incredibly vivid, to the point of photorealism, and the colors seemed to jump off the canvas.

"Kosumi's mother was a talented painter. She had a gift. Work like that, she could do in her sleep. We all have our talents."

Was. Kosumi's mother was past tense. Rachel wanted to ask him why so badly, but she had no sense of how probing she could be with Scallop. Being in his space had made it clear that this was a man whose soul lived pretty close to the surface. If he wanted to share something with her, she was sure he would. A moment of silence made her understand that now was not the time.

"Where's your TV?" Rachel asked, changing topics.

Scallop pointed to the side of his head.

"Right up here. All up here," he smiled as he pressed his index finger against his temple.

"This is all my son and I need, so it's all I have. Now, follow me back outside if you will. Sun should be getting ready to run on us!"

"Sure," Rachel said.

"Kosumi and I have a little nightly tradition here, and tonight you all are going to share it with us."

Scallop called Kosumi and they headed out towards the water. "Guests!" He called out, "I'd love it if you'd all come down to the water with us. Meeting new people and sharing your life and traditions with them is kind of what it's all about. Kosumi and I are going to share our special ritual with you. We do this every night we can as the sun goes down."

Everyone gathered down by the water. Rachel was glad to see that they were all still reasonably sober. Some of them did look as though they were wondering why they'd been dragged out by the water when they could watch the sunset perfectly well from the bar table or the firepit.

Holding Kosumi, Scallop stepped out in front facing the water. He turned his face towards the sun and closed his eyes, Kosumi solemnly did the same. Scallop spoke out loud enough for the nearest neighbors to hear.

"Hello big old Sun. Today was a good day, and I'm thankful for it. Today, I woke up before you rose. I surfed for two hours with my friends. I had breakfast on the beach with my sister and my son, both of whom I love immensely. I worked on my family's farm for ten hours, doing my job as well as possible with diligence, pride and dignity. I had the good fortune to run into Rachel again, and we invited her over. And here I am. It was a privilege to have been on earth today. I've had days beneath your light that have been truly awful. I've lost loved ones. I've killed many people. Those things have broken my heart. But today, nothing bad happened. I'm exhausted. I'm happy. I'm proud. Kosumi?"

"Good day!" Shouted Kosumi towards the sun, "I was at beach, dug BIG hole. I saw Rachel there. On way home thought about whales and the moon in the night. And blue Iced Cream. Then I went to grandpa's farm and grandma took me to town. I had ice cream, but not blue. I cooked. I saw Rachel again at farm. Then all my new friends came over. Fun day. Thank you." Kosumi and Scallop slapped high five and hugged.

Rachel was stunned. It was at once beautiful, incredibly embarrassing, and a little terrifying. Scallop had laid himself bare. "I've killed a lot of people?" It was something to shout that in front of strangers, not to mention his son. That kind of honesty was nothing she encountered, ever. She looked around at her co-workers.

"I hope we didn't weird you out. We try to give thanks to the world each day," Scallop said. She motioned to Scallop that it was no big deal and averted her eyes right into the gaze of Trevor who was smiling at her as if to say, "That was incredibly weird and awesome. Way to go." Most of the others were staring at their feet or murmuring about the beauty of the sunset that had suddenly illuminated the clouds with orange and purple. She looked over at Lauren who was dialing her phone to make a call as she walked away. Scallop turned away from the sun and came over to her. "What did you think?" he asked her, "I imagine some of these people think I'm a complete whack-job," he whispered this last in her ear.

"I like it actually. We should all do more of that," Rachel smiled up at him. She meant it.

"You should take out the paddleboard," Scallop said.

"No, I can't. We have to be at dinner in an hour and I can't get all wet. Besides I've never done it." Paddleboards had come into vogue after she and Tucker had broken up. When she'd been out here all the time everyone had been kayaking.

"Oh come on now, you won't get wet. You won't. Seriously, just go down and get on. Come on now," Scallop said as he guided her towards the boards.

"Yes! Ride the board Rachel!" Kosumi said as he jumped and ran toward the water.

"Yes! Ride the board Rachel!" Trevor echoed. Immediately the rest of the team took up the chant.

Rachel moved toward the water and before she knew it, she was out on the paddleboard. She got on it fine which she knew was probably the most difficult part, and then found it easy paddling towards the sunset. After a few strokes, she looked back at Scallop and Kosumi on the shore, as Scallop put his hand on Kosumi's head. They were a pretty picture with their curly long hair and similar builds. They were standing off from the rest of the group who were still chanting. Rachel lost herself for a moment as she waved to them on the shore. She didn't see the wave that was slightly larger than the others she'd navigated smoothly. The wave hit the board and she jolted forward. As she tried to regain her balance she overcompensated in the opposite direction and went down into the cold water. She came up, grabbed the board, and pulled herself back up smoothly.

"So much for dinner," Rachel shouted toward the shore as her teeth chattered. Scallop and Kosumi laughed and her team cheered. As she came into shore pulling the board out of the water she said, "Go, go. Go to dinner without me and have fun. I'm a drowned rat. I'm calling it a night." She walked over to Lauren and said, "Just make sure that everyone keeps it under control."

"Of course." Lauren said. "Come on guys lets go to town."

By the time they were saying goodbye Scallop had found Rachel a towel, sweatpants and a sweatshirt that belonged to one of his nieces. He graciously accepted everyone's thanks and waited until they'd all gone around the corner of the house before leaning towards her.

"You take a shower right here, get yourself comfy, and Kosumi and I will fetch us a pizza from up the street at Pellegrino's. Sound like a plan?"

"Sounds great," she said "no pepperoni for me. Thanks Scallop."

Father and son left. Rachel took off her wet dress, examined her leather belt, which a look told her wouldn't make it, and jumped in the outdoor shower. The steaming hot water felt wonderful and she listened to Jack

Johnson's "Better Together" play in the background. She was relieved that her team was gone. She was really annoyed that Lauren had been so rude to Scallop. If Lauren had that kind of reaction to Scallop it stood to reason that lots of people in her circle would share Lauren's opinion. She sighed as she gathered her things up and made a quick break across the backyard in her towel. She went back into Scallop's bedroom to change into the sweats, not really knowing what else to do. She didn't think he'd consider it an intrusion. She sat down on the bed. His room was neat, simple and organized. There was one book on the nightstand, "The Old Man and The Sea" by Earnest Hemmingway, and a picture of Kosumi; that was it. The worn wooden floorboards beneath her feet felt good. She thought back to the room she'd woken up in this morning. Scallop's room was a better fit.

An hour later, they'd eaten the pizza and were relaxing outside by the fire pit. Kosumi was falling asleep on Scallop's shoulder as he told him his favorite story, a 'local Shinnecock Native American Legend', about a young boy who fished the Peconic Bay every day of his life. Rachel sipped her wine and gazed into the fire listening to Scallop tell the story, his voice low and serious. When Kosumi was fully asleep, holding a stuffed lamb, Scallop carried him inside to bed. Rachel finished her wine. She didn't know whether she should offer to leave. She didn't want to. Scallop came out, wearing a fleece, popped open a beer, and plopped down next to Rachel.

"So Rachel Jones, what's the good word? Thanks for skipping the dinner and hanging around with me."

"I'm sure they had a great time, and I don't mind staying behind. I eat out too many nights as it is, and they could use some bonding time without me there. It's good for them. When I'm around they all have to be on all the time. This is better. Besides, I'm sure they're not anywhere near as comfortable as I am right now."

"You like it here. So, we're getting to know each other here. Do you have any questions for me?" Scallop asked as he poked the fire.

"Questions? A few."

"I'll give you two for now."

"Ok, *Scallop*?" Rachel asked, obviously asking about the origins of his name.

"Mmm. My name is Walter Kozlowski, just like my grandfather. When we were kids, we used to take a boat out there to the middle of the bay at night and loot the scallop farms. Not many people realize it, but Peconic Bay Scallops are sold all over the world. They farm them every weekday during the season in just about the middle out there. It's about thirty feet down in some spots, but I was able to make it all the way down, grab the traps, and swim back up. My cousins and I would take the Scallops to the docks in Hampton Bays and sell them. Since I was the only one who could make it all the way down there, one day my cousin Joe called me Scallop, and it stuck."

"So that explains how you can stay underwater for so long."

"Part of it. It takes a lot of work. I got started young."

"Question number two 'Walter'. Kosumi? He is beautiful."

"I figured that one was coming," Scallop said as he looked up to the stars. "Kosumi's a longer story."

"I'm not going anywhere unless you're ready to call it a night."

10: Scallop's Walkabout: 1994 – 2008

Scallop looked at the lights across Peconic Bay in Greenport and wondered how much he wanted to tell this woman he had known for a day. He thought explaining yourself honestly and thoroughly was akin to opening a trap door to your soul. You could stand on the edge of the hole and look down at the underpinnings of your life and then close the door again and walk away, or something could trip you up, and you could end up down there with the snakes and moldy cardboard boxes of your past and no ladder. He hadn't allowed anyone new to peer down there in a long time. But he had a strong urge to share with Rachel, an undeniable instinct that compelled him. He looked at the night and let it fly.

"Growing up on the farm, I spent all my time after school and on weekends working. I never really tried in school. I liked being there in class, I was interested, but I didn't have the time after school to devote to homework. I was a good baseball player, but I didn't have the time to do that either. And I sure as hell didn't want to spend my spring weekends doing anything but surfing, hunting, fishing, free diving, clamming…if I had free time, I wasn't going to be playing baseball for Southampton High School. From age ten on, I worked on the farm and was paid for it. I had one goal: to leave here when I graduated high school and never come back. I saved money and got myself an old Volkswagen van that I restored for two years. I put a little bed in there, dressers, a tiny kitchenette. I gotta tell you, I worked hard on that van and was very proud of it. I was set to leave the morning after I graduated from high school, and I didn't know where I was going. My family threw me and my cousins a graduation party in the big barn you saw today, and the next morning, I jumped in my van. I had my surfboard, camping, fishing and hunting equipment, and I was all set. At four AM on the morning of June 24th, 1994, I made a left onto Noyac Road from my farm, and that was it. My parents knew I had to do what I was doing, and I think they knew I'd be back. We all come back," Scallop laughed knowingly.

"By August, I made my way to Denali National Park in Alaska, eventually made my way down to Olympia National Park in Washington State, where I camped, surfed and hung out. I moved south slowly. From Washington, to Oregon, and straight down California I made my way. I picked up odd jobs where I had to. Sleeping under the stars, in the van or sometimes renting a room in exchange for work. Between the skills I learned growing up on the farm and my ability to fend for myself, I was always ok."

"By 1996 I was in Mexico. I worked on a fishing boat out of a small town on the Baja Peninsula. I tended bar and was a surfing guide in Costa Rica. I worked on an environmental expedition that the Sierra Club sponsored on the Galapagos Islands. I lived on Easter Island with the Sierra Club. I did all sorts of things, Rachel, and it was awesome."

"The Galapagos? I hear it's an amazing thing being there. girls there though…" Rachel joked.

"Didn't matter. I had a vow of chastity for the whole wa completely celibate. Scouts honor," Scallop deadpanned back.

"In 2001 I was living in Patagonia, in a town called Tor working as a mountain climbing guide. I was on my day off on the morning of 9/11, I saw it on TV at one of the hotels. I made my way to the nearest airport, which took the better part of a week, got on a plane, and flew to San Diego, where I walked into the closest Nacy recruiting center and volunteered."

Sometimes people alter stories to make them better party entertainment or pickup fodder. Rachel didn't think Scallop was doing that. He was quietly staring into the fire. She could picture a younger version of him hiking out of the Chilean mountains on a mission to serve his country, called to duty.

"Just like that?" Rachel questioned.

"Just like that. My father was in Vietnam, my grandfather was in World War II, and my older brother served in the Gulf War. Service runs in my family. I went through basic training, and based on my background they thought I might be a fit for the SEAL program. I was shipped off to Great Lakes, Illinois, and then to Coronado, California, and by the end of 2002, I graduated and was a full tilt Navy SEAL."

"Heroic." Rachel said quietly.

"No. Not really. But from there, Rachel, things got insane. Afghanistan. Iraq. Four tours. I saw things, and did things, that a person can't undo. You learn to just make yourself numb. But in the end, it gets you.

When I wasn't deployed, I was back in North Carolina at the base training for the next trip over. In early 2008, I got shot, for the third time, this one was in the shoulder, and I was discharged. I did time in Walter Reed. I got out. Then my brother picked me up, and drove me back here. I got out of his truck in the parking lot at the farm where I hadn't been in 14 years. Nothing had changed. I went back to my old room upstairs, and nothing had been moved. Same posters, my diploma was still on the dresser where I left it. My Mom kept things as they were out of superstition, I think, so I'd come back, first from my wandering lifestyle, then from the war. Or the wars. Whatever you want to call that clusterfuck."

"As soon as I got home I couldn't sleep. Nightmares. Night terrors actually. I didn't want to leave my room. I don't know why it started when I got back here, it hadn't happened in the hospital. Maybe it was because there I was surrounded by a bunch of guys who had all been through the same thing. My family didn't know what to do, I stayed in my room for months. Lucy wasn't having it. She tried everything from kale salad, to torturing me with kindness until I took the medication for PTSD they'd given me at the hospital, to sending in the kids to play checkers with me every day. Eventually, I had to open that door and walk outside. I'd had enough checkers. I put on my work clothes one spring day at four thirty in the morning and just went outside and started working. I knew what to do…and I just did it. It felt right to me to be out there plowing the fields and hosing down the stand for the season. Keeping it simple helped me keep my mind right, and it's what I know how to do. In 2010 I started the carpentry business making mostly docks for folks around here on the side. I got back into diving, hunting, surfing, fishing, clamming, all the things I did before, all the things I love. I joined the volunteer Fire Department. Somehow doing those things, here in my home, keeps me calm and grounded in a reality I can get behind. It bonded me to my land, the land and people I set out to protect. It didn't turn out the way I expected, but this land, this place and my people are still worth protecting."

They sat in silence for a long moment as the fire crackled. Rachel stared out at the water but Scallop was in her peripheral view. Was he this open with everyone? She could see why he chose to keep his life simple. Four tours, and shot three times? She tried to find a way to relate to that and came up with nothing. Absolutely nothing in her life was on par with what Scallop had done and stepped away from.

"You asked about Kosumi. And I owe you an answer. That was a long way of telling me how I wound up with my boy. Kosumi's mother was a woman named Kachina who grew up over on the Shinnecock Reservation. Kachina, in case you didn't know, is a Native American name that means 'sacred dancer' or 'spirit' and, with her they sure got that name spot on. Kachina was only twenty-four when I met her. She worked as a bartender at the North Sea Tavern up the road, and in the summertime at a few of the clubs. She was beautiful, and she had a crazy, howling, beautiful laugh. She was a force of nature. Really, she was like a storm. Or like many storms trapped inside a body that while magnificent, wasn't capable of holding all that electricity. We had a brief relationship and Kosumi came out of it."

He paused to catch his breath and to look at Rachel. He knew he described Kachina in graphic terms. It was the only way he could describe her. He'd made the mistake of making people uncomfortable in the past when he talked about her. Rachel either wasn't uncomfortable, or she was skilled at masking her feelings. In case it was the later he switched tacks. "As I'm sure you know, Kosumi means 'fishes for Salmon with a spear'. My Mom just loved that. She tried to change his name to Tim a few years back. Most of the Shinnecock don't even have Native names, she thinks it sounds pretentious. Kachina had been a model when she was a teenager, and some of the experiences she had surrounding that, they really did a number on her. She lived hard. Harder than any girl in her twenties I'd ever met. I was reluctant to get involved with her. Where I was myself at the time, being with someone who wasn't really stable, I knew it was a bad idea. She was a talented painter and an incredible dancer. She danced on the reservation at the ceremonies. She *could* have done some incredible things. But she couldn't…she couldn't. I don't regret any of it, none of it really," he said with an edge, "She brought me Kosumi."

"We had our boy in Southampton Hospital, and we tried to make things work. Kachina couldn't shake her demons though. I tried to help her, I thought having been through what I'd been through I could help. Which in hindsight was an arrogant way to look at things. In reality I didn't know what the hell was going on. Anyway, a few days after Hurricane Sandy hit out here, they found her over in North Sea Harbor, just across from Conscience Point. She'd committed suicide."

Scallop was silent for a long moment waiting to see how Rachel would react. He realized now that he'd finished, that he'd told her not just to open up, but as a test. He was incredibly attracted to Rachel, a kind of attraction he couldn't remember feeling before, although he figured he must have felt at some point. But if his life was too rough for someone like her, if the people they were couldn't find a meeting place, he wanted to know now. He didn't want to embark on a struggle.

"And that, Rachel Jones, is the epic saga that is my life," he paused to look her way. "You want to leave now? No offense will be taken."

He'd said it kindly, in an almost fatherly way, as if choosing to leave would be his recommendation if he had the right to guide her. The song playing in the background switched to Kenny Chesney's "One Step Up", one of her favorites, but a sad one. She didn't like the way the tide was turning. Rachel kicked up some sand with her foot and laughed.

"No, I think I'll stay….hey, is this one of the places where you can catch clams with your toes?"

"You've done that before?"

"Yes, once or twice. I'm a city slicker, but I'm not squeamish, besides what's cooler than a nighttime swim?"

"Well, not too many things are cooler than a nighttime swim right now. You'd have hypothermia in about two minutes with the water as cold as it is. I've got another idea. Did you bring anything other than those crazy shoes you came here in?" he asked.

Rachel gulped back surprise that he'd noticed her sandals. He noticed things.

"Yeah, I guess they don't really go with this ensemble," she joked.

"True, but mostly I don't want you to turn your ankle, and what I want to show you is down the road a bit," he said, smiling at her.

"Wait, we're going to leave Kosumi here alone?", she almost gasped.

"No, it's just a couple houses down, I can hear him from there if he wakes up. He almost never does, and if he does, he'll just shout for me. It's not really any different than me going for a swim. Besides, I know he'll know exactly where we're going."

He got up and rummaged through a covered plastic bin behind him emerging to drop several pairs of flip flops on the ground in front of her. Red flip flops, pink ones with embroidered whales, a pair of Walmart specials with fake gemstones, and some Adidas soccer sandals, which Rachel chose. She'd worn an identical pair every day the summer before her junior year in high school until her mother had confiscated them. Under normal circumstances she would have cringed at the very thought of wearing flip flops covered in some mystery person's sweat, but she was trying to seem game, and when she slipped them on they felt like home.

Scallop pulled two squares with handles that vaguely resembled stuffed tote bags from the bin and pointed towards the road. They walked out in silence. Rachel wasn't quite sure what to say, so she looked up at the sky through the reeds on the edge of the road. There were no lights but the stars and the moon, which was bright enough that they could see the dirt road clearly.

Scallop bumped her leg with the large squares he was carrying.

"What are those things?" she asked.

"These? Oh, they're sit-upons," Scallop said, holding them up and examining the a frayed edge dubiously. "They're old sit-upons."

Rachel laughed. She could tell he didn't expect her to know what they were.

"And, what exactly is a 'sit-upon?" she asked, grabbing one to examine it.

It was made of oil cloth, worn oil cloth that was covered in a late 80's print that would have been most at home on a pair of MC Hammer's signature pants. It wasn't a bag. Rachel had no clue what it was for. "Do you hold it over your head if it starts to rain or something?"

"Nope, although you can in a pinch. You sit on it in the wet grass…sit upon. It's a Boy Scout thing. I went to exactly two Boy Scout meetings as a kid and we made these things. I thought they were stupid at the time, but I've used them ever since. You take newspaper and you fold it up, and then you weave the sheets together, so that it makes a little cushion. You sew it into that fabric, which is waterproof and you can take it with you on your big Boy Scout adventures," Scallop said a little sarcastically.

"I would have thought you would have been all about the Boy Scouts."

"No, Boy Scouts is for kids who need guidance in the outdoors. That wasn't me. I didn't need to get a badge in hunting and fishing. I hunted and I fished."

"Oh, I guess I thought since you were in the Navy you would have been a Boy Scout. I guess they don't really have anything to do with one another though now that I think about it."

"No, not really," Scallop smiled as he stepped in front of her walking backwards. He looked down at her as he took the sit-upon back. "Not really the same at all," he joked.

Rachel was dying to know about his time as a Navy Seal. It was so foreign to her, and sexy of course. She didn't know if he was even allowed to share the details of being a Seal. Was it top secret? Even though he hadn't taken her bait and offered anything yet she felt like this was a good moment to ask.

"So…you were like those guys in Zero Dark Thirty for a while there?" she asked, turning it into a joke. Scallop nodded.

"Not *sort of* like them," he said solemnly, turning to walk next to her again. He didn't say anything else for a moment and Rachel realized too late that everyone must ask him about being Seal, it probably got old for him.

When he spoke again it came out slowly, as though he was exploring a new idea.

"I came out of that experience thinking that we are all like the fish out there," he said slowing, stopping to wave towards the water. "We are each part of a school, and the schools fight one another, the fish attack each other. No one is wrong, no one is right, we just are. When I was doing the things I had to do over there, I wasn't wondering if what I was doing was correct, or right. I did what I was asked to do. When you are in a fistfight, you don't wonder why the fight is happening, you know? You try to win the fight. To be honest, I don't even know if we won that fight or not," he looked down at her and shrugged. "These days, Rachel, I have about all I can handle. I love my son. I have a simple, but wonderful job, and I'm blessed to live in a beautiful place with my family."

"Sounds nice to me," she said, allowing him to drop the fishes and Seals.

"Mmmm. So, what about you, Betty Lou? What's your deal these days? I got the work part of it I think. You raise money for a money manager. But what do you think about these days? Let's get right down to the bone while we are at it! Hear the water? It makes you speak truth."

She laughed, making sure to keep her eyes on the uneven dirt road. "My life is not too exciting. In fact, this is the most adventure I've had in a while, the most mystery too. What exactly are we doing?" she asked.

Scallop took her hand as a chuckled rumbled through him. "It's a surprise. When I tell you, move slowly and very quietly, don't speak. It's just here."

He strode into a large yard, motioning for her to follow him and be quiet. Rachel was startled by how his motions exposed his military background. Scallop saw it in her eyes and changed his demeanor seamlessly, winking at her and tip toeing in a goofy Wile E. Cayote impression. It seemed he could move between laid back surfer and Jason Bourne-like intensity at will.

Rachel glanced nervously towards the house in the middle of yard they were trespassing across. There were no cars in the drive and no lights on inside, she got the impression that it was a summer house. She wasn't used to breaking rules when it didn't come to business, but she also imagined Scallop could talk his way out of any situation they might encounter if they were found in the wrong backyard at the wrong time, so she relaxed as they passed the porch and went behind the house towards the tight row of high hydrangea bushes that stretched across the back of the property. Scallop slowed to a creep and motioned for her to do the same. When they were ten feet from the bushes, he crouched down, lowering himself onto his knees, and handed her back a sit-upon without taking his eyes from the bushes. He crawled forward soundlessly as though in slow motion. It was Rachel's turn to be dubious. She'd never been on a date where she'd been required to crawl across a stranger's grass, but she didn't want to seem prissy, and she was wearing his garbagy clothes, so there was really nothing to lose. She got down on her knees and mimicked his crawl, and then followed his lead when he sat on the oil cloth square at the edge one of the bushes. He smiled at her when she landed next to him and then carefully wedged his face into a space between the bare hydrangea branches. It took all Rachel's self-control not to laugh out loud at the picture of a giant, tattooed man sitting in the dark, with his head inserted in a bush. She bit her lip and followed suit.

Next to her, his breathing was almost imperceptible and she tried to match it even as she wondering what the hell they were doing. The row of hydrangeas was several plants deep and as her eyes adjusted she saw something move a foot above the ground under one of the other bushes. A small head lifted off a white and brown spotted flank and perked up its ears, looking at them, its black nose wet and shinning even in the small amount of moonlight the bushes allowed. Just as Rachel was about to startle, she felt Scallop's hand slide on to her knee, calming her. Another, larger head lifted and nuzzled the small one. Rachel and Scallop sat, watching the mother deer sooth her baby back to sleep. Rachel was fascinated. She felt a part of the intimate scene, a part of a pulse in the neighborhood and the shore that she hadn't realized was there until she'd stuck her head in that bush. She didn't know how long she sat there after Scallop had silently crept away, but at some point, she sensed he wasn't next to her anymore. The deer were both sleeping again and she inched away from the bushes, singularly focused on not startling the beautiful creatures in their home. When she finally dared to stand up she saw that Scallop was waiting out by the road for her, watching her. When she reached him she touched him playfully on the shoulder.

"That was really, really cool," she said whispered, smiling. "How did you know they were in there?"

"Kosumi's had us following that doe around the neighborhood for three months," Scallop said raising his eyebrows at her, "waiting for that fawn to come. We checked early yesterday morning and there it was. I've already been here twice today."

"Well, thanks," Rachel said, not really knowing what else to say, "that was so cool," she repeated.

"You getting cold?" Scallop asked, noticing that she'd wrapped her arms around her middle, not sensing that it was really because she was out of her element.

"Maybe a little. Do you think the fire is still going?" she asked, not wanting to go back to the rental house yet, not wanting to break the spell.

"Sure, if not, I'll get it whipped up again. We'll sit by the fire, but I've got a condition," he said seriously. "I just told you all that stuff. I took you on an adventure, and I showed you a secret. Quid pro quo. You can't just say that your life "isn't exciting". You have to tell me something about yourself that goes beyond the fact that you move money around for a living."

"Alright," she laughed. "Hold onto your hat, this is going to be one thrilling tale," she said sarcastically. "I grew up outside Chicago. My Dad was the CFO of a large consulting firm, my mom is an Interior Designer. Both my parents grew up with money and never knew anything else. I have an older sister who lives in Beverly Hills and is getting divorced. She's an awesome mom and she thinks I'm nuts doing what I do instead of trying to find a husband and become a mom." Rachel scoffed a little at what she considered her sister's old-fashionedness, or small mindedness, or whatever it was.

"I went to a prep school in New Jersey. Lawrenceville. My parents got divorced when I was in college, my father quickly remarried Janet, a woman half his age, and moved to Scottsdale. My mom, of course, just became more difficult. I got a soccer scholarship to Stanford. I got a job on Wall Street out of college, got my MBA at Harvard, and then got this job. I travel once a week at least. I work long days…I work a lot. I love my job. I'm really good at it. That's kind of all there is. Here I am. I have some great friends, a great lifestyle, a great life. What am I thinking about? Many things. Regular things." She felt comfortable talking to him, she was a little disappointed in herself though. She felt like her life story might not be interesting enough for someone who yelled gratitudes at the sunset each evening. She didn't want him to think she was soulless or boring.

"I see. Well, we all are working through our stuff and fighting our battles, aren't we Rachel Jones?"

Just after midnight, Rachel made her way to her car and threw her bag of wet clothes in the back seat. She drove the short distance to her rental very carefully. She was relieved that her team was still out. She took a shower, scrubbing the dirt from her pedicure, climbed into bed and went to sleep. Scallop went into Kosumi's room, gave him a kiss on the head, and went to bed.

11: Easy Like Sunday Morning

Rachel woke up early to the sound of rain on her window and opened her eyes to the antiseptic white of her room.

"Scallop. What a ridiculous name. What a ridiculous person. This is like a reality TV show, and the joke's probably on me," she thought to herself. She imagined introducing him to her mother and buried her face in the pillows.

The rain hastened the Tallmadge team's departure back to the city; most of the group was gone early. Rachel drove to the Country Deli, and picked up three sausage, egg, and cheese sandwiches, orange juice and a couple of coffees. Her plan was to drop them off at Scallop's place, eat with them to say 'thank you', and then hit the highway and get back to reality. Back to the city. Early Monday she had to fly to Austin to meet with the Texas Teachers Pension Fund, then on to Columbus, Ohio on Thursday to meet with the Ohio Pension Fund, with a short layover in Dallas.

Memorial Day Weekend she had a wedding to attend. *Another one bites the dust.* She thought. Her good friend Dana was getting married at the Sebonack Golf Club which happened to be right in North Sea on Great Peconic Bay. Rachel was the maid of honor and many of her friends from Harvard would be there. Most would come with either very significant others or with their husbands. Dana had invited Tucker. Rachel really wished she hadn't, but they'd been friends before Rachel and Tucker had met. While Rachel loved Dana for her fairness and ability to find a way to remain friends with both of them after their breakup, she wished she could have been less fair, just this once. She dreaded seeing Tucker, and seeing his wife. She'd even contemplated making an excuse to be out of the country on business. Dana had given her good reason to do just that by scheduling the wedding for Memorial Day weekend. Why did every woman turn into a Bridezilla? Dana was her best friend but this wedding had tested her patience a bit. The expectation that everyone would be thrilled to put aside their plans and traditions for the holiday weekend, and be grateful that, 'having the wedding on Memorial Day Sunday will give you a day to travel there, and a day to travel back!' confounded Rachel. If and when she got married she wouldn't put people out. But she cared about Dana, and she could hardly skip the wedding when she was the Maid of Honor. At least the wedding was in the Hamptons.

When Rachel arrived at Scallop's cottage, no one was home. The door was unlocked. Without a second thought she walked in and found a piece of paper and crayon on one of the shelves, sat down in one of the beanbags to write a note:

Hello boys! It was great meeting you both. Enjoy these sandwiches when you can. Kosumi – you have a great Dad…Scallop, you have a great son! Talk soon ☺ - RJ

She left the sandwiches on the table in the kitchen with the note.

Scallop and Kosumi had been over at Jessup Neck clamming for three hours. Despite raincoats and boots the Kozlowski boys were soaked to the skin as they made their way back home in the driving rain. It was one of those days where having an outdoor shower was a challenge. They cleaned up, went inside and found the note, which Scallop read to Kosumi.

Kosumi yelled, "YUM!"

"Should we heat them up do you think?" Scallop asked him.

"Yes! And then we will need the ketchup."

Scallop let Kosumi place the cold sandwiches in the oven and then turned it on. They put on dry, comfy pajamas as the sandwiches heated. The rain was so heavy that the sound on the roof was quite loud. As the boys ate their late breakfast, Kosumi was staring at the window with his chin in his hands.

"Daddy, my mommy is in heaven. Will I have a new mommy one day or always Mommy in heaven?"

"You will always have the same mommy. She made you, and she is your mommy. And she is looking down from heaven. She loves you more than you could ever know, Kosumi."

"Will Rachel come back to play with us again? She has a nice face. She is nice."

Scallop laughed.

"She might come back. I don't know. She does have a nice face, my boy. And she is nice. She just might not be our speed."

Scallop had been surprised by the gift of the sandwiches. Not surprised that Rachel had said thank you once again, her well-honed manners demanded she say as many thank you's as possible. But surprised that she'd made herself at home in his house. While clamming he'd replayed some of their conversations from the night before in his mind. She was smart and sexy as hell. He also sensed that she had an enormous capacity for loyalty and joy that she kept in check out of some misguided ideal of "professionalism". But this morning he'd come to the conclusion that the best thing to do with Rachel was to leave it be. Most likely, the difference in their lifestyles was too vast for her to have any more than a passing interest in him.

"Jake at school asks me why I only have a Daddy, and why sometimes Aunt Lucy picks me up from school."

"And what do you say to Jake?"

"That Mommy is in heaven and Lucy is my Aunt. She picks me up when Daddy can't."

"Well that's a pretty damn good answer. Kosumi: who's my boy?"

"This one," Kosumi said as he touched his chest, a tradition they both cherished.

Scallop read Kosumi his favorite book, Ferdinand the Bull, and tucked him in for his nap. The rain pounding the roof helped get the boy to sleep.

"People in the city have noise machines that don't do as good a job," thought Scallop.

He walked to the kitchen, took the clams they'd caught and shucked them. They were the big ones that were good for chowder, which would be perfect for an early dinner on this stormy day.

The emotions and images that had hounded Scallop when he'd returned home from Afghanistan rarely bothered him anymore. He was able to control his mind by rooting himself in a consistent routine. Every morning, he faithfully followed a punishing exercise regimen. It was a workout that most people would find insane, especially since the rest of Scallop's day was also filled with taxing physical labor. But, if he didn't get his workout in, and then work all day, his mind had the energy to wander to places beyond the careful paths he'd laid for it. He steered towards fatherhood and farming whenever possible.

Today, he hadn't exercised at all. He'd been up late with Rachel, and it had been pouring in the morning. Kosumi had climbed into bed with him to cuddle as the rain pinged the roof, and they'd just relaxed, hypnotized by the sounds. They'd snuggled until Kosumi had said he wanted to put on his rain boots and get clams. Scallop thought that clamming in the driving rain and carrying Kosumi around while they did it might be enough to tire him enough to quell his always lurking anxiety for the day.

As he worked on the clams and prepared the broth, his mind drifted back towards his travels. He'd lived on Easter Island in a town called Hanga Roa for a few months. On the boat ride there, he saw giant squid fighting in the moonlight in the Humboldt swells off Peru. Moments like that were frequent occurrences, and it was a magical time in his life. Once on the island, he worked on a fishing boat, and was paid with room, board and fish. Each night, the group in the house would make dinner together, and Scallop became close with a woman named Makohe, a native. They surfed together, and she showed him the island both by land and boat, teaching him about its history as he followed behind her long black hair. Makohe was never going to leave, and she knew Scallop was only passing through, but she was beautiful and interesting. He had only good memories of his time with her. He laughed about how free he'd felt then to spend time pursuing relationships that were never going to go anywhere. He wondered what her life was like now. He imagined that she would approve of the life he'd built for he and Kosumi, living in this little cottage, catching clams, and living each day in a state of appreciation for everything they had.

There were days where he yearned for more. Seeing more. Doing more. He knew himself to be an adventurer, he'd lived as one before he'd returned to North Sea. These days he could sometimes go weeks without leaving the twelve square miles that made up his community. Most days his time with Kosumi made up for staying put.

How his mind jumped from Makohe to the image that left him curled in ball in the corner of the kitchen, freezing and clammy with sweat, just nine brain-searing minutes later he didn't know.

Perhaps it was the memory of Makohe's hair that formed a synaptic bond with the black shrouded body. The body that was pushed by the force of a bullet, his bullet, to ricochet off a sand colored wall. The body that metamorphosed into a pile of black fabric, suddenly shockingly empty and leaking red. It took every ounce of his power to not to scream at the top of his lungs in an attempt to freeze time. If he screamed he might be able to step away from the gun. See if there was another way.

He'd never be sure if the woman who'd been striding purposefully towards an insurgents' home was coming with a weapon, a message, or if she was simply looking for a place of safety. He'd been the cause of scenes far more gruesome than this one. This memory was just the one that had returned to him today, the price he paid for deviating from his carefully crafted norm. It could just as easily have been any of fourteen or fifteen episodes that he revisited again and again. One night last winter he hadn't been able to control himself, he'd screamed until a terrified Kosumi stood beside him yanking on his arm, crying and yelling "Daddy, Daddy, Daddy…Daddy, Daddy, Daddy!" He wouldn't let that happen again.

He struggled to his feet, switched off the chowder and sat down at the table to stare out at the rain roiled water until Kosumi awoke. He hated to use his boy as a life vest. But it happened sometimes.

Lightening flashed across the sky above the Bay that he thought of as his home. He purposely bent his thoughts toward the future. He had a plan parked in the back of his mind. It was a goal he meditated on as a means of pushing himself forward, rather than tumbling back into his troubling past. When his boy was raised, and his parenting was done, he'd leave again. He'd go on another walkabout. Just like he had years ago, he'd pull away from the farm, make a 'west' turn and keep driving until he hit the Pacific Ocean. He was sure the less he moved around now, the more he'd appreciate it when he could once again be free to explore. If he left when Kosumi was twenty-five, he'd be sixty-one, which was far off. Nevertheless, imagining it brought him a calm that allowed him to return to the only present concerns he wanted to take on right now; finishing the clam chowder he and Kosumi would eat before they did some puzzles together, and changing his sweat drenched clothes.

"Comfy pajamas. Dry house. The things that happened in the past, you survived, they can't touch you now. Chowder brewing. Boy sleeping. It wasn't the toadfish. A good day," he thought.

Rachel pulled into the parking lot of Starbucks in Manorville. It was the best place to make a stop for a cup of tea or coffee on the way back to the city, and she really wanted something to warm her up. A mint tea would be the perfect thing to sip while she drove home and listened to Bloomberg Radio, and she was willing to brave the Starbucks to get it. Rachel and this particular Starbucks had a history.

Two summers ago, she'd spent a terrible few hours at this Starbucks. It was a Saturday morning and she'd just flown home from San Francisco on the red eye after a Monday morning appointment in Boston had been postponed. She'd called ahead for her car to be ready for her to pick up as soon as she got back to her apartment. She hadn't even gone in, she'd been so excited to get out to Amagansett. She'd tossed her bags in the trunk and driven straight out to the Hamptons. Tucker's parents were out of town for a wedding and he'd jokingly complained about having to be alone for the weekend, he'd said he'd have to go to the bookstore and find a good read since he'd be solo.

"Maybe *Lady Chatterley's Lover*!" he'd said before giving her a peck on the cheek and returning to stuffing carrots into their juicer as she headed out the door. When she'd arrived, Tucker's car was there, but he wasn't in the house. She thought he was probably down on the beach. She'd just change and go down there and surprise him. She'd gone into their room and put on a bikini and a cover up. Tucker's running clothes and sneakers were on the chair next to the tv and there was a novel on the bedside table with the first twenty pages or so disrupted. *Good* she thought *not Lady Chatterley's Lover!* and smiled to herself. She was grabbing her favorite beach chair out of the garage when she heard Tucker's voice coming from the back of the building. Who was he talking to? She looked through the garage window out to the gravel path that led to the beach and her breath froze below her collar bone, her tongue swelling to three times its normal size in an instant. Tucker was with a woman. He was guiding her down the path by the elbow familiarly. All Rachel could process was a bikini, a perfect pair of legs and a ponytail. By the time they rounded the corner Rachel was filled with a stone-cold fury. She stared at Tucker and he stared back. He was angry too.

"Rachel, this is Melissa, she's a painter I'm working with. She came to stay for the weekend. Nothing has happened...." His eyes challenged her and the unspoken "...yet.", hung in the air. She understood in that instant that any further discussion was unnecessary. Tucker believed with every ounce of his being that his behavior was justified, both what he'd already done and what he would have done had Rachel not arrived when she had. Tucker Pennington could do no wrong in his own eyes. It was his one and only flaw, but it was a big one. Rachel placed her beach chair neatly back in the stack and then resolutely walked to her car and drove away. She left without looking at Tucker or *Melissa* again.

Melissa! Was there ever a talented artist named Melissa? Melissa was a name for an elementary school teacher with a disproportionately large ass. Not a slim painter with perfect legs and a tiny plaid bikini. Rachel never took in her face. There was just a bright light of fury where the face should have been when she tried to conjure it so she could make a comparison between *Melissa*

73

and herself.

By the time she'd gotten to Southampton the rigidity of her fury was loosening its grip, and she was beginning to feel nauseous. As she drove into the town of Manorville she knew she was going to be sick. She ran into the Starbucks crying hysterically. It was a ridiculous place. Someone had decided that the lobby of a bank was a good spot for a Starbucks. It was always overcrowded with people coming and going from the Hamptons who needed their caffeine and sugar fix. There was always a line for the ladies room. Rachel ran up to the line of women waiting in the hall to use the bathroom.

"Please, please, do you mind if I go first?" she blithered.

The stunned woman at the front of the line said, "Of course Honey, go ahead," and then awkwardly patted her arm as they waited for the bathroom to become vacant. On the way out she hung her head and walked quickly to her car knowing that every eye in the place was trained on her. She was too upset to worry about who those eyes belonged to: clients, friends, acquaintances, Tucker's family members?

When she got back in her car, she'd taken a few deep breaths to calm herself and then made a call. The only person she trusted to see her in this state was her longtime personal driver, "Easy" Eddie McGillicuddy.

A deep scratchy voice with a New York accent answered on the second ring. "Toots! Do you need me today?" She hated the sound of her own voice as she asked Eddie to come pick her up an hour outside the city on his day off. "You sit tight kiddo, have a lay-down in the backseat or something. I'll be there in no time."

Eddie was a seventy-year old retired cop and piece of work, from Sunnyside, Queens. He chain-smoked, loved the New York Mets, despised Hillary Clinton – and he made his opinions known on both to all who would listen. He reeked of an intense mixture of menthol cigarettes and Vitalis hair tonic which Rachel found oddly comforting, and was a proud father and grandfather. He enjoyed his retirement gig driving Miss Jones around. Eddie was the only person Rachel shared her feelings and the daily episodes of her life with. In turn, he told her what was what with gusto. He'd been driving her to and from work for over three years, and he treated her like his daughter, and he loved her.

By the time Eddie rapped on her driver's side window an hour and a half later, Rachel had gone over the past few months with a fine-tooth comb. How could she not have seen that Tucker was unhappy enough to seek out someone else? She believed him that nothing had happened. Tucker wasn't a liar. What he was, was someone with such a practiced charm and an unpracticed magnetism, that it would have been impossible for *anyone* to have seen his seemingly facetious remarks about her travel, her work ethic, and her absences for what they were – hints that he wanted something more than what Rachel was providing. She didn't think anyone would have seen it coming, but she still felt like an idiot.

Eddie opened her door and said, "Oh little darling, please get in the car." She climbed in the back seat of his town car and found a box of tissues and a fleece blanket waiting for her. Twenty minutes later Rachel had poured out the tale of her afternoon to Easy Eddie, who listened intently before letting his thoughts be known. She knew it was coming.

"Jesus, Mary and Joseph. Please kiddo, consider it a blessing. Nice guy. Not threatening enough. He had no bite to him. He had some money, but hell in case you haven't noticed you've got plenty of dough. But there was a reason you weren't feeling it for all that time, sister. Not enough history to that guy, you need someone who's seen some real life. He was a schmuck. Maybe it was his man boobs, or the stupid whale logo that sat on top of his man boobs on every shirt he wore. Maybe it was his skinny legs. Maybe it was the fact that you could kick his ass from here to the Verrazano Bridge. He was handsome, sure, but I could never figure out if he was the skinniest fattest guy ever, or the fattest skinny guy of all time. Maybe it was the pain in the ass mother out in New Canaan. Whatever his deal was, you didn't take the bait for a reason. Pick yourself off the floor. Life is going to lead you down some dark alleys where you walk into walls. You gotta find your way back to the street, figure out the way to go and out one foot in-front of another. I'm sorry but the guy was a privileged, preppy pretty boy. Not a real man. And you, darling, you are something special. I tell my grandkids about you all the time. The hardest working and most successful woman on Wall Street, that's you Rachel fucking Jones."

Rachel knew Easy Eddie's comments were meant to cheer her up. Right now, they didn't make her feel any better, she was hurt, offended, betrayed and in shock. But even though she wasn't cheered she did understand that there was a truth to Eddie's assessment of Tucker, and of their relationship. She'd never embraced Tucker's vision of their future and it was clear now that it hadn't been built on a foundation of anything more than conventional expectation. If Tucker had had any passion for a future together with her, he would have pursued that future with something more than light hearted, teasing objections to her lifestyle choices. He hadn't.

"Toots. Be honest. Are you feeling any real heart break here? Or are you just surprised?"

At the time Rachel told him she was heartbroken.

Having to drive past that Starbucks was one of the major reasons Rachel hadn't spent much time in the Hamptons the past few summers. But today she walked in and ordered her mint tea, grabbed a snack, and chatted with the other customers waiting for their overpriced beverages. She felt like herself for the first time in a long, long time. Being outgoing was in her nature. After her breakup though, she'd sometimes felt like she had to manufacture her own personality in order to live up to expectations. Today, she felt great.

When she got back to her car she held out the snack she'd picked up, chocolate covered expresso beans, and snapped a picture of it with the infamous Starbucks in the background. She loved getting Eddie hyped up on chocolate and caffeine. He came up with his best stuff when he was popping his favorite goodie. She texted Easy Eddie the picture.

"A treat for you Eddie." He immediately sent her a return message.

"Nice to have you back Darlin'. Who's the guy?"

12: Plus One?

Rachel was in a taxi on the way to LaGuardia Airport to catch a plane to Austin. She was contemplating whether she should ask her friend Dana to grant her a "plus one" to her wedding. She was torn. Big time. Dana had already stated a clear "no ring, no bring" policy. Rachel herself found it annoying when people brought someone who was just "a date" to a wedding. Years later the bride and groom would have to look back at their pictures and debate the identity of the mystery guest at their own wedding. It was an intrusion. But, Scallop lived just minutes away from the wedding venue, she wanted to see him again, and most importantly, she didn't want to attend this wedding alone.

Tucker was going to be there with his wife. The painter with the ponytail, the perfect legs, and the twins. When Rachel tried to envision meeting them again, a diluted version of the stony anger she'd felt that day in the garage invaded her chest, but there was no image to accompany the emotion. She honestly couldn't predict how she was going to react upon seeing them. She didn't relish the thought of exposing herself in front of her old friends from business school. While they were old friends, they hadn't always been one hundred percent friendly.

Dana had kept in close touch with almost everyone from their time at Harvard. Dana was not one to let someone get away. She was one of those people who felt her life was only full if it was full to brimming with other people. Rachel loved her for it. But they both knew their friendship was due to their differences, not their similarities. Rachel was self-aware enough to understand that while she'd been friendly to almost everyone they'd gone to school with, she'd been friends with very few of them. She'd crossed paths with many of them over the past few years, the world of finance is a lot smaller than people think, but the business encounters rarely turned into friendship at the end of the day or anything else social.

Rachel attributed her lack of popularity to a combination of jealousy and a misinterpretation of her focus. Everyone had understood why Tucker and Rachel were together, they suited one another. But that didn't mean that some hadn't been jealous, either because they wanted Tucker, or because they wanted Rachel. Jealousy has a potency that cuts right through logic.

Since childhood Rachel's focus had been consistently misinterpreted. She told people what she was going to do, then did it. She didn't step on others in order to reach her goals, and she didn't gloat when she achieved them, but somehow her heightened focus made other people uncomfortable. In her thirty-four years she'd been an All-American Soccer player, an elite level student, and one of the 'the 5 hottest women in Hedge Funds'. She had become very accustomed to walking into rooms where not everyone liked her. She knew that her breakup with Tucker had been big news for the crowd that would be attending the wedding. She could stand the unwanted attention, but she preferred to give them all something else to talk about than her aloneness.

Was Scallop a good solution to her problem though? While everyone would certainly think he was handsome, and be impressed by his Navy Seal pedigree, could his presence net her just as much negative attention as flying solo? She could hear the whispers wafting across the tops of cocktail glasses now.

"Who is that with Rachel? A farmer?"

"A surfer who never went to college?"

"A guy who is a North Sea redneck townie? Great tats! I wonder how he fits into the life plan of total planetary domination?"

"Rachel Jones, you can be a real asshole," she chastised herself for considering using Scallop as a solution to her problem. Exposing him to her "friends'" snobbery wasn't a kind thing to do to someone who had not only shown her kindness, but generosity and trust. Would Scallop even want to join her? Did he own a suit? He probably didn't. *Jeez, I am just as judgmental as they are!*

By the time Rachel got out at LaGuardia, she'd bagged the idea of asking Scallop completely. If they'd been dating for months, and she had felt sure that there was something between them, it would be different. Or if there was some sort of sign from somewhere, the universe she guessed, that something with someone from such a totally different world might work out, she'd risk it. But as it stood, she would have to suck it up, grin, and bear it.

Sitting on the tarmac half an hour later, Rachel was getting back to a slew of unread emails. She'd been so busy recently that she wasn't getting back to everyone immediately, which irked her. Tallmadge was launching a new energy-based fund and Rachel had been assigned the task of meeting and screening potential portfolio managers. On this trip to Austin, she was seeing three candidates who were all driving from Houston to meet her. She also had meetings with The Texas Teachers Fund, and The Dell Family Foundation and then two dinners with individual investors scheduled.

Rachel skimmed her inbox. There was one from Dana that jumped out at her. The subject line was "Plus One?".

"Hi Ray Ray. I can't believe the big day is almost here. I'm excited but ready for it to be over. My mom is making me bonkers with the seating chart. The band refuses to play Mustang Sally and it's my sorority theme song from college. First world problems....anyways, Claire McFall and her husband just told me they can't make it. Her doctor told her to not fly given she is 8th months prego. So I wanted to throw it out there...if there is anyone you'd like to bring we have the space now. LMK. See you Friday love ya Ray Ray."

Well, that could be considered a sign.

Rachel consciously put aside her thoughts about Scallop and the wedding and spent the flight working. She had always been grateful for her ability to compartmentalize, concentrating exclusively on whatever her priority was at the moment. She read some research reports, went over pitch books, and caught up on commodities and energy market for her interviews.

Once she landed, she allowed herself the length of a moving walkway to arrive at a decision. *Enough "hemming and hawing".* It was an expression her mother used that irritated her, but it was effective. The thought of being ineffectual enough to warrant being told she was "hemming and hawing" always made Rachel decide, fast. At the end of the walkway she pulled over to the side of the terminal and dialed the home number Scallop had given her. There was no answer. She wasn't interested in facing another moment of indecision later in the day so she googled the number for North Sea Farms and called it.

"North Sea Farms, this is Lucy."

"Oh good! Hi Lucy. I was hoping you'd be the one to answer!" Rachel meant it, the moment she heard Lucy's voice she felt like she was talking to an old friend.

"It's Rachel Jones."

"Hey Rachel! Kosumi's been talking about you nonstop. He keeps going on about you leaving him the best egg sandwich ever and your "nice face"."

"Man, he's so cute." Rachel hadn't even considered Kosumi. She realized she needed to. "So Lucy, I want to ask Scallop to go to the wedding of a friend that's coming up next weekend. It's at Sebonack. But I don't want to put him in a tough spot when it comes to Kosumi. I don't know how often he goes out at night." Rachel wasn't fishing for information on Scallop's dating frequency, as soon as Kosumi had been mentioned an image of him in pajamas weeping because he wanted his Dad had popped into Rachel's head. She had no interest in being the cause of that little man's distress.

"Oh, don't worry. Scallop *doesn't* 'go out' much, but Kosumi's used to him not being at home every night. He's on duty for the fire department at least one night a week. Inga and Veronica sometimes watch Kosumi at Scallop's and he sometimes stays here with us. Don't worry about that. If you're looking for something to worry about though, I'd choose Scallop's outfit for the wedding as a major cause for concern. Were you thinking board shorts and a North Sea t-shirt?"

Rachel laughed. Nervously. "I was thinking a suit. It's black tie optional, the toughest dress code there is, no one ever knows what to wear. But I'm quite sure a bathing suit is not what my friend Dana has in mind."

"Don't worry. I'll handle his ensemble," Lucy promised. "Weddings are such a blast. I haven't been to one since my husband passed away two years ago. People don't invite me because they think I'm going to be sad. I'd welcome the chance to dance my ass off and hang at the open bar! I'm sure Scallop would love to go. Let me find him Rachel. I think he's out back by the compost area. Normally I'd send the girls but they are at school, give me a few minutes. And....good luck with this. You're going to need it...." Lucy said with a laugh.

Rachel moved through the airport as she waited. How did this family do it? Tell you their life story, painful details and all, as nonchalantly as they might discuss an episode of their favorite sitcom. After about ten minutes, Scallop surfaced. They chatted for a few minutes. It was a bit awkward. So awkward that Rachel almost made an excuse to end the conversation and make another plan, but she thought Scallop could be one of those people who was completely flat on the phone, maybe that was why he resisted cell phones. That, or he wasn't interested in either her or the wedding. But Rachel wasn't one to back away from something she'd started.

"So, I'd really like you to join me if you aren't doing anything. As I said, it would be great to get to go out and have some fun, and I'd also like to have a date since Dana gave me the ok. No pressure at all...I just thought I'd ask since its right in your backyard, down the street."

Silence. Scallop gave it some thought. He *wasn't* good at talking on the phone. Rachel felt like an idiot as she waited while walking in a small circle around her bag.

"I think that'd be very fun. I have just one thing to do this weekend and that's early Monday morning for the Memorial Day Parade. But that's no worry. They are honoring my Grandfather, my Dad, and Kosumi's Grandfather from the other side of the family this year. But no worries. I'd like to go. Thanks for asking me."

"My pleasure."

"Before that course existed, my cousins and I used to take boats over there, hunt and camp out up there right where the clubhouse is now. Great spot. Thanks for asking me. I haven't done anything like that in years. I'd love to join you!"

Rachel smiled. How many times had he said thank you? "Thanks for saying yes! Is Lucy still there by any chance?"

"Sure. You want to talk to her?" Scallop asked sounding a bit surprised.

"Yes, please."

Lucy grabbed the phone from Scallop, who walked off back to his work.

"Ok lady, I'm trusting you. No board shorts and t-shirt with a tuxedo printed on it."

"You got it. I've never seen Scallop in a suit. A uniform, but not a suit. This will be a real treat for me. Bye Rachel." She laughed the sort of low mischievous chuckle that only a big sister who's up to no good can, and hung up.

Scallop rolled out of bed at 5:30 AM to begin his warm weather workout. He'd never needed an alarm clock; he always rose a few minutes before the sun. Scallop kicked Kosumi's door open and began to sing, first quietly and then with increasing volume.

"Kosumi my boy…RISE AND SHINE AND GIVE GOD YOUR GLORY GLORY! RISE AND SHINE AND GIVE GOD YOUR GLORY GLORY! RISE AND SHINE AND: GIVE GOD YOUR GLORY GLORY!!!!" he sang doing his worst impersonation of an opera singer as he tickled and woke the sleepy boy, excavating his feet from beneath the covers and giving them a gentle pull.

The morning air was cold as he stepped onto the beach wearing only his bathing suit and carrying Kosumi, who was wearing the same plus his life preserver. He took one of his paddleboards, threw it in the water and tied the strap to his ankle, and he began his two-mile swim to "The Bluff", with Kosumi sitting "crisscross-applesauce" on the board, holding the paddle and occasionally helping their cause by rowing a bit. The swim took about thirty-five minutes as the sun rose up over Peconic Bay from the east. Schools of bunker disturbed the glassy water while seagulls, ospreys and blue herons eyed them from above as potential breakfast options. Kosumi dipped his hand in the water and let single drops fall from his fingertips, watching the rings they made until they hit the board's wake. It was rare that the bay was this calm. It could have been a mountain lake. Scallop focused on the hill of sand in the distance with a determined intensity.

Holmes Hill, surrounded on three sides by the Conscience Point National Wildlife Refuge, had been formed by a glacier during the last ice age. A steep incline completely covered in sand several feet deep, the bluff ascended from the water at an angle that even the most fitness obsessed Hamptonites found challenging. The spot was famous. It was both a rite of passage and a historical landmark. English settlers had anchored at Holmes Hill in 1640 before taking smaller boats into North Sea Harbor and making landfall at Conscience Point, where they were greeted with open arms by Shinnecock Indians. In modern times, a personal tale of being greeted with open arms by someone else was currency for local teens and for adults who didn't have the good sense not to kiss and tell.

Once they reached the bluff, Scallop grabbed Kosumi, and sprinted the incline ten times, alternating between holding Kosumi in front of him, on his back, and on shoulders. After the eighth scaling, Scallop felt light headed and had to slow down temporarily to keep from vomiting. This moment was the whole point of the daily pilgrimage. If he did his best for the final two repetitions, the resulting endorphins would hold his demons at bay for today. If he didn't push himself to his absolute limit, he could end up on the floor again, and this time Kosumi might not be napping. He pushed.

Swimming back, his lungs burned and his calves twitched. He only slowed when their cottage was in site. He pulled them slowly forward as Kosumi began to sing their morning song on his own. Eventually Scallop climbed carefully onto the board and paddled them slowly back to their cottage singing Harry Belafonte's "Jamaica Farewell" quietly so that he could listen to Kosumi's little voice echo across the water.

> *"But I'm sad to say I'm on my way*
> *Won't be back for many a day*
> *My heart is down, my head is turning around*
> *I had to leave a little girl in Kingston town"*

When he reached shore, he slowly walked up the beach towards the outdoor shower, Kosumi running in front of him. The morning air was colder than the water and as soon as Scallop had slowed down his pace he'd begun to feel it. Kosumi had some toy trucks right outside the shower that he played with while Scallop cleaned up. The hot water was both a reward and a comfort. Today would be a good day.

Inside, he flipped on the coffee percolator, a relic from the 1950s that had been in the house when he'd moved in and began making their breakfast. They ate only eggs from the farm, vegetables, and meat or fish they caught themselves. Today, Scallop put together some hearty omelets to the sounds of Kosumi playing with his dinosaurs. The smell of eggs, bacon and coffee filled the house. Today would be a good day.

Scallop kept his clothes in a wooden chest at the foot of his bed. He had three pairs of jeans to wear to work, and two pairs of overalls. He had a pair of work boots for the summer and one for winter. In summer, he wore short sleeved collared shirts that bore the logo of the farm, and in winter he wore the long-sleeved variety with thermal underwear. That was it - no variations. Simple, clean and consistent. He kept Kosumi's wardrobe equally uncomplicated. This morning they dressed, and father and son headed outside to the truck.

He'd bought his red Ford pickup truck from his cousin Tommy in the summer of 1992, the first summer he was old enough to drive. It already had some years and some mileage on it, but eager for his own wheels, he'd been proud of it. When he left North Sea in June of 1994, the family parked the truck behind one of the barns under an open shed roof toward the back of the farm. It sat there for a decade and a half. Once Scallop became a SEAL no one would touch it, out of superstition. They had an unspoken understanding; as long as the truck was there, Scallop was coming home. Through all four seasons for fifteen years, there it sat. Weeds grew around it, a Raccoon family lived beneath it, and birds made nests above the tires.

When Scallop turned on the truck in 2009, it didn't start. Tim thumped on the hood a couple of times as if he was giving a friend an encouraging pat on the back, and said, "I'll be right back." He pulled his own truck around the barn and they gave Scallop's a jump. The truck turned over and Counting Crows "Mr. Jones" blared through the speakers. Tim whooped and they both laughed at the song. Scallop remembered purchasing the cassette single at Long Island Sound, the creatively named, long defunct record store in Southampton because a girl he had a crush on liked it. There was only one other cassette in the truck, "August & Everything After" by Counting Crows. He'd bought it the same year at the same store.

Seven more years had passed, but those two cassettes where still the only music in the truck. There was no CD player, and the radio didn't work. Every morning on the way to school Kosumi insisted on blasting "Mr. Jones" on repeat for the entire ride. They sang together as loud as they could, Kosumi singing lead and Scallop singing backup. As soon as Kosumi was dropped off, Scallop would turn up the Counting Crows. Stories of Mr. Jones, Anna, The Rain King, Sullivan Street and Omaha provided the daily soundtrack to the first part of his workday. This was just fine with Scallop.

Heading to work, he always took the short cut on Mary's Lane to Majors Path which lead back to Noyac Road, and stopped at the Country Deli for a coffee. Keith Hernandez was sitting at a picnic table outside the Deli reading the Wall Street Journal and drinking coffee. Scallop got his coffee and sat down across from him.

"Morning. How'd it go with that woman Rachel the other night? I stopped by yesterday, but you guys were out clamming, I guess. In the rain – because that makes a hell of a lot of sense. You didn't have any beer, and for some reason you still don't have a TV, so I left."

"Went well, I think. She seems cool. I don't know. She called yesterday and asked me to join her at a wedding she's going to next weekend over at Sebonack."

"Nice. She seemed cool to me. When I got home that night, I Googled her. Google, by the way Scallop, is what they call a 'search engine' which exists on this thing called the 'internet'…"

"Very funny asshole."

"And I found some article where she was hailed as the 'Hottest Hottie of Hedge Funds' or something like that a few years back. You got your work cut out for you with that one Grizzly Adams. Let me know when you need help, because you will. For all the Pinot Noir in Santa Barbara wine country you will partner."

"Hmph," said Scallop. Thinking Keith was probably right.

"You make chowder?"

"Yeah. Coming over?"

"Wouldn't miss it brother. I'll bring you some decent beer. Time to do my thing. The mighty Brewers of Milwaukee clash with the Metropolitans this fine day. Man, I wish I'd gotten paid a bit more when I played. I wouldn't have to do this. I'd much rather stay here."

They both got up. Keith began his trek to Queens to do color commentary for the Mets day game, and Scallop to drive the tenth of a mile to his childhood home. A few minutes later he was parking in the farm's dusty parking lot as two cats and five chickens ran to avoid the truck. He had to deliberately avoid the peacock who was stubbornly fanning his plumage in Scallop's usual spot. It was 8:15 AM when he walked into the office at the back of the farm stand.

The office was decorated with hundreds of pictures of the family and staff, spanning decades and generations. A hand painted wooden sign with red white and blue lettering hung above the desk. "Celebrate the Bicentennial with Some Fresh, Local Food from North Sea Farms". Dust coated many of the decorations and the room smelled of dry dirt. There was a space heater by the door for the winters, and a ceiling fan above for the hot, sticky summers. This was the heart of the farm. The place where decisions were made, employees gathered, and plans were hatched. The small room had sentimental value for everyone in the North Sea Farms clan.

On the wall next to the front door, a hand drawn height chart was marked up with dates that went all the way back to the 1950's. More than a dozen markings lay punctuated each inch. Every family member, every employee's child, and every kid from North Sea who was friends with a Koslowski had their name there. Scallop and Kosumi were there of course. They were exactly the same height at age four, their etchings lay one right next to each other, the dates on them separated by 36 years.

Scallop didn't say anything when he entered. He went over to a filing cabinet where he'd stashed the pieces of a trimmer engine he'd been trying to fix and pulled it out. Lucy was at her computer entering numbers in a spreadsheet and Tim was there reading the paper, his feet up on a stool. Scallop kicked Tim's feet off the stool and sat down to take a fresh look at the small engine. The three saw each other almost every day of the year, they didn't need to greet one another in the morning or say goodbye at the end of the day. They were in the midst of a long conversation. Tim nudged the Scallop's stool with his foot.

"Looks like the Shinnecock Nation is trying to claim all of the land across to the bay, straight through Shinnecock Golf Club and Shinnecock Hills. They say that the golf course is on ancient Indian burial ground," he whistled between his teeth. "Yowzers. The total value of the land, according to them, is a billion dollars. Scallop, you might want to pay attention to this, get involved in whatever suit they have cooking. It might be important to Kosumi."

"They should get paid for it. Back in the day their winter camp area was right where the Shinnecock clubhouse is now. They'd move back over to where the reservation is now during the summer months. It was all taken from them just like everything else. You're probably right, I'll have to look into it."

"You may just have to," Lucy said glaring at the QuickBooks maze in front of her. "We can't go on like this forever brothers. This needs to be a big season, bigger than we've ever had, and I don't see how it's going to be. I've renegotiated with the bank for some better rates for the short term, but it's the 3rd time I've done that, and they kill us with fees. I have Pedro and Luis working six days, but I cut back Luisa and Hector to part time. I said no to my friend's daughter to work the register at the stand, Inga and Veronica can have all the hours and it's all we can afford to be honest."

"We'll make it through. We always do," Scallop said.

"Not really, Scallop. And that's what you just don't understand, and it annoys me because it's all I think about, you have no appreciation of the facts and it's driving me bonkers. We manage to pay our staff, and we have months that we make money, but it's getting worse and worse I'm afraid. We can't spend forever in the red. We have kids that are going to want to go to school. And even if they decide not to, we don't want to hand them a failing business and property with multiple mortgages. We need to start making money here." She looked at Tim and he pursed his lips.

"We could always sell to Wallace. Every time I see him, he reminds me of how much he'd be willing to pay for this land. Part of me thinks we should just take him up on his offer. We could each make enough money to retire." Both Tim and Lucy were looking at Scallop. It became clear to him it was not the first time his brother and sister had had this conversation. Joe Wallace was the owner of Wallace Building Company in Bridgehampton which had dominated the high-end spec and custom housing business in the Hamptons for the past ten years. Joe was a well-liked guy, and his children had grown up close friends with Tim's children. It made sense that Wallace would approach Tim to buy the farm. He wasn't surprised or offended that he hadn't been included. Tim would already know how he felt. But he had always thought that Lucy would never want to give up the farm. He put the engine down on the floor so he could give them attention.

"I don't want to be the generation that gave up. We were handed this farm with good faith. I'd hate myself each time I drove by and saw those big Wallace homes on our farm. Lucy, you'd feel the same way. Tim, maybe not you, but you know, you might."

"Scallop, I don't have too much left in me. Kim and I were talking about it the other night. Our kids are gone, and there's just not too much reason to be here all the time. Kim's eligible for retirement this fall. We've been talking more and more about going to St. John for the winters. We'd come back up here in May and stay until Thanksgiving."

Tim's wife was a nurse at Southampton Hospital. She'd grown up here with all of them, but her family, through some connection Scallop had never quite figured out, had a home on St. John and Kim had inherited it a few years ago.

"Honestly, Wallace's offer sounds good to me Scallop." Scallop looked at Lucy who looked at Tim. "Things change, you know. Times change. People change. We aren't the same people our great grandparents were. And our kids aren't either. And maybe if we did pass along the place to our kids...is that looking out for them? Do any of them even want to live this life? They're surrounded by people who work less and make more money. I don't see why any of them would choose this."

"What exactly is Wallace's offer?"

"He says the land is worth about fifteen million and he'd give us a small percentage on each of the houses, which will go for around five each depending on approvals and all that. We owe about four hundred and fifty thousand dollars, which sounds like nothing when you think in terms of paying it back after selling to Joe. But it sounds like a whole lot when you think of having to pay it back from the profits of the farm. There are no profits."

Scallop picked up the engine again. He focused on the shape of the fuel tank in order to stifle the panic that was percolating in his belly. Lucy touched his knee.

"Scallop, there is something to be said for making one's life easier. We choose to live this life of endless work, and we can make a different choice. A way out is being offered to us, and a lucrative one at that."

"Mom and dad can't be interested in doing this."

"You'd be surprised," said Lucy. "When I talked to Mom about it she was actually excited. I couldn't believe it. She said she wanted to travel and learn pottery. I don't know what she's planning on doing with Dad while she does that," she laughed.

"And Dad isn't who he used to be Scallop. Fifteen years ago, you're right, he would have shouted us down. At this point I doubt he'd look up from the news. He won't be around forever, I think he realized that when he decided to sign everything over to us. It's our decision, we three need to make the best decision for the whole family."

"I got some years in front of me," Scallop offered. "I'm not sure what I'd do if we didn't have the farm. I don't have enough carpentry work to make that my only source of income. And a lot of that work comes from here...from the farm. People seeing me here, all of that. I'd have to change my whole setup. That's for sure."

"That may not be a bad thing there, Johnny Recreation," Tim constantly teased Scallop about his surfing, paddle boarding, hunting, and diving, but he knew it was one of the ways Scallop coped. "But I don't think you're hearing us. If we sell none of us will be worried about where our income comes from."

"What we'd be thinking about is what kind of different life we'd like to have. I think it's something we should consider ok?" Lucy said looking at Tim and clearly ending the conversation. For now.

"Yeah, gotta make hay while the sun shines' as Grandpa would say," Scallop said dropping the engine back in the file cabinet and heading outside.

Scallop started where he left off Saturday, repairing the pig fence. A particularly snowy winter and rainy spring had taken its toll on several of the cedar posts. Two had rotted and a few others looked like they might not make it another year, so he decided to replace those too. It took a good forty-five minutes to dig out a rotted post. They were sunk four feet deep which put them below the frost line and decreased the chance that they would lift up in the winter, causing the rails to split. The rotted wood splintered as he dug it out. Sometimes he'd excavate a large hunk, but most of the time he was breaking the post up as he dug out the ground around it. It didn't make any sense to move the posts' locations. If he did he'd have to replace rails, and that was an unnecessary expense.

On the farm, there was always a maintenance to be done. Maintenance and all the other daily, weekly and monthly work: plowing, picking, and planting, feeding and watering the animals, weeding. All of this fell to four people, Tim, Scallop, Pedro and Luis. They were off from Christmas through March first, but other than that, rain or shine, heat or cold, they worked all day.

Scallop planted the new post and leaned on it, looking out across the field towards the stand. A woman he knew from Kosumi's school was helping her toddler out of their mini-van. She picked the little girl up and walked her over towards one of the peacocks who was standing near the corner of the farm stand showing off his plumage. She pointed at the bird and she and the little one laughed. Scallop knew they were probably there to buy strawberries for their strawberry muffins. She'd told Scallop one day at drop-off that it was their Tuesday tradition to stop and get whatever fruit was in season at the Koslowski's and take it home to make muffins in the afternoon. They ate them all week for breakfast. What would happen to their tradition if instead of a farm stand there was an oversized luxury home owned by people who would use it only six weekends of the year? Would they go to King Kullen for some artificially ripened strawberries from who knows where? Where would Kosumi get his strawberries?

Scallop was upset, but he didn't think he was being dramatic. Their farm was a beloved place in the community. Generations had come to get their watermelons in the summer, pumpkins in the fall, turkeys at Thanksgiving and eggs for Easter. Fifty years ago, there had been small farms like his all over the South Fork of Long Island. North Sea Farms and a few other farms were almost alone now, it served as a last bastion of the way things were. Every piece of free land was being sold to house people for whom this would never be home. Many of them were wonderful people who Scallop enjoyed knowing, but they weren't here often enough to become a part of place. Most of them would never hear the cadence of the land, the sea, and the marshes, the rhythm that he and Kosumi, his parents and his grandparents, all lived by. Their lives might be easier if they took Wallace's money. He'd probably never have to dig four feet deep to ferret out chunks of rotted cedar wood again. But he didn't believe that making their lives easier would make them better, and he liked digging holes.

14: Gordon Lightfoot on WEHM

At about four thirty, Lucy called out to Scallop across the field to come into the house and see her. Scallop walked over, expecting to be told that he had to drive to the Fairview Farm at Mecox in Bridgehampton to look at their chisel plough and decide if they should invest in a new one, which had been something Lucy had been threatening verbally for a while. After this morning's conversation, he was particularly uninterested in going. He and Pedro had figured out a way to MacGyver their plow this spring and it had already made it through the vast majority of the planting. What was the point in buying a new one if they were going to abandon the farm?

His mom was on the front porch mixing compost into the long rectangular planters that sat between each of the porch columns. She had some early impatiens and ivy on the side ready to plant, the same colors she'd used since he was a kid. He put his hand on her shoulder as he walked by. She made a "hmmm" sound but didn't look up from her work. He could tell from behind that she was smiling.

Scallop swung open the screen door and walked past the entrance to the living room where his father was watching Fox News. In the kitchen there were two overdressed women in their twenties sitting at the table drinking tea with Lucy. He didn't recognize either of them.

"Scallop, this is Katie and Diana. They work at Ralph Lauren in East Hampton and they are here to fit you for a suit for the wedding you are invited to this weekend. Ladies, this is the man in question, he may resist."

"Hi," said Scallop, shaking both their hands. He looked at Lucy and shook his head.

"That's ok. I have the blazer and the nice pants from last year..."

"No, you don't. You are getting a nice new suit. I'm paying for half, Tim and Kim are paying for half. That's all there is to it. Ladies do your thing."

When the girls finished measuring Scallop, Lucy handed them each a pint of strawberries "for the road" and they left. Scallop poured himself a glass of iced tea from the 1980's fridge. He sat down at the kitchen table across from his sister, leaned back in his chair and let his leg sprawl out in front of him. They both sat there for a few minutes without saying anything, Lucy sipping her tea and reading the mail. They were done for the day. They watched their father limp through the kitchen onto the porch, where he settled into a rocking chair in the shade, his afternoon spot. The old man was very limited these days. He didn't talk much and didn't go anywhere. He was happy watching their mom plant the impatiens.

The local radio station, 92.9 WEHM, was playing softly in the background and Gordon Lightfoot's "If You Could Read My Mind" came on. Lucy looked up from the mail and took off her glasses and starred out the window toward Noyac Road.

"Listen to this." She began singing along.

"I never thought I could feel this way
And I've got to say that I just don't get it
I don't know where we went wrong
But the feeling's gone
And I just can't get it back"

"When I finally gave into the reality that Bill was going to pass away, I was shopping at Schmidt's in town. This song came on, and I didn't even know it really at the time. I mean I'd heard it, but that's about it. And I was looking at my grocery list and trying to focus. My husband was going to die...and I was going to be alone, raising my girls, all alone. I couldn't keep it together and I started crying, and I thought I might pass out. When I lost my breath, that was the moment it all hit me. What was coming down the pike, straight in my direction, was crystal clear. Don't ask me why this song struck me so strongly, I think it's about divorce not death, but it was just so sad."

"An older lady dressed in Lily Pulitzer, I remember the pattern on the fabric perfectly, came up to me and helped me compose myself. She grabbed my list and led me down the aisles and she gathered the items, even holding my arm at times. I didn't know who she was, and I still don't. She wasn't from town, and it wasn't the time of year you'd see summer folks out here during the week...but she grabbed my list and helped me find everything and helped me check out. She never asked me what was wrong, she just helped me because she saw I needed it. I thanked her, she winked, and just left. I've since wondered if she was real. I mean, this wonderful woman arrives from nowhere to help me out. You can't make that stuff up."

"I'm sorry Luce, I wish I'd been there to help you," he said.

Determined to get her point across, Lucy took off her glasses and looked right at her brother with her piercing blue eyes.

"That's not why I'm telling you this. Listen to me. Walter, this may be your last chance. After all you've chosen to do, and how you've chosen to live, this woman has now walked into your life out of nowhere. She seems to be considering taking a real look at you. She knows about Kosumi. You told her about Kachina?" Scallop shook his head yes. "Right! So I'm not going to allow you to show up at a fancy wedding she invited you to in a blazer and chinos. You will have your best foot forward for this. I need you to for my own peace of mind. This might be the universe giving you what you need my brother."

"I appreciate that. I do. But at this point I've seen her three times and really only spent a lot of time talking to her once. You're making a pretty big deal of this. No?"

"I am, because I have a feeling this has happened for a reason. You wandered the Earth doing whatever you wanted. You joined the military, got holes shot in you and survived. You came back, had a child with the craziest person east of the canal, and yet you have a beautiful wonderful son who isn't scarred by her death. I suspect there are other things that are worse than all of that. Most women, especially women like Rachel, wouldn't take a second look at you. She is. And she should...but you have to do your part. You don't have to change who you are, but some effort is going to be required on your part here kid. Believe me, I know what it's like to go through life as a single parent. The feeling of being alone can be overwhelming, and it's every day and every night. I don't think you want to be alone. And while finding a way to make this work with Rachel is a long shot, it's one you need to take seriously. So, I got you a nice suit. The end."

15: Pellegrino's

Tuesday after work, Scallop and Kosumi rolled into Pellegrino's restaurant to meet Tim for a quick drink. Pellegrino's was a small family owned Italian Restaurant midway between the farm and Scallop's house. They were regulars. During the summer the brothers had two softball games a week, their team "Joe's Garage" played on Mondays and Thursdays. Wednesday night they had duty at the North Sea Firehouse, so Tuesday night was their drink night. Kosumi ran back to the kitchen to play with his friend Guzman. Sometimes they played out in the backyard, and sometimes Guzman's father, who was the head cook, gave them some "work" to do in the kitchen. A Corona was waiting for Scallop on the bar next to Tim who didn't look over when Scallop sat down next to him, he was engrossed in the Mets game on the TV above the bar.

If there had been a New York Islanders game on that day they would have made the trek to Sag Harbor. Tim had to watch the Islanders at Murf's Tavern. In the winter the local guys crowded into the tiny cape that was Murf's to play darts and cheer on the often ill-fated Islanders. But, the season was over, and today neither Tim nor Scallop wanted to drive that far, so Pellegrino's it was. Tim kept his attention on the game while Scallop started in on his beer.

"Thanks for helping to get me a suit," Scallop said when the game went to commercial.

"Not a problem brother. I hope the wedding is fun. Sounds like a nice fish on the line you've got there, huh?"

"I guess so. I'm not sure why Lucy is so amped up about it. As usual she's got the cart way before the horse. At least she didn't make me go take a look at that plough today."

"She's just looking out for you, and wants to make sure you look good, that's all. She really seems to like this Rachel woman."

"Yeah. Not sure what there is not to like. But I think we both know she isn't going to find this whole scene amusing for long. You know?"

"One step at a time brother. One step at a time. Go on the date and then you can think about all the ways it won't work out. Look, I have something to tell you, and I haven't told Lucy yet, but after this morning I think I'd better tell you sooner than later…"

"I knew it. You're gay. I always thought it was possible, but it's good to see you've come to terms with it. I'm proud of you Tim!"

"Freaking comedian this guy is," Tim said to Dan, the bartender.

"Ok. That's not it. Let me think…it was you that robbed the Otto's North Sea Deli in 1984 that night? Took all the beer and Twinkies? I knew it!"

"No Scallop, I think I'm done. This is going to be my last season. It's definite"

"Come on."

"Kim and I decided this afternoon. We can sell the house, move to St. John full time. I'm going to run the charter fishing boat, and we can just live the life we've been looking forward to living. It's like Groundhog Day here for us. The farm all day, the firehouse, softball, the seasons come and go and we do the same thing. So what I'm telling you is, I want to sell to Wallace."

Scallop looked at his beer bottle as he listened to his big brother. Tim had been heavily recruited as a baseball player by several colleges. He'd decided on the University of Rhode Island but had only lasted a year in Kingston. He was a fish out of water away from his community and he'd concentrated more on booze than on his classes and baseball combined. After skipping an exam due to a massive hangover, he packed his car and drove to New London to catch the Cross Sound Ferry to Orient Point.

He'd joined the Army, mostly because he felt like he couldn't go home to their father without a plan, and was shipped off to Camp Lejeune, and served in the Gulf War. When he returned from duty he married his high school sweetheart and they became rocks of the community, just like his parents had been. Tim coached all his kids' teams, was the head volunteer fireman at the North Sea Fire Department, a board member at the Peconic Land Trust, and one of the main figures at the Southampton Polish American Hall. To say that everyone in town loved him would be an understatement. Scallop had always looked up to him. He trusted him. He couldn't understand why he would want to leave the community and the life that had supported him.

"The winters out here are killing us. It's fucking depressing, Walter. The heavy lifting should be done, you know what I'm saying? And I'm still doing it. It's time for me to live in the islands, fish the pilings and drink my green label each day, as a wise man once said. Hear me?"

"You really want to sell?"

"Scallop we are in the unique situation. We own acres of valuable, coveted land. People out there are struggling. Life is short, and there is something to be said for making one's life easier as our sister says. You guys could buy me out if you both really don't want to sell. But I don't see how that makes any sense. Going deeper into debt for the farm isn't a smart move."

"I don't know what I'd do. I suppose I could get a job at a security firm or something like that. That's not what I want to do though."

"Walter. It wouldn't matter. You'd make enough money from your share of the sale that you wouldn't need to work at a security firm or have the carpentry business. You wouldn't really need to do anything. Maybe doing nothing isn't an option for you, but you'd have the choice. You and Kosumi would have some money to upgrade a bit. You catch me?"

"I'm not sure I want to upgrade, Tim. I'm raising my boy in a way I think is consistent with how I see the world. We have only what we need. Nothing more."

"That's going to get old as he gets older. Trust me."

"There is also the farm, Tim. Generations before us worked that land. That land has a spirit; that land is our friend, and it's been good to us. We can't just pass it on for money. We can't."

Tim laughed and lovingly hit the end of his little brother's cap.

"I'd love to live in your mind for one day. Just to see what the hell goes on in there. Is there reggae music constantly playing? Birds chirping? People eating dirt and standing on their heads humming? Maybe the chirping birds fly out of the asses of the people who are standing on their heads eating dirt and humming?"

Scallop was used to Tim teasing him about his philosophies.

"Close! People are standing on their heads humming, and they are eating dirt, birds are chirping, but the people are farting, but when they fart…a fart sound doesn't come out, instead its reggae music. Usually early Jimmy Cliff. 'Many River to Cross" most of the time."

Tim snorted and they both laughed into their beers. Tim smiled at Scallop.

"Seriously Scallop? The farm is our friend and has a spirit? The farm is just land, some dirt which the generations before worked because they had no better options. That's it. Now we can make the most of the fact that we own it, or continue to bust our asses to work it when it doesn't make us any money. You heard Lucy today. Being all weird and sentimental about it isn't smart."

They both took a break and watched the game, with Keith Hernandez providing colorful commentary.

"My kids are grown and they've moved away, they ain't coming back, and I'm fifty. Lucy's girls are beautiful and brilliant, the way things look they'll head off to some Ivy League schools and become Wall Street wizards. That leaves you and your boy. You are doing a great job of raising him all by your lonesome Walter. I mean that. I'm proud as hell of you and each time I look at you with him. I'm amazed at how great a father you've become under some trying circumstances. But you can't really go on this way forever little brother."

"I think I can. And I think it's important that I do," Scallop said, getting upset for the first time and nervously fiddling with his hat.

"You haven't thought it through. It will be hard on Kosumi. One day in the not so distant future, his friends will ask him why the house he lives in isn't insulated and isn't heated. He won't be able to have any friends sleep over because their parents will be afraid their kid will freeze to death. He isn't going to be four forever. Just like that you are going to look up and he is going to be sixteen, and you are going to wish you'd made different decisions about money. Why? Because you aren't going to have any and you are going to want to give your son more. Take it from someone who knows."

Tim patted Scallop kindly on the back. He didn't want to upset his little brother, but he needed a dose of reality. They all tried to keep Scallop's life as even keeled as possible, he'd been through a lot. But Tim needed to take care of the whole family even if that meant disrupting Scallop's carefully crafted routines.

"Change is a constant in this world, and those who adapt with the times and accept it survive. Yes, it would be sad that there would be no more North Sea Farms. That's for sure. End of an era? Yes. But time moves on brother. Adapt or perish."

They watched the game for a while and talked about anything else they could think of, surfing season, fishing, softball. Anything but the twenty acres across the street.

16: 666 5th Avenue

Rachel walked into her office on the 34th floor of 666 5th Avenue at seven am Friday morning and put her bag down on the couch. Lauren had already been in and dropped her coffee and the papers on her desk. A white post-it, monogrammed with a modern LM, was stuck to her coffee cup, "Tallmadge in today. Wants to see you around ten." Rachel shrugged and stuck the post-it on her desk. She was happy to be back in New York and had expected to see Tallmadge at some point today. Her trip to Austin and Columbus had been a mixed bag. The Texas Teachers Retirement Fund and Ohio Teachers Retirement Fund had agreed to allocate more capital to Tallmadge, and she'd met with two family offices in each city; three were a sure thing, one she thought had a fifty-fifty chance of happening. The meeting with the candidate for Commodities Portfolio Manager hadn't gone well though. She'd done her own research prior to meeting with him and she felt there were massive flaws in his strategy. Plus, the clandestine background check they'd run had revealed he had waged an on and off battle with cocaine addiction. He was sober at the moment, but he'd been sober before and fallen back. He didn't strike her as someone whose force of will could overcome the powerful pull of addiction. Working in the hedge fund world she'd seen so many cases of addiction that it made her upset to think about it; but with all that exposure had come an ability to sense those who had a chance, and those who didn't. This guy was at once arrogant and insecure. She could feel him questioning his own analyses, even as he presented them to her. She'd made it clear at the end of their meeting that Talmadge wasn't interested in him.

She lowered the blinds on the windows facing the hallway and kicked off her Jimmy Choos. She always wore Jimmy Choos to the office when she returned from a trip. It was a summer casual Friday but she'd chosen not to dress down, Jimmy Choos made her feel like a bad ass, and she liked to make sure no one had forgotten who she was while she was away. But, in the privacy of her own office she had to admit they weren't comfortable. She'd been up at 5:30 with her personal trainer making up for the couple of days of lame workouts she'd had while on the road. Her feet weren't onboard with her decision to dress to impress. She got comfortable on the sofa.

Rachel treated her office like a second home. She was there all the time, so she felt justified sitting on the couch while shuffling through her emails, skimming the morning research provided by the major bulge bracket banks, and drinking her Starbucks Iced Trenta Americano. Her coworkers understood that if she was in the office, she was working, even if she looked like she was relaxing on the sofa. She sighed as she saw an email from Talmadge's Vice President, Sterling Thorngood, marked *urgent*.

"Welcome back. Good job. Let's chat after lunch, when you get settled."

Since the blinds were closed Rachel indulged in an eye roll. Sterling Thorngood marked all of his emails *urgent*. Sterling was Rachel's least favorite person at Talmadge. If she really thought about it, he was one of her least favorite people - period. He was a self-important, melodramatic, Park Avenue WASP who spent his days sending ineffectual, urgent emails and annoying the productive hard-working people at the company who were trying to do their jobs. Sterling's role as Vice President was purely ceremonial. Even though he'd come to the fund in the mid-nineties he was a throwback to the time when having the right connections could garner you a high-level position at a fund. Sterling's father was close friends with Tallmadge from Fishers Island and while the world had moved on, and legacy employment had all but disappeared from the industry, Tallmadge was both old fashioned and uninterested in conflict. At his father's behest Sterling had interned at the fund in college and begun working there as an analyst upon graduation. But he had quickly proved himself so untalented that Tallmadge had moved him into the position of "Vice President" before eighteen months had passed, just to keep him from doing any damage.

The only function Sterling served was as an unofficial talent scout. With his "Town & Country" upbringing he was both connected socially and hyper-focused on appearance and perception. Sterling could attend a Hampton's polo match and zero in on the one young person in the crowd who would be able to sell Tallmadge's funds to their ideal client and never rock a single boat. He'd been instrumental in Rachel's hiring. Rachel knew he sincerely regretted it – she was much more than Sterling had bargained for. Rachel 's value to the fund had become immediately apparent and it was born of hustle, persistence and intelligence. An asset like Rachel cast a shadow that eclipsed someone like Sterling. A life built around a father's Skull and Crossbones membership was precarious, and naturally, being shown up made Sterling apprehensive. Instead of working harder and displaying his value, he dealt with his feelings towards Rachel in the only way he knew how, he condescended.

Within a month of her hire Rachel and Sterling had come to loggerheads. Rachel's opinions had already become more valuable to everyone who mattered at the fund and decisions were made based on her opinions, not Sterling's. There had been no love lost between the two since then. Rachel might have felt sorry for him if he weren't such a tool.

By ten o'clock, Rachel had gotten through the news and the reports she needed to read and was ready to meet with Tallmadge. She always enjoyed their meetings. She knew he had absolute faith in her and he had taken such a step back from the day to day operations of the business that their meetings had become a kind of family check in; her the accomplished granddaughter, he the grandfather just checking in to make sure that all was well.

When she entered his paneled office, so different from the rest of the contemporary space, he stood up to greet her.

"Rachel, my dear, how was your trip? I hear we dodged a bullet on that commodities prospect."

"Yes, he's *not* a good fit for us," she said, kissing him on the cheek. It was a custom they'd fallen into years ago, and while such a thing would be taboo in many professional relationships, it was not for them. She sat down across the desk from him.

"I wanted to tell you how much I enjoyed the outing this year. I had a wonderful time with that Stewart fellow. I think all our guests enjoyed themselves."

"I'm glad you liked it. I thought it went very well."

"I hear you met a fellow while you were out there? Something to do with Swizzle and some jewelry?"

Rachel was shocked. Someone had told about Scallop and the incident with the watch to Tallmadge? Perhaps it was one of the guests. She could not imagine that one of her team would have had the opportunity or the balls to mention it to him.

"Oh yes!" she said. "Swizzle dropped a watch she loved in the water, and I found a local guy to fish it out for us. Everyone was very impressed, he stayed under water a really long time."

"Ah, well good. I hope you thanked him. I'm sure Swizzle regaled him with her thanks. Hopefully she wasn't too much the worse for drink."

"No, it was fine, she was fine," she assured him.

"Good, good. Well dear, I wanted to let you know that Sterling will be speaking to you about your contract. I know, I know, he isn't always sweet to you, but he did hire you, and I generally let him follow up on these matters when he brought someone in. If anything goes in a direction you're not comfortable with come and speak with me right away. Ok?"

"Of course. Thank you for letting me know. I'm sure that Sterling and I can work things out without bothering you. Are you going back out to the island this weekend?"

"Yes, I'm going to stay out for a couple of weeks I think. Take a little rest and watch the summer come in."

"That sounds lovely. Have a great time, just call me if you need anything."

"I will Dear, if you come out to see that diver fellow, bring him out to the island and have a glass of wine with me."

He patted her on the hand as he walked her to the door. Now she was sure! Someone on her team had said something about her taking the team to Scallop's or her flirting with him at the bar. Someone had gone over her head. Who? Talking out of school was not something that her team did. Not if they wanted to stay on her team. Discretion was such an important part of what they did for their clients, and that discretion had always extended to personal details about coworkers. Rachel felt panicked. Someone was breaking the unwritten rules, and she had no idea who it was. There were only two reasons someone would tell Tallmadge or someone else who would have in turn told Tallmadge; one, a member of her team had no control over what came out of their mouth when presented with the opportunity to talk to someone in power, two, someone was deliberately trying to pull her star from the sky. Either way, it had to be handled.

She laughed it off. "Oh, that's so nice of you, I'm sure his dance card is far too full of daring dives for treasure to stop for a drink with the likes of us."

"Alright Dear, well, you know where to find me, " Talmadge said as he stood up and walked over to the cabinets where he kept everything from golf clubs, to waders, to a "My Pillow" for napping on his couch. They were done.

Rachel walked briskly from his office back towards her own. Her team's desks were in cubicles outside her office. Almost all of them were on their phones. Trevor looked up and gave her a nod as she passed by. She gave him an encouraging smile and went into her office and closed the door. She flopped down in her desk chair and swiveled around to take in the view. *Who?* It was possible that dingbat Kendra had crossed paths with Tallmadge in the hall and had verbal diarrhea. But something was telling her there was more to it than that. Someone could have mistaken Sterling for someone you could tell things to, he would have loved to relay any story that made Rachel look bad straight to Tallmadge. Was there anyone on her team that was egotistical enough to think they would be in line for her job if she left? Yesterday she would have said no. She popped back out of her chair and headed down the hall determined to get her meeting with Sterling over with and hopefully leave with a better idea of who needed to be cut from the team.

Rachel steeled herself as she gave a quick light rap on Sterling's door. She knew he would be wearing the infamous Sterling Thorngood casual summer Friday ensemble: Salvatore Ferragamo loafers, khaki pants that were just a tiny bit too snug across the front, and a light blue Fishers Island Golf Club shirt that clung in all the wrong places. Sterling's physique vaguely resembled a vertical pile of marshmallows. She marveled that the Town and Country set were so accepting of Sterling considering his "sparkling personality" and "outstanding looks". But Rachel understood that if you were born in, you were in. If he'd been in the middle class, sitting on the bench on every sports team, mediocre grades, and nothing interesting to say he would have been at the bottom of the social strata. Rachel was sure that if it came down to it, she could beat the living hell out of Sterling with her left hand. But, a life of privilege, surrounded by enough peers with similar motivation and intellect had made him a fixture.

Rachel entered Sterling's office without looking at him, her eyes locked to her iPhone, she needed something from him, but he didn't need to know that.

"Hi Sterling. What's the good word?" she asked.

"Nice work on your trip. If they both up their allocations that's splendid. Well done. You, Rachel Jones, are a marvel of modern capitalism at its best."

She smiled tersely. "How can I be of help this morning Sterling?" She braced herself for the unctuousness she knew was about to begin.

"You've had a great year. You and the team you've created, and molded in your image, is simply magnificent." The *in your image* had a perceptible sarcasm behind it. "It's not just the money you raise, but it's also the way you go about it. Presence. Poise. An incredible intuition for knowing when to call on whom based on macro market trends. We want you to know that as your contract winds down, we are very interested in making sure you are happy here at Tallmadge."

"That's good to know, Sterling. If I wasn't happy, you'd certainly know about it. Yes, the team has done a great job, and I believe we can get better from here. But things are harsh out there, the competition is brutal and I know that I'm the reason we're beating it back right now. We both know that. Since you brought it up I want to be clear. With my contract extension I expect my floor to be double what it is now. If that's not possible, we have from now until the end of the year for both of us to make different arrangements."

He stared at her blankly, sweat beading at his brows and his anger filling the room with a pressure that made Rachel slightly sick to her stomach. She was demanding quite a bit. In her current contract, Rachel's "floor", the minimum amount she could be compensated over the course of the year was 1.5 million. She'd asked for double, plus the percentage on all the funds she raised that was already in her current contract. If Tallmadge agreed, which she believed he would, she could be looking at ten million over the course of the next two years. Rachel had not become so jaded by her work on "the buy side" that she was desensitized to the fact that this was an extraordinary amount of money. The reality of this business was that anything could happen. Global markets could sour. Regulations could change and turn investments or the entire industry on its head. She could let her guard down and some crafty person with hearty ambition could find a way to push her out. Pushing for what you needed to sustain you over the long haul while you were on top was the only way to protect yourself. Thinking you were always going to be on top was naïve.

"So, you off to Fishers Island this weekend?" she asked, knowing that a change in tack would throw him off guard.

"Uh yes. Indeed. We are. Tibby and the boys are there already are probably playing the back nine as we speak." Sterling let out a loud awkward laugh, something he habitually did when there was nothing humorous about a situation.

"Right." Her tone let him know she'd caught him feeling awkward. She switched tacks again. "Have you had the chance to meet Kendra, the newest member of my team? The outing was her first real trial."

"Uh, no. I haven't had the pleasure. You know, I let your team be your team. How did she fare?" His eyes hadn't shifted, nothing had changed in his tone of voice. He was not the one that had passed any information about Scallop or the watch incident on to Tallmadge. There was no use continuing the conversation. His anger with her blunt delivery would cause him to relay her salary demands to Tallmadge in a way that exposed him for the sniveling, jealous, hanger-on that he was. Tallmadge would be expecting her to negotiate her contract and to ask for the moon. Why would she not? Sterling would look like a whiner, she would look like a winner.

"She did just fine. Listen Sterling, thanks for the talk. Please let me know if you can work with my terms."

She left the door of his office wide open and purposely walked across the trading hall to get back to her office. She paraded the guys on the desk loudly saying hello to each, she had a particular ritual with every one of them which she went through loudly and with enthusiasm for Sterling's benefit. It was quite the performance.

"Jonesy! When are you coming over to meet the twins?" asked Steve Ledbetter, the Distressed Credit Portfolio Manager.

"Bedwetter! Whenever you invite me. The pictures are gorgeous. How's Vicki feeling?"

Ajay Desai, the Indian Quant Trader who Rachel recruited from Goldman Sachs, blushed as she walked by, getting ready for what he knew was coming.

"Bye bye Mr. Ajay Desai. He trades futures he trades options in the blink of an eye. And if your returns don't hit the blue sky Ajay this will be the day that you die. This will be the day that you die," Rachel sang as she massaged his shoulders, the desk howling with laughter. She kept going through them all until she reached her office on the other side of the floor, at the door she blew them all a kiss, kicked up her heel and closed the door behind her to the sound of male laughter.

As soon as she closed the door to her office she grabbed her phone and sent a text to Heddy Lesslaw, a headhunter who Rachel had known since her time at Goldman Sachs. Good headhunters like Heddy knew that someone in her position could decide to jump ship at any time for any number of reasons. Rachel had been in touch with Heddy for years, and Heddy was always prepared with opportunities for Rachel. Heddy lived two blocks from Rachel and every time they ran into one another Heddy always had at least one interesting opportunity on the tip of her tongue. She had the most impressive mental rolodex Rachel had ever encountered and Rachel liked her and trusted her. Rachel was 99.9% sure she'd be offered exactly what she'd just demanded at Tallmadge. Heddy was a necessary safety net, who would also be a pleasant coffee date.

"Coffee/lunch/drink next week? It might be time to have a look around" Rachel pressed send.

As Rachel plowed through the remains of her day, she pushed down a nagging anxiety about taking Scallop to the wedding. She wanted him to come, she didn't want to be rude, but Tallmadge's mention of him had made her extremely unsettled. Perhaps he was truly only interested in her happiness. Perhaps he disapproved. She had a feeling he wouldn't be the only one. What would her friends think? She knew what Tucker would think. Snob. That was it. She was going to go, enjoy looking at him for the evening, and enjoy spending an evening with someone who was the antithesis of Tucker and most of the other guests.

On the way home Rachel told Eddie all about her battle with Sterling and her decision to say "screw it" to public opinion and take Scallop to the wedding.

"Good girl. I know you talk big talk about "reaping what you sew", and crafting your own goddamn destiny and blah, blah, blah. But honey, I gotta tell you. Life is random. It's *random*. Sometimes you gotta just jump into the river and see where the current takes you. Just say "fuck it" and float."

"Thanks Miyagi. "Fuck it and float." She said, laughing as she got out of the car and ran into her building.

17: Sebonack Wedding

By four in the afternoon on Saturday the two hundred and fifty guests had gathered on the lawn of Sebonack Golf Club, overlooking Great Peconic Bay. It was a perfect day at seventy-seven degrees; National Golf Course's famous windmill sat picturesque in the distance. The sky was perfectly blue, dotted with the fluffy white clouds that would make for unbelievable photos and Rachel looking down, marveled at how her purple floral Badgley Mishka evening gown, the same one all the bridesmaids were wearing, complemented the particular green of the grass.

As Rachel looked out across the lawn, dotted with groups of guests in cocktail dresses and well-fitted suits sipping champagne and greeting one another, towards the water and the ceremony area she had to admit that Tracy, the obsequious wedding planner who had been hissing questions and commands into her ear since the bridal party had arrived at seven in the morning did indeed know what she was doing. Sited to catch the best possible view of the water was a triple arch of purple peonies and white orchids, some the size of a thumbnail, some the size of a dinner plate, and hundreds of them in every size in between.

She'd watched the clever and daring floral designer weaving shining strips of seaweed into the display from the windows of the suite of rooms on the upper floor of the club house where they'd spent the day having their nails, hair and makeup done. The florist and an assistant had worked with incredible speed during the hour before the guests began to arrive, pulling dripping strips of the seaweed from large white buckets. They wore laminated aprons to protect their clothes from the water and wide brimmed straw hats to protect themselves from the sun, but she'd seen them lug their buckets out to the service parking lot about twenty minutes ago red faced and dripping. The sun gleamed off the seaweed in spots and streamed through it in others, lighting it up like light green stained glass. The effect was a combination of wild and refined that can only be achieved through a willingness to spend an enormous amount of money on something that could only last a short while.

Placed in front of this masterpiece were a dozen purple plaid picnic blankets with purple velvet cushions carefully placed in a symmetrical layout that gave the impression of being casual and random. Rachel felt for the guests who would shortly be asked to become subject to Dana's quirky sense of humor and plunk down on the ground wearing their finery and sipping champagne and then have to find a way to stand up gracefully and either take off their shoes or risk putting their heels through the plaid blankets.

At least Dana had made a concession for the older guests; on the edges of the whole setup eight Victorian sofas upholstered in the same purple velvet as the cushions were sitting incongruously amidst the golf course backdrop. When Dana had told her what the sofas were for as they'd been toted across the lawn by the rental company that morning, Rachel had started to protest. How was Dana's eighty-seven-year-old aunt who Rachel knew couldn't put her own shoes on going to struggle out of a low-slung Victorian sofa to watch her walk down the aisles. The ever-present Tracy had hissed in Rachel's ear, "Don't worry, I've got a cater waiter posted at each sofa to help the seniors." Rachel had a moment where she began to understand just how annoying she must be to Sterling Thorngood. Rachel was the financial world's Tracy. *Except I don't hiss!* Rachel told herself. Then she decided to cut the officious Tracy endless slack. The fact that she was good at her job had allowed Rachel to spend the day enjoying time with Dana and the other bridesmaids instead of having to run around making sure everything was the way Dana would like it as she had the one other time she'd served as the maid of honor for her sister. Aside from having to deal with her Tracy had made everything gorgeous. It was perfectly Dana and perfectly charming.

Because she was free, Rachel hadn't had such a fun day in recent memory. There were four other bridesmaids. Three of them were friends from business school, the fourth was a friend of Dana's from her summers in the Hamptons. Rachel felt almost buoyant being with her own friends. There was nothing like spending time with people who supported you with a wellspring of shared memories. She felt the most herself when she was with them, her strongest and, at the same time her most flexible. They'd spent the day holed up upstairs getting ready, gossiping, and *eating cheese*. At exactly twelve fifteen that afternoon three waiters had come in carrying trays piled high with cheese, bread, pate, fruit, fig compote, and nuts and set them around the room. Dana smiled blissfully as they set one down directly in front of her.

"I've been eating kale and grilled chicken for months. It's past noon. How bloated can I possibly get in three hours? Cheese me! Thanks boys!"

After Dana *mmmm'd* and *oh my god'ed* over the cheese for a few minutes she slathered a big pile of pate on a piece of baguette and dropped the bombshell Rachel knew she'd been dying to let fly since this morning.

"So...Rachel is bringing a new beau to my wedding," she bit her baguette dramatically.

"Really? Oh, do tell Miss Rachel," said her friend Sarah who although she was four months pregnant was recklessly eating a hunk of stilton with obvious delight, "is he guaranteed to make Tucker wish he'd dressed a little smarter today?"

"Oh please," said Jenny, "nothing could make Tucker regret his polished disarray. Tucker is Rachel's ex," Sarah explained to Leslie, Dana's childhood friend from her summers in the Hamptons. "He was at school with us. So, who is he? Poor guy. Does he know what he's walking into? Tucker will probably try to be his new bff. He won't be able to suppress his tendency to be disingenuously awesome."

"Let's not stray from the point here. You need to brace yourselves," squealed Dana, "his name is too good. It's unreal."

"His name is Walter," said Rachel.

Sarah laughed, "Is he like the Walter in *Sleepless in Seattle*? Bill Pullman's character? Thrilling Rachel."

"Come on," shouted Dana, "that's not what they call him! You told me he goes by his nickname." She turned to the others looking like the cat who ate the canary as she thickly smeared another piece of bread with pate. "He lives here in town, a farmer. He surfs, of course, and he's got some sort of underwater super powers."

Leslie gasped a little. "Oh, I think I know who you're talking about! It's not Scallop is it?"

"Oh my GOD. You know him? Scallop! Scallop!" laughed Dana.

"Yeah, we went to elementary school and high school together. He's nice. He's always been nice. He's absurdly good looking. It's almost obscene. He's been through some things since school…", she looked up at Rachel. Rachel could see that she was trying to gauge if she knew about Kosumi and perhaps Kachina as well. Rachel smiled at her. Leslie smiled back. "I'm glad he's found someone."

"Oh!", Rachel's breath caught a little, "I wouldn't say he's *found* someone. This will only be our second date. The first date wasn't even really a date." She felt like she needed to be clear about exactly the place she and Scallop were at, although she didn't know why she felt that way.

"I imagine that's how most dates with Scallop are. Not really dates," said Leslie. "He's not likely to ask you to dinner at the Maidstone and choose the wine."

"Well, so much for my 'no ring no bring policy'. Rachel's bringing a gorgeous, weird stranger to my wedding, to make Tucker wish he weren't such a dumbass."

"Whatever." Rachel kissed Dana on the head as she reached over her to grab a hunk of cheese.

"Hey, the hair! The hair!" Dana grabbed the cheese out of Rachel's hand and popped it in her mouth.

"I can't imagine anyone fabulous enough to knock Tucker out of the narcissistic construct he's been living in his entire adult life. It's not gonna happen," said Jenny. Jenny had been the only one of Rachel's friends who had been disapproving of Tucker when they'd been dating. She'd tried to warn Rachel that Tucker's moral compass was warped by his temerity. She'd been right. She felt free to point out she'd been right whenever the opportunity arose. This didn't bother Rachel. Jenny loved her and Rachel knew she was still worked up about Tucker hurting her.

Several hours later, a harpsichordist and a violinist were providing unobtrusive accompaniment as guests mingled drinking lemon water from crystal glasses. Tucker and the woman with the ponytail were walking down the hill towards Rachel, arm in arm. Sometimes in life there is no way around an awkward moment; all you can do is keep breathing, live through it, and be thankful it doesn't last forever.

Rachel put her hand out and found purchase on one of the few trees that dotted the landscape. She took a deep breath and realized she didn't need steadying.

Tucker's wife didn't look a thing like she remembered. The perfect legs, tan, bikini and long straight ponytail, burned so indelibly into her mind by thousands of repeated remembering's, were not only absent, it seemed impossible they had ever existed. Those legs were covered by the conservative navy jumpsuit Melissa was wearing, in a cut calculated to disguise a middle that was disproportionately thick. Her curly hair was a natural shade of red and her dimpled face was dotted with freckles of the type that guaranteed she'd never be taken seriously. This was not a woman who tanned. Rachel knew she looked far more glamorous than Melissa did. Melissa was what people called "cute".

Rachel's memory had failed her; turning Melissa into someone Tucker had chosen as an equal substitute for Rachel, maybe even a step up the ladder of young, glamorous, hard-ass, New York business women. She'd always thought he'd swapped her out when she didn't measure up to his expectations. Looking at Melissa it was clear that Tucker had chosen an entirely different animal. She looked softer, sweeter, and far less confident than Rachel. Right now she also looked terrified. Her face had just blanched and she'd nearly stopped coming down the hill, pulling Tucker up short with her. Melissa had seen Rachel and she clearly wanted to change directions or even leave altogether. But it was too late, Tucker had seen Rachel.

Tucker waved and shouted, "Rachel!" as he lopped downhill, his white shirt, tucked into his seersucker suit just loosely enough and slightly askew enough to make it look like he didn't care all that much, stayed perfectly amiss. He pulled Melissa along behind him, hair bouncing, boobs bouncing, blush rising. Tucker reached Rachel and pulled her in around the waist for a tight hug and a kiss on the cheek, pushing the wind out of her.

Rachel had spent so much time thinking about how she'd react to seeing Tucker again, she hadn't spent a moment considering how he might react seeing her. No matter, had she spent hours fantasizing about it she never would have imagined him greeting her like a best friend who'd been out of the country for several months. Hugging her breathless and leaving both she and Melissa dumbfounded.

"You look *great!*", said Tucker. "It's so good to see you! Melissa, you know Rachel!"

To Melissa's credit she recovered herself quickly. Seeing Rachel's shock at Tucker's behavior she took hold of the situation. "I don't actually.

We've never been introduced. It's nice to meet you Rachel." She shook Rachel's hand. "Tucker mentions you often," she said without any subtext. Rachel was impressed, she was feeling like Tucker might have made the right choice. Melissa was certainly nicer than she'd ever be.

"This is one of Melissa's first big nights out without the twins," Tucker said. He was speaking calmly and matter of factly. "You know I have to be out for openings all the time, but she really hasn't been anywhere but in the trenches. Perfect timing for Dana's wedding. I think she really needed a night out. It's been a lot of yoga pants, granola bar dinners, and spit up in the hair. I saw the Deal Breaker article on you a while back. That must have made your compliance guys go crazy. Hey Rachel, did you notice the chaise lounges at the pool...?" He was waiting for her to wow Melissa with her special gift. He'd always loved that she could identify design with a glance. Rachel started to fill in the blank out of habit, but stopped herself.

In a single, charming breath Tucker had done everything a reasonable person would have avoided in this situation. He'd belittled his wife. He'd held her trials with their children up against a magazine article in which Rachel had been named one of the "5 Hottest Women in Hedge Funds", an article he would have known made Rachel both angry and proud. Then he'd referenced their old private joke. *He just completely insulted his wife and now he wants me to play the furniture game with him?* How could Tucker be oblivious to the fact that he was making both women uncomfortable?

Rachel looked at Tucker and then over at Melissa. Their eyes locked, understanding flashing between them. The two women had expected to be uncomfortable meeting one another. Melissa had always felt guilty about the small part she'd played in Rachel's unhappiness. She'd Googled Rachel after that terrible encounter in the Amagansett garage when she'd been blindsided by the fact that Tucker had a girlfriend. She hadn't known a thing about Rachel when she'd agreed to spend the weekend in Amagansett. She'd only met Tucker a couple of times before that. She'd actually left the house shortly after Rachel drove off embarrassed and upset. But Tucker had pursued her for months after, and she'd finally decided to see him again only when she was sure that Rachel was fully out of the picture. She wasn't someone who went out with other women's boyfriends. She'd read the article in Deal Breaker when it came out a few months ago and seen the recent picture of Rachel in it. Tucker assured Melissa that she was "just as gorgeous" as Rachel, but the reassurance was unconvincing. On the ride to the wedding, Melissa felt so nervous she had nearly thrown up. Tucker had taken her arm as they got out of the car, kissed her, and said, "Stop worrying, there will be so many people we probably won't even talk with her." And then he'd made a bee-line.

Tucker had, as he always did, expected to have his cake and eat it too. He expected them to like each other. He expected that Rachel had forgiven him. He expected Melissa to share the intimate details of child rearing with his ex-girlfriend. He expected to make private jokes with that ex-girlfriend and have his wife find it loveable. He expected. Rachel wasn't going to deliver.

"Outdoor furniture's not my specialty." She said, purposely keeping her eyes on Melissa. "Melissa it was so nice to meet you. I really want to see some pictures of your twins. Mothering two at the same time. That's such a major responsibility. I bet you're great at it. I've got to go see if Dana needs anything right now though. It's almost…" Tucker cut her off.

"Who is that? Are they coming here? Are you allowed to bring boats on this beach?" He was looking past Rachel toward Great Peconic Bay, squinting a bit, trying to make out something on the water.

Rachel turned to see Scallop arriving in his twenty-five-foot center consoled Zodiac. Two hundred some odd guests all spread out to get a better look as Scallop expertly landed the boat on the beach, threw on his jacket and walked towards them into the grass. Rachel turned back to Tucker and Melissa.

"Excuse me, my date's arrived." She smiled at Melissa who smiled back, both of them aware that for once Tucker Pennington was the one who'd been blindsided.

The crowd watched as Rachel, dark and tan standing out against her purple bridesmaid's dress, made her way towards Scallop. He pointed to her confidently, then to his dapper dark blue suit. With his long curly hair, sunglasses, and tall, chiseled frame they presented a striking contrast to one another and quite a picture and Rachel knew it. They kissed on the cheek.

"Nice ride. Excellent to see you!"

"Thanks. It's only a few miles, and the bay was perfect today for it."

"How do you plan to get home? Does that thing have lights?"

"I'll be just fine. I've done it many times. What a day for a wedding."

"It's perfect. Dana is doing great. Nice suit you have there. Your sister did a good job."

Scallop laughed. Rachel motioned to the crowd.

"Shall we enter the fray? I'll introduce you to my friends. I know most of these people from business school. Some of them I haven't seen in a couple years. Some I see a lot for work."

Sarah and Jenny were facing her standing in the midst of a clump of a dozen old friends from school that included Tucker and Melissa. They had linked arms and were staring intensely over their water glasses in unison as Rachel and Scallop walked up the hill. They looked like runway versions of the "Witches of Eastwick" cooking up some trouble. Rachel rolled her eyes, grabbed Scallop's hand and said, "Brace yourself." Rachel and Scallop breached the circle, catching everyone's attention. Her friend Abigail was there with her husband. Rachel hadn't seen them since their own wedding over a year ago and she'd been excited to see her today. She was kind, effervescent and intelligent and was rarely if ever sarcastic. An anomaly in her group of friends. Abby seemed like the best inroad to Rachel and she went in for a hug.

"Abby, how are you? I'm so glad you're here. I can't believe it's been so long! This is my date, he goes by 'Scallop', we could tell you his real name, but then we'd have to kill you." Scallop shook Abby's hand.

"You can call me Walter if you like. I don't want to seem too mysterious." Rachel introduced him around the circle, not surprised when Jenny and Sarah simply shook Scallop's hand and let Rachel move on to the next introduction, an undercurrent of glee running between them. They were waiting for her to get to Tucker! Of course. This was epic drama at its best - so much better than any reality show. Jenny and Sarah had been waiting all afternoon to see an epic, standalone episode of "The Real Graduates of Harvard Business School" play out against the backdrop of one of the most exclusive golf clubs in the country. Would Tucker Pennington's shield of entitled narcissism be penetrated by the stunning local farmer who'd arrived on the scene like a low rent 007? Would there be a twinge of jealousy? Or would Tucker carry on, believing in his own perfection, never even considering whether Rachel had upgraded or downgraded her package? Their money was on Tucker's conceit; they'd never seen it fail before.

"Ahoy there Captain. Tucker Pennington. Welcome ashore!" Tucker said. Sarah and Jenny gripped each other's arms. It was happening. Abby, who'd turned away to whisper something to her husband, snapped back to attention and Rachel took a small step backwards. Tucker had been unsettled.

"How's it going Tucker? Scallop Kozlowski," Scallop said as he shook his hand and slapped him on the back.

"Sorry. Scallop?"

"Don't be sorry Tucker. You got it."

"Huh." Rachel had *never* heard Tucker speak in a monosyllable. He awoke articulate. "So, you have a house right nearby? Your, ah, boat, you came in that, must not be too far."

"Not far at all. The conditions were perfect for it and, to tell the truth, I've never been out in the boat in a suit, seemed like a novel thing to do."

"Yes, yes. Nice boat. So, ah, how long have you two known each other?"

"Since last Friday night."

"I see. Work? Are you at Tallmadge as well?" The rest of the group was completely still and quiet, too stunned to even be uncomfortable.

"No. I'm a farmer."

"Oh. Okay!" said Tucker. He'd found something to look down on. It was obvious he felt he had the upper hand now. It was obvious. None of them had ever seen Tucker question where his hand was. Ever. "Ah, which farm would that be?"

"North Sea Farms, right down the road," Scallop replied.

Tracey, headphones and mouthpiece in place and a frozen smile on her lips thrust her head into the circle.

"It's time to begin. Guests would you mind taking your seats? Ladies, would you come with me?" Oblivious that she'd interrupted the denouement of a saga they'd all watched for years, Tracey placed a hand on each of Sarah and Jenny's backs, guiding them back towards the clubhouse, breaking the moment.

Rachel turned to Scallop. "Sorry about that. Tucker and I used to date. Obviously. Sorry if that was awkward. I didn't expect that at all. I've got to go do my duty. Find yourself a good seat and I'll see you at the cocktail hour after the pictures."

"Sounds like a plan."

Scallop found a seat, surveyed his surroundings, and introduced himself to a few people. The groom, Mark was a television ad salesman for NBC, but he'd come from Ohio originally. The family business was a small empire of car dealerships in Cleveland and Akron. Scallop sat next to Mark's sister-in-law Marcia, a bookkeeper at the dealerships. He could tell she felt out of place in the Hamptons. She had the wrong hair, the wrong dress, the wrong shoes. If she were in Cleveland she would have been considered the height of style. But Dana worked for DKNY and many of the wedding guests were from the fashion world. Scallop told her about his day at the farm, planting lettuce, and fixing the turkey pens. By the time the music picked up for the beginning of the ceremony he thought he'd made her feel a bit less like a whale that woke up in Wichita.

Scallop was still on his own while Rachel took pictures with the wedding party during the cocktail hour. As Scallop grabbed a Heineken from the bar, Abigail and several friends of Rachel's from Harvard and their significant others circled Scallop. Eventually, it was the entire Harvard crew, less Tucker, treating Scallop as if he was a guest on "Inside The Actors Studio".

"Where did you grow up?"

"Right here in North Sea."

"So that makes you a Southampton High School grad?"

"That's right."

"Have you always worked on the farm?"

"No sir. I left here the day I graduated from high school and drove to the west coast to surf, wander and just live life man. From Alaska to Washington state and on down to Argentina I did it all. Surfed. Climbed mountains. Tended bar. Worked on the Galapagos for the Sierra Club. Then 9/11 happened, and I flew back to the U.S., volunteered, and became a Navy SEAL. I served four tours in Iraq and Afghanistan, was discharged and returned home here in early 2009. So, since then, I've just been here working at the farm. I have a small business making docks also. But mostly I enjoy the land out here. It's God's gift to us, and I use it daily. Surfing. Paddling. Diving. Fishing. Clamming. Hunting. I do something each day that binds me to the land in some way. And, I have a beautiful son who is four years old. That's me folks. Now how about some details about you all?"

"What do you hunt for out here?"

"Mostly over educated city guys who come out here for weddings," Scallop said making the crowd laugh.

The wedding party joined the rest of the guests as cocktail hour drew to a close. Rachel sought out Scallop and found him explaining his background to two of Mark's uncles who were trying to convince him he'd make a terrific used car salesman. She pulled him aside as the guests made their way to the tables.

"Having fun? Sorry I've been preoccupied with my duties. After this speech, I'm pretty much done."

"No worries. I'm having a great time. Nice group of friends you have here. We have the whole evening ahead of us. Ready for your speech?"

"Is anyone ever ready to give a speech at a wedding? It's a torture we inflict only on those we love the most. No. I'm not ready. Not at all."

"You'll be fine."

Several minutes later, Rachel was introduced to give her speech.

"Hello everyone. My name is Rachel Jones, and I met Dana on the first day of classes at Harvard Business School. We were instantly friendly even though we had almost nothing in common. She ate all my food, borrowed all my clothes, studied half as much as I did and got the same grades, and she was a golfer for god's sake. Raise your hand if you loved the picnic blanket/floor cushion seating arrangement she set up earlier?" Rachel walked the dance floor with the microphone in hand like a seasoned politician at a town hall meeting before the Iowa caucuses.

"No one, *no one* knows how to have fun like Dana. Maybe that's why so many of us here today count her as one of our best friends. She has a special way of relating to people. She makes you feel great about yourself. If you need something, she'll help you get it. You don't know how to do something; she'll teach you. I finished in the top ten of the friendly little golf tournament we had yesterday. You know why? Dana insisted I learn to golf, "for business". I think it was really so that she could beat the pants off me every time she drags me out on a course. She seizes opportunities when they present themselves. Like when she met a nice young man from Cleveland at a bookstore, and decided then and there he was the guy for her. And here we are, years later, celebrating with them. Making the most of the opportunities that present themselves to us? Seizing situations. That's really living life isn't it? I believe it is. Look at this beautiful couple in front of us today. They're two people who made the most of a situation. They fell in love in Boston, they were able to sustain a long distance relationship for years, they found a way to shape their careers so that they could be together and here we all are today. Dana even voluntarily visited Cleveland…many times! That *had* to be the clincher. Optimism and perseverance triumphed. These two committed to one another whole heartedly, pig headedly, and enduringly years ago."

"Usually these speeches are about how getting married is massive decision, how it takes hard work, compromise and sacrifice every day. Everyone says a silent prayer that the couple will find a way to navigate the rocky path of life together, and then lifts a glass while wondering if they've got a chance. Look at these two. They've been skipping down craggy paths hand in hand with smiles on their faces for years. Save your prayers for someone who needs them. I don't think that these two need anything more than for us to celebrate a love that has already conquered all with a real big party. I love you Dana, and Mark….I don't have to tell you how lucky you are. Cheers to you both. I won't wish you luck…you don't need it."

Rachel finished her speech to shouts and applause filled with love and enthusiasm for her friend who ran over and tackled her as fast as the Badgley Mishka would allow. Rachel laughed locked in an ecstatic embrace with Dana who had gone from zero to ten on the drunk scale in minutes, and whipping off the lipstick and slobber she'd just shmeared all over both cheeks. Dana grabbed the microphone and tiptoed over to Mark's brother Herb, who was loudly applauding and shaking his yes, quite carried away by Rachels' speech. Dana held the microphone out to him like a challenge, expecting him to grab it and meet the challenge, somehow out-do a wedding speech that had actually hit the mark. Poor Herb, he looked terrified. Herb was the least outgoing of Mark's family, which was saying something. He knew he couldn't follow Rachel with her command of an audience, charm, beauty and the legs that terminated in red shoes the like of which Herb had never seen in Akron. Herb stuffed the sweaty piece of paper that held the speech he'd worked for weeks back in his pocket and sheepishly raised his glass.

"To the happy couple!" he shouted at the very top of his lungs.

The guests laughed and shouted "Cheers" as the band started up – "It's Not Unusual" by Tom Jones. Herb was treated to a bear hug from Dana as Rachel headed across the room to Scallop, sitting at the table next to Jenny smiling at her as he downed his champagne. By the time she got over to him he had her champagne in hand, ready to go. He let her down it, placed it carefully back down on the table and saying, "Let's go!" put his arm around her waist, lifting her just a bit of the ground and swung them both around to face the dance floor.

Dana had hired her favorite local band, The Nancy Atlas Project, who did regular stints at The Stephen Talkhouse in Amagansett and the Bay Street Theatre in Sag Harbor. Rachel and Tucker had used to make a point of seeing them when they'd been Out East in previous summers. As the band got going, the dance floor filled up with people and energy. For the briefest moment Rachel felt Tucker's eyes on her. Funny she thought that being faced with the band they'd both liked seemed to affect them. But the second she began to dance with Scallop any thought of Tucker was driven from her mind. Scallop was a very involved dancer. He was spinning, twisting, grabbing her, and turning her. At one point he did the worm, his long body cutting a wide path across the floor as the other dancers moved aside clapping and laughing with astonishment. There was no time to breathe or think. Her hands in the air, his hands on her hips, Rachel felt the music, herself, and this other crazy human being and everything else was blurred. After the sixth straight fast song Scallop pulled Rachel to the bar where he convinced her to do a shot of tequila. Don Julio was swimming to her head as they sat down for dinner.

Father Vinny, the plump mustached priest who had performed the ceremony, stood in front of the bride and groom's table, blocking the couple from view as he gave the blessing. After the "Amen" he continued.

"I had an interesting conversation with someone during the cocktail hour. I spoke to a guest who happened to know the entire history of this very ground. I don't want to put him on the spot...but I thought perhaps he would like to share with us? Mr. Kozlowski?" Father Vinny motioned to Scallop, who was taken off guard, but nodded solemnly and with no hesitation walked up and grabbed the microphone.

"Howdy. Thank you, father. This ground we are standing on is sacred to the Shinnecock people. The areas that are now Sebonack, Shinnecock and National golf courses have great historical significance to the tribe. The site of Shinnecock Golf Club served as their sacred burial ground. Just back through the woods behind us was where the tribe lived during the winter months. Right over there, where National's windmill stands today, was the site of the fall and spring celebrations that drew tribes from across the island, including the Montaukett and Poospatuck tribes. Europeans arrived here in 1640, just around the corner from us here at Conscience Point. They were welcomed with open arms by the Shinnecock, which was probably a mistake, but that's another story for another day." Scallop took a pause to let the gravity of his words have their impact.

"Where we're standing was a site for religious ceremonies, including weddings. You can see why. The Creator's work is truly on display here. Dana and Mark, how humbling is it to know that exactly where you said your vows today, people have been getting married for literally thousands of years. There's evidence that weddings may have been performed here since Before Christ. I bet all those people, going back all those years, who got married here, are looking down here today at you both and wishing you luck. And peace. And happiness. I'm sure they are. Make those things yours and enjoy your day...and thanks for inviting me to your party."

Scallop received a quiet round of applause. Rachel looked around expecting to see people whispering behind their drinks wondering at the giant hippy surfer dressed up in a suit. But the applause was respectful and many of the faces she saw were not looking at Scallop, but out to the site of the ceremony and at the water beyond. Scallop sat down beside her and took a big swig of his tequila on the rocks as a waiter placed the salad course in front of them.

"Father Vinny's going to want you to come to all of his gigs now," she said.

Jenny leaned over. "He really put you on the spot, didn't he? But I didn't know that about this golf course. Thanks for doing that Scallop. That will be one of those things that people remember from this wedding."

"I'm always happy to share what I know about this land. People should know where they are."

They ate the dinner of local striped bass, potatoes and al dente green beans companionably. Rachel felt both comfortable and excited sitting next to Scallop, and everyone in the wedding party seemed to enjoy his company. Jenny and Sarah had stopped winking and nudging one another, and Leslie and Scallop chatted like old friends but were polite enough not to exclude anyone else at the table from the conversation. They talked about upcoming local events and the way the area had changed since they were children. Rachel was pleased to find that having Scallop at the dinner table with a group of her friends was more or less like having any other date from the city doing the same.

Once they were done with dinner though, "Saturday Night Scallop" turned back on. He was ready to dance. Nancy Atlas was in the middle of singing "It's Five O'clock Somewhere" by Alan Jackson, as Rachel and Scallop wound their way through the crowd towards the front of the dance floor. Nancy Atlas saw Scallop coming and sang.

> *"I could pay off my tab,*
> *pour myself in a cab,*
> *and be back to work before two.*
> *At a moment like this,*
> *I can't help but wonder,*
> *what would Scallop Kozlowski do?*
> *And what the hell he is doing here?..."*

The band held its drumroll which caught the attention of every guest. Scallop stopped walking and spun around. Rachel, whose hatred of country music was rivaled only by her disdain for being surprised, looked on half horrified half hysterical. Scallop walked over, kissed Nancy on the cheek and grabbed the mic and sang.

> *"Funny you should ask that,*
> *Nancy Atlas, because I'd say:*
> *Pour me somethin' tall an' strong,*

Make it a 'Hurricane' before I go insane.
It's only half-past twelve but I don't care."

Then Nancy and Scallop sang the rest of the song in duet as everyone danced and sang along. Rachel saw how much of a hit this was while her embarrassment and horror subsided. Dana draped her arms around Rachel from behind.

"Quite the mollusk you found here," Dana said as they swayed along and watched.

"What do you think?" asked Rachel.

"Oh, don't get me wrong. That guy's a freak! Does he have tattoos? I think I saw a tattoo on his chest. He's a weirdo. But I think I like him. How about you?" she asked pointedly over her shoulder as she boogied away.

Scallop hopped down from the stage.

"Well, you're a fun date," Rachel said.

"Thanks. Sorry. I know Nancy from surfing and I had no idea she was going to do that."

"Not a problem. I...."

"I really want to thank you for your service. My friend's nephew is a SEAL and I just want to thank you for all you do," one of the relatives from Ohio, a short, dark haired woman with a helmet hairdo, had shoved a hand in between the two of them. Scallop shook it.

"Nice job singing up there I have to say. You two should do a duet later on!"

"I love that you did the worm!" said her husband.

Rachel sat and ate her wedding cake, while Scallop chatted with a couple of Dana's co-workers who wanted the scoop on the best surfing spots, she was thinking that this wedding simply wasn't turning out as she imagined. Rachel had envisioned leading him around by his hand, introducing him to a group of people. He'd be shy and intimidated by the intelligence and wealth that surrounded him. Why had she thought that? Why had she romanticized that vision? Would she really be interested in someone who would struggle with her crowd? No. But, besides the bride and groom, perhaps even more than the bride and groom, Scallop was the talk of the reception – "The Most Valuable Partygoer."

While one part of Rachel liked that Scallop was quite the personality, another part of her simply wasn't used to not being the center of attention herself. A lifetime of being the prettiest girl in the school, the All-American Soccer player and the Hedge Fund Hottie had left Rachel always at the center of all things, but tonight the maid of honor was playing the role of Robin to Scallop's Batman. She caught a glimpse of Tucker staring across at her eating her cake, Scallop holding court behind her. Tucker was clearly wondering what was going through Rachel Jones's mind.

They danced the last few songs. Dana and Mark had wisely chosen to exit via Irish Goodbye, slipping away unnoticed as the party came to a close. Dana had warned Rachel they planned to make an exit before the after party down on the beach. As they danced to Nancy Atlas' partly tongue in cheek "Stairway to Heaven", Rachel felt completely relaxed in Scallop's arms as they got truly close for the first time in the evening. She'd forgotten who was watching and stopped thinking about whether or not she was a horrible person for expecting Scallop to fail their date. She felt her purple dress sliding against her skin, Scallop's calloused hands like hot magnets on her waist and hips as he spun her around, and her hair brushing her shoulders. She barely noticed as the officious Tracy announced that the after party, bonfire, s'mores and beers were down on the beach.

They sat together legs touching on a log near the bonfire, shoes off, talking. Even with the time approaching midnight lights from surrounding homes and docks blinked against the water and music from another party floated their way.

"Look at that," Scallop said looking out across the water. "Have you ever seen anything prettier? There are times when I like to imagine it as it must have been when there was no electricity and almost no people. Some days in the spring and the fall when it's quieter here, when there's fog on the water when Kosumi and I are out, starting our morning, the fog dampens what sound there is, and you can't see all the houses, it's actually like we're the first ones to discover this shore. I love that. It makes you feel powerful, like you can't fall, the land, the water will catch you. But looking out on it now, with the lights from everyone enjoying the night. I love that too. A great night. I'm glad I came. Even with the suit ambush my sister pulled off. I'm surprised she didn't make me take dance lessons. You'd think I'm a family embarrassment."

"Well, you're quite the dancer." Rachel giggled into her beer, swaying slightly towards Scallop then back away.

"Life's too short not to get down when you want to sweetheart. You know what I mean? I like your friend Dana she seems like she gets it. I have to admit I was nervous about coming to this. I thought you'd be looking for some man candy with a side of upper class cheese to parade around to a bunch of pains in the ass, and I knew I wouldn't be able to deliver on either of those things. But, I've enjoyed this night, the view, the dance and the freedom. Singing with Nancy was a bonus. Nancy…your dress…and this."

He ran his finger down her spine where her dress dipped down in the back, leaning back to look at the part of her that he'd decided he liked the best, based on what he'd seen so far. He leaned forward and held her eyes. She broke the glance only because there was nowhere to go with it at the moment, and wrapped her arm through his. But she quietly held onto that feeling of magnetic heat running down her back, pulling all the other parts of her body towards it while she took another sip of her beer.

After a couple of minutes Scallop bent over and rolled up his pant legs. He got up, taking their shoes, and walked down to his boat. She watched him go. A group of men were standing smoking cigars near the fire. Scallop stopped to talk to them, keeping his eyes on Rachel, he was making her wait. She smiled at him. The hands weren't the only part of him that were magnetic. She could hear most of the conversation. The men had left their ties, jackets, and inner editors under the tent and they were talking politics, specifically, Syria, ISIS, and America's now precarious position on the world stage.

"Scallop...when you were serving, did you ever wonder about what sense your missions made? Does that cross your mind?"

"I thought about it after the fact. But never during. You buy into everything and put full faith in the mission or you die. Period. If I tried to strangle you right now, you wouldn't sit there and wonder why I was doing it. You'd fight back, try to save your life. A split second of indecision and you're dead. When I was moving into enemy villages with my team, there was no time for contemplation. Finish the mission. Do what needs to be done. There is absolutely no point to having a conscience about what has to be done when you're in the middle of it... now, you ask me what I think of all of it? There is no right side, there is no wrong side...there is our side and there's their side. We pretend to be more logical than the animals that we share this place with. We're not. We're no different from the animals in the forest or the ocean. You play for your side. He plays for his side. I don't play for the other side, I play for my side. Know what I'm saying there ke-mo-sah-be?" His eyes shone in the firelight and as he swung them back towards Rachel who he'd forgotten about for a short moment he saw that everyone on the beach had heard most of what he'd just said. They were all looking at him.

"And with that folks, I am out of here. And you, my lady, are coming with me."

Scallop picked up Rachel, and threw her over his shoulder. She gasped, startled, winded and swept up. She didn't look up to see anyone's reaction, she didn't resist. She just let him carry her, the entire length of her body draped over him, feeling that magnetic pull. She could not have imagined herself enjoying being manhandled in this way. Scallop grabbed the anchor, pushed the Zodiac into the water, placed Rachel in the boat, cradling her as he put her down and jumped in, turning on the lights. He shouted "Goodnight all. Enjoy the night" and hit the gas, driving off into the night, leaving the late night guests laughing around the bonfire. Rachel looked out towards the water at the lights leaving the beach behind.

Scallop easily navigated Peconic Bay's waters aided by the light of the moon and his headlight, as he'd done countless times. After they pulled away from the beach he silently handed her a knit cotton blanket, their hands touching as he passed it over. She silently wrapped it around her, leaving the bit of her back he'd touched at the fire exposed and then turning out towards the water again. Within fifteen minutes they were on the beach in front of Scallop's cottage. Scallop beached the boat as he killed the engine, and helped Rachel off the boat. She held her dress up to keep it from snagging on the tall grasses with one hand and Scallop held the other. As they walked up the yard she stepped on something sharp and Scallop said, "Stop." He picked her up and held her in front of him, like a little kid, carrying her as they look at each other. There was no question in either of their minds about what they were about to do. No nervousness and no hurry.

It had been a long time since Scallop had been in a situation like this. He wanted to eat her alive, literally ingest her. He'd felt that way since she'd come to the farm. He carried her up the stairs to the back door and stopped. The light was on in the living room sitting on the floor, her back to the door was Inga. She hadn't heard them coming. He was tempted to turn, walk back down the steps, and take Rachel to the outdoor shower. But he knew there was only one reason Inga would be sitting in his living room. He let Rachel slide down him slowly, not breaking eye contact, pulled her face to his and kissed her so fast and fierce that he stole her breath and then he turned her towards the opening door and whispered in her ear from behind.

"I'm sorry about this."

Inga and Veronica were sitting on the sheepskin rug one on either side of Kosumi rubbing his back. He was sleeping in his "Jake and the Neverland Pirates" pajamas, snuggling a worn teddy bear next to a face puffy and red from crying. Inga looked up at Scallop.

"Sorry Uncle Scallop. He woke up crying and wouldn't stop. He kept repeating 'daddy comes right back' and 'go see daddy' over and over again. Eventually we just decided to bring him here before Grandma and Grandpa lost their minds. We thought being at home might calm him down," Inga said. She leaned down next to his ear, "Little Kosumi, Daddy's home buddy, Daddy's home." Kosumi lifted his head and stood up and crawled towards his father, who knelt in front of him on the carpet. Scallop held out his hands to Kosumi's   cheeks.

"Hi Daddy, I dreamed. I dreamed that you went to the woods and didn't come back. I waited until dark and you still didn't come back. I got cold and I walked home but didn't know the way."

"Daddy's home big boy . I didn't go into the woods. Daddy doesn't get lost and he always finds his way back home. I love you. Who's my boy?"

Kosumi hit his chest with his hand and solemnly said, "This one." Scallop picked up his son and carried him down the hall to his room.

"Sorry, Rachel. I hope we didn't ruin Uncle Scallop's night," said Veronica as they put away the few toys on the floor and gathered their things.

"Of course not. Thanks for watching Kosumi girls. We had a really good time. You go ahead home, I'll finish cleaning up here for Scallop."

"Thanks. That dress is awesome," said Inga.

"Yeah, my friend Dana has pretty good taste. Drive safe girls."

Rachel closed the door behind the girls and thought, "Great. Now what?" Should she try to get a cab or an Uber back? She felt terrible that Kosumi had been upset and every part of her body felt unsettled by what had almost happened. She was certain that she and Scallop weren't spending the night together now. That little boy needed his Daddy and he didn't need her distracting him.

"Rachel." Scallop stuck his head around the corner. Why don't you find something comfortable to put on. I'm just going to get Kosumi back to sleep. Just stay here." He disappeared back around the corner.

Since she didn't know what else to do, she went into Scallop's room and found the same t-shirt and sweatpants outfit she'd worn the last time and put it on. Apparently, no matter what you thought your plan was going to be, hanging out with Scallop Kozlowski was going to be a casual affair.

She fell asleep in one of the giant beanbags listening to Scallop tell his son bedtime stories. Forty-five minutes later, after Kosumi had loosened his grip on Scallop's waist he found Rachel asleep in the living room. He pulled up a beanbag and sat looking at her in silence feeling horribly guilty that he'd not been there for his son. Today, he'd chosen to leave his son for the night and get drunk all day at a wedding with privileged, snobby strangers who probably viewed him as a novelty at best, and a local circus attraction at worst. Did Rachel feel that way? Gorgeous, competent, confident, and no-nonsense. She was so far away from who he was, who he was willing to be, how could he risk a moment of his son's happiness on anything so unlikely to turn out well. Despite what he hoped, Scallop also knew this relationship, if that's what it was, was a pipe dream, and one with potentially serious side effects for his son. Tonight may have been a fortunate preview.

18: Scott Cameron Beach

Early the next morning Rachel was awoken by a small hand on her face. "Rachel, it's time to go to the beach," a little voice carried on hot wet breath whispered into her ear. Rachel giggled, partially because that warm breath tickled, partially at the situation.

"Oh, is *this* when we go to the beach?" She sat up and motioned for Kosumi to sit on her lap. "How are you this morning? Are you feeling better?"

"Yeah, we went to bluff this morning and I saw a fox!"

"You did? You've already been to the bluff this morning? What were you doing there?"

"We did the morning paddle board."

"Ah, I see." She didn't really, but having this little boy wrap his arm around her neck while he told her about her morning was much more comfortable than she would have imagined. Comforting in fact.

Scallop came through the front door smiling. "Ok my boy, go grab your beach pail and put it in the truck." Kosumi shot out the door with a squeaky whoop. Scallop turned to Rachel. "Well, that wasn't the evening you bargained for. Sorry about the couch. You fell asleep and it seemed like the best place to leave you under the circumstances." His look was largely apologetic, but there was an undertone of self-censure in his voice that hit Rachel in the chest. He was alarmed that Kosumi had been upset, and that he had seen that Rachel was spending the night. She understood. But she also felt a warning tingle. She may have been worried that her friends wouldn't accept Scallop, but she hadn't considered that he might have some equally valid reservations about her. If she was really honest with herself, she had to admit that his reservations were *more* valid than hers. He cared for his son. Even regular dates with her could disrupt his little boy's life. A relationship might upend the carefully balanced motherless cart Scallop was pushing around.

"How about if we go meet Lucy at the beach? Grab some breakfast on the way?" She could tell he was trying to get her out of the house as quickly as he could, to keep the situation from becoming more awkward.

"Sure. That sounds good, umm, what should I wear though?" she looked down at the sweatpant-t-shirt outfit that she seemed to descend into whenever in his presence.

"At this time of the morning it's still "come as you are" at the beach. So, come as you are. I've put your clothes from last night in a bag in the truck and here's a pair of flip-flops I think will fit."

Really? He'd already loaded her things in his truck? She bristled as she stood up, pointedly folding the blanket he'd laid over her the night before. "Yeah, sure, give me just a minute in the bathroom and I'll be ready to go."

He grabbed her hand as she tried to blow past. "Hey," he made her look in those eyes that had made every single woman at the party last night take a long second look, "last night was the most fun I've had in a very long time. I know it seems like I'm rushing you out of here. That's for Kosumi, not for me. Me, I wish we could rewind to just before we walked through that door last night. We'll go back there, for now though, let's get some breakfast and go to the beach." She gave him the practiced smile she used in work situations when someone made a valid argument and she didn't like the consequences of their point.

"Sure, I get it. I don't want Kosumi to be confused, or you for that matter. Let's go check out the beach, I can't stay too long. I'll have to get back for the brunch at Sebonack by ten thirty, can you drop me off there on your way back from the beach?"

"My pleasure," he said. As she turned, he put his hand between her shoulder blades, covering the majority of her back, one long finger reaching up to the base of her neck. Almost all of her annoyance dissipated as warmth flowed through her catching in her breast bone.

After the leisurely drive past a few austere farms owned by old family friends and many mansions behind hedges, Scallop pulled the pickup onto to Scott Cameron Beach, where Lucy has already set up shop. Scallop tossed a tinfoil wrapped egg sandwich into Lucy's lap. She was sitting in the same spot, on the same blanket, wearing the same outfit as when Rachel had met her. Rachel carefully handed her a coffee. Lucy had been swimming despite the cold ocean water temperature, which made Rachel shiver just to look at her.

"Hey! So?! How was it? I hear you had quite the welcoming committee. There was wailing, there was gnashing of teeth. Super romantic stuff. Poor guy," Lucy said, her eyebrows doing a Groucho Marx as she tossed her strawberry blond curls behind her in a come-hither pose.

Rachel laughed as she sat down next to Lucy, whatever annoyance she had about this morning's events had dissipated with that eyebrow raise. How did Lucy do that? She'd taken a moment that was gaining traction in Rachel's mind as a real *moment* of hurt and disappointment, and shined a light of clarity on it. It was nothing.

"Well, it was rotten luck. Kosumi stays with us all the time, I don't know what it was about last night that upset him. Maybe it was just that it was a different day of the week." She shrugged her shoulders and took a good look at her sandwich, "Ahhhh, the mother of all egg sandwiches," she said, "it's an *investment*, but it's a gift that keeps on giving. No OJ?"

"No my sister, no OJ," said Scallop sitting down next to Rachel, letting Kosumi sit between his legs as he ate his sandwich. The ocean was calm and the sand was already heating up. It was going to be a hot day. Rachel thought they were probably there at the best time to be there. Before the spikeball playing hordes arrived. While what she was wearing wasn't going to be the object of snooty comment after snooty comment. She looked at her sandwich in her manicured hands and knew that in another circumstance she'd be the one making the snooty comment.

"So, how was the wedding?" Lucy asked.

"It was really nice," said Scallop. "Nice people! Nancy Atlas was there. We did a little tune. I was asked to speak about the history of the land."

"You did a little tune....?," Lucy said incredulously, turning to Rachel, "Exactly how much of a spectacle did my brother make of himself?"

"He was provoked. Actually, everyone enjoyed having him there. My friends from business school are probably gossiping about him over mimosas right now. Quite the dancer, your brother," Rachel laughed.

"Yeah, I'll bet they *are*." She shot Scallop a censorious look. Rachel caught it.

"So Rachel, are you staying out here for the week? Or are you headed back to the city?" Lucy asked.

"I'm on the road for the next month," Rachel said, her eyes focused on Kosumi who'd begun digging a hole in front of the blanket. She didn't want to look at either Scallop or Lucy. She wasn't upset with Scallop anymore. But, despite what he'd said earlier, she wasn't sure they would see each other again. She turned to Lucy, "I'm looking forward to it. London, The Isle of Man, Düsseldorf, Zurich, Geneva, Monaco, then two weeks in the Middle East. Qatar, Abu Dhabi and finally Dubai."

Scallop snorted. "I bet they love you in the Middle East. Nice, pretty, young aggressive American woman - must go over great."

"Exactly!" she laughed.

"Well, I hope we'll see you later on in the summer then. Kosumi and I will be whipping up some mean raspberry tarts once they're in season. Won't we kiddo?" she hit Kosumi on the bottom with her toes. He lost his balance and fell to the sand giggling. He jumped up, his hands on his hips.

"Aunt Lucy, why you did that to me?" he asked smiling.

"I want to go on a hunt with you, that's why! Let's make a turtle coming out of the sand! We need five rocks like this," she held out her fist, "one rock like this," she made a shape the size of a dinner plate, "and one, well kind of in between."

"Alright, well, Kosumi and I are going to make a turtle sculpture, so you two just do whatever suits. Rachel, come back for the raspberries and that drink we talked about. It was great meeting you and thanks for giving my little brother a turn around the dance floor last night. It's truly an act of charity. You might be canonized. Why don't I watch the little guy and you can take Rachel to the train or her car or however she's getting back to *Manhattan*," Lucy said Manhattan as if it was the very worst place a person could want to go.

"Thanks Lucy, I'll see you for the raspberries."

Lucy and Kosumi tore off down the beach, weaving towards the water then away from it. Scallop and Rachel watched them go. Rachel thought they were beautiful running together. These people led a daily life that was so different than hers. While she was stopping off at Starbucks they were running in the sea air.

"He's such a sweet kid. What a life for him here. To come here every day and be outside, and free, and grow up with a big family. He's lovely."

"Yup, he's pretty awesome. So, when you go to the Middle East you don't travel alone do you?"

"No, they hire me a guide, or two, depending on where I'm going to be. You're right, smart ass American women aren't everyone's favorite over there."

"Good. I can assure you, that if some group takes you hostage, I'll be there within 24 hours. I'll drop right in from the skylight just like you see in the movies...throw you over my shoulder, and take you home. I promise."

"I leave tomorrow afternoon and I'm gone for a month. My assistant emailed me on my way out here that I'll fly back Friday, July 1st," Rachel said as she sipped her coffee. Scallop looked at the ground.

"If you want to, why don't you come straight here from the airport? I mean, I don't know if you want to, or if you will want to, but I take that weekend off every year. And I'd love to have you out for the weekend. We could try a rewind on last night....", he paused, nervous, waiting for her to say something. "I mean, I'm sure staying in my place for the weekend will be a bit different for you, I guess you can think of it like camping sort of, but we'd love to have you. I'm enjoying getting to know you. We'd get some grown up time, maybe not the whole night, that didn't work so well," he smiled wanly to himself, "but *some* time. You can sleep in the bed, I'll take the beanbags."

Rachel smiled at him. She loved his house, she liked his kid, she wished last night had gone the way it was headed when they'd gotten out of his boat. But it hadn't. She sighed.

"Not to get too deep on you here, but I feel a little bit like I'm spinning my wheels in life. No, maybe that's not right. I think I just don't know what my next step is. I've got to be cautious and think about what I'm willing to get into right now. Does that make sense? This isn't a 'It's not you, it's me' moment," she smiled at him, "it's just that I would like to come see you again, but I don't know if it would be anything more than that, and that might not be something you're comfortable with." Scallop rested his arms across his knees, and looked out at the ocean.

"That makes sense. And thanks for saying it. We are different. From different worlds. But let's back that up a bit and just look at the here and now of it...look at that boy out there playing. Look at him. He's golden. He is my whole life. He doesn't recall his mother, and I'm very hesitant about bringing anyone new around. I don't allow my focus on him to wander. It's why I keep things so simple. He needs normality, routine, love and attention. So the one thing I want to be clear about is that I'll never want to run back and forth to Manhattan. My life is here, you should know that before you decide if you want to come back here with us."

"You're doing a great job with him. And I hear you about not having the bandwidth to deal with too much else right now."

"Bandwidth. Yes. I know all about bandwidth." He reached in front of her and made a dreamy motion with his hand, "Kosumi and I have the cloud back at the cottage so I don't need bandwidth." He put his hands in a solemn prayer position, then peaked at her through one eye. The ability to make light seemed a Koslowski trait. It wasn't something Rachel encountered all that often.

Through his cocked eye Scallop could see that Rachel hadn't completely understood what he'd said. He found that people who didn't have kids just didn't get it. It didn't matter how old they were, it didn't matter if they were involved aunts and uncles or godparents. Even teachers without kids didn't get it. The only people who get having children are other parents.

"Rachel, this isn't about bandwidth. I have endless bandwidth for more. More conversation, more experiences, more people…more love. But I won't trade my son's happiness or compromise on how I think he should be brought up to get any 'more' for me. Do you hear what I'm saying? It's important and people with no kids don't get it. It's not your fault, some primal gene turns on as soon as your kid hits the air. It's shocking."

"Ok. So why don't we leave it at this: I will come back here for the 4th of July and we'll take it from there. I will absolutely follow your lead with Kosumi. I don't even mind taking the beanbag. I can't believe how well I slept in that thing."

Rachel walked towards the club house at Sebonack. Scallop had just dropped her off and they'd shaken hands over the "deal" they'd made at the beach before she hopped out of the truck carrying her Badgley Mishka dress and in a canvas tote bag with a line drawing of a dog reading a book, "Southampton Library", and some unidentifiable stains that had probably been there since the early seventies. She was going to go up to the room she'd been meant to stay in last night, gather her things and head back to the city to pack for her trip. Engrossed in the replay of the last twenty-four hours that was playing in her head she didn't notice a golf cart behind her, crawling along, waiting for her to clear the driveway.

"Excuse us please." Rachel turned quickly to find three women, in full brightly-colored golf regalia and a sparkling clean golf cart behind her. It took Rachel a second register Lauren was the woman driving the cart. Her red hair was pulled in a ponytail through a golf cap that sat just above the Versace sunglasses she'd shown Rachel the week before. She had on a large scale floral top, a white golf skirt, and a shocked look on her face.

"Hi Rachel! Ha! I did not expect that to be you!"

"Yeah." Rachel laughed, but she was annoyed to be caught in her current state by a member of her team who looked exactly like she would expect them to look – put together, fashionable and in league with their clients – Rachel wouldn't have gone to one of her college soccer practices in this getup, and she was about to walk into one of the most exclusive golf clubs in the country looking at best like a Good Will shopper. And She knew what Lauren meant was not that she didn't expect to *see* Rachel, but that she didn't expect to see her wearing *that*. Lauren knew Rachel was going to be at Sebonack for the weekend. Lauren played golf here with her mother and aunt, who were members. It seemed likely they were the two perfectly preserved older women in the cart who were looking off in the other direction, pointedly avoiding being introduced to whoever this sloppy girl with the dirty tote bag was. Lauren's Hamptons connections were one of the reasons she'd been hired. "Yeah, I'm on my way in to change right now. The wedding was quite the event last night."

"Well, memorable, that's good!" said Lauren, "That outfit looks a little familiar."

Oh god! That's right, this is the same thing Scallop gave me when she was at his house.

"No, it's just one from my broad collection of baggy men's vintage tees and pilley Walmart sweats," she said playfully. She looked at Lauren, letting her know this was going to be the end of the conversation. "Well, you ladies have a good game, and I'll see you at the office Lauren."

"Ok, see you first thing," said Lauren, taking the hint and pulling away quickly. Rachel walked off quickly but stopped at the door to the clubhouse to look back where the cart had headed. She could see Lauren lifting her head to look at her. She didn't like being judged by someone she supervised, and she knew she shouldn't be walking into the Sebonack club house looking like a high school dropout. She should know better. She knew better.

19: June on Both Sides of the Pond

During his Navy SEAL training in Coronado, Scallop learned the power of controlling his mind. If you can control your thoughts, you can withstand almost anything. He learned to block out pain, cold, exhaustion, and fear. His commanders at SEAL training saw that he had come to understand this crucial element of their training regime early, and they dumped punishment on, and he rose to the occasion. This skill came in handy.

When he began to feel restless with his life as a father and farmer, living in a place where almost nothing seemed new unless you focused in on the miniscule changes in nature, he used his training to quell the urge to seek out the new and extreme. But now, for the first time in four years, he opened the steel trap of his mind to the idea of Rachel. He knew there was risk involved but he let his mind recreate there anyway. For the next month, Scallop thought about Rachel almost constantly. When he was with Kosumi he focused in on him. But when Kosumi was occupied his mind wandered to Rachel. He didn't know what it *was* about her that had captured his attention. She was beautiful, certainly, but he could show up to the Coast Grill any Saturday night and find a beautiful woman who would be just as interested in him as Rachel seemed. It was her toughness. It was sexy and at the same time safe.

He was also aware that his preoccupation with her was totally premature. While her self-control would prohibit her from causing drama if things went further and then took a downturn, he was a different story. The small part of himself that functioned in the same way most people operate, with a preset of doom and gloom, whispered that he was inevitably setting himself up for a train wreck of heartbreak, disruption and possible depression. The larger part of him screamed, "You met this woman for a reason, you wouldn't be feeling like this, after all this time, if she wasn't someone who was right for you. Every day."

In London, Rachel sat looking out the window of a lobby in the Gherkin, the forty-one-story rocket ship-phallus that is the sparkling eye-catcher of London's financial district. She arrived a few minutes early for a meeting, was ushered to a seating area with some mid-century inspired sculpted walnut and stainless steel armchairs cushioned in turquoise velvet by a designer she didn't recognize. That happened more and more these days. She didn't see her parents much, and she ignored the nonsense her mother posted on Facebook, so she was losing her game when it came to calling out the newer designers; vintage though she was still spot on.

She was offered an espresso and as she sipped it she looked out on the Thames and wondered if Scallop had some fatal flaw. Was he secretly an alcoholic? That seemed unlikely. Did he suffer from severe PTSD? His reaction the night of the crash had been extreme, but he hadn't freaked out, he'd obeyed a natural reflex to duck and cover. That was just good sense and good training considering his background. Did he have violent tendencies? She'd seen and felt nothing from him but kindness. Would his family be as loving and trusting of someone who they knew might turn on them? She didn't think so. Would he be unbending when some of the elements of his simplistic, minimalist lifestyle wouldn't work for Rachel?

And one question niggled at her even as she tried to push it below the surface of the others. Why was he single? While he may have been heartbroken by the death of Kosumi's mother, it had been several years. She hadn't had to twist his arm to get him to go out with her, if anything had actually happened afterward she was certain that the final score would have shown that Scallop was the instigator. He wasn't reluctant to go further with her. And while many women who came to the Hamptons on the weekend weren't looking for anything beyond some summer fun, surely there had been local women who Scallop had grown up with who'd have jumped at him, quirks, child, and all. But it seemed like she was one of a very small club. For a second, she let herself entertain the thought that she was just *that* fantastic – the first woman tempting enough to make him abandon his priorities and convictions. After the short moment of self-indulgence, she reigned herself in and decided there was no way that was it. There was something else, something that she didn't understand about his personality or his history that she didn't know about yet.

She stood up and walked to the window in order to clear her head. She was disgusted with herself for spending so much time thinking about this. Last night as she flipped through channels and went over some briefs she'd spent the better part of an hour running through the same sequence of questions. She'd done it on the flight to London, and she'd done it on her drive from Southampton back to the city. It was a complete waste of time. She wasn't going to get any answers when she was half way across the world. She was giving far too much of her focus to something she couldn't control and was unlikely to result in anything worthwhile anyway.

Last night she'd googled Kosumi's mother, Kachina, and found a few pictures from Facebook, a memorial website that her friends from the reservation had made, a few police records including a DUI from when she was eighteen where she'd been found in possession of marijuana and cocaine, a domestic violence situation involving a boyfriend named DaVeshon Brown, and a few modeling pictures promoting local bars. In almost every photo, modeling and personal, Kachina was dressed in a bikini with a cut Rachel wouldn't have considered wearing at a private Brazilian resort. Every part of her body was on display. She was beautiful, gorgeous even, with long dark legs and arms and a mane of big, wild, curly blonde hair. She had a sexuality so overt that Rachel felt like she was intruding on an intensely intimate moment as she looked at an ad where Kachina leaned into the camera, offering an overflowing plate of cheese covered nachos. Rachel understood now why Scallop had described her as storm-filled. There was something primal and a little bit intimidating about her. Wherever this woman went, "sturm und drang" would certainly follow.

She'd googled Scallop too. There was surprisingly little to be found. An article about his Navy SEAL service that had run in the Southampton Press as a Veterans Day feature was accompanied by a picture of him in the same diving getup he'd worn to retrieve Swizzle's watch. He smiled for the photographer, looking like the world's most handsome dingbat. And while the article attempted to paint him as a war hero, a courageous man with a weighty past, the photo made it impossible to take him seriously. There were a few other mentions of him on the Southampton Press site, items from the police blotter when he'd been a first responder to a fire or accident, a couple of articles on the farm and its place in the community, and a couple of pictures of him on his nieces' Facebook pages. That was it. There were no photos or mentions of Scallop and Kachina as a couple. There was nothing placing him anywhere besides Southampton. She was so accustomed to combing through the LinkedIn and Bloomberg profiles of the men she dated until she'd killed any chance of a revelatory conversation that she felt like she was somehow at a disadvantage with Scallop. If he wanted to he could track every single one of her movements for the past decade via google search; she imagined he knew how. The only thing that kept her from being completely annoyed by their disparate levels of transparency was the certainty that Scallop would never bother to do any type of search on her. He'd never do something so invasive and unromantic. So, she became annoyed instead about their disparate levels of morality, shut the lid of her laptop and went for a workout.

Rachel called Scallop's landline, there was no answer. She jabbed at her cell phone to hang up and forced herself to take a deep breath. She'd been traveling for over two weeks and it was beginning to wear on her. She checked in with the office in New York two or three times a day and she'd just finished what should have been a routine call with Trevor. She'd gotten through giving him instructions about onboarding a new client and he'd said, "Rachel, let me just step out of the office here for a minute. Can you hold on?"

She was in a hotel in Geneva between meetings, her shoes off and Bloomberg TV news on mute. She could tell from Trevor's voice that whatever he was going to tell her was going to piss her off. Normally he'd just spit it out. Why was he going outside?

"Listen," he said, "I hesitated to tell you about this when I first noticed it because I thought I might be imagining things. But I'm not. I want to remind you, I'm just the messenger," he paused, waiting for her to say something.

"Got it. Tell me what's going on."

"You have a problem with Lauren. I hate having to say this. I thought she was loyal to you. I don't know, maybe she's getting to the age where she thinks she should be up a few rungs higher."

"Trevor, cut the psychological analysis. *What* is Lauren doing?", she asked. But she already knew. She'd trained Lauren, she'd taken her under her wing because Lauren was her four years ago, and Lauren was doing exactly what Rachel would have done in her position. She was trying to push her out. If Lauren was as good at manipulating a situation to her advantage as Rachel would have been, she did have a serious problem with Lauren.

"She's become chummy with Sterling. *Really* chummy. And she's wheedling her way into Tallmadge's heart as well. I didn't think anything of it until I heard her telling Kendra about Tallmadge taking her out to dinner with Jeff and Linda Everhardt. She was talking about how she felt terrible, but she'd felt she *had* to tell Tallmadge about your 'liaison' with the diver-surfer guy the weekend of the outing, and how you'd spent the weekend with him instead of bonding with the team, which was what we were *there for*. I still thought nothing of it until I walked by Tallmadge's office the other day. She'd brought him some book on *birds* that she was pretending to be fascinated by, and he called her 'dear'. You are 'dear'. Not her. So, you have a problem."

Rachel wasn't surprised, but that didn't mean she wasn't hurt by the betrayal. It didn't help that Trevor did an impressive Lauren impression, mimicking her refined, clear way of speaking while inserting just the hint of viper slithering beneath the surface. She wondered how long Lauren had been waiting for Rachel to do something wrong, watching for anything she could use to tarnish her reputation. Buying her coffee, arranging her newspapers, helpfully setting up bloody Mary bars and plotting. Rachel would have someone else get her coffee from now on.

"Thank you, Trevor. Thank you for your loyalty. I appreciate you telling me. I'll deal with Lauren," she said coldly. Damnit! He was right. She was furious, and there was one way to make herself feel a bit better, "Is Kendra doing anything miraculous that I don't know about?"

"No, she's fine, but the mouth doesn't stop. I know you were concerned after the outing that she couldn't control herself. I think that's true. She jumped right on Lauren's bandwagon. The two of them went on for forty-five minutes about you, that guy, how you're 'checking out', and how it's not good for the firm."

Rachel seethed. She was checking out? Because she hadn't gone to dinner and got blasted with the team?

"Don't tell me. I don't want to hear it. Alright, I'll get rid of Kendra as soon as I

get back. She's got to go. I don't want Lauren to have any cohorts. Anyone else on their team yet?'

"No way, the rest of us have either been around the block enough times to know the likelihood of Lauren ousting you is pretty low, or they're new enough that they're simply trying to keep their head above water, and the rest actually, well, we actually like *you*."

"Thanks Trevor. That's nice of you to say. Alright. I hate to ask you to do this, but could you keep an eye and let me know if it gets any worse?"

Trevor agreed, and as soon as they hung up Rachel sat down and wrote an email to Kendra, criticizing some correspondence she'd sent to a client, and beginning a chain of documented displeasure with Kendra's work that would lead to her dismissal as soon as Rachel returned to New York. If Lauren had managed to ingratiate herself with Tallmadge, she'd be more difficult to dispense with. Rachel would have to catch Lauren in a mistake, so that firing her would not appear to be the act of self-preservation it was. There was only one more part of this that she could take care of from a hotel room in Switzerland.

Rachel wasn't surprised when she couldn't get through to Scallop. Someone with no cell phone who spent most of their day outside was tough to catch. She might have the best luck getting a hold of him if she called the pay phone in the parking lot of the Country Deli and hoped he answered as he walked by it at 7:45 each morning, or if she called the Coast Grill to find out what time he was *supposed* to show up with the vegetables.

Instead she called North Sea Farms. Veronica answered the phone and turned the phone over to her mother.

"Rachel?" said Lucy. "I thought you were halfway across the planet!" When Rachel said she was in Geneva, Lucy said, "Isn't technology nuts. I remember when I was in elementary school, I had a friend who moved away and I wanted to call her. My parents said I couldn't, that we had to write letters, because the long-distance call was too expensive. And it really was. Now you're walking around with a computer pressed to your face that calls me across the ocean for practically nothing. Crazy. I guess you're probably calling for the golden boy, yes? INGA! Go and see if you can find Scallop!", she shouted.

There was a pause on the line while Lucy waited for Rachel to say something. When she didn't Lucy jumped back in, "So, we're super psyched for you to come for the fourth of July. Kosumi especially, he keeps talking about your hair. First he liked your face, now he likes your hair. I managed to talk Scallop into having Kosumi stay with me one night to so that you two can go out. Hopefully it will go a bit more smoothly this time. I think he's pretty happy that you're willing to stay in his mangy cottage."

Rachel had called with every intention of telling Scallop that her plans had changed, and she couldn't make it out to Southampton for the 4th. While Lauren was completely out of line Rachel was angry that she'd given her anything to use as ammunition. But, there was a very simple way to make it a non-issue. If she didn't date someone who would embarrass the firm, in fact didn't date at all for a month or two it would take the wind out of Lauren's sails. But as she listened to Lucy, she thought of sitting between her and Scallop at the beach, eating and watching Kosumi dig. It had been the nicest moment she'd had in the past year. Well, almost, she thought of dancing with Scallop, his hand on her waist as he turned her. That had been the nicest moment.

"Screw Lauren," she thought. "I'm going to go have a nice holiday weekend *and* I'm going to get her."

"Hang on Rachel," Lucy put her hand over the receiver of the mustard colored rotary dial phone that hung on the wall of the farm stand office, "Rachel, Scallop went over to the marina to help Joel put in a new dock post."

"Well, of course, where else would he be?" Rachel asked. "That's ok, just tell him I called Lucy."

"Wait! Don't go, tell me about the coolest place you've been or the weirdest person you've seen in Geneva. I've never been there. Never been anywhere really. What's the most interesting thing from your trip so far?"

They spoke for half an hour, laughing over Rachel's stories of the strange and unusual on the streets of Geneva and London. Rachel's description of the Gherkin had Lucy in near-tears. Rachel couldn't believe how easy it was to while away the better part of an hour talking with Lucy. She couldn't think of another woman she'd been able to connect with like that as an adult. Perhaps part of their rapport came from the knowledge that they had a vested interest in one another. They had a man in common.

Rachel hung up with Lucy with a light heart. Her determination to crush Lauren like the preening insect she now understood her to be had not waned, but she'd decided she was going to do it without ruining her chance to spend time with these people. She liked them. It was as simple as that.

Lucy hung up, found Tim, and gave him an update. They didn't want to hover, but they were going to do everything in their power to help Scallop pursue Rachel. They had their collective caring fingers crossed that their younger brother just might be able to pull this one off. He'd sacrificed far too much for a woman who'd been too broken to fix. It was time to trust that the past would stay where it was, and hope for a time to come that included the love their little brother and his son deserved. They hoped at this point his conscience wouldn't get the better of him.

20: Rhiannon at Heathrow

Rachel stood on the sidewalk at Heathrow looking up as thousands of raindrops slammed into the glass overhang above her. Other travelers hurried past her, looking up, harried by each distant rumble of thunder. Rachel calmly waited as her taxi driver, an ancient little man who came up to her chest, struggled to pull her bag out of the snub-nosed taxi cab. She was in no hurry. She was early for her return flight and she hadn't seen any planes leaving as they'd approached the airport; a fair sign that she wasn't going anywhere anytime soon. She decided to check her bag. Normally she'd keep the bag with her, but she was tired of hauling it around, tired of the clothes and shoes inside that she'd been wearing for a month, and tired of its business-like efficiency. She wanted to get a martini at the bar without the bag invading her personal space.

Ten minutes later she sat in the Virgin Atlantic lounge sipping a chilly dirty martini. She popped an olive into her mouth with a sigh, grateful for her favorite travel outfit, a chic navy jersey jumpsuit that draped perfectly, but felt like pajamas. Not much of her trip had been enjoyable. Between the discomfort of a hotel-to-hotel lifestyle, the stress of making the trip a success, and the emotional turmoil of Lauren's betrayal Rachel was done in. The briny, boozy relaxation had already flowed out to her extremities and for the first time in weeks she relaxed. Her conversation with Lucy was the last breath she'd taken before plowing through the remainder of her trip. Client meetings, clandestine calls with Trevor, meticulous reporting, and covert extracurricular research had left absolutely no time to recharge. She knew she was on top of everything, her trip had been a success, she'd had emails from Tallmadge, that putz Sterling, and several board members congratulating her on two coups she'd pulled off, signing clients that had been considered extreme longshots. She'd managed to control the Lauren situation whilst appearing oblivious to its existence, and she'd put a few personal wheels in motion.

She asked the bartender for more olives and swung around on her bar stool to take in the lounge. This room always amused her; how a giant room reminiscent of Star Trek's bridge, decorated with a medley of mid-century modern's greatest hits, and lit like a high school gymnasium managed to be a comfortable place to hang out she would never understand. But it did. And today she was glad for its comforts because the departures board indicated she was going to be enjoying Virgin Atlantic's hospitality for a few hours yet. Half the seats were already taken. A mother and daughter with New Jersey accents and blow-outs were swapping *US Magazine* and *People* on adjacent Eames loungers, and a grouping of beige swan chairs held a pair of nearly identically dressed thirty something men, who Rachel surmised must be on their way back to Brooklyn. Pretty soon, the only seats in the house would be the hanging lucite egg chairs that no one ever sat in. Rachel's mother had insisted on putting one in her room when she was a teenager. She'd hated it. The entire lounge was filled with the very type of furniture Rachel's mother always used in her designs, she could identify every piece. Though she'd hated it as a kid, it was now, ironically what felt like home. As Rachel wondered what sort of nonsense the Brooklyn hipster boys in their plaid shirts and jeans rolled up at the bottom were selling, she was surprised to see a familiar face walk through the door.

Ted Jacobs was one of the best third-party marketers in the business, he had the same job as Rachel, but instead of being on staff with a single firm, he worked for himself and raised funds for various investment management firms. Rachel had known Ted for several years, they crossed paths frequently and they not only respected one another, but genuinely liked each other. Ted had a reputation for being the nicest, most earnest, kind and welcoming person on Wall Street. He looked like an aging movie star, complete with a full head of silver hair. Ted was about fifty and the boyish good looks that predisposed people to like him had thickened just enough to predispose people to trust him as well. If he ever took it into his head to run for public office, he'd easily win based on pure likability and trustworthiness. Once upon a time he was a college lacrosse star for Johns Hopkins, now he was a doting dad, a good husband, and a great fund raiser. But tonight Ted wasn't looking so great, he looked a bit tired, and his left arm was in a cast supported by a sling.

"Ted!" she shouted and waved enthusiastically across the lounge.

"Miss Jones!" Ted exclaimed, obviously just as glad to see her as she was to see him. The wait for the flight had just gotten a lot more interesting.

"What the hell happened to you?" she asked as she shook his good hand and looked at his bad one.

"What?! No, 'how you doing?', no, 'nice to see you Ted?', no, no, no, *this*," he tapped his cast, "is a long story that I'll only tell you after a big, tall drink. Flying in this thing is unbearable - I need to fortify."

Rachel called the bartender over and Ted ordered a vodka on the rocks, then downed half of it before setting it down on the bar. The two road warriors were weary and Rachel was relieved that she didn't need to turn her A game on around Ted; they knew each other well enough to just be themselves.

They talked some business, but not much. Ted asked Rachel what was happening in her personal life. Rachel was always reluctant to open-up, even to her close friends. There was always judgement and advice, and while she loved Dana and her other friends from school, she'd spent years watching them make incomprehensible personal decisions. Was she really going to take their advice? Being judged by people who were completely unqualified to judge was infuriating. The only person she really talked to was Easy Eddie and she hadn't been in the back seat of his car for a month. She'd been itching to share with someone, and as she considered Ted, she decided he might be the best person amongst her acquaintance to talk with. She might even walk away with some actionable advice she could trust. She knew he was happy, she knew he was discreet, and she knew he was a good guy.

"Are you really asking? Because I could use your thoughts?"

"I wouldn't ask if I weren't interested."

"Ok then, let's girl talk," she took a big sip of her martini and then let it pour out. "Lately, I'm wondering what's next. I don't think I need to be falsely modest with you, you know I'm at the top of my field. I'm astronomically good at my job. But it's beginning to bother me that that's all I do. It took me a lot of energy to get where I am, and of course, I still need to work hard, but it's not the same as making the climb you know? So, what's next? I feel like my life is a little empty. Do I need to take up some cause? Do I need to get obsessed with some hobby? I don't like to think that my happiness resides in another person, and I'm disgusted with dating, and I hate clichés, but maybe I need someone."

Ted sipped his drink and listened. She could tell he was *really* listening and that he knew her well enough to know that she wasn't the type of woman who had a "problem of the week". This was something that she was generally working on and trying to solve. "I get a feeling that you've got someone in mind," Ted said.

"I do. But I don't know if it's just that he's ridiculously good looking. I don't know if it's that I'm going a little batty and I find him attractive because he's such a departure from what everyone expects me to choose. He's also got a son who's lovely, and I don't know if I've just got some uncontrollable Mommy instinct kicking in. On the other hand, I could just be looking for a reason not to see him again because I really like him, and I'm afraid, deep down, of upsetting the balance of my life and jeopardizing everything I've built."

"Miss Jones, I don't think you need a hobby or a cause, unless you really want one. Tell me about the guy you met."

"Alright, although I feel like the living embodiment of a cliché," she said, only then realizing that part of the reason she was torn at all about pursuing her interest in Scallop was that it fit the cliché of 'city girl meets a rustic outdoorsy guy and discards all her ambitions along with her clothing'. "He's a farmer in South Hampton," she finished lamely.

"Mmmm," Ted nodded knowingly, "sexy."

Rachel giggled into her martini, "Yes. Definitely. He's also a surfer, a carpenter and a king of Zen minimalism and he came to my rescue when I felt like a damsel in distress for the first time in years."

She went on to tell him about Scallop, Swizzle and the watch. Ted knew Swizzle and Hooper and he had a good laugh at Rachel's description of Swizzle's distress. She told him about taking her team to Scallop's cottage and taking Scallop to Dana's wedding.

ood grief Rachel, I think I understand women better than your
an, and he sounds to me like every girl's wet dream. What's the
s he not so bright?"

aven't noticed," she deadpanned. "No, really, he's smart and kind
us. It's just not what I expected. And I don't know if I'm looking
to stick a square peg in the round hole that I've got. And while he's intelligent
and kind, he might oversimplify his life, and my life can be complex. It might
just be a bad idea. Also, he doesn't seem all that keen to leave Eastern Long
Island unless he's forced to. But, there's something about spending time with
him that makes all the things I worry about and focus on seem inconsequential.
Have you ever experienced that?"

Ted took a big drink, smiled and put his hand on Rachel's shoulder,
Fleetwood Mac's Rhiannon began playing in the background which Rachel
thought added to the feeling of living a cliché.

"I gotta tell you sometimes…yeah, sometimes unexpected…actually,
forget that…unimaginable things…happen to us. Situations that we never
dreamed for an instant we'd be in. My life has been irrevocably changed by
being in the wrong place at the wrong time and the right place at the right time.
Chance encounters can change everything."

"Early 2008, I'm on top of the world. I'm a Managing Director at Bear
Stearns, my family is happy and healthy, and everything is just coming up
rainbows. We'd settled out in Bronxville, and I've got myself the life I'd
always dreamed of."

"Then the crash happened, I didn't get taken over to JP Morgan in the
merger, and suddenly I'm out of a job, and I've lost the vast majority of my
net worth. My marriage, which I had always thought was rock solid, was in
trouble. We started arguing about literally everything under the sun, and things
deteriorated quickly. I got a job at a riskless principal broker dealer, so I had
no base salary and I was working one hundred percent for commission, and I
couldn't write a ticket to save my life. Six months of working my ass off and
nothing to show for it. My marriage gets worse, suddenly we're separated and
I'm living in an apartment in town as we sorted through the details of our
upcoming divorce. I was a train wreck. All my thoughts were of my kids, and
how to just hide all of this from them, like that's possible. I get fired from my
job crossing bonds, and Rachel, I mean, I'm at a place I never dreamed I would
be at just a very short time before. I was looking at all sorts of jobs out of sheer
desperation. It's 2010 now. I jackassed into the city on a rotten rainy day just
like this one to meet with a recruiter, and afterwards I just ducked into the bar
at the Roosevelt Hotel on 46th street, ordered a martini, and I sat there, spent.
If there were more tears to cry, I would have been crying. But those days, I
spent my nights crying, and sweating, so there were no tears. I thought I had
nothing left. No enthusiasm. No hope. No confidence. I'd failed my wife, my
kids and myself. I gave a good thought to drinking another ten of those

martinis, and not caring what happened to me. I even thought about the money sitting in my multiple life insurance policies, and how my family might use it to regain some happiness. It was dark."

Rachel could see Ted's dark green eyes watering up, so few people really let you see their soul, but looking into Ted's eyes, she could see his. She was glad he was he was the person she'd confided in. Ted took another sip, clapped his hands, signaling a turn of the page.

"And what do you know…who walks in but Doug Morgan, who I knew from my time at Bear, who'd started his own third-party marketing firm. We'd always had a good relationship, we had a drink and agreed to talk the next week. Doug had just lost one of his guys to a competitor, so there was an opportunity there. He offered me a job and I took it. We wound up getting lucky with our first few clients rooted out from contacts and acquaintances, then we had a track record, and then over the course of the next year we were doing great. My wife and I got back together, we went to counseling and things are good again, really good. The kids are great. And here I am, gainfully employed, running my own book, making more money than I ever had, and I'm back. But had I not dropped into the Roosevelt Hotel that day, I don't know what would have happened to me. I would have probably gotten divorced, and been a sad sack living in an apartment by the train station, embarrassed to have my kids over. But it happened. Who knows what might happen with you and this guy. Your life is already pretty great, maybe it just gets way better. Maybe he fills a hole. Weirder things have happened. If my life pivoted for the better because I wanted to be sad and have a martini at the Roosevelt, yours could change because *that ditz,"* he whispered looking around knowing that one of Swizzle Hooper's sorority sisters could be sitting down the bar, "*Swizzle Hooper* dropped her watch and you met a nice guy. Cheers. Good luck, the right choice will present itself. That's what I tell myself, at least. I've come to believe that."

He took a long pause and considered Rachel over the rim of his glass, "Hunh. I don't know Rachel, maybe this is too much, maybe you'll think I've become a new-age kook, but looking at you I have a feeling about this. Like it's going to be a good thing for you."

Rachel pondered that for a moment and took a big drink of her martini. She did think Ted had wandered into the realm of new-age kookiness. But, she could tell he believed that he had a sixth sense about her and Scallop and she appreciated his care and thoughtfulness.

"Wow brother. This is what layovers should be all about, Ted! Thanks for the advice. I'll take it," Rachel said as they both laughed. "So, what the hell happened to your arm?"

"I'm a lucky guy and a total idiot at the same time. Memorial Day weekend I'm headed out east. Maggie and Molly had gone earlier, I picked up Patrick from his baseball game and we drove out later. I was driving down

Noyac Road, and what do I do? I text Maggie to say something of no importance whatsoever. I veer into the other lane, look up and see a truck about to hit us. I veer back over, off the road and into the woods. A tree branch came through the window and hit me right through the shoulder blade. I was knocked out cold as was Patrick…."

Rachel stared at Ted as he continued. She felt as if she was floating and Ted's words were being broadcast through a loud speaker just for her. She recalled every detail of that night; watching from across the street as Scallop saved Ted and Patrick's life. Suddenly she knew Ted was no kook. In fact, years later, she'd think about this moment, the surrealness of it, how odd she'd felt, and how she thought it must be like what people felt when they got a message from God. She'd remember that she hadn't thought about the next plot point in every story that included a message from God, a trial of faith.

"Luckily for us, a local fireman, a retired Navy SEAL of all things, was across the street and was able to save both of our lives. I'm so lucky. They said another minute or so for us and we would have been toast. I owe that guy my life."

Rachel raised her hand, ordered two more martinis, and took a deep breath.

"Ted, want to hear something ridiculous?"

21: The Sun Always Shines in North Sea

Rachel awoke as Easy Eddie's Cadillac Escalade hit one of the many unpaved potholes on East Shore Drive. Eddie pulled into the yard of Scallop's house and incredulously leaned over his steering wheel, his meaty face screwed up in a squint.

"What the *hell* is this? This can't be the right place! This is a shack for the love of God!" he craned around in his seat to yell at Rachel.

"Thanks Eddie. This *is* the place."

"Is he a fucking squatter or something? Some kind of hippy?," he gripped the steering wheel anew, "Jesus H. Christ Rachel, this place could float away. There are holes in the roof - I can see them from here! Is there a bathroom? Ho-ly shit, I thought I'd seen it all. Maybe the preppy kid from Connecticut wasn't so bad after all. Call him and try to get that thing going again."

Rachel snorted, "Thanks for the well-considered advice Eddie. Eloquent as always. There's a bathroom. It's actually very cute and simple on the inside. And the views are great. Scallop lives here with his four-year-old son. He's a farmer *and* a former Navy SEAL; he could kill you with his left hand, so if, and when you meet him, I wouldn't mention the holes in the roof. Help me grab the bags and get settled, you fucking pain in the ass."

It was close to noon, a beautiful day, and a not too humid 88 degrees. The door was open and Eddie put Rachel's bag in the bedroom, his head craning from side to side as he took in the details of the cottage.

"You better hope there aren't raccoons or other wild animals living in here for the love of God. Jonesy, you could be in Hawaii right not if you wanted…dating the Prince of England, and instead you're here with Daniel Boone. It doesn't make any sense to me. This guy can't even afford a TV! Jesus."

"The Prince of England in Hawaii. Daniel Boone on the seaside. These are good analogies Eddie. They make no sense you realize. But thank you, it's nice to know you care," she said, giving him a warm hug. "You're a good kind man, and I'll see you Monday night when you pick me up. Have a great 4th with the family."

He kissed her on the cheek shaking his head with bewilderment. She watched as he drove slowly away pointedly avoiding the tiniest potholes while waving and pointing out the window and through the sunroof, as a stream of expletives flowed from his open windows. She walked inside, phone in hand, to send out a few final texts before she attempted to shut down for the weekend.

Eddie had picked her up at JFK. Her weekend bag, packed by her new assistant Aaron, was in the car waiting for her. Rachel sent Aaron a quick text to say thank you and good job. He was the younger brother of her friend Jenny, gay, gorgeous and fresh out of college. Jenny had mentioned that he was looking for an entry-level job in finance, Rachel had bypassed human resources and hired him from the road. Picking out her fourth of July weekend wardrobe had been his first assignment. Rachel didn't really care what he packed, she just didn't want Lauren in her apartment. Lauren had been given the promotion that had been in the works for some time before Rachel had discovered her scheming. Subsequently she had been relieved of her duties as Rachel's assistant and temporarily lulled into a false confidence while Rachel decided exactly how to crush her. Meanwhile Rachel had regained her privacy. Rachel Jones was familiar with the adage, "keep your friends close, and your enemies closer," but allowing your enemies to choose her undergarments was too close for Rachel's comfort. As she sorted through her bag she felt doubly good about her decision to hire Aaron, he'd packed perfectly; probably better than she would have herself. He'd managed to put something for any occasion she might encounter over the weekend, short of a state dinner, into a weekend bag and included a few accessories that would work with anything she pulled out of the bag. Impressive. He obviously had experience with a holiday weekend in the Hamptons.

At JFK, exuberant American self-indulgence had been on full display. Everyone she encountered had been in a good mood (a minor miracle for JFK airport) and either on their phones discussing weekend plans happily wishing a fellow traveler, "Happy Fourth!" Rachel saw more than one person pull flip-flops out of their bag before hopping into a cab. Fourth of July weekend is one of the few times a year when the elite of New York's financial machine take a break. Rachel changed her clothes, put on flip-flops of her own, and shoved her phone into the bottom of her bag, knowing that for once it would be alright if she only checked it every few hours.

On the center of the dining table, was a drawing from Kosumi. He'd drawn three stick figures against the backdrop of the sea, and written 'well come Ray chill' in green crayon. Next to that was a note from Scallop, in large square writing, "Be home after 5. Backyard BBQ. Make yourself at home.", also in green crayon.

It was nearly one, so Rachel had some time to kill. She sat at the table for a while, just staring out at the view as a light breeze came through the open windows around the dining area. She could have laid her head down on the table and gone to sleep it was so silent and peaceful being alone there in the house. But she felt it would be lazy to take a nap, so she "motivated" and changed once again, this time into her bathing suit, and headed out on the paddleboard that had dumped her into the frigid water back in May. This time, the water was calm and she maneuvered the board with ease. She paddled along the shore going west, checking out the homes dotting the beach. There were two types; large, beautiful custom made homes that were probably built in the last twenty years, and the smaller summer bungalows and cottages like Scallop's. The cottage/bungalow variety still outnumbered the bigger homes, but she knew that couldn't last for long; the real estate was too valuable, the views too good. The families that had inherited the little cottages from relatives that had come from a different class than Southampton now attracted, stood to make a fortune by selling. This was the way of things all over the east end of Long Island. The landscape had changed. The Kozlowski's weren't the only ones grappling with the question of whether to sell their valuable property and move on. Rachel felt a little guilty as she calculated the profits to be made here. She wondered if any of the modern showplaces provided their inhabitants with the tiniest portion of the peace she'd just experienced at Scallop's dining table.

After a half an hour of paddling she turned back, not wanting to get too far away from the house. The sun was high and she'd worked up a sweat on the paddleboard. She pulled it up on shore, out of reach of the tide and took a swim. As she floated in the bay, she realized she'd never been in the ocean by herself. She'd been alone in hotel pools late at night, fitting in a workout whenever and wherever she could while she traveled. But this was different. The biggest weekend of the year in the Hamptons would begin in just a few hours, but the water behind Scallop's home was quiet. She could hear the voices of children in the deep distance but she could also hear the voices of birds nearer by, and feel the occasional nibble of a small fish on her toes. Her hair splayed out around her, brushing against her face and neck as she floated on her back, looking up at the clouds. She didn't know how long she floated there but eventually she realized she was nearly asleep in the water. She walked slowly out, her limbs weighted down with the exhaustion of a month of travel, stress and a level of uncertainty she didn't enjoy. She wrapped herself in a towel, and went inside, changing into a long flowing sundress that didn't require anything underneath and digging through her bag to find the autobiography of the Federal Reserve Chair, Janet Yellen, that she'd asked Aaron to pack for her. She wandered back through the house hugging the book to her chest and helped herself to a big glass of water.

She was looking forward to Scallop and Kosumi coming home. She'd been fantasizing about another night of talking by the fire, and to Scallop's hands. His sensation of hands on her were the one thing that kept coming back to her in London and the Middle East. If she was honest with herself the way those hands felt were the main reason she was here right now. She settled into a hammock placed in the shade and ready with a pillow. Within moments, jetlag and a distinct lack of drama in Yellen's life story dragged Rachel into sleep.

Two hours later, she awoke to the sound of wind chimes blowing in the breeze. The wind had kicked up and Rachel sat up, hugging her knees to her chest and resting her chin on them as she had as a little girl. Groggy she looked out, mesmerized by the small waves on the bay.

She heard a car pull into the driveway, and realized what she probably looked like. She'd fallen asleep with her hair wet from the water, and while the dress she'd thrown on felt romantic when she walked through the breeze, it might not look it after being crumpled beneath her for the past few hours. She'd made it to the back steps when Inga and Veronica came around the corner.

"Hey Rachel," Inga called, spotting her on the stairs, "our Mom and Uncle Scallop sent us to get you. We're having a big family dinner tonight at the farm, and we have to buy the wine and drinks. Scallop had to pick some people up for the dinner, and our mom is working the register until closing time. So, mom thought you could go with us to buy the wine."

"Oh. Ok. Sure, that sounds like a plan. Just let me change. Are we in a hurry?"

"Not a huge hurry," said Inga, "but we should get back to help Mom as soon as we can. There are like fifty people coming for dinner."

Rachel was a little thrown. "Wow, well ok!," she said to the girls, "I'll just change really quickly and we'll go. Just give me three minutes."

"Well, I guess I'm going to have dinner with fifty people," she said to herself,   "

"Surprise!" Five minutes later, her fantasy of having a private moment with Scallop anytime soon destroyed, Rachel was riding shotgun in a North Sea Farms pickup truck that was being driven by a high school girl. She'd managed to freshen up quickly, putting on a more structured dress and some sandals. Luckily her hair didn't look as insane as it might have. The salt water had given it a nice wave and it was passable, as long as you didn't touch it; it had a grungy feeling salty crunch to it, and when strands caught in the wind from the truck's open windows, they slapped against her face, irritating her skin.

"So you work on Wall Street?" Inga asked.

"Well, yes. I work at a hedge fund. I raise money for my firm."

"That sounds cool. I want to work on Wall Street," Veronica stated with confidence.

"Well, Wall Street isn't what it once was. The industry is retracting, it's getting smaller. With all the new rules and regulation, there's not as much opportunity as there was once. By the time you two get done with school who knows where it will be. The way business gets done is changing so rapidly it's impossible to guess what things will look like ten years from now."

The girls asked Rachel a litany of questions about her life, job and background. Rachel was surprised by how comfortable they both were with her, and how mature they seemed compared to other sixteen year old girls. Rachel thought if her friends saw her now, driving to get wine in an old, dirty pickup truck with two teenage girls, they'd have a field day. None of them had grown up like these two girls had; working every day side by side with their family members, catering to the needs of a higher class. They'd been groomed to be who they were. So had she.

They went into North Sea Liquors and the girls went straight to the counter where an ancient beagle sat on a small dog bed. Behind the counter was a casually dressed middle-aged woman who obviously knew the girls. They giggled over the beagle and chatted while she rang up a small line of customers. The store was a standalone building no bigger than a living room and its theme was "The Sun Always Shines in North Sea." A faded fiftieth anniversary sign sat on the dark wooden shelves behind the and there were at least a dozen people shopping. Rachel squeezed past two women a bit older than her loading up on Tito's and Don Julio for the weekend. She stacked two cases of Cake Bread white wine and one case of Whispering Angel next to the counter and placed a few other miscellaneous bottles on top of them. When she was ready she came up to the counter and Inga introduced her to JoAnn Rogoski, the owner of North Sea Liquors and Ginger, the well-aged beagle.

"JoAnn is here every day with Ginger," said Inga. "I remember when Ginger was a puppy. Our dad used to bring us in here to play with her while he bought drinks for parties when we were little."

"It's nice to meet you Rachel," Joanne smiled at her. "It looks like you girls are having a pretty big to-do tonight," she said, helping Rachel put the wine on the counter.

"Just the usual fourth of July party. This is Rachel's first Koslowski fourth. I think you're going to *really love* the sing-along," Veronica said slyly to Rachel as she pulled her wallet out of her small purse.

Rachel stopped Veronica's hand with her own, "I've got this, girls."

"No," said Inga, "Mom told us to pay for all of this."

"Nope. I've got it. It's my contribution to the party. It's only fair anyways. If there really is a sing-along, I might drink all of this, and leave none for anyone else."

"The total will be 527.35," said Mrs. Rogoski.

Rachel saw shock pass over both Inga and Veronica's face. She was glad she'd offered to pay, but wondered if she was going over the top. Maybe fifty Kozlowski's didn't go through several cases of wine in a single night.

They loaded the wine in the flatbed and Veronica gunned the engine, skidding out of the dusty unpaved parking lot onto North Sea Road as she took advantage of a brief break in the steady traffic. Rachel was nervous that the bottles of wine would never make it the few miles up the road to the farm.

"Either of you two have a boyfriend?," she asked, in part to make conversation, in larger part because the combination of the crowded liquor store, the traffic, and the wind streaming through her fingers as she draped her hand out of the pickup's window had brought on an unexpected excitement for the holiday weekend. Totally gone were thoughts of her job, Lauren, even Scallop. She was just happy to be in a truck, in a sundress, and free to gossip with girls.

"Inga does. But he's totally random," Veronica leaned over the wheel to look at Rachel in order to deliver this information with the proper level of disdain.

"Hardly. He's a very talented musician. He plays five instruments, and his parents own a jazz club in the city, and a restaurant out here."

"Um, he can't swim. He's *random*," Veronica laughed, "He just arrived at school this year from nowhere. He dresses weird. He wears way too many layers of clothes. He must be hot all the time. I'm telling you…he's weird."

"Whatever." Inga glared at Veronica and sulked for a few seconds before she said,
"Speaking of weird, my mom's *really* excited that you're dating Uncle Scallop. She's almost intense about it. Are you going to stick around? She keeps saying she hopes you stick around. As if…you probably won't. I don't know if she'll be able to take it if you decide you don't like us all after this party, and there's any number of things you might not like about us after this party." Rachel wasn't exactly sure how to respond. She was flattered that Lucy wanted her around, but she didn't want to say anything to these girls that wasn't true.

"Your uncle and I have only known each other a month. And we only really have spent time together for two days and change. He's a great guy. Unique. I'm enjoying getting to know all of you. But Scallop and I might have to go on one normal date before we commit for life!"

"Well tonight you get to meet the entire extended family which might make you want to turn right around and go back to your apartment in the city!" Inga said.

"Entire extended family?"

"Of course! No one told you! Every 4th of July weekend we have all my aunts, uncles and cousins over for dinner. This year everyone is busy for the weekend so the dinner is tonight."

"I see," Rachel said. She was regretting that she hadn't taken a shower. She also fervently wished that she had not become so attached to her imagined itinerary for the night, because it wasn't happening.

"If Uncle Scallop had to attend a wedding with your people, I guess it's only fair you have to be at this dinner tonight," Veronica said sensibly as she pulled into the gravel parking lot of the farm, which was packed with cars.

In the small azalea-lined yard behind the farm stand, five long picnic tables were laid out with red, white and blue tablecloths. Tim Kozlowski and his son, Richard, who'd flown in from Florida, were working the large grill at the far end of the yard. Several other people were darting about, carrying piles of plates and pitchers of water. Three young boys were on the porch shucking corn as Lucy burst through the screen door from the kitchen carrying a giant platter laden with six whole chickens

"Hello Rachel Jones. Thanks for going with the girls to get the wine, I hope you weren't afraid for your life. It's so good to see you. How was the rest of your trip?"

"It was good. I'm glad to be back. I heard you were stuck in the farm stand."

"My mom took over for me. She's going to close up early in just a little bit. Welcome!"

"Thanks for having me at your family party. I was expecting pj's and pizza by the firepit tonight."

"Listen, Scallop forgets about this party every year. I sent him to pick up Pedro's and Luis's families in town. They are joining us for dinner and the family doesn't have a car. He should be back soon. Why don't we get that wine on ice over there in the ice chest if you don't mind? Make yourself comfortable, it's great to see your smiling face tonight!" Lucy said with a wink as she moved off to the grill.

Rachel and the girls unloaded the wine. Within a few minutes several carloads of families had arrived. Kids of all ages ran in every direction, and parents dressed in shorts and t-shirts delivered watermelons, cases of beer, salads and other contributions to dinner. Rachel felt a little better about how she looked because everyone else had dressed more casually than she had, but otherwise the scene was overwhelming. Rachel was from a family of four who wasn't close with their extended relations. Her mother had stopped talking to her father years ago when they divorced. Her mother also didn't talk to her aunt, who had no children. Her father had one brother with a son in Seattle and they didn't keep in close touch. She barely spoke to her own parents recently. The only member of her family that she talked to on a regular basis was her sister who lived in Beverly Hills. Rachel felt untethered in a sea of Koslowski without Scallop, like she'd shown up at a college frat party where she knew no one, and wasn't pretty enough to get noticed.

Before long, at least thirty people were bouncing between the yard, the house and the barn. A few stopped to say hello to Rachel who had positioned herself by the fence where she could keep an eye on the parking lot. A tall woman with wild curly blond hair carrying a coloring book and a Ziplock baggie full of crayons, stopped short as she walked by her.

"Oh, hi! You're Rachel, right? I've heard about you. You going to make it through this fiasco?" she laughed, "Hang in there and have a few drinks. I'm Cousin Olga Cooper," she thrust out her hand and grabbed Rachel's firmly, suddenly loud and cheerful. "My maiden name's Kozlowski, my father and Scallop's father are brothers. Four of the small lunatics running around here belong to me. You can have them if you want them," Olga said as she noticed a toddler about to wander out into the parking lot and took off after the little one.

Around the corner came Scallop. Somehow she'd missed him pulling into the drive in all the chaos and his truck wasn't in the lot, he must have parked elsewhere. He was wearing his work clothes and a broad smile. On his shoulders he carried a small boy she didn't recognize, and hanging from his lower half, his little arms wrapped around Scallop's waist and his legs around his thighs was Kosumi. Pedro and Luis stood up to greet their wives and children and Scallop saw Rachel standing alone by the fence as he put both boys on the ground. As he walked towards her the atmosphere seemed to adjust around her, the party taking a completely different shape. She took a deep breath, smelled the rich smells of farm and the barbeque, felt the warmth and excitement of Scallop's family, and stepped away from the fence.

"You made it. Welcome. It's great to see you Rachel." Scallop reached down and kissed her on the cheek. Pressing his face against hers for just long enough to make her blush, but not long enough to attract the attention of the women in his family, all of whom seemed to be purposely looking away from them.

"It's great to see you too. And it's great to be here. Hotels, planes and meetings were getting old. I wasn't expecting you to throw me a party! So nice of you."

"Yeah. Sorry I guess this was all news to you. We have a dinner each fourth of July, and this year for whatever reason it's tonight. I had to grab Pedro's and Luis's families, so sorry I wasn't here. We try to make sure they all know they are part of the family."

A child shot in between them and then another one chasing the first, "Christian! You have to be careful! Sorry Rachel!" Olga yelled from the porch where she was opening a bottle of the Whispering Angel. Scallop put a hand on the back of her neck that sent a pleasant shock down her spine and led her into the fray. People continued to arrive, Rachel met many "in-laws", "outlaws", some cousins who were cousins and more who weren't really cousins but went by the title. She drank her wine and held on for dear life. The Kozlowski's seemed to consider conversation a light-hearted story telling competition. People shouted across one another's heads interjecting in exchanges taking place all the way across the yard, calling one another out on inaccuracies or adding a detail to their story. Rachel found she didn't need to be "on" as she usually did during a party. She just needed to sit back and watch the show.

Eventually, a little girl rang the bell that hung from a post on the porch and everyone found a seat around a row of picnic tables set end to end to make one long table set with paper plates, paper napkins and plastic silverware. Rachel found herself across from Scallop and between Veronica and Scallop's cousin Jake. Rachel was relieved that the din seemed to have subsided as they sat, then shocked when Veronica grabbed her hand and Cousin Jake offered her his. She took it. With no announcement and no leader they all, even Pedro and Louis, began to tunelessly sing in the style of a children's nursery rhyme. Voices joined in the chant, or prayer, as their clasped hands formed one big circle.

"Every morning seems to say,
there's something happy on the way,
and God sends love to you,"

Scallop's mother helped his father out of his chair at the head of the table. Rachel had been introduced to them both earlier. Scallop's mother was short and muscular curly grey hair. She'd given Rachel a friendly but non-comital greeting and hurried off saying she needed to bring out the potato salad. His father had only acknowledged her handshake with a slight lift of his head. He'd been saving his strength. Now, sandwiched between his wife and his son Tim, he spoke in a belabored, quiet voice, determined to get his words across.

"Tonight, we thank God for this country. The greatest country on God's green Earth. Bless all of you for being here. It is my great joy seeing all of you, together, on my farm. Smell the sea air, eat some of my wife's layer cake, enjoy your work, enjoy your play, enjoy every day in this land of opportunity." Then, he began to sing, "God Bless America, land that I love…" the rest of the family joined him during the first line, holding hands again and looking at one another and at Scallop's father with palpable emotion. Rachel was unaccustomed to such an unjaded show of feeling. She felt embarrassed. Not for them, but for herself. She didn't know how to take part in a scene like this. Rachel's family didn't behave in this manner. There were no family barbecues, prayers or song singing at Jones family gatherings. In fact, there were no Jones family gatherings.

The final chord of "God Bless America" rang out in exuberant cacophony. The Koslowski's weren't great singers. But they were enthusiastic. Veronica gave Rachel an unexpected quick hug and they sat down to dinner.

The food was plentiful; most of it from the farm. Barbeque chicken, macaroni salad, potato salad, corn on the cob, oysters, clams, crabs and scallops. Despite the number of people, more than half of them children, the dinner was orderly. Bowls and platters were passed down the tables, lemonade was poured for the children. The food made its way around quickly, and the conversation was less boisterous than it had been before, and focused in large part on politics. Lucy sat at the end of their picnic table. Her passion for the environment had led her to join several local groups including the Bay Keepers and the Peconic Land Trust. She was a liberal who was for gun control. She sat diagonally across from her brother Tim and her Cousin Richard, a local builder. Both of them owned several guns each and identified as Libertarian. Rachel was surprised by the divergent viewpoints within the family and impressed that the conversation stayed somewhat academic and respectful, flowing seamlessly between calm debate and effusive admiration for the dinner.

After they ate, the kids spread out across the farm to play "Manhunt", while the older generation moved the party to the porch doubling down on wine. Rachel found herself caught up by conversations with different family members while Scallop talked fishing with one of his cousins. She talked to Scallop's Mom about a bestseller they'd both read, and to Lucy and Pedro's wife about breast feeding, of all things. As she nearly snorted some rosé out her nose at Pedro's wife's impression of some upper-class woman trying to untangle herself from a voluminous cashmere breastfeeding poncho that she was really enjoying herself.

Scallop came around refilling people's glasses with wine and beer and Cousin Joe Gminski broke out his guitar to lead a sing along. His song list started with Hank Williams "Family Tradition", went to "Pink Houses", and then on to "Friends in Low Places". Country and folk music were not Rachel's thing, but listening to a chorus of tipsy cousins, aunts, uncles and grandparents belting Jimmy Buffet's "One Particular Harbor" had an undeniable charm. She was shocked to notice that it was getting dark already. As they wound their way through Joe's repertoire, children danced and then settled down to snuggle in laps. They didn't seem to be all that concerned with whether or not the lap belonged to their parent, they were comfortable sitting on any leg, and three little ones found a spot together tucked in behind the chairs on a plaid blanket.

Suddenly it was ten o'clock and despite her nap in the hammock earlier, Rachel's jet lag had joined forces with the wine; she was exhausted. The porch swing on the far side of the porch from the sing-along was empty and she stretched out on it. She'd begun to doze off when she felt a small hand on her arm, followed by a pointy little knee digging into her leg. Kosumi climbed up and laid his head on her stomach. She had an intense moment of panic. If this had been her family, judging eyes would have scrutinized whether or not it was appropriate for Kosumi to be showing her such affection when she and Scallop barely knew one another. As she looked around wondering what she ought to do she caught Lucy's eye. Lucy waved drunkenly and then pointed at Kosumi and laughed at Rachel's predicament. No one was judging here. Rachel relaxed. She leaned back letting the weight of Kosumi's head anchor her to the swing and they drifted off.

Sometime later Rachel came-to as cool air brushed her stomach. The heat of Kosumi had been lifted off her center and Scallop stood over her holding the boy to his chest. He pantomimed that she should stay where she was, he would take Kosumi upstairs to lay down. She groggily straightened her hair and clothes, cold and nonplused to find that she half wished Scallop had left them as they were until the morning. The sing-along had ended and Cousin Joe had subsided into quiet strumming and humming to himself as a diminished band of Koslowski adults talked. A hand clasped hers through the darkness behind her, and she turned to find that Scallop had come around the back of the house. He was standing just beyond the reach of the porch lights, again pantomiming for her to say nothing and to come down to him. She glanced back at the remaining partygoers. They were too absorbed in their conversation and probably too far gone to notice if she and Scallop disappeared for the night. He lifted her down off the porch and pulled her towards the back of the house. She wasn't sure where they were going, but everything about him told her exactly what they were going to do. She followed him, pulled by the current of electricity that ran between them emanating out into the night, into the fields. The moths drawn to the windows at the back of the house seemed to know what they were about to do. Every hair on her body stood on end with hypersensitive awareness. She felt the ridges of his fingerprints against the back of her hand, felt the air that the movement of his hair pushed through space, she noticed the sponginess of the earth beneath her heels.

Behind the house they picked up the deeply rutted dirt road that went out towards the barn and the pig pen. As Scallop silently pulled her down the road, she glanced back at the group on the porch to see if anyone was watching them, but they seemed a mile away. Then Rachel knew exactly where they were going. The two-story door to the big modern pole barn gapped open. The moment they escaped the glow from the floodlight at the front of the building, stepping inside the cool silent space, Scallop lifted Rachel up, wrapping her legs around his waist, kissing her with the pressure of a month's worth of waiting. He carried her as he slowly, silently pulled the giant door closed.

The darkness inside the barn was absolute. Scallop let her slide down his front bringing her dress up over her head as her feet touched the ground. She couldn't see where she ended and where he began, she didn't know where the walls were, if they were three feet from a tractor blade or if they were in the company of a family of raccoons. For a second she didn't know where Scallop was. She laughed breathlessly, "The barn," she said, "of course it's the barn."

"Yes, the barn," Scallop's voice came to her from a few feet away just before he lifted her off her feet again. He'd shed his own clothes and his body was hot, dry and fluid against hers as he carried her through space until they landed against a wall covered in something slightly spongey and smooth. For a split-second she wondered what the hell it could possibly be, and if it was clean. But an instant later she didn't care. This kiss lasted longer than she could have imagined possible, long enough to lay to rest all the questions, anxiety, fear, hope, doubt and curiosity that they'd both allowed free reign since they'd met. As they touched in the blackness they both understood they had met their match. Rachel had a heightened awareness of her own muscle, bone and sinew as Scallop swept his hands from her shoulders out to her fingertips. They made almost no sound as they explored every piece of one another, sensing their way from the skin to the other's core. In the end, when they took each other it was like a conflagration resulting from a slow burning chemical reaction.

They leaned against the padding, for what must have been a quarter of an hour, Scallop still holding Rachel off the ground, both exhausted beyond speech. Eventually Scallop pulled her away from the wall and carried her somewhere, she still had no ability to get her bearings. He set her down and a second later pressed her dress into her hands. She didn't know what to say, didn't really want to speak and break the silence, so she said nothing. She felt for the seams of her dress to make sure she was putting it on properly and when she finished she could feel him at her feet.

"Step forward" he said. She moved her foot slightly forward and felt her sandals with her toe, slipping them on. She could hear him a few feet away pulling his clothes on. Then he stood for a moment just breathing.

"Rachel," he said, reaching out and grabbing her neck. He pulled her toward him and then slid his hand down her arm, taking her hand in his. And then the door slid open. She tried not to squint as the flood light stung her eyes. She imagined her hair was wild after what they'd just done, it was possible her clothes weren't on properly, and squinting was not her best look. But Scallop didn't look back at her. He shielded his own eyes from the light as he looked across the field towards the farmhouse porch. Everyone was gone and the porch light had been turned out. Still without looking back, he lead her around the side of the barn where she was surprised to see his truck under a shed roof. He opened the passenger door for her and she climbed in. As he turned on the engine he reached over and grabbed her hand again, fiercely bringing it to his lips and kissing it.

Scallop pulled the truck around to the front of the house and quietly said, "Stay here Rachel, I'll be right back with Kosumi."

It took Scallop a few minutes to return but Rachel didn't mind. She felt outside of time. She was stunned. She had a new awareness of herself. She knew it was insane, but it felt as though Scallop had opened the cage of her body in that barn and placed her soul back inside it. She didn't know where it had been before, but she knew now that it hadn't been where it was supposed to be. It was staggering to realize what she had been missing. It was terrifying to know that someone could change that much for her in the space of an hour.

Scallop opened the door and gave Kosumi to Rachel, making sure that all his parts were inside the cab before he closed the door. Kosumi seemed to break the spell over both of them. Rachel felt at least able to carry on a conversation again.

After a few minutes she said, "So, that was quite the party," with light sarcasm in a voice low enough not to wake Kosumi, "really, I enjoyed meeting everyone. Does Cousin Joe always serve as entertainment?"

"Yeah, unless you don't invite him," Scallop said matching her tone.

'I guess letting me know the plan for the night would have involved you participating in some form of modern communication..."

"True," he smiled, "but, I forgot all about it to be honest. Lucy came out to the barn said she'd sent the girls to get you. At that point I just figured you'd be able to roll with it, and you did. But, for the rest of the weekend we are free of family obligations. It's just us."

It was well past one in the morning as they pulled into Scallop's yard.

"I know it's really late, but I think I need to take a shower. My last one was over forty hours ago in Abu Dhabi. I've been *in* Abu Dhabi, on a plane, in the Peconic Bay, and up against a *mysterious cushion in a barn*," she said, knowing she was blushing, "I still feel more drunk than seems possible, and I can't imagine putting my feet against clean sheets."

Scallop laughed, "The shower is great at night. I'll turn it on for you, and jump in after you. And don't think you're winning any contests, I actually worked in a pigsty today for Pete's sake. You should know that I'm going to win that one every time." Scallop lifted Kosumi of Rachel's lap and carried him into the house, Rachel followed.

By the time Scallop had placed the sleeping boy under the covers, kissed him on the forehead, and walked to the kitchen, Rachel was standing looking out the window holding a travel bag of toiletries. The consummate traveler she was clearly able to take care of herself and be ready for anything at a moment's notice. Scallop found it incredibly attractive. He'd brought a towel for each of them.

"This might be the nicest shower you've ever had," he said as they stepped out onto the back stairs, "look at the stars tonight."

She'd been so focused on him and his family that she hadn't thought to look up at the sky. It was stunning. Layer upon layer of stars extended out beyond sight and understanding. They walked to the shower both looking up. Scallop pulled open the slat door and reached in to turn it on. She followed him in, it was roomy enough for them both to navigate. She took the towel from him, a fresh electrical current, stronger than a riptide passed between them as Scallop stepped back out.

Rachel slid out of her clothes, hanging them on one of the rusted metal hooks, and stepped under the hot water as she looked up at the stars, a half-moon providing more than enough light. She felt every droplet of water hit her body. She was still tipsy enough and shaken enough from the barn that the force of the water seemed strong enough to push her. How could there be anything left after what they'd just done? She'd been surprised by the fresh current between them and wondered what, if anything, Scallop was going to do; the charge he'd left behind was not something she could ignore, but she was curious to see whether or not it had the same pull on him.

Scallop's heart was racing as he walked around the front of the house to grab the bag he used to bring clothes and miscellanea back and forth to the farm. He walked it inside, doing battle with his better self. He was sure Kosumi was so exhausted after all the activity with his cousins that fireworks wouldn't wake him. He could picture Rachel out in the shower. He wanted her, and this time he wanted to look at her, and he didn't want to be quiet about it. He stood in the living room, his eyes closed listening to the shower roaring outside. For the previous month, he'd imagined her. In his mind's eye, he knew the shape of her hips, the contour of her back. He tried to breathe slowly and control himself, knowing his son was asleep only feet away. But, he found himself in front of the shower despite himself. Better the shower than the bedroom. This couldn't wait until tomorrow night when the girls would have Kosumi.

Rachel's face was tilted back under the water when Scallop entered. She didn't hear him come in and her eyes were closed against the stream. He was able to look his fill, unobserved. What he saw caught him in his throat, his belly, his feet and his hips. He had imagined her as soft. She was smooth, but there was nothing soft about her. He understood now why they'd felt so perfectly matched in the barn. Her dark skin was wrapped around the type of graceful muscle that only came from a lifetime of the kind of focused physical activity that made up his own days. Her center was darker than he'd pictured, and he realized she used her wardrobe to cloak some of her true nature. When she opened her eyes suddenly the whites of her eyes shone against her darkness. Rachel stood still as Scallop pulled off his work clothes. Now that he'd really seen her, the intensity of her stare and the wall of energy that was coming at him didn't surprise him. He let it flow over him for a moment, standing back at her. When they came together this time it was an onslaught. Two separate forces displaying their singularity, their power, in a passionate, ferocious bout of consuming.

When it was all over, they stumbled to the bedroom exhausted, passing out in one another's arms, with no thought of anything outside themselves.

22: The 4th of July

Scallop heard Kosumi pad up behind him and take two plates from the shelves near the dining table, and place them carefully, one at a time, on the table; his job at mealtime. Scallop turned around to find him sitting in his usual spot at the table looking sleepily out towards the water.

"Good morning my boy, don't forget to put out a plate for Rachel."

Kosumi hopped up excitedly and carefully picked out the plate he thought was right for Rachel. Scallop had been loath to wake the little boy at their usual time for Scallop's workout, Kosumi had been up so late the night before. He'd been sound asleep when it was time to head out and Scallop was positive he would stay that way, so he put on an old stop watch he'd had since junior high school and gave himself forty-five minutes to run hard, leaving a note for Rachel. If Kosumi woke up and wanted him they'd be able to find him. Since he was giving himself less time to exercise than usual he ran full-out trying to exhaust himself so that he could be sure to have a calm day. When he got home he was relieved to find he'd been right; both Rachel and Kosumi were still sleeping. Before long, the little house was filled with the smells of coffee, frying eggs, bacon and sausage.

"I dreamed last night Daddy. Again. About the boat and the big, big truck!"

"Really? Was it the same dream you've had before, or did the truck do something different this time?"

"The truck smiled at Grannie's cat and then drove into the water to meet the boat. Again!"

"Ah. So, it *was* the same again! That's a pretty special big truck. Who's my boy?"

"This one," Kosumi said as he touched his chest.

"And how much does Daddy love you?"

"Up to the sky."

Scallop squeezed Kosumi and then solemnly handed him the silverware to place at each plate. He was a bit young to do it, but Scallop made it part of their routine. He didn't care if the silverware was straight and properly set. He cared that Kosumi felt useful. It was amazing to Scallop how fast his little boy was growing up, he could see him change from day to day. He ran his hand through the long, curly blonde hair that was one of the many markings of his Koslowski genes. Kosumi was undeniably Scallop's.

Sometimes, particularly when Kosumi was dancing, he'd feel a tug of guilt that the only physical trait Kosumi had inherited from his mother was her dark skin, striking against his blond hair. So little of her peculiar beauty had managed to triumph over his own genetic code. It had died with her. Kosumi did seem to have some of her dancing spirit though.

"We are going to have a great day today my boy. Rachel is here to play with us, and we are going out in the boat, we'll show her all the fun things we do! Then, we'll go to the carnival with Uncle Tim and your cousins. When you come back, we can have prayers and then sit by the fire. It will be a fun, full day for you and maybe we'll see some fireworks. Are you ready for some booming?"

"Yes. Boom! I want to see Rachel, I'll go see her."

Scallop had no idea how Rachel would react to one of Kosumi's wake up calls. For Scallop it usually included hands on his face and a knee is in his groin. And, unless she'd gotten up while he was out he was positive she didn't have any clothes on.

"No, buddy, you stay out here. Let Rachel sleep, she was very tired."

Scallop finished making breakfast and Kosumi played quietly with his trucks in the living room.

Rachel could hear them out there. She hadn't spent much time around small children. She'd only visited her sister in California a few times when her niece was Kosumi's age. Her sister was a stay at home mom who never stayed at home. She went from activity to activity, dropping her kids off to be exercised and supervised by other people. Rachel found the atmosphere her sister's parenting style generated irritating. She listened to Kosumi quietly playing with cars in the living room, driving them back and forth along the windowsills; it was actually soothing. She closed her eyes again, giving herself a little more rest and the boys a chance to have a little bit of normalcy. Half an hour later, she emerged from the bedroom looking and feeling refreshed.

"Morning," she said as she walked into the kitchen, peeking into the living room to see if Kosumi was looking and then kissing Scallop. In her mind this egg-cooking dad was now her boyfriend. It was so natural, she'd made the transition without any of her characteristic weighing of pros and cons. She poured herself a cup of coffee and sat down at the table, admiring his back as he finished making breakfast.

"So is there a newspaper? I know there's no wi-fi. Any magazines to read?"

"No magazines. If you really want, we can go down to the deli and get a paper. But, you could also just do nothing. You might just like it. All that bullshit people choose to drown their minds in erodes their soul. You could shut off the phone for the weekend and just be here, just be happy to be alive and have another day. There are people out there who are leading desperate lives. We're lucky to have this food, this place to be and the life we have. I know I'm happy to have another day with you," Scallop said as he worked the eggs around the frying pan, not looking at her as he spoke. There was no judgement of her behavior in his voice but there was the slightest edge. She knew he lived what her friends would consider a "Zen" life: surfing, living simply, not caring about things. He seemed to believe his own dogma, and it was a pretty harmless dogma to be living by. But she knew it must have grown up around some trauma, she imagined it must have been his time in the military.

Kosumi climbed up next to her, silently placing a miniature Ford F150 at the top of her plate and smiling at her.

"Hello little guy. What are we going to do today? Have you made a big plan for me?"

"We're going on the boat. I show you the bluff and I will show you the beach. We can swim and then the carnival!"

"The *carnival*. We're going to a carnival?"

"Yes! You'll go on the rides with me?"

"Sure! If you'd like me to."

"Yes please!"

They ate a companionable breakfast. Rachel was struck once again by the
difference between this house and her sister's house. Kosumi did not shout or make a mess with his food to catch the adults' attention, there was no need. Scallop made him part of the conversation without making it all about him. He asked Kosumi what he thought they should show Rachel on the boat and he included some of his suggestions in the plan. They decided they would show her the bluff and the beach, teach her to fish, and then show her how fast the boat could go.

"How long does it take to get to the North Fork?" Rachel asked Scallop.

"Depends on where exactly you want to go, and whether or not it's rough out there, but it's usually under half an hour. Why? Do you have somewhere to go over there?"

"A friend of mine always talks about a place called Claudio's Clam Bar as though it is the be-all-end-all. I'm just curious," Rachel said casually. Trevor was actually the "friend" who waxed poetic about Claudio's on an almost weekly basis, he and his partner took their kids there all the time, and she relished the thought of finding a way to tease him about it, and she thought if she happened to run into him it would be a good chance to have an in-person chat about what Lauren had been up to in the past few days while she'd been wrapping up her trip.

Scallop rolled with it, "I know Claudio's. Haven't been there in years. I used to hang out at the bar, when I hung out at bars. It was the oldest family run restaurant in the country, but they just sold it recently."

"Aha! Well, already I have the local dirt to rub in Trevor's face! Can we go there for lunch? Is that alright?"

"Yeah sure," Scallop said gamely. Rachel was again struck by how easy going he was. Many men she knew would have been put out by their date railroading their plans in a different direction, but he actually seemed excited to do something different as he bent down to Kosumi.

"My boy, we're going to go to a special lunch with Rachel, so you'll want to bring these things: a shirt, some flip flops, a book, and some paper and crayons. Can you find all those things and bring them to the table?"

As Kosumi sprinted to his room to find the flip flops, Scallop stood and pulled Rachel in for an enthusiastic kiss. "Good idea. I forget you're not used to staying at home and digging up your own dinner. You should feel free to remind me whenever you don't want to do that."

She laughed, "Ok, don't worry, I won't be shy about it!"

Scallop's Zodiac N ZO 760 was made for days like this. He pulled it in as close to the shore as he could get so that Rachel and Kosumi could climb in and then waded back to shore to get towels and bottles of water. Kosumi showed Rachel how to navigate the inflatable sides, pulling himself up on his belly like a beached sea creature and then rolling over and flopping on the floor between the pontoon and the driver's console. Rachel scrutinized her options and knew that whatever she did wasn't going to end up looking much better than what Kosumi had just done so she followed suit hoping that Scallop was looking somewhere besides her backside. Rachel had been on plenty of boats but never on a Zodiac. While it's hull was inflatable, it was comfortable with seats like a regular boat, and it seemed secure enough. Kosumi showed her where the adult life jackets were stored and he put on his own, dramatically clicking each closure, proud that he was the sort of boy who knew how to do these things himself.

Scallop climbed in the boat. Rachel was relieved to see that even he had an awkward time of it. He handed towels to Kosumi who resolutely stowed them under a bench, struggling with the bench top just a bit while Scallop started the motor.

He looked up at Rachel, "Alright! Let's show you the sights!"

"How fast can this thing go?" she called over the noise of the engine.

"Go sit up front with Kosumi and we'll show you."

They flew over to Robins Island, with Scallop pointing out different points of interest to Rachel as they went. It was just after ten in the morning and the temperature was already above ninety. The bay was calm and they passed by another boat every few minutes. Rachel held her hair back as it whipped in her face and she and Kosumi giggled as they waved and shouted "hello" in funny voices to the other boats going by. Scallop kept his attention focused on driving, he was going fast while giving other boats a wide enough birth, careful and considerate of his wake. Rachel did not know how to handle a boat, but it was apparent to her that Scallop did. After they'd taken a few turns around the bay Scallop killed the engine.

Scallop pointed to the top of "The Bluff", which was several hundred yards up from the beach, "That's where I swim to most mornings with Kosumi. It should also be noted that in the early 1990s, a certain local boy did something for the first time up there," he side whispered with wink.

"Really? I'll keep that in mind," Rachel said trying to be flirtatious and charming while pushing an unpleasant visual to the back of her mind.

"Rachel, do you want to go swimming?" Kosumi asked, tugging on her cover-up.

"Sure. Do we go right here from the boat?"

"Yup. Watch this!" he shouted as he jumped off the back of the boat into the water.

Rachel followed suit and so did Scallop. Together they floated around the boat for a good twenty minutes talking about the other boats passing by. Scallop told Kosumi and Rachel about the different features of the different types of boats, if they were good for fishing or speed, and if they were reliable or temperamental. They got out of the water once Kosumi's fingers started to pucker up like the skin of a prune, and Scallop and Kosumi set up to fish off the front. Rachel begged off saying she wanted to sun herself, but really she liked to listen to them talk to one another. She silently chastised herself for being a living cliché, getting all hot and bothered over a man being a good dad. She'd made fun of friends in the past for doing the same thing. But it was sexy. She got it now.

At noon, they started towards the town of Greenport on the North Fork. As they went Scallop pointed out the fine homes on Shelter Island, as well as the famously chic Sunset Beach Restaurant. Rachel politely didn't tell him she'd been to both places before, because in between pointing out the man-made wonders of the bay, he also pointed to harbor seals, three dolphins, and a wide sloping lawn where Kosumi claimed to have seen a hundred rabbits last summer.

As they slowed to approach the long pier at Claudio's they could see it was already getting crowded. It was early for lunch in the Hamptons, but people who planned on spending the afternoon came in early to stake their claim on a table. Claudio's had an indoor restaurant, with an old-fashioned bar and an interior that hadn't been updated anytime in Scallop's lifetime, but the summer action was outside on the covered pier. Half the tables were already filled and a band was doing a sound check. Scallop laughed, "We're probably here at exactly the right time. In two hours or so this place is going to be a complete zoo. By four o'clock people will be squeezed in here like sardines either hitting on the person next to them, or becoming "BFF's" with them," he laughed heartily, "I haven't been here since before Afghanistan. I like it, it's a totally mixed bag of people. Biker guys, *your* buddies, locals, families with kids. You never know what kind of music you're going to get either."

"Country? Do they have country bands?" Rachel asked dreading the answer. Had she actually suggested they have lunch somewhere with a bunch of bikers and loud country music? She was going to kill Trevor.

"What's wrong with country?", Scallop asked.

"Meh, I'm just a suburban born city girl," she poked Scallop in the bicep as she gathered up her things in the boat, "Maybe if you give me a tractor driving lesson I'll suddenly love it," she joked.

"I'm not sure that'll do it," Scallop laughed, "but you might learn to like some new swear words on the tractor. It's harder than it looks." While they'd been talking country music a reggae drum beat had started up and Kosumi was squirming along to it where he sat in the front of the boat.

"I think you're in luck. Sounds like we've got reggae today. Ok to dock the boat city girl?"

"Yes, proceed!" Rachel sat down next to Kosumi and began to wiggle along with him. Scallop navigated the boat down the narrow channel formed by the two piers that made up the Claudio's campus; a big operation, with a clam bar, restaurant, marina, and a take-out booth. Once he reached an open spot on the pier he floated out beyond it and then expertly swung the boat around to the dock, avoiding the boats docked in front and back of where they were pulling up, as well as another boat looking for a spot, and ending with the bow of the Zodiac facing out towards open water. He tied them up and Rachel hoisted Kosumi up to him and then let him pull her up on the dock. As they walked towards the restaurant Scallop stopped to help a young couple in their twenties tie up their boat. The dock was busy, and not a good place for a rookie boater to cut his teeth, and the kid was a rookie. He had a mid-size speed boat, a "Nordic Rage", emblazoned with yellow and red flame details, and he was struggling with the throttle as he tried to pull its pointed bow back and away from the classic wooden Chris Craft it was drifting towards. He was visibly frustrated and glaring at the young woman he was with as though it were somehow her fault that he didn't know how to park his toy.

"Why don't you two go find us a place to sit and let me help this kid out," Scallop said quietly to Rachel, "This weekend is always an amateur festival. These people are lucky they all don't drown, but the least I can do is get that poor girl out of the boat with that punk. He'll either learn to drive that thing someday or he won't come here again."

"Alright. I see you make a regular habit of rescuing damsels, just remember, you're meeting me at a table in a few minutes and plying me with a lobster roll and a margarita. I'm your damsel of the day. Where should we sit Kosumi?"

"Can we sit next to the band, right close?" Kosumi pulled Rachel off in the direction of "Stir It Up".

He chose an empty table close to the dance floor and put his little backpack full of crayons and paper on the chair. Then he stood gripping the back of the chair, bopping up and down and looking anxiously at Rachel, unwilling to sit.

"Do you want to dance Kosumi?" she asked.

"Yes!" he yelled throwing his hands up in the air, unable to keep his enthusiasm down.

157

"Alright then," she laughed, "I don't want to lose our table so you just dance right here in front of it where I can see you, and I'll sit here and save our seats."

Kosumi joined the few other people already on the dance floor and launched into full body movement, throwing his arms and hair around to the beat, sometimes on it, sometimes in syncopation, launching his whole torso towards the floor and then up again and spreading his legs wide. He was a sight, and Rachel could hear people at the nearby tables commenting on how gorgeous he was and how beautiful and *involved* his dancing was. Scallop came and sat down next to her.

"Everything alright at the dock?" Rachel asked him.

"Yup, that poor dude doesn't have a clue about boats. I guess it took them an hour to get out of the small marina there were in when they started, and it will probably take him another hour to navigate out of here. I told him to call a cab if he was going to drink. So, what's on the menu?"

"Well first we have entertainment...I present you with 'The Great Kosumi'," she said, pointing at Kosumi who was presently dangling his arms down to the floor and alternating kicking each leg out behind him, "I think he might have a career as a dancer, he's talented. Everybody's watching him."

"Mmmm," Scallop said. He barely looked up at Kosumi and there was something in the tone of his monosyllabic response that brought Rachel up short. Usually anything to do with Kosumi took Scallop's attention.

"Should we have him to sit down with us?" she asked, concerned that maybe Scallop felt it was inappropriate for Kosumi to be dancing, although she couldn't imagine why he would feel that way.

"No, no. He can dance. He comes to it naturally," he said quickly. "Let's get some drinks," he said as he motioned to a waiter to come over. They ordered drinks from their college age waitress who Rachel was certain was from some upscale town in Connecticut judging by her haircut and earrings. She hoped there were enough summer jobs to go around for both the locals and the kids whose families owned summer homes here. She brought a Dos Equis and a shot of tequila for Scallop, and a margarita for Rachel.

One bowl of clams, three burgers, and one ice cream sundae later Claudio's was jam packed. They'd finished eating so they abandoned their table and danced with Kosumi for a few minutes. Rachel was again treated to Scallop's dance stylings. As she danced along with him she wondered if he might think that Kosumi had inherited his natural rhythm and connection to music from Scallop. He had rhythm, that was true, but he did not have the same deep understanding of the tone of the music.

As they pulled away from the dock Rachel realized she hadn't even searched the crowd for Trevor. She'd been so absorbed by Scallop and

158

Kosumi. They had spent most of the time making observations about the people at Claudio's; someone had a silk shirt that reminded Kosumi of a dolphin, someone else had the type of hair that flies straight up in the wind. They were not finding fault or making fun, they were just 'wondering'. She realized she hadn't spent a second thinking about what people thought of her and Scallop.

"Team nap!" Scallop announced as they walked back into the cottage. The house was pleasantly cool from the fans Scallop had left running in each room. Scallop took Kosumi into the bathroom and helped him wipe the sunscreen off his face. "Hey Rachel, can you grab Kosumi a glass of ice water for his bedside?" he called realizing too late that he was treating her with a familiarity she might not feel. His heart sank as he recognized what was happening, he was treating her like she was his girlfriend. He had already made the assumption that she was committed to both him and Kosumi. At lunch she had helped Kosumi cut up his burger, she dropped her guard, eating clams with her fingers and wildly doing the twist on the pressure treated dance floor with his son. "That doesn't mean she's going to be here every weekend doing that," he told himself, "and she's made it pretty clear that she definitely won't be doing that during the week." He met her at the door of Kosumi's room and thanked her for bringing the water, he wasn't going to include her in the most intimate of he and Kosumi's rituals, it was a bad idea.

"Why don't you go stretch out in my room while I tuck him in?" he asked, casually enough so that he was certain she didn't realize he was purposely sending her away.

When he came to the bed a few minutes later she smiled up at him, offering him her hand. He took it, wondering how it was that they had somehow changed places. Since she'd flopped into the boat this morning she'd been living in the now, just as he'd suggested she do and he was suddenly mired in the past and struggling with what might happen in the future. He smiled back at her forcing himself to reenter the present through the feel of her skin and the smell of her neck.

Fifteen minutes later Rachel was curled up on the bed with a sleeping Scallop next to her. It felt so incredibly comfortable, like she was at once anchored and cushioned by him and this place. Her skin was hot against the breeze from the fans. She could smell the sun and the sea spray on Scallop and on herself. "It can't be this easy," she thought as she dozed off. In less than twenty four hours she'd met people who she'd genuinely liked and who hadn't expected anything of her, she felt comfortable in Scallop's house, and she'd had the most intense intimate experience of her life; she had no choice but to fall asleep with her mind at ease and her body satisfied.

"Ahem, Ahem, Knock, knock! Hey! Cousin Richard is here and I'm not leaving until I have my little rascal cousin Kosumi ready for the big carnival!"

Rachel had been startled awake by a loud knock at the door. Someone was at the front door yelling, and Scallop wasn't in bed next to her.

Blearily she walked out into the living room. Scallop's nephew Richard, who Rachel had met the night before was leaning sheepishly against the front door frame, letting the door hang wide open.

"Oh, hey Rachel. I hope I didn't disturb anything. I tried to, you know, let you know I was coming in."

"Not at all Richard. We were having a nap, but I think I might be the last one sleeping. I don't know where Scallop and Kosumi are…," she also didn't know what Richard was doing there. Richard was a twenty-six-year-old policeman in Naples, Florida who had been a college football player and now coached high school football. She'd spent a few minutes chatting with him the night before and had found him charming, intelligent and refreshingly unjaded in his excitement to be home with his family. He was back for a week's vacation and he seemed more interested in chatting with Veronica and Inga and helping his grandmother than in going out and ripping it up in the Hamptons like every other handsome guy in his mid-twenties Rachel knew would. Maybe this was how the Koslowski's did it. Maybe they just showed up anytime at one another's houses. She guessed it wasn't a bad thing, it just wasn't something she was used to. Scallop and Kosumi came in the back door, fresh from the shower.

"Hey!" Richard said enthusiastically. "Aunt Lucy sent me over here to pick up Kosumi for the carnival. She knows I need someone to go on *all* the rides with me, and she thought you two might want some privacy for a bit," he said conspiratorially from behind his hand.

"Oh," said Rachel, her confusion cleared up. Lucy was engineering private time for her and Scallop. "You know, we can all go the carnival! I don't think I've ever been to a country carnival."

"No way," said Richard, "Aunt Lucy's orders. So, what do you say little buddy? Do you want to go eat ice cream and fried dough with me and Inga and Veronica? Let's go see if we can win one of those giant stuffed bananas."

Rachel looked over at Scallop to see what his reaction was to the change in plan. Maybe he wanted to take Kosumi to the carnival and her presence there was getting in the way. Maybe he wouldn't like his sister intervening. But, he seemed completely fine with it.

"What do you think Kosumi? Do you want to just go to the carnival with your cousins?" Scallop asked him.

"Sure!" shouted Kosumi.

"Great," said Richard. "Uncle Scallop you *know* if you go there you're going to end up in the dunk tank for Dad. Rachel, if you want to have a good time tonight you better make him steer clear!"

"Normally I help out at the carnival," Scallop explained, "it's run by the fire department. Tim and I take turns in the dunk tank. It's a good way to cool off."

Richard ushered Kosumi out the door. As he picked Kosumi up he leaned in to Rachel, "You sure you know what you're getting into?", he asked, "I mean I'm a part of this family and I live in Florida by choice," he finished dramatically as he ran down the steps.

Scallop waved out the door smiling as they drove away and then turned to Rachel, "So, my sister, in her infinite wisdom thinks we need the night alone. Did you want to go to the carnival? I don't want to deprive you of bad hamburgers and friend dough just because my sister thinks we should be doing *something* else."

She'd been happy to go to the carnival, but she was just as happy not to. A night filled with ridding the teacups and eating cotton candy wasn't her first choice of entertainment. "Lucy's just trying to be nice and give you a break I'm sure. What do you say we take those paddleboards over to that big bluff you showed me today?" Rachel proposed.

"Ah, Lucy has enchanted you I see. She does that. But, yeah, that sounds great to me," Scallop said happily, and suddenly he looked like a thirteen year old boy presented with the adventure of his life. Before long, they were paddling side by side as the sun began to move further to the west, giving the sky a ruby red tinge. The water was just a little rougher than when they'd been out earlier in the day. They had to work to move through the water, laughing as Rachel nearly lost her balance, not being as practiced as Scallop. She appreciated that he stayed right next to her, breaking his rhythm whenever he started to pull ahead so that he wouldn't leave her behind. In turn he was impressed with her stamina, he didn't have to hold back much for her to stay with him. As they went Rachel asked Scallop about the different members of his family.

"So, Richard…," she said, "he seems to really like hanging out with his family. It's nice, but is it just a *little* weird?" she laughed.

"Nah," said Scallop. "I remember being the same when I was a kid. No party was as fun as a family party. I had a bunch of cousins and second cousins my age and we all would play hide and seek in the barns and house until the middle of the night and then when we were older we'd sneak beers and play drinking games up in the hay loft. No one paid any attention to what we were doing. We were together and safe."

It took them about forty-five minutes to make their way over to the bluff, working against the tide. As they passed the private beach at Southampton Shores, they watched as a group of people set up plastic tables and party decorations around the pavilion on the beach.

"What do you think they're up to there?" she asked Scallop.

"Must be a party I guess," as he stopped paddling, "Wait!," he said laughing, "I actually know exactly what they're doing. They're setting up the annual community cocktail party that they do at The Shores every fourth of July weekend. It's probably happened every year for the past century. When I was a kid, I used to play with the kids in that neighborhood in the summers. We'd stuff ourselves with chips, dip and strawberry shortcake at that party and then we'd play "kick the can" after all the grown-ups stumbled home to eat dinner."

"Your childhood sounds like so much more fun than mine. My Fourth of July's were spent sitting on a picnic blanket in an uncomfortable, fancy dress, watching the fireworks in Chicago. My sister and I were only allowed fruit roll-ups as a treat, no ice cream, no popsicles, so that we wouldn't make a mess of our dresses. My mother would spend the entire time making rude judgements about everyone around us. It was zero fun."

When they reached the bluff they pulled their paddleboards ashore, "Now," said Scallop, "comes the hard part. Climbing up this big old sucker. Most mornings I swim over here, run up this thing a few times, and swim back. I say we skip that tonight. We can walk it. The view from up there is something else."

It was an hour until dusk and there were only a few boats left anchored off the beach below. They had the bluff to themselves as they slowly walked their way to the top. It was a tough climb and they were quiet as they pulled themselves up the slope, sliding backwards five or six inches with each step. When they reached the top, Rachel's lungs were screaming. She turned around to look out towards the water, the red sun was seeping into the sky turning it pink almost to the water line. Her breath was ragged, and there was a lump in her throat that she needed to release.

"This is beautiful," she blurted. It came out louder than she'd expected, and it was tinged with an anger she didn't understand. Scallop looked at her from the corner of his eye and said nothing, he could see something was working in her.

"This has been the nicest day Scallop. Can you tell I never uncoil? I'm always chasing the next thing. I spend so much time running around like a lunatic," she paused for a few seconds, "I don't get to look at anything. It's rare I spend a week in just one place. Occasionally I'll make it a week where I don't leave Manhattan. But I never relax. You get to live right here. And see this, every single day. If it's a beautiful summer day, you climb up here and look at *this*. If it's a snowy, cold winters day, do you come over here and watch the snow fall on this landscape? It must be so quiet then." She sat down on the slope and he sat down next to her knowing that she wasn't finished.

"You enjoy your life, don't you? I don't really. I'm proud of my accomplishments, I feel a competitive triumph when I kick ass at my job, but I don't *enjoy* my days. I don't enjoy being me. I've been wondering a lot recently about what the hell I'm chasing. What's my end game? Am I just working to make money that I'm never going to spend on anything worthwhile?" She looked at Scallop knowing it was impossible he'd have an answer. He didn't know her well enough to know if she was just having a moment of self-absorbed self-examination or really thinking about making a change. How could she expect someone she'd spent a few hours with to be able to hand her a personal "why"? But she did expect it. She believed he was that intuitive, she believed that they were already so connected that he could feel things about her that he had no business knowing yet.

He took her hand and smiled down at her, pressing it to his lips, "Listen, routine isn't necessarily a living death. My life, for fourteen years, was one adventure after another. My travels. Surfing, rock climbing. That might have been the most epic thing I ever saw. After a while it was almost like I didn't feel alive if I wasn't jumping out of a plane, or storming an enemy outpost in the mountains of Afghanistan. When I came back here, I found that in order for me to adjust to not doing something extreme five days out of seven, I *needed* to root myself in routine. Sometimes now, I get so stuck in my ways just being here, that I don't want to meet anyone new. And since Kosumi, I depend on routine even more to create a rhythm of life that works for me and for my boy. I've constructed a reality for him that makes him feel safe and secure so that he can grow in a way that's natural for him, not warped by his circumstances. I want to teach him to live with the seasons, with the currents and the wind, and with a feeling that he belongs to those things. I hope I have. That's my reason for doing what I do every day. I do it for him. Right now my life just seems more exotic to you than your own. Sure, it's possible that you've spent the last decade of your life doing the wrong thing in the wrong place. But I think the fact that you are proud of what you've accomplished and that you relish "kicking-ass" at it means that it's likely what you're supposed to do. Maybe you're just doing it for the wrong reasons. I know every foolish magazine article you've ever read has probably told you to 'take care of you first'. That's nonsense. I don't believe that's what makes human beings happy. I think what makes human beings happy is caring for people and things outside themselves. And *that* my lady is why I let my sister mess with all my plans tonight! So that she could go to bed feeling like she helped her poor little brother have a good date. And also because it would allow us to do what we're about to do up in that little stand of trees. Which incidentally was where I did this particular thing for the very first time with a very forward city girl when I was seventeen."

Rachel laughed out loud. He hadn't exactly given her an answer, but she felt better.

"Oh I see. You took me on a little tour so that you could re-live your glory days?" "Hey, it was you who suggested the bluff."

Another moment and they were in a secluded stand of trees at the top of

163

the hill. In the center there was a perfect circle that had been cleared down to the soft dune sand by deer decades before. Scallop smiled and pulled Rachel in for a kiss.

"I can't see any reason you shouldn't enjoy being you every single second," he whispered in her ear. Their exchange started slowly and built with intensity. Rachel could feel every element around her from the ripples on Scallops knuckles as she guided his hand to the soft sand beneath her and stuck to her fingers. When it was over they simply stared at one another for a long time. She might have felt self-conscience, naked out in the open. But she didn't. She felt free, like a nature goddess with her nature god.

Scallop looked in her eyes and wondered if this was as good as it was going to get for him. Inevitably, this was going to end. And he would have to live through it, which he would. He remembered in 1997 he'd thought he had it made when he and a girl from Norway, whose name had now slipped from his memory, had shared a room in a youth hostel in Patagonia and made love for days on end as a snowstorm passed over the mountain. The snowstorm had ended and they had parted ways. This was different. This was adult life. She made him and his son feel like something that had been missing was suddenly there. He knew he would lose it. But he was committed to living in the fantasy while he had the opportunity.

After a few moments of holding one another, they struggled into their bathing suits and headed back down the bluff. Halfway down Scallop had fallen a step or two behind Rachel and he called out to her, "Rachel, hold up a minute! I see something. I'm not being funny, but I need to check you for ticks."

"What!" Rachel said louder than she'd meant to, feeling distinct sensations of ticks' legs in her hair. "There were ticks in there?" she said, treating Scallop to one of her cutting glares for the first time ever.

"Yeah, probably. I'm sorry, I didn't even think about it. There didn't used to be as many ticks around, but they're all over the place now. We're both going to have to check each other."

He stood behind her sifting through her hair bit by bit. Moments before he'd been touching her in a way that made her skin bloom and now she felt like she was being roughed up by a middle school gym teacher who had a hundred girls to check for lice, and to top it off he was humming as he sifted.

"Um, searching for bugs a little hobby of yours?" she asked unable to keep the acerbic tone out of her voice.

"Kind of," he said, "do you know that song by Brad Paisley? It's called "Ticks". It's kind of a joke song, 'I'd like to see you out in the moonlight; I'd like to kiss you way back in the sticks; I'd like to walk you through a field of wildflowers; And I'd like to check you for ticks," he sang. Rachel had never heard it before but it was unmistakably a country song, Scallop sang it with a bit of a twang for authenticity.

"Oh God. You *really like* country music, don't you? I *knew* there was something! Some fatal flaw. You didn't say this morning at Claudio's. You were waiting until I was completely in your thrall right? Until you'd taken me out and had your way with me in the tick infested sand! I'm glad I found out so early on. It's best to get the deal-breakers out in the open right away!," she said, jokingly.

"Again with the country hating? I thought everyone liked country music now," Scallop said earnestly.

"No! Grown up frat boys who make millions of dollars a year like country music. Singing along with some drawling 'dude' going on about guns, God, football and drinking crappy beer makes them feel ok about the fact that they have to hire someone to put their kids crib together because they can't figure out how to use an Allen wrench. It's sad and annoying all at once. I can honestly say without reservation that I *hate* country music."

Scallop laughed so hard he had to lean over. "Well, I guess we hit a nerve there. I've never seen anyone get so scrappy about a country tune."

"It drives me nuts," she laughed as she began to sift through Scallops hair, "I also hate sitcoms. Ah!", she shouted, flinging a tiny black bug as far away from them as she could.

"Well, you know I won't contaminate your day with those. The last sitcom I watched was "Cheers" and it wasn't a rerun."

As they paddled back towards home they could hear the sounds of the Southampton Shores community cocktail party drifting across the water. Scallop was mostly concentrated on moving his board through the water, but Rachel caught him craning to see the details of the party.

"Should we go in there and have a drink?" she asked Scallop nonchalantly. She'd had a full day of doing things she never did, she thought, why not round it out by crashing a party in her bathing suit. Maybe the ladies in Lily Pulitzer on the beach could use some Rachel and Scallop. Scallop paddled pensively.

"Nah. Let's just head home," he said. But Rachel could feel that part of him wanted to go to that party. Something in his voice made her know she was right.

"Come on, let's go in. You know people in there don't you? It'll be fun."

"You really want to go? You won't know anyone. Do you do this all the time? Is crashing parties a little hobby of *yours*?" he joked.

"No, but I could use a drink and I'm having a different kind of day here. What the hell?"

A few minutes later, the new couple was walking up the beach toward the pavilion. Clumps of people stood on the sand and on the boardwalk. The older women were perfectly coifed and wearing shoes in the sand, the children had all been bathed and were wearing belts and dresses; no one was in beachwear. As they made their way towards the bar, a large, slightly pudgy guy in a bright pink Vineyard Vines shirt and curly grey hair broke away from a group and came towards them squinting.

"Scallop? Is that Scallop Kozlowski?"

"Hey there...," Scallop smiled at the man but it was obvious that he didn't know who he was.

"Hey! It's Patrick Reagan! Remember me?" Patrick said, shaking Scallop's hand and giving both he and Rachel a quick once over with his eyes. What he saw was a much better looking version of the boy who had single handedly built the tunnel beneath the pavilion, and one of Patrick's favorite childhood memories. The fact that Rachel was a gorgeous woman who judging from her suit, hair and nails was someone who likely belonged at this party anyway didn't escape Patrick either.

"Holy shit. Of course I do! What's up Patrick?" Scallop said, genuinely happy to see his old friend.

"Well...Tons! That's my wife over there. Three of these kids running around here are mine. Come on let's get you a drink," Patrick lead them over to the three fold-out tables that were covered with red and white checked tablecloths and laden with top shelf liquor and bottles of mixers. While two jovial retirees made their drinks, doing a poor but humorous impression of Tom Cruise and his buddy in "Cocktail", Patrick kept talking, "I heard you became a Navy SEAL? I can't believe you're here. I was literally just telling those people over there about that fort you built under this place that had a tunnel that went all the way over there! Funny you just walked in from nowhere man."

"Yeah. I guess I did. Patrick this is...my girlfriend, Rachel Jones," Scallop smiled at Rachel. She could see she was right to insist they come ashore, it had taken him exactly thirty seconds to get comfortable, and he was obviously thrilled to see his old friend.

Patrick looked startled, "Oh Jeez, *Rachel,* I knew I knew you from somewhere. We've met before. I run the High Yield Corporate Sales at Credit Suisse," Rachel smiled politely hoping she wouldn't have to start discussing business in her swim suit, but she didn't need to worry, Patrick just plowed on.

"Wait until everyone sees that you're here Scallop. It's been way too long. Are you in town here?

"Yeah, I'm back at my parents' farm, are all the other kids we used to run with around? You still see them?"

"Do I see them? Some weekends I wish I saw less of them. Jim and Eric Murray are right over there, with way less hair and way more weight than they had in 1985. And scattered around this shindig are the Spinelli's in their various forms. I'll go find them."

The next hour was a reunion of the kids from the 80's in the Shores. Scallop caught up with all his old friends. Watching Scallop talk with all of them she could tell he'd been missing this, he had a real connection with these people. He lived here, right amongst all his childhood friends, but for some reason he hadn't seen any of them in years. Rachel chatted as well. A few of the group were Wall Street people who knew of Rachel. One drink became five, and before they knew it everyone was having a drunken, rollicking time.

"Hello everyone! Hello, can I have your attention please!" Jim Murray shouted from atop a bench in the middle of the pavilion. Jim had come a long way from when he used to play man hunter and go fishing with Scallop. He was now a successful lawyer in New Jersey and the President of the Shores Community Association.

"Before we commence with our time-honored tradition, you *know* what's coming, I just would just like to take it down a notch and genuinely thank all the people here who have served our country. In particular, I want to recognize my old friend Scallop Kozlowski from the farm up the street, who stopped by to see us tonight with his girlfriend Rachel. Scallop used to fish and play dodgeball with us every day when we were kids, then he served as a Navy SEAL in Iraq and Afghanistan. I'm so glad he stopped by tonight because it's been way too long and it gives us the opportunity to say thank you. Thank you for your service, Scallop!"

Scallop put his hand up a bit embarrassed as if to say, "it was no big deal," but the crowd clapped, and then Jim led everyone into a loud and heartfelt rendition of "God Bless America" in unison. Rachel was positive this was the only time in her adult life where she'd sung any song in unison on back-to-back days. She was beginning to think unjaded patriotism must run through the water in North Sea.

The party broke up with promises to get together soon and Rachel and Scallop paddled back home. It was tough going several cocktails in. Although the water was calm Rachel's legs felt shaky and she was pulling far less water with each stroke than she had on the way to the bluff.

"I'm not sure this is the best idea," Rachel said about an eighth of a mile off the beach.

"It's not," said Scallop seriously. "If you need to you can sit down on the board and I'll swim between the two boards and pull us home."

This was an absurd thing to suggest, he'd had at least six beers, but Rachel had no doubt he could do it if it was necessary. She shook her head no.

"I think I can do it, but let's just take it slow." Scallop nodded solemnly and they were quiet. Rachel spent the rest of the return trip trying to imagine something that she though Scallop *couldn't* do if it was necessary, coming up with one ridiculous romantic scenario after another. Could he kill a bear? Definitely. If someone attacked her on the street would he stop it? Absolutely. If her mother came to visit and behaved abominably, as she always did, would he call her on it and toss her out? Rachel had no doubt that Scallop would not even allow her own mother to treat her badly. Rachel took a steel-edged pride in being able to handle every situation that came her way. But she felt a sense of weightlessness when she thought of allowing Scallop to handle some things for her. As they pulled up to his beach she was trying to come up with scenarios in which his fence-building skills would come in handy as part of her city lifestyle.

They found Keith Hernandez passed out in the hammock in Scallop's yard, a copy of "War & Peace" on his belly, and two bottles of Opus One empty on the ground beneath him.

"Did you invite him over?" Rachel whispered.

Scallop snorted loudly, "No. But he comes and hangs out a few nights a week. There's no need to whisper, he'll wake up when he wakes up. Nothing we do one way or the other is going to make any difference. Just leave him there, he'll probably wake up when he smells the food."

They showered, had another drink, and Rachel got cozy by the fire as Scallop worked the tunes and lit the charcoal in the gigantic half drum BBQ that looked like something straight out of a country music video. All the while Keith slept on in the hammock. Rachel watched as Scallop pulled a rolling cooler around the corner and began to toss clams on the grill and clean more bluefish then they could possibly eat. He had crabs and scallops and shucked corn on the cob and a little pot to melt butter. She wondered when the last time he cooked for a woman was. How much did he think they ate? He was stacking it all high on baking sheets when Kosumi arrived with Lucy, Inga and Veronica. Scallop lined up four big sheet pans of food down the center of picnic table with the pot of butter in the middle and then plunked down a pile of napkins and a pile of mismatched forks. As they sat down Richard arrived with Kennedy, a girl he'd met at the carnival (Rachel was relieved to find that Richard was in fact a 'real live boy'). Rachel wasn't sure how Scallop had known people were going to roll in at dinner time but he'd been right about the amount of food to make. Everyone ate the clams and fish, dipping it into the butter and putting it straight in their mouths, no plates; it was a free for all. Keith woke up midway through the meal, helped himself to a beer and tucked in some clams. When they'd finished they sat around the fire and made s'mores to the accompaniment of the same old mix that was heavy on the Bob Marley, Jack Johnson, Kenny Chesney and a few outliers.

Rachel laughed at Keith as he did an impression of Scallop; she realized she felt perfect, she had never been so happy. She'd been proud, she'd been triumphant, but she'd never been this light hearted. She was clean, comfortable, physically exhausted and a bit tipsy with Kosumi on her lap, his little hands on her knees, sticky from s'mores. She knew what friends were doing right now, running around the Hamptons, rushing to get to reservations and high-end parties, and she got to be here, in front of a fire on the beach, with her boyfriend's son in her lap, telling silly stories with his sister and nieces. She had no desire to be anywhere else.

At that moment she knew the truth. She loved Scallop. She would turn her life upside down to be a part of his. She knew it could work. She knew she could do it without sacrificing everything she'd worked for.

23: Chicken Fried Summer of Love

Rachel looked up from her desk at her new favorite photo. She'd printed out an eight by ten copy for herself when she'd been in the city a few days back. It was a photo of her and Kosumi with their heads sticking out of the sand atop the bodies of mermaids they'd sculpted. Scallop had dug deep holes in the beach for them to climb into and then he and Inga and Veronica, who'd gotten a rare day off from the farm, had buried them atop their sand sculptures. That had been beach day number ten of the summer. Rachel was keeping count.

The photo was in good company up on the wall of the farm stand's office amidst the decades of Kozlowski memories. Rachel pushed in the vintage farmhouse chair she'd been using at the long counter-style desk she was now sharing with Lucy at the farm.

A few Saturdays ago, she'd asked to use the wi-fi in the office to do some quick research. Her laptop perched on a corner desk; she'd used an overturned plastic bucket as a chair. She left her laptop there to charge while she and Scallop had taken Kosumi to the beach, and when she'd returned to retrieve it, she'd found it sitting centered on 3 feet of cleared desk space. The desk had been whipped down and decorated with some farm flowers in a mason jar. Pulled up to the desk was an old-fashioned kitchen chair that had been painted a sage color at some point, its wooden seat softened with a floral pillow.

Lucy had brushed off her thanks in what Rachel now understood was her typical fashion, but Rachel had been deeply touched. She didn't think anyone had ever cleared their decks for her comfort and she'd been surprised to find how well she worked in this rustic space.

For the past few weeks she'd been working two days a week to the sounds of people coming and going at the farm stand. She'd gone back to the city for three days for meetings and to make an appearance. She and Lucy worked well next to each other. Lucy seemed to be able to sense when Rachel was concentrating and when she was ready for a good laugh.

It was Monday afternoon and Rachel had been working since early in the morning. She'd gotten up when Scallop and Kosumi headed out for Scallop's insane workout. Rachel had done it with him once and vowed never to do again. She worked with a trainer in the city and rarely went a day without an intense workout, but Scallop's routine was masochistic. She also felt it was a space and time he needed to himself.

It was after five and the farm stand sounded quiet. She imagined that Kosumi was in helping his grandmother make dinner, they were planning to stay for spaghetti and meatballs. She closed her laptop and went to find Scallop. She knew where he'd be, he was always in the big barn from four o'clock on. He preferred not to be wandering the farm just before dinner time when the stand was at its busiest, the consumer facing part of being a small-scale farmer did not interest Scallop all that much.

As she neared the barn she heard the first few plucked out measures of "Chicken Fried" by the Zac Brown Band. "So much for surprising him," she thought, "he's seen me coming."

After their conversation about her rabid disdain for country music, Scallop found opportunities to test out songs on her until he found "the one"; the song that would make her go "nuttier than squirrel crap" as he cheerfully put it. He'd picked her up at the Jitney Bus station one night with "Chicken Fried" blasting out the windows of his truck and he knew he'd found it. Rachel had been pulling her bags towards his truck without hurrying, thinking she'd let him enjoy the anticipation, when she realized a country style racket was attracting attention, and that it was coming from where she was headed. She rushed to the truck, head down, hoping no one would notice her and climbed in next to Scallop rolling her eyes at him.

"Well, just go would you, Country Joe?" she said, somehow simultaneously annoyed with him and amused. He obligingly pulled out of the bus station with a squeal of truck tires and a double honk of his horn, and then turned to give her a dazzling smile.

"God this song is annoying," she said, switching it off.

"I like the sentiment," said Scallop, "all you really need *is* a cold beer on a Friday night and a pair of jeans that fit just right. That's what I've got. Kosumi has two pairs."

"Good grief. Well, I guess that's true. But I think most of the people who listen to *that* have more than just one pair of jeans. They probably have about twenty bought on sale at Walmart for $2.99 each."

"Wow! Well, we're feeling a little snobby tonight aren't we? Ok my lady, from now on that's our song," he said, laughing at her in a way that made her exasperation disappear as he put his arm around her shoulders. She had to laugh. The irony was that years later, when Rachel thought back to that summer, the memories of the thirty two trips to the beach, conference calls to London from the farm office, reading Kosumi books in the hammock and falling asleep with his little head on her chest, and chatting with Lucy by the firepit would all be accompanied by "Chicken Fried".

From the barn Scallop sang along with an enthusiasm that Rachel thought would have waned by now; he'd been playing it at least twice a day, every day, since he'd made his discovery. She got ready to play her part in the charade and ambled into the barn door opening. To bait him in turn, she'd developed a mocking caricature of a country line dance in which she did a series of repeated shuffles and knee slaps whilst miming actions to the song lyrics. She sashayed across the opening and mimed eating fried chicken, she galloped the other way stopping to pretend to pull on a pair of jeans that "fit just right", on her next pass she swilled beer. Tonight, she added a couple new moves, finding a way to mime an American flag flying in the wind.

Scallop stood inside the barn, watching the show, leaning his shoulder against the old gymnastics mat that hung against the wall.

"You look like a really sexy, mentally ill pterodactyl." He ran over and stopped her convulsions with an embrace. "We could close that door and make better use of that gym mat than we did last time. How about it? Spaghetti and meatballs are probably going to be a good forty-five minutes yet."

"Oh no!," she said disentangling her arms from his hug. "For one thing, I saw Pedro out there picking the corn, he'll be headed this way soon. For another thing, I only touched that mat the first time because it was pitch dark. Now that I've seen it in the daylight it'll never happen again. You're going to have to come up with a better option than that ratty old thing!"

By the end of fourth of July weekend Rachel had found a moment to go back into the barn, curious what the cool cushioned wallcovering she and Scallop had "used" that first night had been. Apparently, Inga had been a gymnast through middle school, up until she'd decided that soccer was her thing. She'd used the huge blue mat to practice tumbling in the barn. No one had bothered to dispose of it because it came in handy for some purpose or other every once in a while. It was reasonably clean by farmyard standards but Scallop could understand why Rachel didn't want to spend much time pressed up against it..

"Well, here's the thing," he said grabbing her, "after that freaky pterodactyl dance I have to have you. So, we're going to make a run home while Mom has Kosumi making meatballs."

He picked her up and threw her over his shoulder and carried her out to his truck behind the barn. Rachel was game. She was certain she would never get tired of his unique combination of responsibility and wildness. He'd have her back in their seats around the long dining room table in the farmhouse by the time the rest of the family was ready to hold hands and sing the little grace song she'd come to love. She'd take hands with whatever family member she plunked down next to with her entire body singing.

Early Saturday morning they went to Flying Point beach, they set up camp on a blanket long before the crowds started to arrive. Scallop spread the blanket out on the sand for them and unfolded Rachel's Tommy Bahama beach chair for her, placing the giant mesh bag of beach toys she'd picked up in town for Kosumi a few weeks before in the chair before running into the surf with his surf board. Rachel and Kosumi dug holes, made sand castles and played in the surf together all the while watching Scallop as he rode in on waves and swam back out. Rachel could tell the waves were good because Scallop wasn't spending much time sitting on his board looking out for a good one. Scallop didn't really talk about surfing much, using the lingo she heard the other surfers come out of the water throwing around, bragging about "shredding" and being "in the soup", he just surfed. He'd offered to teach her and she'd gone out with him one day when Lucy was watching Kosumi. She'd gotten up on the board a couple of times before being tossed by waves. She knew that if she practiced she'd be able to do it well by the end of the summer. But she also knew that helping her slowed him down and took away from his experience. Watching him was entertainment enough.

Saturday mornings Scallop had to be at the farm for a while to help keep the stock fresh in the farm stand, so Rachel had begun taking Kosumi to Sip-n-Soda in town. It was an old-fashioned luncheonette and soda fountain shop in the village, a local staple in town, that had been run by the Parash family since 1958. It was packed each weekend with families from the city who were at their beach houses for the weekend. Rachel loved sitting with Kosumi while parents around them ate with their children. It was something they could do together in Rachel's territory. Kosumi loved his pancakes and milkshakes, a special treat for a boy who had rarely eaten in a restaurant before Rachel came along. He would smile proudly whenever someone who knew him from school, town or the farm would stop at their table and say hello.

This morning Rachel just ordered an oatmeal and picked at it, helping Kosumi with the maze on the back side of his menu. She and Lucy were planning on taking the boat to the Lobster Inn in the late afternoon. Scallop and Lucy had taken turns giving Rachel driving lessons on the boat and she was going to try to drive it without Lucy telling her what to do tonight. She wasn't ready to pull it up to the dock yet, but she was ready to try to handle what came her way when she was out on the water.

They'd taken the boat to the Lobster Inn before. It was Scallop's favorite restaurant on Earth, and for good reason. It was casual in an any-town America type of way. You could show up in Gucci or a rumpled cover up tossed over a wet bathing suit and sit at one of the many closely packed, thickly lacquered tables that were made of a knotty antique wood that had been splattered with butter by thousands and thousands of diners before you. Rachel always split the Lobster Inn's house special, "the splat", a gigantic pile of steamed seafood and corn, with someone they were with. Two weeks ago, she had invited Scallop's nieces to dinner with them and she and Veronica had spent five minutes debating over who was most worthy of the final lobster claw in their splat. They'd ended up flipping a coin. Rachel had won the toss and slowly eaten the claw, dipping the sweet meat in extra butter and eating it with dramatic relish as Veronica watched in mock astonishment at her callousness.

Scallop and Tim had a softball game tonight and Kosumi was going with them. Mid-way through the morning Lucy had placed her hand down firmly on a stack of papers as if to demonstrate her power over them, and spun towards Rachel in her office chair.

"Rachel, any chance you'd go out with me tonight and talk a little business? I'd love to hear your thoughts on making this place a little more profitable, or on the best way for us to move on if that doesn't turn out to be possible."

Rachel's instinct was *always* to offer business advice when she was asked. But in this case, she was reluctant. She knew from a very brief conversation with Scallop, it hadn't even been a real conversation, more of a comment, that the farm was not profitable and that there was an offer on the table to sell it. When she'd tried to ask questions he'd uncharacteristically shut her down. "That's really Lucy's department, I'm the heavy lifting." The family had not discussed their troubles in front of her, but she had felt a ripple of tension flow through a circle around the fire pit the other night when Inga had asked if she could bring friends home from college in the summers to work at the farm stand. Was there a chance there would be no farm stand by then? The Kozlowskis probably needed the input of someone from the outside, there was no way they could make an accurate assessment of their own situation, too many emotions. She decided to throw herself on the sword that was being offered up and dive into the family business.

"Yeah sure," she said, "Scallop's sick of going out with me anyways. Last weekend I convinced him to go to The Bell and Anchor and you'd have thought it was a medieval torture chamber. It was like being part of an awkward social experiment. I think I'm going to have to limit myself to low key places except on very special occasions."

"Yeah, he can't really sit in a restaurant all night. He wants to eat and then do something else. Ironically, he can sit for hours at that firepit and not get antsy, but if there's a white tablecloth, he's gotta go."

Rachel laughed. "Yeah, maybe if we sit down and take the tablecloth off. Do you have a P&L I can look at before we get on the boat? I don't really know what the state of affairs here is, without that I'd just be taking an uneducated stab in the dark. That won't be helpful."

Lucy looked a little embarrassed. "I've got the one from two years ago that I put together with the help of the Small Business Development Center. I didn't do last year's because, honestly it was going to be too depressing. Profits were almost identical to the year I'm going to give you, and in the meantime I had to take out a home equity line of credit to finance general operating expenses."

Rachel nodded sympathetically, and Lucy printed her out the two-year-old Profit and Loss statement and then left it with her to read while she went to inventory the farm stand. Rachel read through it. It was bad. They were almost three hundred and fifty thousand dollars in debt with no new sources of income that might contribute to paying it down. The salaries the family members drew were so small Rachel's stomach churned as she read through them. Scallop lived cheaply by choice, but it was lucky he had his peculiar outlook on life because there was no chance of him living any differently with the poverty level salary he took. She noticed that his was smaller than the other siblings as well. The amount they were paid seemed to be based on what their families needed. Lucy, with two teenage girls about to go to college had the highest salary, Tim was second, he was probably still paying off whatever he'd contributed to his kids' college, and Scallops was the lowest. It appeared that their parents lived on next to nothing. The fact that they all survived on so little, in one of the most expensive places to live, spoke of a personal commitment to the farm that she'd never heard any of them verbalize.

Rachel glowed as she and Lucy walked into the restaurant. She knew that at some point tonight she would have to deliver bad news to her friend, but she'd just successfully navigated the Zodiac from Scallop's backyard to the Lobster Inn. She was so ecstatic she thought she might have a beer to celebrate. There must be something about being a sea captain; you craved beer. Lucy had parked the Zodiac for her so that they'd be sure to end on a high note. Lucy looked gorgeous in a simple cornflower blue linen dress which had probably been her go-to for years, and her hair in a messy bun. Rachel had on a black jersey dress that while completely comfortable made her look far more formal and more metropolitan than Lucy.

"Alright. Let's both have two beers before we get down to it. I could tell from your face when you came out of the office that you think we're all nuts and you're feeling a little sorry for us, so let's have enough to cushion the blow first," she said after they were seated.

Rachel reached across the table and grabbed her friends hand, giving it a squeeze. She met Lucy's gaze squarely but sympathetically, "I *don't* think you're nuts. I do not think you're nuts," she repeated, "I think you love each other and love your farm, and I also think we should drink several pitchers of beer."

After they'd both had a pile of salad from the salad bar, famous for its deliciously gloppy dressings and pickled beets, and were about halfway through beer number two Lucy finished up her analysis of Veronica's new boyfriend, which boiled down to one word, 'weird', and asked Rachel what she thought about the farm.

"So, do you think it's hopeless?"

Rachel sighed, "First, I want to say that I think you guys live a remarkable life. You get to spend your days working alongside your family and I can see you've all made sacrifices to hold onto your heritage. I think that's noble; I don't think I know many people who have made, or would make a sacrifice like that."

Lucy breathed in audibly and out slowly.

"I don't know anything about farming," Rachel said. "But I can easily see that if everything stays the same you won't be able to continue with the staff you have and pay yourselves. It seems like there are some places where you can expand we need to research if they would make you more profitable. Basically, what I have right now is a bunch of questions. Would finding a few more revenue sources cost just as much in labor and improvements as they'd bring in income? Would you be interested in pursuing those revenue sources or are you guys just tapped out when it comes to collective energy? Do Tim and Scallop have any thoughts on what should be done? Scallop has never shared anything with me. How much of a say do your parents have in the farm? Would they be willing for things to change quite a bit?"

Lucy took a big sip of her beer and then leveled her eyes at Rachel, "I haven't even told my mother this, but Tim wants out. He wants to retire and move to St. John. His wife has a decent pension and they have a house that they can sell here and make some money. He wants to sell the land. In his opinion it's a done deal."

Rachel nodded. She liked Tim but she could see now why he seemed a bit separate from the rest of the family. He was done. He was working the farm, but she'd never seen him stand out amongst the plants hatching a plan for an improvement as she'd seen Scallop do.

"My parents took a back seat after my husband died. My mom used to do the same job I do on the farm. My dad had his stroke and my Mom said that the bulk of the income needed to go to Tim and to me because we needed it the most. Scallop was gone then. But she also said with the bulk of the income came the bulk of the responsibility. She'd help out, but she needed to be in the house more. At that point she was around the same age that my grandparents had been when they'd taken a backseat, so it was our turn. She hasn't said a word about any decision we've made since then and when Dad says anything she lets us know that we don't have to defer to him. I think she faced more than one time when she considered selling it too."

"And Scallop?" Rachel prompted.

"I think Scallop needs the farm Rachel. I feel weird discussing this with you because you two are obviously in love. It's what I've wanted for him for a long time. The Kachina thing was such a mess. Really. As if he didn't have enough demons to deal with when he came back from Afghanistan he had to go get involved with a she-demon. I don't want anything I'm sharing with you to affect how you see him. The farm healed Scallop when he came home, enough so that he was recognizably our brother. He needs the farm, and the water, and the fire department, and softball and his rituals with Kosumi. They connect him to the good things in the world. I think he's seen a lot of bad things and done some bad things too. I don't know what the hell could have been awful enough to turn my blessed brother into the person he was when he came back to us. I mean it. *You* know, it *seems* like he walks and the angels sing. It was always like that growing up. Everything seemed to go his way and he never had an ego about it. He was just pure joy. But let me tell you, it wasn't like that when he came back here. I don't know how to describe how he was except that instead of exuding confidence and light he seemed to exude "sick". He wasn't crazy or erratic or mean, he just had an aura of ill."

Rachel couldn't imagine a version of Scallop that fit that description. But, it was becoming clear why he so cheerfully maintained a schedule that while filled with recreational skills rarely deviated week by week. She had colleagues who were recovering alcoholics who functioned that way. Maintaining a routine that avoided triggers and controlled putting themselves in an unpredictable situation.

"It was scary and none of us knew what to do. Eventually he started coming out of his room and doing things around the farm but he was only half there. He stayed that way until Kosumi started to be a real little person, talking and learning things. Kachina certainly didn't pull him out of it. Actually, I think a lot of the time she made it worse. I knew when Kosumi was born and she didn't become a real mother that she'd never be right. Have you seen that happen? A fairly immature or selfish woman becomes a mother and really *becomes* a mother? Kachina stayed the same messed up girl with a baby."

"What kind of person doesn't step up to be *Kosumi's* mom?" Rachel asked incredulously. It seemed impossible to her that Scallop would choose to be with someone as screwed up as Kachina sounded. Women of every ilk threw themselves at him. Why would he pick a trashy, depressed girl who didn't fit in with his family? He wouldn't. Well, the Scallop that she knew wouldn't.

"What I'm telling you is nothing was the same as it is now. This financial stress is tough but other than that we're all happy. The past couple of years Scallop has been a great father, not just to Kosumi, but he and Tim have been there for my girls. We've all supported Mom and Dad as Dad's health has failed, and we have the joy of having Kosumi around. Sell the farm, and all that falls apart, fall deeper in debt, all that falls apart. I want to keep everyone together and happy, I'm just not seeing a way to do it. I guess part of the reason I'm asking you for help is because you and Scallop seem so happy right now and I think you deserve to know he might not be the same without the farm to ground him."

Lucy was hunched over drawing stripes in the condensation on her beer glass. It was the first time Rachel hadn't seen Lucy sitting tall, and her heart ached for her. Only someone with as good a heart as Lucy would not be resentful in her situation. She carried the weight of her family's happiness on her shoulders and didn't begrudge them anything. Rachel did wonder though if some of her concern for Scallop was just the overprotectiveness of a big sister. Her own sister sometimes overdramatized Rachel's situations.

"Lucy, I don't think any of this is your fault. Don't lose heart. Does Scallop understand the situation?" she asked signaling their waiter for two more beers.

Lucy looked up at Rachel and nodded. "Yes, he knows, but he's pretty set on pretending it's not happening, it's not helpful honestly. It just makes me feel worse. Mom knows, but I think she thinks it's possible to just continue to carry on as we always have."

"Alright, well, let's do some creative thinking and see if we can come up with any viable revenue streams that will be enough to pay back these loans and start building instead of losing. While we do that, you also try to work on Tim. How are things structured? If he wants to sell and you guys don't what will happen?"

"I think Tim would be fine being bought out. You know, not for the same amount as a third of the sale would be. I think deep down he's not insensitive to the fact that the farm is a big part of who we all are."

"Good, that's good," said Rachel, "we'll think of every possible option so that you guys can make an informed decision, ok?"

Lucy nodded and smiled through the first bit of teariness Rachel had ever seen from her.

"Alright. But for now, we're eating clams," she said as the waitress carefully lowered the "Splat" down on their table, taking care not to lose any clams over the side of the plate. "I can't believe I'm not sick of these things yet. I've probably eaten more clams these past few weeks than I have in my entire life put together, and I just want more."

Lucy smiled. "Better watch it. You're going to end up with gout."

Rachel sloshed a clam in butter and pretended to consider the merits of eating it, then looked up at Lucy and said, "Totally worth it," as she popped it into her mouth.

Scallop didn't quite know how it had happened, but going out after dinner for ice cream had become something they did several times a week. Every night, as Kosumi put the last clean plate back on the shelf at the farm or at home, he would turn and look expectantly at Rachel or Scallop and say, "are we going to get ice cream tonight?" They would pile in the truck and drive into Sag Harbor to Big Olaf, or into Southampton Village and visit The Fudge Company. Scallop would have preferred to spend the rest of the evening in the backyard sitting by the firepit talking, on the paddleboard watching the sunset, or reading a book. But he'd noticed that Rachel got antsy if they didn't leave North Sea every few days, and he found it amusing to watch her navigate the Hamptons scene that he'd always avoided; she did it so well. She also managed to make him feel a part of it, which he never had.

Scallop and Kosumi found Rachel already back from her date with Lucy and sitting at the dining room table scrolling through her phone. Over the past few weeks Scallop had been happy to see Rachel's dependence on the little blue glowing box wane. He was certain that the pocket-sized super computers were eating holes in the fabric of society at worst, and best case scenario, were distracting everyone from what was good right around them.

He'd always loved the beach, but now he appreciated it as one of the last places where people just talked to the guy next to them. Between the natural instinct to look out at the waves and the fear of getting their seven-hundred-dollar lifeline wet, almost no one at the beach pulled their phone out of their bag. The more time they were on the water, the less time Rachel was on her phone. He smiled thinking that her lack of connectivity didn't make her any less intense. It just directed her intensity at him and out into the world.

When she looked up at him he felt his head swim; something had changed. She saw him differently. She knew, or thought she knew, something about him that she hadn't before tonight. She was agitated about something, and it was something to do with him.

"Hey! How was dinner? You two spend the whole time talking about how handsome I am, what a great surfer, how you're both so lucky to have me?" he asked in a lame attempt to discover where the sands had shifted.

Rachel rolled her eyes at him. "Actually no, you didn't come up at all as a matter of fact," she said without teasing but also without looking up at him. So, they *had* talked about him. What the hell had Lucy said?

He had been shocked by Lucy and Rachel's friendship. They couldn't be more different, and yet, not only did they enjoy each other's company, he could see a bond forming between them that was rare. Their instinct seemed to be to lift one another up and support one another. It was like what he had felt for the guys on his SEAL team and he was sure it was an uncommon relationship for grown women who had only just met.

"We spent the whole night watching a group of college boys try to impress their dates. The poor girls came to the Lobster Inn looking like they expected to be taken to a club. They girls looked miserable, and the guys spent the whole time talking to each other about football. It was like watching an updated version of "Saved By The Bell" with beer. Train wreck."

This time she looked up and gave him a little smile with so much less behind it than usual. Jesus.

Rachel was being truthful. She and Lucy had ended the conversation about the farm once they'd dug into the "Splat". Rachel didn't have any solutions to offer right then. As they'd searched for the next topic of conversation Lucy had noticed the group of six young people sitting at a booth far enough away to watch them, but close enough to hear most of their conversation. It had provided them with the outside distraction they needed. They'd both had another beer and left the restaurant laughing.

As soon as Rachel had gotten back to the cottage she'd changed into cutoffs and the t-shirt she'd worn the few times she'd helped Scallop around the farm. It smelled like the hay, it looked like something a farm girl would wear, and it made her feel connected to the place that she now understood was in very real danger of not always being there for these people she loved. And not just for them! Rachel loved being at the farm. She loved the energy of necessity being tended to that pervaded the place. When she did her own work there she loved to feel the contrast of what she was doing with what they were doing. It was like all of America on a few acres.

She sat down at the table and dug into research. She began by looking at real estate sites and tax records to see if the number Wallace was offering the Koslowskis was a legitimate offer. She'd gotten far enough to feel confident that while his offer was a little low, it was in the ballpark of the farm's market value. For some reason this made her angry. Irrationally she'd been hoping that it was way off base.

As she smiled up at Scallop she laid her phone face down on the table so that he wouldn't see what she'd been doing and pushed it away from her with more force than she intended. Scallop gave her a side eye and said, "How about some ice cream? I could go for a peppermint stick cone, how about you Kosumi?" Kosumi had been standing in the middle of the living room throwing a softball a few feet in the air and trying to catch it with a glove that was much too big for his hand. He hastily grabbed the ball that had just hit the floor and yelled, "Yes! Peppermint stick!", while he did a little dance that looked like the mountain climbers Rachel's trainer sometimes made her do.

Rachel smiled at Scallop. He never ate any ice cream. He was offering because he could feel her agitation. When she looked at him all she saw was a confident strength, a soft power. She couldn't reconcile that with the person Lucy had described. A damaged man whose environment needed to be managed and protected.

"Let me just change out of this," he pulled off his baseball cap and ran his fingers through his loose hair. "I could probably smell better. But we kicked some ass right Kosumi? Why don't you take the ball out front buddy?" Kosumi ran out the door, and hopped cheerfully down the steps from the stoop. "You going to change?" Scallop asked turning at the bedroom door.

"Nope," she said, "I just changed into this. I'm ok not winning any best dressed awards tonight. I've had a lot of beer and a lot of clams and I'm going to go have a lot of ice cream. That's my plan."

"Ok then," he said. He glanced back at her again when as she picked up her phone, completely absorbed in "swiping" things closed with determination. He stepped inside the door of his bedroom and stopped, feeling the press of anxiety in his neck. A cord of nervous energy ricocheted from the fingers of his right hand, up through his shoulder to his jaw and back again. Why was it there? What had her so agitated? What on earth had Lucy shared with her? Her energy had been directed at the phone, not at him. Scallop was overwhelmed by that toadfish feeling, sick to his stomach and alight with anxiety.

Roughly he stripped down and rubbed away the dust of the baseball diamond with a wet towel. He needed to feel how deeply the change he'd seen in Rachel's eyes had penetrated, now. Checking the window to see that

Kosumi was occupied with digging a dirt pile for his Tonka trucks to drive over, he walked quietly to the dining room. He gently took the phone out of her hand and pushed it aside.

As Rachel looked up, "Ready for ice cream?", died breathlessly on her lips. It was twilight and soft light streamed through the windows refracting off the particles floating in the air around him. He was beautiful, like a carefully sculpted marble statue that had power and movement, and he was looking down at her with worried eyes and an obvious readiness for something other than ice cream.

She stood up slowly running her hands along his collar bone and shoulders, with the strange thought that perhaps she could expose the truths of his heart by opening his chest. He didn't give her time. He picked her up, wrapping her legs tightly to him above his hip muscles and pulling her in so that she would feel his need. It was powerful, but unnecessary. She could see it in his eyes.

He carried her into the bedroom and put her down against the span of wall he knew wasn't visible from any of the windows and slowly, purposely removed each item of her clothing, never breaking his gaze. When he was finished, he stood back and looked, with the expectation that she would look as well, see who he was, what he was. He searched her, trying to identify what had made her see him differently, first with his eyes, then with his hands and mouth testing each part of her from her knees upwards. When he reached her mouth he was inside her seeing if it lay deep within, purposefully driving it out. She let him. When they finished he knew it had disappeared with the light particles in the darkening gleaming. Whatever it had been, he was now sure Lucy had kept his deeper confidences.

As Rachel put her cutoffs and t-shirt back on feeling again each of the places Scallop had touched, she dismissed Lucy's characterization of Scallop as damaged goods. Big sisters never saw their younger brothers clearly. She couldn't fault Lucy, it only came from love. She pulled her hair up into a messy bun and shoved her feet into some flip flops laughing at her reflection in the mirror, she was going to go out wearing the North Sea Farm stand uniform.

Southampton Village was so crowded they had to park Scallop's truck in his friend's empty driveway, leaving the keys in the ignition in case he came home and needed to move it. Rachel and Kosumi got matching peppermint stick cones and as they walked through town they prompted one another not to let it drip. They walked cheerfully past the jewelry stores, clothing boutiques and galleries packed with the works of "listed artists."

The Southampton Arts Center was holding its annual gala. Photographers and guests in formalwear mingled on the red carpet in front of the terraced entry and carefully decorated tents were set up on the side lawn.

Guests wandered in and out stopping to take an hors d'ouvre from the trays offered by young, good looking waiters.

"Bullshit like this is why I never come into town in summer. Look at these people. Wow. What a scene. I remember when that building was the library. I used to sit in there all day and look at National Geographic on microfiche on rainy days," Scallop said.

Rachel could see three people she knew from where they stood on the sidewalk. Elliot Metzger, the Global Head of Fixed Income for Goldman Sachs, who had once been Rachel's boss was standing with Patricia King, the US Head of Equities for Bank of America not to mention a friend she met frequently for drinks, and George Spiegel, the founder and owner of Flagpole Capital, a hedge fund that was similar in size, scope and strategy to Tallmadge. Patricia caught Rachel's eye and did a double take, gave her a mischievous look and waved her into the party. Rachel wished she had changed out of the farm costume she'd been so eager to wear earlier, and put on something acceptable before they'd left the house. She also knew that Patricia knew exactly what she was wishing. She waved back and motioned that she'd be there in a minute and turned to Scallop. Somehow, he managed to simultaneously raise his eyebrows and squint at her as if to say, "do we *really* have to go in there?"

"We have to go in," she said hastily. "They've seen me now and it would be rude of me not to say hello. Very bad form. I promise we'll get out of there as quickly as possible without anyone else noticing me. Trust me, walking into *that* dressed like *this* makes me just as uncomfortable as you and Kosumi will be. I should have listened to you and changed."

She handed Scallop her cone and swiped the paper towel across Kosumi's face, plucking the last of his ice cream cone from his little fist and handing that to Scallop as well. "Hey Buddy, we're going to have to stop eating these now and go into that party for a few minutes. If you want we can get you a whole new ice cream when we get out. How does that sound?"

"Ok," Kosumi gamely said smiling up at her.

"You are the *best* little kid in the whole world," she said as she grabbed his face and kissed him. She stood up and came face to face with the faded lettering on Scallop's frayed, sleeveless, "Peconic Marina" t-shirt. He was also barefoot. She turned towards the party hoping that the little group had forgotten all about her in the past twenty seconds but they were all standing, framed beneath a hanging flower arrangement looking expectantly at her. She took a deep breath and plowed towards the tent hoping that her hands weren't peppermint stickie.

"Rachel Jones! The one and only! As I live and breathe!" Metzger said.

"Rachel! Great to see you! Elliot here was just telling us how he taught you everything you know. We don't believe him. After all, you moved on and he's still at Goldman," Spiegel said as he laughed and drank his champagne.

"I'm so happy we came into town tonight, we were just hanging around in the backyard and then we decided to come in and get a little ice cream, and here you are!

This is my boyfriend, Scallop Kozlowski, and this is his son, and my friend, Kosumi," Rachel said watching Patricia's appraisal of Scallop. She was the first to offer Scallop her hand, and as she shook it she placed her other hand midway up his forearm giving it a firm squeeze. As the others shook his hand in turn Patricia turned to Rachel and gave her a smile and a sly nod. "Well," Rachel thought to herself, "good thing Swizzle didn't drop her jewelry on Patricia's watch. I'd be having a very different summer."

Rachel exchanged a brief catch-up and a few pleasantries and they had turned to leave when a photographer practically dove in front of them before they could make it out of the tent.

"Excuse me…can we get a picture of you three? We'd love to put you in Dan's Papers," he continued as he grabbed his camera. The last thing Rachel wanted was to wind up in the society pages of the one magazine that practically every Hamptons regular read.

"Totally. I want one too. This family is made for Hamptons Magazine!" a second photographer said as she prepped for a shot.

Scallop ran his hands through his hair, giving Rachel a look. "No. Really." she said, "I'm sure your assignment was to take pictures of the Arts Center event, we're not even attending the gala, my friends just grabbed me off the street."

Patricia was suddenly at her shoulder. "Aren't they lovely looking?", she smiled ingratiatingly at the photographers. "Come on Rachel, let them take your picture." Patricia was having far too much fun. Then the men joined in. "Just take the picture Rachel, who cares? This kid's really cute, people love that stuff."

Trying to avoid an out and out scene she gave in to the pressure and posed for the picture; Scallop and Rachel flanking and holding Kosumi. An assistant to both photographers asked for names, which Rachel provided as quickly as possible. Within five minutes of entering, they were gone and headed home. Kosumi hadn't wanted another ice cream and both Scallop and Rachel were done with town for the night.

24: Jessup Neck

By the second week of July Rachel had decided to take two weeks' worth of saved vacation days off during August. The first week of August she was back in the office for a streak of twelve-hour days where she made enough phone calls, held enough hands and stroked enough egos so that she could enjoy her vacation relatively undisturbed. She wished that she could tell people she was going somewhere exotic where there was no cell service, but the escapade at the Southampton Art Center had made it clear that just because she was starting to feel like a part of the local landscape on the East End, it would probably never be possible for her to disappear into it.

She'd begun to enjoy the pace of life in North Sea. She felt at ease when she was there, like time and responsibilities stopped when she entered the hamlet. She was shocked to find that the more she slowed down her own pace the more details she noticed. The pace of life in New York City was lightning fast. She realized now that she'd been throwing herself into a rat-race competition where whoever was living the most frenzied life won. She'd bought into the New York City dogma that if you weren't "balls to the wall" you weren't working hard enough. But spending weekends in North Sea she found herself staring out at a bird on the water and noticing the rhythm it adopted as it ducked its head beneath the water in time with the lapping waves. One afternoon Kosumi fell asleep on top of her in the hammock and rather than wiggling out from under him she spent an hour and fifteen minutes watching the clouds float out over the bay. And it seemed that giving her mind a chance to wander resulted in a keener focus when it was time for work. She could absorb information more quickly than before, and then turn it into a clear course of action without having to hash it over several times. She was happy for the discovery, but a little annoyed that all those New York Times articles about taking breaks and unplugging had been right after all.

Her vacation plan was to be a local. It was rare, but when she took a vacation, she liked to learn to do something new and have a little adventure. She told Scallop that she wanted to learn to do all the outdoorsy things he'd done growing up. She'd never ridden an ATV or fished for anything and it was exciting in more ways than one to learn from Scallop. Watching him drive the boat or bait a hook never failed to make her anxious for Kosumi's nap time.

She'd been attracted to him from the start, so strongly that every time she looked at him from a distance, she felt a pull as though he was her personal magnetic pole, but the importance of that purely physical attraction had waned over time as she grew to know him better. She liked that he could fix things. She liked the fact that Scallop could live off the land if he had to. If Armageddon happened, or a cyber-attack that crippled supply chains, Scallop would be fine; he'd probably enjoy it. She had found herself what she never realized she wanted: a throwback, minimalist, survivalist and a badass.

Some of their adventures went off better than others. Richard was back in town and he joined them on Rachel's inaugural ATV adventure. Kosumi rode with Scallop because Richard insisted that Rachel ride with him, it only took Rachel half a mile of skidding and rumbling down the dusty system of paths that ran cross lots around the farm to understand that Richard was messing with her. He left Scallop and Kosumi in the dust and pushed the ATV's speed to its limits. When she dug her freshly manicured nails into his stomach from a combination of fear and fury he did a one eighty stop and turned to her with a giant white grin on his dusty face and said, "Welcome to the family!" It was difficult to be angry with Richard. She gave him a punch on the arm, "Don't you dare move," she laughed, "I'm switching with Kosumi, I know you won't drive like that with him."

Fishing was fine. Even with her new-found ability to relax she couldn't fish for hours on end. The first time out she'd been focused on learning how to bait the hook and watch the pole. Scallop had shown her how to reel it in if she caught something, but she hadn't. The second time she stopped watching her pole and fell asleep in the boat. Little Kosumi had to jump over her when he saw something tug her pole and begin to reel it in. She guessed she wasn't going to be much help in the fishing department if Armageddon did come.

When Scallop had to work, she took walks on the beach, had a cup of coffee with Lucy, wandered into town to get her nails done, and got lunch with friends. Her first week she went to three softball games, and the monthly meeting of Scallop's Dart League at Murph's Bar in Sag Harbor.

Every morning at seven thirty she checked in with Trevor just to make sure that everything was going smoothly at Tallmadge. Every morning Trevor cheerfully told her the same thing, "Don't worry, everything's fine. Enjoy your day, have a beer for me." The only thing that changed each day was her drink of choice, one day a beer, the next a margarita, the next a mojito. Rachel was relieved that with Lauren's appeasement her own absence merely meant that her team wouldn't have any large new clients to deal with for two weeks; it was a break for them as well.

Early one evening in her second week, they took the Zodiac to Jessup Neck. The South Fork of Long Island never comes closer to its shorter sister to the north than at Jessup Neck, where a narrow spit of sand and trees juts north from the hills of Noyac, separating Little Peconic and Noyac Bays. At the tip, its rocky beach subsides into a sandbar several hundred feet long and then eventually to a deep but narrow channel between the two forks, a choke point through which huge numbers of striped bass, fluke, weakfish, and bluefish squeeze together each spring as they enter the Peconics from Long Island Sound. The bottleneck forces the water in the channel to move like a river. Swarms of fish cruise through during summer to ambush the silversides, rain minnows, killifish, squid, and bunker heading into the bay. At dawn and dusk, they spring into the air and dart around, visible just beneath the surface.

Scallop and Kosumi loved to come here, anchor the Zodiac on the sandbar, and play in the strong currents. Rachel was astounded at the sheer volume of fish hurrying around her ankles like New Yorkers funneling into the subway at rush hour. It was at once fascinating and cringe inducing; there were a lot of fish touching her legs. "This is so cool!", she laughed, "But, should I worry about any of these guys giving me more than a nibble?"

"No. You'll be fine. Don't some women pay to get the dead skin on their feet eaten off by little fish?" Scallop asked.

"Yes. But, I've never done it."

"You're tasty, but I think you're safe," said Scallop. "Kosumi, let's show her how it's done." They walked to one edge of the sandbar and then lay down in the shallow water, holding hands, and let the current sweep them through the channel to the other edge of the massive sandbar. Rachel joined in after the first pass and they spent the next hour doing it again and again. At first Rachel was nonplussed by the sensation of fish swimming beneath and around her. That faded on the third pass. The three of them held hands silently, gliding passively through the water looking up at the sky. She felt as though she was being carried just as much by the fish as by the water, a part of a natural process she'd never participated in before.

They made their way back to the Zodiac, Kosumi leading the way, kicking the water in front of him as he moved against the current, Rachel and Scallop walking behind holding hands silently. When Kosumi reached the boat, he climbed in and pulled something from beneath one of the seats, pressing the play button on a paint splattered boombox CD player, which had been a hand-me-down from Tim to Scallop when he left for college. The only CD was Dire Straits "Making Movies", and Kosumi played track number two, Romeo & Juliet, on repeat while he searched for starfish for the few minutes of daylight that remained, it was tradition. Rachel laughed at Scallop and both his lack of musical selection and he and Kosumi's unwavering adherence to their little rituals. Scallop grabbed Rachel by the arm and pulled her to dance as Mark Knopfler's voice and resonator guitar gently echoed off the water.

"You ever square dance, my land lubber lady?" Scallop said starting the question in a bad pirate impersonation but dropping it as he looked into her eyes.

"No, I can't say that I have, my swashbuckler," she said, meeting his deep gaze.

"Well it's a fine night to try my lady," he whispered huskily into her ear as he led her to dance.

As they moved together in the current, Rachel looked out over the deep blue shallow water, juxtaposed with the pink and purple sunset. The moon was full and rising. Almost every day here she felt something she'd never felt before. Tonight, it was as though she was spread out and intermingled with Scallop, the water, the fish, the breeze and Kosumi. It was at once liberating and empowering. Perhaps Scallop felt this all the time.

"I don't think the finest painter or poet could capture this," he said, "Jesus Rachel, you're perfect. Do you wonder how this happened? You and I?" he asked her.

"All the time," Rachel said.

"The last time Kosumi and I were here, in the spring, I didn't know you. I couldn't imagine that there was a feeling like this, that someone could come into our lives and fit so well into a place I didn't know was waiting for someone. I want us both to feel like this every second of every day. I think the fish can feel us."

"I can't believe I'm saying this, but I think they can," she rested her hand on his chest. "I wish this was my every day. I worry a little about the fall, when I will really need to travel again and be in the city. Do you think about that?" she asked, touching his back with the tips of her fingers, not wanting to lose the sensation of being together.

"Hell yes, I think about that. I'm terrified that you are going to decide this isn't going to work, or that it's just not practical for you, and you'll be gone. And I'll be left to live with your memory. I've got enough experience to know I'm not going to find someone else that I have this with. I'd spend the rest of my life missing you. I love you," he said picking her up and wrapping her legs around him, seating her in the place she'd come to the think of as rightfully hers.

"I'm in love with you too, Walter Kozlowski," she said kissing him hard, pushing away any thoughts of how things might change with the weather, with the music playing behind them.

"When you can fall for chains of silver
you can fall for chains of gold
You can fall for pretty strangers
and the promises they hold"

25: Kay & Rachel

On Tuesday at noon, Rachel volunteered to work the cash register at the farm while Lucy took her girls shopping for school clothes at the outlet stores in Riverhead. Rachel was disgusted with herself for being nervous about working the cash register and scales efficiently. Lucy had shown her how to do it before she left and Rachel had studiously taken notes, but she didn't want to be the cause of the first vegetable riot the farm had ever seen. Sometimes the stand would be empty for a half an hour and then suddenly there would be six people lined up to pay at once. The produce was sold by weight so each item needed to be weighed and rung up. Veronica and Inga did this so smoothly, and with such good humor that their customers left the stand in a better mood than they'd come in. Rachel knew how easily that tide could turn though. While they were dressed casually and had a few extra freckles from the beach, these were the same people who spent the other three seasons honking their car horns at one another and stealing each other's cabs on the streets of New York City.

Luckily it was the slowest afternoon of the week. The few customers who came in were locals and in no hurry, by three o'clock Rachel was getting a little bored and sleepy between the heat and the hum of the fans that were pushing the August air around the stand. She was tempted to go get her phone from her desk in the office and read the paper but the girls weren't allowed to use their cell phones in the stand and she didn't want to cause any problems.

Scallop's mother Kay came in the back door carrying a wooden crate of peppers in from the field. For a woman in her early seventies Kay Kozlowski was in remarkably good shape. Lucy's had inherited her build and eyes, and while her years working in the sun had aged her skin in a way most of her customers would never allow, Rachel thought she was the most beautiful older woman she'd ever met. While most of Kay's time was spent caring for her husband "The Captain", she managed to work two or three hours outside every day, wearing the same faded lilac plaid Columbia button down shirt, made for gardening, while she fed the chickens, picked, kept the flowers around the house and stand looking nice, and arranged the inventory in the stand. After she put "The Captain" to bed she somehow found time to make quilts and paint watercolors. Rachel both liked and admired her. She was talented, hardworking, loving, and fair. Rachel had no idea what Kay's opinion of her, or her relationship with her son was, because she was so unfailingly pleasant and kind that it was impossible to get a read on her. Rachel didn't have any customers so she ran over to help Kay with the crate. Kay set it down and brushed her away, beginning to take each pepper out one by one, making sure each was in good condition.

"Thank you dear, I've got it. It really was so nice of you to volunteer to help here while Lucy and the girls got out. They hardly ever get to do things other mothers and daughters do during the season. They were all very excited about it. We all help each other, but I feel that sometimes Lucy gets the short end of the stick."

"I'm happy to. It was this, or go help Scallop and Pedro in the field. I don't think I'm quite ready for that yet. At least not in this heat."

Kay smiled at her and handed her a pepper she'd just given the side eye, apparently, it wasn't good enough for the stand.

"Well, I'm glad you like it. I've been watching you and Walter. I have to admit, that I wasn't sure that we'd see you again after the fourth. We are quite a scene, and I think it's quite a different scene than the one you're used to. But, I don't know that I've ever seen Scallop so happy."

Rachel had felt a momentary sting that Kay hadn't expected her to return after the family party but it faded as she realized that Kay had just noticed the same obstacles for her and Scallop that all her friends had. Kay put her strong weathered hand on Rachel's arm.

"My Walter has had a rough time. I know right now the glue is holding in the places where he's been broken. It hasn't always been that way," she smiled kindly at Rachel who was wishing at that moment that Kay had been *her* mother, "It's made me happy to see him having a nice time with someone who cares about him and is as smart and put together as you are."

Kay took off her glasses to push the hair that had strayed from her hastily done French twist out of her eyes, and then seemed to consider whether or not she should continue. Looking Rachel in the eyes, she made her decision. "I'm sure you've heard something of Kosumi's mother?" Rachel nodded, wondering what could possibly be coming, Kay was too nice to speak harshly about a dead girl or the mother of her grandson.

"She was what the kids call a 'hot mess'", she said looking heavenward, "one of the hottest messes I've ever met. She was angry and scared and unhappy. She was a beautiful girl and she had no one to guide her in that or in the difficulties of being poor and an outsider here. She needed help, so did he at the time, and while they liked each other well enough they couldn't help one another. I thank God every day that Kosumi is a joyful little boy who seems to have inherited only the good from both his parents and none of the bad."

Rachel nodded, again struck by how differently the women in Scallop's family saw him than she did, than the rest of the world did.

"Family is important to us Rachel. I guess I'm trying to tell you that you are welcome to be a part of it, such as it is, if you'd like. But I also want you to understand, because I don't think that you do right now, that the places where Scallop is broken could come unglued. I don't think that you would do anything on purpose to make that happen, but I want to ask you to please be careful. When he left after High School, we didn't think he'd come back. We hoped and prayed, but we doubted. We were sure he'd settle someplace in South America, somewhere he could surf and climb mountains. Then he joined

189

the service. And yet he made it back here. So we are both blessed, darling," she finished kindly patting Rachel's hands. Rachel knew she needed to respond but wasn't quite sure what to say, it was rare that someone was so straightforward, it was one of the things that she liked about the Koslowskis.

"Kay, I've loved being here and getting to know your family. My family isn't close. My parents had an unhappy marriage and a bad divorce, and none of us really found a way to be together after that. I don't talk to any of them much," Kay motioned her towards the metal carousel that held the greens and began inspecting the lettuces, placing the wilted heads in the crate she'd come in with, she motioned Rachel to continue. "My mother still lives in the Chicago area, alone in a condo. My father is remarried and lives in Scottsdale. I have a sister who lives in Beverly Hills who is married with a daughter but, to be honest, we're the polar opposite of what you have here. Lots of things about me are different…" she trailed off, suddenly sad and not sure what else to say. Kay filled the empty air for her.

"I met my husband when I was in grade school, and we've been an item since then. I think we're the anomaly, not you dear. Even with our closeness and everyone supporting one another we never quite figured out how to properly run this place. We've done our best to raise our children. Tim, Lucy and Walter do a great job raising theirs. What we're not is good business people. Decisions Peter and I made," she smiled at Rachel's confused look, "That's 'The Captains' name, no one calls him by it now but me, poor decisions we made decades ago are the reason our kids are struggling with this farm now. Had we bought more land when we were young we would have been able to expand and do a lot more wholesale. But when land was still affordable out here the kids were little, and we feared the added risk. Peter remortgaged the house after it was paid for to pay for equipment that seemed like a good idea at the time but was probably more than we needed. We gave our children a lot of love and encouragement but we made mistakes too."

"I guess everyone does," Rachel looked steadily at Kay, "but, I will try not to make them with Scallop. I know you feel he's special, and I feel that too. And so is Kosumi. And so is Lucy, and so is this place. I've never been this happy, this feels like a whole new life for me. I honestly don't know how I'm going to make it fit with my job and the many places that I need to be, but I know that I am going to find a way. I'm good at that sort of thing."

Kay smiled broadly at her.

"I hope so. We're glad to know you. Now I must water the Sunflowers because God knows no one else will if I don't, and I think your phone has rung a few times while we've been talking dear." Kay Koslowski said as she walked away.

Rachel realized Kay was right. It hadn't really registered but she had heard her phone, more than once. She ran back to the office to get it. There were three missed calls from Trevor and a text, "Change out of your overalls, get in a car, and get to the office. You need to be here. Now."

Rachel ran to the side door of the farm stand and shouted for Kay to come back.

26: Hurricane Kachina

She pulled her knees up under her chin, resting her cheek on the back of her hands. She wished she'd had the fortitude to stand up to her mother and wear something different than the tight t-shirt and jeans she knew made her look like exactly what she was, an underage townie cocktail waitress. But, her mother's happiness with their new source of income hadn't caused her to stop hurling insults at Kachina. She knew that if she'd even *tried* to dress appropriately by emulating the "rich assholes" her mother drove around the East End in her ancient cab, her mother would have dug into her until she'd hit pay dirt - the tiny nugget of self-respect Kachina kept carefully hidden. You don't poke the beast. Her mother's moments of lucidity were laser focused on Kachina's destruction. She did everything she could to keep from pressing her mother's buttons.

She was so nervous she was consciously keeping her fingernails from drifting between her teeth. She didn't want to ruin the nice manicure she'd gotten during the prep for last week's shoot. At least her nails looked nice. It was Saturday morning and the steel grey train car where she sat wedged against the window with her feet on the torn vinyl seat was empty except for the little old lady who was asleep and smelled weird. There was nothing to distract her nerves.

She hated the train. She knew most of the girls in her class at school would have killed to be allowed to take the train into "the city" on their own. A few parents in town might have allowed their fifteen-year old daughters to ride together in a large group without a chaperone, but not many. Kachina couldn't think of *any* mother beside her own who would allow their fifteen-year old daughter to take a two-hour ride on the Long Island Railroad to go to a business meeting all by herself. Not that she would really know, she thought, she really didn't know anyone else's mother.

In the past four months she'd ridden by herself a dozen times for the small print modeling jobs the Pinnacle Agency had booked for her. They were trying her out for something bigger. At six foot one, with bright green eyes, dark skin, curly blonde hair, high cheekbones, and a culled together ethnic look that came from a combination of polish blood on her mom's side and a mixture of Shinnecock Indian and African American on her dad's, it was clear, even to Kachina, that she had the looks for the runway. Linda, her agent at Pinnacle said she was "fascinating", and "of the air". Kachina didn't know what "of the air" meant. Her dad used to say she was *like* the air, she could tell what he meant, that was the way he talked.

She guessed that in the modeling world it meant something different, maybe it had something to do with the fact that she didn't smile and mug for the camera like the other girls who'd been at the Abercrombie and Fitch shoot she'd done a few weeks ago. The photographer had given them an impatient lesson in "aloof". She'd gotten a water break.

She'd met Linda last summer at the beach. Linda's twenty-three-year old son had invited her to spend the day with him the night before when she'd been his designated Jägermeister shot girl at Neptune's Beach, the bar in Hampton Bays where she worked on the weekends. She was fifteen but she'd lied her way into the job. She needed a job, and she knew she could pass for eighteen when the person she had to pass with cared only about how much booze her looks would sell.

Linda had taken one look at Kachina sitting next to her son on a beach blanket at Coopers Beach and sent him for some ice creams. Linda, quite beautiful herself, a shrewd woman whose late fifties were the new late forties, had looked down at Kachina for a moment and said, "Stand up dear. Let me get a good look at you."

She'd stood up, pissed off because she was embarrassed. She was positive this fancy lady was just like the rest of them; unhappy they were getting older, uninterested in anyone outside their own circle, and worst-case scenario, a racist "bee-aitch". She figured she was about to be told to leave the beach and never speak to this lady's son again. But, she'd been wrong.

"Well," she said, "Look. At. That. How old are you sweetheart? Fifteen? Sixteen?"

Kachina lifted her chin defiantly. "I'm eighteen."

"Oh dear," Linda said kindly. "No, you're not. I'd say you're fifteen. My son should *not* have asked you to come here with him. It's inappropriate, and one hundred percent his fault, *not yours*. Shame on him. You work at a bar? Shame on the man who runs it. I think you and I will take our ice creams to go. I want to talk to you about something that will be much more exciting for you than spending an afternoon with my son. He's not all that interesting, I'm sad to say."

Linda searched through her beach bag, her white cover up flapping in the sea breeze and produced a business card; she was a modeling agent.

Linda gave Kachina a ride back to the camper-trailer that passed for the house she and her mom had shared on the reservation since her father had died almost three years ago. They sat in Linda's BMW and made plans for Kachina to go into the city the following week to do her first modeling job. Since then Linda had been getting her some work every few weeks.

When Linda knocked on the door of the trailer that first day, Kachina had been mortified when her mother, June, had stumbled to the door in a cloud of pot smoke, her hair wild, her breath stinking of stale whiskey. Linda had kindly acted as though nothing were at all out of the ordinary and gotten her mother to sign a contract document on her phone. When Kachina had come into the city for her second job, Linda had taken her to a Bank of America branch and shown her the account she'd set up in her name using the document her mother had signed.

"You can share whatever you like with your mom dear," she'd said. "I bet you'd love to help out at home. But you should get used to managing some of your own money. I think you're going to be making enough that you'll want to be in control."

Kachina wished she was meeting Linda today, but she wasn't. Linda had called her earlier in the week, "My dear, I have news, you'll be so excited, but it's a little sad for me. *Ted Frears* has been watching the work you're doing and he's taking over your management! You've heard of Ted haven't you? He's Talia Scott's agent. He launched Cheryl Sylvan. He takes his girls to the top faster than anyone else in the business. I wish I could keep handling you myself but I deal mostly in print and you're already better than that. Ted's the best person for you. This is a real opportunity."

Kachina had heard of Ted Frears. At a couple of the jobs she'd had in the past few months other girls had remarked on how lucky she was to have been discovered by Pinnacle, because she'd have a better chance of being noticed by Ted from within his agency. He was one of the top three agents in the business and she felt nauseous at the thought of meeting with him. Linda had explained that his schedule was really tight at the moment, but he was keen to meet her and asking to see her that Saturday afternoon.

She knew if her dad were alive, she wouldn't be sitting on the train alone. Jonas Rogers would have been sitting right next to her. Even if he hadn't been as excited about her being a model as she was, he would have been right by her side. She honestly didn't know what he'd think of the modeling. No doubt he would have made some connection between modeling and their heritage, she thought. Her dad had been the most knowledgeable member of their tribe about Shinnecock History. When she'd been little she'd helped him give tours at the museum. Few visitors to the Hamptons, were willing to glance away from the shinning trappings of the American luxury lifestyle that had overrun the place, and focus on the real history of the land that now played host to endless opulence. But those that did had gotten an earful from her dad. Of all the things her father had been proud of her for; she was pretty good at school, she helped other people without being asked, she knew the thing he was proudest of was her dancing.

Since her very first pow-wow at two years old it had been obvious to everyone that Kachina carried the spirits in her dance. She'd followed along with the dancers performing traditional tribal dances almost as though she knew them already. She was at once controlled and so free she seemed possessed. By the time she was five she'd become the featured dancer at every pow-wow. Her dad had found every excuse to trot her out to dance at other parts of the year. If there was an event, he found a reason for her to dance. He probably wouldn't love the modeling, she thought. It wasn't exactly spiritual. But in her present circumstances, making money any way she could was necessary.

Jonas Rogers' death had been a shock to his community. He'd been in great shape. He was a great golfer, in fact he'd been an unofficial member of Shinnecock Golf Club and played there often despite never having paid a dime in dues. He'd been the face of his tribe to the community of Southampton and the rest of the East End, and he was Kachina's hero. But one steaming hot summer day three years ago, she'd come home from her friend Jane's house at lunch time to find her dad lying face up on the chipped linoleum floor of their kitchen. By that night her father was gone, and some well-meaning member of their community had tracked down her mother.

June had walked in the door of the three-room cottage Kachina had shared with her father for the first time in Kachina's memory, and begun smearing peanut butter on the graham crackers her father kept in a special plastic container for her so that they wouldn't get stale in the sea air without a word to Kachina. She felt the light being sucked out of the cottage, sucked out of her, sucked out of everything and everyone she knew. There was no more light, and Kachina knew it would never come back. She'd hidden in her room for days, only coming out when she could hear her mother snoring drunkenly in her father's old bed. She'd been forced to come out weeks later. Within three weeks of her father's death her mother had sold their cottage for enough to do some repairs on the taxi she drove, and settle a few of her many debts. They'd moved into a camper-trailer one of her dad's friends had for rent a few doors down. Her mother told her it was temporary until she could get enough money together to get a real house off the "god-forsaken reservation" ("I didn't want to live here when you were born, and I *sure as hell* don't want to live here now!")

Her mom and dad had split when she was a baby. Kachina had only realized her mother lived right in Southampton when she was nine years old. She'd spent all week cajoling her dad into taking her to the Stop & Shop to buy brownie mix so she could bring something to her class bake sale. Jonas didn't always concede to conforming with the traditions of Southampton public schools, but in this case he'd buckled to her persistence and they'd been picking out chocolate chips when a harried woman backed into them. She was remarkably beautiful with dark skin, blonde hair, blue eyes and delicate feature but a meanness that hit Kachina like a wall flowed out of her in every direction. Kachina was startled by it and stepped behind her father, using him as a shield for the first time since she'd been a toddler. The woman glared at her father, then she looked Kachina up and down scowling and left the aisle. Kachina remembered her father picking her up, clasping her in a bear hug and whispering in her hair, "I love you my beauty – you are the air and the spirit of this place, let's go make the best brownies Southampton has ever seen." She remembered putting her head on his broad shoulder as he carried her back down the aisle her long legs dangling below his knees. When they got to the register, Alice was their cashier. She was Kachina's friend Sandy's Aunt. She rung them up shaking her head and scowling. Kachina looked up at her and smiled. Alice reached across the conveyor belt and touched her dangling leg, looking at her dad.

"How a mother could run away from a child this gorgeous I can't imagine. That bitch was in such a hurry she didn't even stop to buy the two packs she gets here every day. Unbelievable! You're both better off without her. We all love you honey," she said giving Kachina's leg another squeeze. On the way home Jonas had told Kachina his version of the story.

Most days she missed her dad so much it was like she had a case of mild food poisoning; her stomach upset, a lump in her throat and a headache. Her life with her dad hadn't been what people traditionally think of as comfortable. He worked at the Seven-Eleven in Southampton. They lived in a place where they were surrounded by wealth, and privilege. It was their home, but they were outsiders. Even within their own community Kachina was sometimes discriminated against. Her mixed race, darker than normal skin, and the disdain the community held for her mother, kept her separate from the group. But, she had been safe. With the passing of her dad, she'd completely lost her place in the community. She stepped away from the friends she'd had, and her mother made it her business to rebuff every overture from the adults in the community.

Linda was the first person since her dad who had made her feel protected. Kachina stared out the window as the train lurched through the dark underground tunnels beneath Penn Station curling her finger around her hair. She wished again that Linda was going to be with her at the meeting today making the introductions. Helping her answer any questions this new agent was going to ask her in a way that didn't expose how little she knew about, well, everything.

Kachina got off the train involuntarily covering her nose and mouth when she stepped onto the platform in the bowels of Penn Station. It was August and it was more than ninety degrees outside, hotter in the station and definitely smellier. Kachina had never been in the city on a day like this. Normally she'd be at the beach, surfing or babysitting, she did that occasionally to augment the money from Neptune's that she used to pay the rent on the trailer.

It was a little cooler when she got outside, but by the time she'd walked the fifteen blocks to Pinnacle her t-shirt was clinging to her back and her jeans were sticking to her outer thighs. The lobby of the building was deserted when she arrived and the swishing sound that Kachina's sandals always made echoed off the marble walls and floors. The weekend guard barely glanced up at her when she told him in a mock whisper that she was going up to the thirty second floor. When she got out of the elevator, she could see through the glass entry to Pinnacle that the office was empty. The lights were out in the reception area that was usually filled with girls waiting for an appointment and agents coming and going. She could see that a couple of offices were open, the natural light from their windows spilling into the reception space; Ted must be in one of those.

She knocked softly on the glass wall and waited. When no one came out of either of the offices she knocked harder, her knuckles stinging, and called out "hello?"

Through the glass she heard a muffled "It's me," and a second later a man came out of the office on the right, raising a hand up in peremptory greeting. He wasn't what Kachina had expected. She didn't know why, but she had imagined being greeted by a paunchy, balding man in late middle age wearing an ill-fitting grey suit. This guy had to be somewhere in his late thirties. He looked like a character from the romance novels they had at the Southampton library; like he belonged at the helm of a speed boat on the Italian Riviera in his light linen shirt and perfectly cut trousers. He had smooth dark hair and the muscular build of someone who didn't have to try too hard. He opened the door for her.

"Kachina," his voice was low and his words clipped, he didn't offer to shake her hand. "I recognize you from your shots. I'm Ted, why don't you come into my office and we'll get to know one another."

His office was just like Linda's which made Kachina feel a little more comfortable. She was sweating so much she wished she'd found a bathroom to splash water on herself before she'd gotten here. Ted sat down across from her looking worried, which made her feel worried.

"So Kachina, I've been watching you," he paused and looked her in the eyes with a gravity that made her feel like she was ten years old, "I think you have a lot of potential. I think you could make us both quite a lot of money. How does that sound?" He cocked his head to the side waiting for her answer.

"Um, that sounds good," she said simply. What else was she going to say?

"Good. I always want to be sure that my girls really *want* it. If you're not going to take this seriously, if you're not going to be able to handle little bumps in the road there's absolutely no point in us going forward. You can stay with Linda and make a little money to save for college and I can move on if you're not feeling one hundred percent committed to the path I'm going to offer you," he said.

Kachina felt panicked. Who wouldn't want to do this? Why was he asking? Maybe he hadn't liked her on site and he was trying to get rid of her. He saw her panicked look and smiled kindly, "It's *a lot* of travel. It's a lot of hours. People imagine modeling to be an incredibly glamorous life, but I'm going to be honest with you, there can be some stress, and there can be some tedium to it. Tell me about your family. If I send you abroad will you be homesick? Are they going to allow you to have a real career in modeling? You might miss school, you might be away for weeks at a time. It hasn't escaped

197

me that you're here without a guardian, is that because they don't ɛ

Kachina snorted out of nervousness. Did her mother not appr Absolutely. Did her mother not approve of Kachina being go making enough money to buy the groceries, pay the rent on their smoking trailer, and pay to fix her taxi cab? Those were all things her mother would approve of. They were also things it was easy for Kachina to talk about. She told Ted that her father was gone and that her mother wasn't here because she couldn't *possibly* care less what Kachina did. Her mother was a drunk and a drug addict. If she disappeared for months she would only notice because she'd eventually be evicted from the camper they lived in.

Ted looked at her appraisingly and she realized she may have said more than she should have.

"Well Kachina," he said seriously, "It sounds like you're in a tough situation. I'm going to help you. In six months, you'll be making enough money to either really help your mother if you want to, or to support yourself. How does that sound to you?"

All Kachina could do was nod. Verbalizing just how good it sounded to her would mean crying.

"Great," said Ted a huge smile transforming his face into something from a teen magazine. He suddenly looked just a few years older than her, like a guy she'd meet at the beach. It was so shocking it made Kachina giggle.

"You look like you could use some lunch Kachina. Should we go to lunch?"

"Sure," she said thinking how much she liked him. Lunch might actually be fun.

"I have a reservation at Blue Water Grill in a half an hour. You look fine, but you're not really dressed for it. We've got a room full of samples down the hall. Would you like to go down and find something to change into while I finish up a few things here? Just go three doors down on the left and pick out whatever you like. There's a bathroom in there, makeup, shoes, everything you need."

This *was* fun. Kachina searched through three long rolling racks of clothing not sure what was appropriate to wear at lunch time to the Blue Water Grill. She didn't know anything about the restaurant but something about the way Ted had said the name made her think it was going to be a really nice place where she'd need to be dressed in a certain way. She just wasn't sure what way that was. She choose the simplest thing she could find, a black pencil skirt slit up the side, a white sleeveless wrap blouse and a pair of five-inch stiletto pumps. Even though they were simple, she was sure they were the nicest clothes she'd ever worn. There were a few department store-style makeup displays set on a long counter with a mirror. She put on some makeup, again not knowing if she was putting on too much or too little for the time of day and the place they were going. When she was finished she stood nervously in the doorway to Ted's office.

He looked up. "Hunh. Well, people are probably going to think you're my intern, not my date. But I guess that's alright," he laughed, "Let's go."

When they got out on the street his energy changed. They walked the several blocks to the restaurant with Ted holding her elbow, leading her along. She caught him glancing at her appraisingly. She was several inches taller than him in her heels. She wished she could tell if he liked her or not. He didn't say much as they walked, and his expression was not quite a scowl.

When they got to the restaurant the maître'd obviously knew Ted. He looked Kachina up and down and raised his eyebrow at Ted approvingly.

"Your latest protégé? Very nice. Welcome, my dear. What's your name so I can tell people I met you when you're famous?"

"Kachina," she said blushing. She liked the Maitre'd.

"Good name even," the Maitre'd said as he led them to their table, "enjoy!"

Kachina sat down and immediately picked up her menu. She didn't know where she was supposed to look or what she was supposed to say. The restaurant was about three quarters full, but she didn't want to rudely stare at people just to have a place to rest her eyes.

"So Kachina," Ted said loudly, "have you ever had oysters?"

"Um, yes. You know, I'm like an Indian. I don't think there's an animal that comes in a shell that I haven't eaten, most of them just a few minutes after they came out of the ocean. My dad used to cook clams every night on a fire in the summer. I've probably eaten more shellfish in my life than everyone in this restaurant put together."

As long as they stuck to conversations about mollusks she'd be alright.

"Your dad used to? He doesn't anymore?"

"Um, no. He died a few years ago," she said. She was used to saying it by now. She always tried to say it in a way that would make people stop asking her questions. It didn't work on Ted.

"I'm very sorry to hear that. So you really have no one looking after you. I have to tell you from the standpoint of your career that may be better, it can be very difficult for us to develop you when we have a parent who wants to interfere and limit the scope of what I can send you out for," he said seriously.

"Mr. Frears, really, mother will not care what I do. You could send me to Australia for six months and she'd think I just went out to buy her cigarettes."

"Well, that will give us lots of room to maneuver. Also, that means she won't mind if you have a glass of wine with me."

As if on cue a waiter brought a bottle of wine to the table and poured Ted a sample. He tried it peremptorily and then motioned for the waiter to pour the glasses. "Thanks Charles, this for now, and then my red with lunch." Then he motioned for Kachina to drink pushing a basket of bread towards her and holding up his index finger, indicating that she shouldn't eat more than one piece. Kachina bristled a little. She was hungry, but she didn't want to do anything that would make Frears think she couldn't do what she needed to do to be a success. She didn't take any. He nodded approvingly.

For the next half an hour Ted talked about all the jobs and designers he thought she was right for. All the while she talked she drank her wine which seemed to refill like the cat feeder one of the families she babysat for had.

By the time the salad Mr. Frears had ordered for her arrived, she felt dizzy. She tried not to bolt it down. Taking just a few bites to settle her stomach, and stop her mouth. She had some sense that she was talking too much, like the twenty-three year old guys she served shots to every weekend. But she couldn't stop herself.

"Mr. Frears, how is working with you going to be different than with Linda."

"Well Kachina, first you need to understand that you need to do *exactly* what I tell you to. Linda and I have a very different style. First, I'm the expert. I know how to do this. Second, you need to understand you *don't* know what you're doing. You won't get anywhere in this business without someone to guide you. Here's what I'm going to do. I'm going to tell you precisely how to act in every situation I send you into. You're going to act that way. Once I'm certain you can do that, I'm going to put you in front of every designer you can imagine. I'm going to send you places you've never been. If you don't want to stay with your mother, within six months I'll have you in an apartment in the city. You might have to live with a couple of girls, but I can make it so you're on your own. You can make enough money to go to college if you want. Maybe you can make enough money to never do anything else but endorse products, I can't say that yet. But I will help you get there if it's possible, I've done it many times before. But *I* am the boss. Do you understand that?"

The thought of not having to walk home past her old cottage and spend the rest of the night looking out the filthy windows of the trailer caused a complete chemical change in her body. A lump of hope rose up from her stomach and cut off her air supply, making her dizzy. "Mr. Frears, I understand, I'm going to do whatever it takes, I swear," she said, the lump made it hard for her to talk as well. She knew she was going to cry. She didn't want Ted Frears to think she was a baby, or any trouble.

"Excuse me Mr. Frears, um, I just need to use the bath....the *ladies* room. I'll be right back." She passed a waiter and asked him where the ladies room was. As he pointed to it she reached out and used his outstretched hand to steady herself. The heels were higher than anything she'd worn in any of the shoots she'd done and at home she wore sneakers, or flip flops when she was working. She tried to walk in a way that was grown up and attractive as she made her way to the bathroom in case Frears was watching her go. She sensed that he was.

When she returned to the table, smiling, trying to give them impression she was a professional Mr. Frears was standing waiting for her. She guessed he'd paid the bill and was ready to leave.

"Alright Kachina, I think we'd better get back to the office and sign some papers." He took her elbow again and adjusted his body to accept the weight she was putting on him. She'd never drunk wine before. She'd never drunk much of anything in fact. She wasn't allowed to drink at work so she'd never had any more than the little sip of vodka she'd been pressured into by the older waitresses at Neptune's. She'd only taken enough to satisfy them. She'd spent the past three years living in the midst of an after school special on the realities of alcoholism.

When they got outside Ted hailed a cab and helped her in. When they arrived back at Pinnacle he ushered her through the lobby, quickly passing by security without an acknowledgement. Ted had to use his key to get into the office. Kachina vaguely noticed that there was no longer any office doors open. Whoever had been there earlier must have gone home. A moment later she was slumped in a chair in his office.

"Kachina, I'm just going to get some paperwork together," he said as he walked back into the reception area, closing the door to the office behind him. Her head was swimming, her feet were killing her in the shoes. She was afraid to take them off in case Mr. Frears thought she should have them on, and the pencil skirt she had thought looked so sharp made her feel like she was in a straightjacket. She could hear him out near the main door and then opening and closing doors to the other offices. She imagined he was searching for paperwork. When he returned, closing the door behind him she managed to sit up straight in her chair and cross her legs, ladylike. He passed behind his desk closing the blinds on the windows as he went. There were no papers in his hands.

"Now, there is just one more thing. All my girls go through this. I don't want you to think that I'm treating you differently, or that this is special in any way. I need to see you without your clothes on. I need to see exactly what you look like so I can understand what we're dealing with here," he paused to wait for a reaction.

Kachina's head had gone from swimming to pounding. Was she really supposed to take her clothes off? Maybe she was. She had no idea. She felt desperate. She wasn't afraid of taking off her clothes, she just didn't know if this was some kind of a test, if this really was something that all the girls did as a matter of course or if he was trying to see if she was slutty and might act inappropriately on jobs.

"If you're uncomfortable with this then I'm not sure we can work together. It's impossible for me to know exactly what you're suited to without truly seeing you," he said. His tone told her this was a one-time opportunity, the choice was hers.

She didn't know if she was choosing rightly, but she quickly turned away from him. In less than ten seconds she had unzipped the skirt and pulled it off, pulled off her own cotton underwear, pulled the blouse over her head and unhooked her bra. She turned around slowly her bra dangling from one hand. She held her arms out from her body, thinking that it would make it easier for him to "see" her as he walked around the desk in a wide circle appraising her. When he had made it all the way around to her backside, and was standing at the door of his office he said quietly, "Turn around please Kachina." She turned slowly with her head down. Being looked at in this way was not a comfortable thing. She stood there for a few seconds, wondering when he would be done. Finally she raised her eyes to his and knew in an instant that she'd made a terrible mistake.

Every bit of air flew from her lungs as he slammed her against the desk, his forearm across her throat. How he managed to rip into her so quickly she would never be able to imagine, no matter how many times she replayed the sequence of events in her mind later. Her head bounced of the desk and before it had cleared, a searing pain shot up from between her legs and radiated everywhere. She tried to cry out but now his other hand bore down on her mouth and chin. Her ears were filled with a buzzing mixed with the sound of her own vertebrae grinding against the desk. Pain was everywhere and her body performed the one and only action it could, forcing her to pull enough air through her nose between the grinding thrusts at her hips and throat to keep her from suffocating. It continued until she felt sure that her skin had split and her bones were making contact with the desk. Then it stopped suddenly as an inhuman sound pushed across her face. Frears made a low triumphant growl as he held her down with renewed force for a second. In an instant he flipped her over, pressing her torso and face into the desk.

"Now I know you," he whispered into her ear before lifting her again and letting her flop on the floor.

She lay there quietly crying, focusing on the pain radiating from her spine. Barely aware of him as he straightened his clothes, unlocked the door and strode down the hallway. Moments later he returned with the clothes she'd come in. He stood over her, folding her jeans and t-shirt neatly, and placing them on the chair nearest to where she lay curled on the floor. Talking to her in a calm authoritative tone.

"I will do everything I told you I would do. I will give you a career that will allow you to make your shithole home and your drug addict mother a distant memory. But please understand, there is no point in telling anyone about this. This is the price you pay. All my girls have paid it, by the way. And they will all deny it. The agency will not allow someone like you to tarnish our reputation, so I suggest you take the train home and wait for me to call you with the next opportunity to change your shitty life."

He walked around the desk and picked up the phone, pressing a few buttons. "Gerry, can you get my car ready?" He went to a closet and took out a bag and a jacket, then stood at the door.

"Here's what happens now Kachina. I'm going to wait out there while you put those crappy clothes back on. I'm going to take the service elevator down to the basement, and you're going to take the regular elevator and be on your merry way. Make it merry, you understand? Then I'll call you this week."

He closed the door behind him. Kachina wanted nothing more than to get out of there. As though possessed she pulled on her clothes and staggered to standing so she could stuff her feet into her shoes. In her peripheral vision, she saw her bra on the floor. She'd forgotten to put it on. She dropped painfully to the floor and crawled to it, ramming it in her back pocket before dragging herself to standing again using the desk as support. Not crying anymore, she stumbled out of the room and out of the office. Frears was standing in the door of the service elevator. As soon as the office door clicked locked behind Kachina he let the elevator door go and disappeared from sight. Kachina frantically pressed the down button on the elevator he'd said she should take. She barreled her way out through the lobby and down the sidewalks, filled with a wild energetic rage that she wished she'd felt while it had been happening.

She hadn't stopped moving until she got home; she'd stood by the door of the train car, she'd walked from the train station home, she'd staggered down the dirt road to her house knowing she needed to get there before her entire body seized up. Her hips, back, and chest felt like bruises that were reaching out for one another, trying to form a single giant, disgusting bruise. When she opened the door of the trailer there was silence. Her mother wasn't there. The same dirty dishes her mother had left from a sandwich 3 days ago were still where Kachina had left them. The same half-drunk bottle of whiskey was on the table. The same pile of drug crap was right next to it.

She climbed into her elevated bed, the mildewed smell of the cushions that had been meant for occasional use on camping trips irritating her more than usual, and she stared at the stained plastic wall. She was so angry she had no room for thought. She was angry at her mother for not giving a shit about her or even about herself, she was livid with her father for leaving her, she wanted to kill that bitch Linda for sending her anywhere near Ted Frears. She was so angry with herself for being such a stupid naïve idiot that she wanted to do herself harm. She kicked at the walls of the trailer until it rocked alarmingly. But it didn't help, and it hurt like hell.

There was nothing she could do. She jumped down from the bed, and sat at the table pulling her mother's dirty glass towards her. She filled it and filled it again until the bottle of whiskey was empty and then she laid her head down on the table.

On Cinco de Mayo in 2011, Scallop had been out drinking with Pedro and Luis, who worked at the farm, celebrating a Mexican military victory, even though they were Paraguayan, in a local establishment known as Fellingham's on a back street in the village. His friends had headed home, and Scallop was alone at the bar waiting for his friend, a local cop, to drive him home. It was nearing midnight and he was the only person at the bar. Kachina walked by him as he stepped outside to track down his ride home. She stopped straight in front of him.

"Well look here. It's Scallop, the farmer solider. You know I live right across the parking lot in an apartment above the garage. You came here hoping to see me, didn't you?"

"I didn't know that. How are you Kachina? I was pretty close friends with your cousin Jason Johnson. And I remember your father well. Jonas was an awesome guy; he was my baseball coach when I was eight. I used to hang out at the rez all the time when I was a kid," Scallop said as he took a swig of Blue Point, suddenly feeling old.

"Get out. Jason moved off the rez a while ago. He taught me all the tribal dances. We still do them every year at the pow-wow on Labor Day. I heard Jason might be moving back soon. He'd been upstate or something for a while, working at one of those casinos someplace."

Kachina moved closer to Scallop, sizing him up like a shark gazing at a bluefish, her beauty and raw sexual power undeniable. Looking at her on this particular night, it was as if she stepped out of the pages of Playboy, or more accurately, Penthouse, and into Fellingham's on this Cinco de Mayo. She kissed his cheek, then blew in his ear and bit his earlobe, as her hand moved between his legs. It had been a long time for Scallop, and he'd become somewhat used to it. He knew he should walk away. His ride would be there shortly, and he'd feel better about himself in the morning if he just ejected himself from this situation. One thing he learned all too well in SEAL training was self-control.

But why not? The woman across from him was as explosively attractive as one could imagine. He wasn't in a relationship, to his knowledge she wasn't either, and they were consenting adults. This stuff happens. Scallop gave in and spent the night with Kachina. Over the course of the following few weeks they rendezvoused several times, which was exhilarating for both parties. This wasn't a relationship, it was a no strings attached arrangement, and both viewed it as such. But, as always happens with such situations, Kachina eventually wanted more, Scallop had no interest in moving in that direction, and things ended. It was fine by Scallop.

Just before Hurricane Irene hit the East End, Kachina showed up at Scallop's cottage out of nowhere, saying that she had nowhere else to go. This was actually true; her landlord threw her out for not paying rent for months. She'd spent the money she earned bartending on drugs and alcohol. Her mother had shacked up with an ex-convict in a trailer park in Hampton Bays and they hadn't spoken in a year. Scallop would have turned her away, but Irene was hitting shore and the roads were extremely dangerous. She was holed up with Scallop for the storm. And it was there that Kosumi was conceived. Had it not been for that hurricane, Scallop wouldn't have his boy, the light of his life and his reason for living.

It was when they were holed up for the hurricane in the cottage that Kachina told Scallop the story of the modeling agent Ted Fears, what he did to her, and what he said to her. Kachina lost all control as she broke down in Scallop's arms after her admission. As she wailed incessantly, Scallop thought about Jonas Rodgers, and how he owed the old man something as he watched from heaven as his daughter stumbled through her life rudderless since his passing. As Scallop watched Kachina cry, he didn't see a sexy twenty-three-year-old woman. He saw the young, scared, violated girl that Fears had raped. Her faith in mankind was stolen that day, never to return. Kachina told Scallop that not a half an hour goes by where she didn't think about that day and what had happened to her. It dawned on Scallop that Kachina probably hadn't been Fears only victim. As Scallop held Kachina close and whispered in her ear that it was ok, he thought about what he would like to do to Ted Fears.

One week later, Scallop experienced the highlight of his relationship with Kachina. He attended the annual Labor Day pow wow on the reservation, at which Kachina led the parade ceremony, as she danced the traditional tribal dance flawlessly. Her headdress was immaculate, her deerskin outfit a unique sight, and Scallop was genuinely impressed with all that he saw that day. He had no idea that woman was carrying his child, and neither did she.

When Scallop told his family of the developments, that he was going to be a father, they were less than enthusiastic, to say the least, but eventually they got on board and accepted the reality of the situation. They were happy that Scallop was going to be a father, and while there were questions about Kachina and her mother, she was the daughter of the great Jonas Rodgers, who was a friend of the extended Koslowski clan in his time and a beloved local fixture. Kosumi was born in April of 2012, a beautiful boy who was exactly eight pounds. When Scallop held his son for the first time, he immediately started crying. Looking in his son's eyes, he knew that his life from this day forward would be different. From now on, his reason for being was this boy, and his motivation and rationale for all he did needed to reflect that.

Scallop was worried about Kachina. While he found her to be insanely attractive, entertaining, quite sincere and endearing, her behavior was erratic and there was certainly a problem with substance abuse that she came by honestly. Kachina was diagnosed as bi-polar in high school, but nothing was ever really done about it, thus her periodic self-medication via her actions, which obviously weren't in her best interests. As Kachina began to know and trust Scallop, she began to confide in him about her battles with depression.

Her confidence in Scallop was so strong that she revealed she tried to take her own life on more than one occasion; and would have succeeded on her most recent attempt if not for a neighbor on the reservation stopping by her unit by chance and quickly called an ambulance.

In October of 2012, Hurricane Sandy moved up the East Coast and morphed into Superstorm Sandy. Scallop insisted that they ride out the storm at the farmhouse, an idea Kachina wasn't thrilled about as she found Lucy and Kay quite controlling. Eventually, Kachina agreed as there weren't many other viable options. Monday morning Scallop left his baby boy in the dry, warm comfort of the farmhouse with Lucy, the twins and his mother and headed to the firehouse. As Sandy started to hit, the first of fifty calls began to the Southampton Fire Department. The overflow was passed along to North Sea as the day wore on and the intensity increased. The power eventually went out, forcing North Sea Fire Department onto a generator.

There were five others on call through the night as the storm infamously ravaged the Jersey shore, Staten Island, Manhattan, Brooklyn, Queens and parts of Nassau County. The eastern end of Long Island was lucky by comparison. Tuesday morning, the cleanup began and the North Sea Fire Department was very busy. Trees were down, power was out and danger abounded. Downtown Sag Harbor was completely flooded. Waters from the bay also heavily damaged Noyac, with entire neighborhoods being flooded. With the exception of some flooding, a downed tree and the roof blowing off a shed, the farm emerged unscathed.

In the middle of the day on Monday, as the storm began to ramp up on the East End, Kachina put Kosumi down for a nap. She then went into the living room, where she had a forced conversation with Lucy and Kay about the storm. Lucy and Kay both noticed that Kachina seemed off, but they assumed it was just because she felt out of place. Kachina mentioned that she had to get something from her car, and she headed outside into the driving wind and rain. It wasn't until nearly half an hour later that they realized she'd driven off into the storm. Scallop drove to the reservation just after the storm ended, which was completely evacuated. No sign of Kachina anywhere.

Tuesday afternoon, her car was located in the parking lot at Conscience Point by Southampton Cop and longtime friend of Scallop, Sargent Tom Brown, who summoned Scallop. Tom put his hand on Scallop's shoulder; a cold gust of wind blew a smattering of brown leaves between the old friends as tears moved down Scallop's cheeks.

A woman was kayaking in North Sea Harbor, surveying the damage, when she came upon what looked like a body in the dense weeds and brush at the end of Conscience Point National Wildlife Refuge. She called the police, who arrived quickly. The body was badly disfigured and decomposing, and had been preyed upon by fish, rodents and perhaps birds. But when it was properly identified, it was indeed positively identified as Kachina Rogers of Shinnecock Reservation.

The news of Kachina's suicide had made all the local papers; they ran old pictures from her Facebook page, mostly of her bartending in her bikini. The police had done a proper investigation, questioning Lucy, Kay and Scallop before officially ruling her death as a suicide. The letter she left behind for Scallop and Kosumi was all they really needed. There was only one other casualty in the Hamptons from Sandy, which happened in Montauk, where a woman walking her dog Monday was swept into the sea and found Wednesday in Easthampton.

No wake was held, but a large funeral service was held at the Presbyterian Church on the reservation. Scallop sat in the front row with Kosumi and watched as several senior members of the tribe spoke about Kachina, how special she was to her lionized father, Jonas, and how Kosumi now carried the Rodgers family torch. Scallop's memory took him back to when he was eight and playing Little League for the Barristers Barracuda's, which was coached by Jonas Rodgers. After a game one spring day, Jonas invited the team back to the reservation for a tour followed by a pizza party. The players were shown the sights of the original settlements, an area on the shore of Shinnecock Bay where whales were cut up after successful trips to sea. Scallop recalled the incredible detail and uncommon eloquence on display as Jonas gave the tour that day. He spoke of events long ago as if he were a participant, and truly had a gift.

Scallop's friends, family and community paid their respects with proper formality; most of them knew that Kachina was troubled. Her recent centered, motherly behavior was an exception to her historically erratic behavior. Most feared that the road ahead for the couple would have been filled with potholes at the very least, and that the challenges of parenthood would eventually wear on whatever relationship the couple could have generated.

As Scallop looked at Kachina's casket from the front pew, he thought of the few times she talked about her rape, and how badly it affected her already somewhat unstable psyche. She told Scallop about its effects on her several times, and she even referenced it in her goodbye letter, which most people would more accurately call a suicide note.

At the cemetery, when Kachina was being lowered into the ground next to her father's grave, members of the tribe danced and sang loudly. Scallop watched, holding the boy that was the byproduct of the person being buried and himself. As the sounds of the singing and dancing filled his ears, he thought about how this isn't fair. Here was a person who never had a chance. Due to her uncommonly good looks, she had a small ray of hope that perhaps her life could be different, but the world can be a cruel place. After she was raped at a young age by the predator in the city, she fell into self-medication, to which she was massively predisposed. Like a minnow swimming into a trap, she was simply caught. From there it was only a matter of time before she was dead. Scallop's thoughts began to focus on what he could do to honor Kachina and her father.

Last night, despite the crazy day she'd had, Rachel had decided that since she was in the city, she should follow her regular Wednesday routine. When she wasn't on the road, she liked to stack her Wednesdays with activity. Many of her colleagues purposely kept Wednesday light, but something about having a packed "hump day" gave her a feeling of self-satisfaction that she loved, even though she knew it was a little "holier-than-thou." Wednesdays started with volunteering at a homeless shelter on the lower East Side. She'd worked the early breakfast shift there once a week since her days at Goldman before graduate school. Now she was on the Board of Directors for the shelter as well. But, she kept her Wednesday breakfast shift in order to set an example for the other board members and volunteers; and because she enjoyed it. Every week, Eddie picked her up at the crack of dawn and drove her downtown. He used her shift to sit in the car, listen to sports radio, and drink cup after cup of bodega coffee while he waited for her. He was always in fine form by the time she climbed back in for him to take her to work – Eddie on five cups of coffee was a wild ride. She was supposed to be there by 4:30am. This Wednesday that wasn't going to be easy. As she fumbled to turn off her alarm clock she felt nauseous and wished that just once she could let herself screw something up.

When she'd gotten home last night she'd put together an outfit to take in the morning so that she could be in the office by seven thirty, ready for a full day of calls, meetings, and interviews. That wasn't going to be easy either. How was she going to maintain her famous professional demeanor when what her mind, body and soul wanted, more than anything, was to knock heads together. "Actually," she thought to herself, "It might be better to just smash the one head, repeatedly, against my desk!

She was embarrassed that she'd had to run out on the Koslowski's yesterday, leaving Kay to mind the farm stand when she'd committed to do it. Kay had been completely understanding, seeing that Rachel was frantic to get back to the city, and to her office. Rachel could only imagine what Kay thought of her. Best case scenario she just thought she was a type-A maniac, worst case, that she was obsessed with her own inflated sense of importance. Kay had come back into the farm stand to find Rachel on the phone with Trevor, balancing her iPhone between her chin and shoulder as she pulled a whole chicken out of the refrigerator case for a customer, with her half-packed computer bag slung over her shoulder. Rachel had blithered something to Kay about Lauren and her scheming, handed her the chicken, and walked out the back door, grabbing her laptop as she passed her desk.

She had run to Scallop's and changed, and driven recklessly back to the city, weaving between lanes to save a few seconds, and even using the HOV lane while alone, something you have to be desperate to do on Long

Island. She was on the phone with Trevor for the first half of the ride getting not only the details of what had happened, but also Trevor's full blown analysis of where *she* had gone wrong, where *he* had gone wrong, and exactly what sort of a treacherous bitch Lauren was. She was ready when she arrived at the office at quarter past five looking like she'd spent the full day there thanks to the hair products she kept stashed in her car and the accident on the Long Island Expressway that had slowed her down enough to allow her time to put makeup on in her rearview mirror.

When she walked into her office, Sal Silvestri, the Chief Compliance Officer for Talmadge was sitting at her desk, waiting for her with his shirt sleeves rolled up, looking like he'd had a day that had required him to get elbows-deep. Sal's sparse light grey hair almost exactly matched the shade of his suit pants. If it weren't for his intense green eyes, he would have blended in with the furnishings. But those eyes, framed by dark horn-rimmed glasses were sharp as a knife's edge when he looked up on her entrance, and Rachel knew, that for the first time ever, she was in trouble at Tallmadge.

Sal got up and shut the door behind her, following her back to her desk where he stood over her, placing a thick green folder down on the desk. He glared over the rim of his glasses as he pushed the folder across to Rachel. She didn't need to open the it to know what was inside. The spines of several magazines were sticking out the open length, and one of Lauren's obnoxious engraved post-it notes was stuck to the top. "This might be a problem for us," was written neatly in her small, precise handwriting. Rachel pulled out the magazines to find that Lauren had helpfully marked the important pages with more pretentious post-its. She wanted to claw them to tiny shreds with her fingernails and then stuff them down Lauren's throat. But, they *were* time-savers, and in seconds she had three spreads fanned out across her desk, each of which included the photos of her, Scallop and Kosumi at the gala for the Arts Center in. Dan's Papers, Hamptons Magazine, and 27 East all had shots of her in those cutoffs, with Scallop in that truly awful t-shirt. In the background, elegantly dressed guests were gliding past in soft focus. The photos were terrible. It looked like the Beverly Hillbillies had shown up at the Beverly Hills Hotel, except much, much worse. Rachel's face turned red and she chose to keep staring at the photos, because the only other option was to meet Sal's glare. She wouldn't have blamed him if he'd thrown his glasses at her head. Every photo identified Rachel as an employee of Tallmadge, which was why Sal was vibrating at a fever pitch.

"Why the *hell* were you, our Head of Marketing, at an event like *that* wearing "Daisy Dukes" accompanied by *Crocodile Dundee*? I don't think you have any idea what you've done here. Burnham has been so disengaged this summer, I thought he'd pack up his office this fall and finally retire! It's time. I don't have to tell you that that's something that *needs* to happen. You know all of this. But having *these* delivered to his desk on, the one day he was in the office in two weeks by little-miss-prissy-perfect-pants has *revivified him*! I don't know if it was the guy's tattoos, lack of shoes, or the fact that he could see George Spiegel in the background of this one, but he's apoplectic. So now *I'm* apoplectic."

Sal had been at Tallmadge his entire career. Burnham Tallmadge had hired him fresh out of Harvard when Tallmadge had been in his forties and Sal had been with him ever since. Sal was his friend, confidant and most loyal employee. He was also the one pushing Tallmadge to retire for his own sake, as well as for the company. People needed to see a slightly younger man at the helm of a fund like the one he'd built, and Tallmadge should have the opportunity to enjoy the birds and plants he loved so much. Sal was a good guy.

"Sal, he was a Navy Seal! That's where the majority of the tattoos came from," Rachel blurted. She couldn't believe it as she heard it leave her lips. She sounded like a teenager defending her pot-head boyfriend to her mother. In Sal's face she could see what an idiot she was being.

"'The majority?" Sal asked, pausing for effect. "Lauren handed these out today. She casually dropped them on anyone's desk she thought would take up her mantle. Honestly, I wouldn't have put it past her to have shared it with clients! Some of them have seen this. I had calls today Tom Webber and Cal Quincy asking if you were *still with the firm*. What the hell are you doing?"

Sal waited for Rachel to say something. She didn't have anything to say. *What was she doing?* She was making a mess of things. When she didn't answer Sal jumped back in.

"Obviously, this isn't really a compliance issue. I don't think the guy in those pictures is any kind of security risk. It's a reasonable bet that guy hasn't touched a computer since high school. I know you way too well to think you'd share anything inappropriate with him Rachel… I hear he's a farmer or something?"

Again, Rachel didn't answer. She knew absolutely deserved a bigger dressing down then Sal was dishing out.

"I guess I'm the one sitting here because this is a *PR problem*, and that's _your_ department. Since you can't reprimand yourself for *this*," he puckered his face and waived emphatically at the magazines to indicate just how little he thought of "*this*", "I've got to do it. And I'm telling you, you've missed your window to deal with Lauren. You should have fired her months ago. Were you just not paying attention? I know she's been angling for a while, and you've just allowed her to ram her foot in a door that was solidly shut in her face up until now. She just gained Burnham's trust at *your expense*. If you make a move to get rid of her now, it won't look good. We're all stuck with her. Thanks for that. She's cold hearted that girl, and I wouldn't trust her to get you a coffee."

"Sal, obviously I've made some mistakes! I knew it was a mistake to let those photos be taken. I should have known it was a mistake to go *anywhere* dressed like that," Rachel swallowed what she realized must be low-level hysteria, she was so unaccustomed to it she didn't even recognize it. She was scared. "So what's the message Sal? Are you telling me I'm done?"

"No! Anyone else would be. Just be careful, that's all. Protect the firm. I wish your personal life were none of our business. But you know that's not how it goes. When you show up in the society pages identified as one of our key employees, and you are by far our most public employee, you *know* what you should look like."

"Noted," Rachel said flatly, fighting back and almost irresistibly strong urge to be combative. She knew Sal was right and she knew she was really angry at herself, not at Sal.

Sal could see Rachel had recognized her mistake, and he immediately simmered down. "Look. Your personal life is your personal life. It's not my businesses. But, these are *your* choices Rachel. You should know some of the board has seen it too. I had a couple of emails today. Basically, they said, 'what is Rachel Jones doing at *something like that* with *someone* like that?' That's your reality."

Rachel ground her heel into the carpet trying to steady her hands as she stacked the magazines, George Spiegel's smirking face catching her eye in one of the offending photos. He'd probably tipped off the photographers, told them where Rachel worked. He saw an opportunity to make rival Tallmadge look bad and his own Flagpole Capital appear the secure choice with him appropriately dressed in the background of the photo while in the foreground she looked like Daisy Duke. How could she have forgotten that she needed to behave as though she were at war?

"I know all of that Sal," she said looking him in the eyes. "Honestly, we were walking by and I saw a few people and popped in to say hello. The photos weren't expected, and we reluctant to do it, it just sort of happened."

"Well, you should go see Burnham, you'd think he's been personally injured. I think your reign as his perfect pet is over. Go make it up with him, and next time think about where you are. Southampton is Southampton, regardless of who you're spending time with. Do you think this relationship has legs?"

"Does this relationship have legs? That's your question after you just said this wasn't any of your business?"

"I'm just asking off the record. We are just two people talking here, and I care about you. I've been feeling bad all day about having to talk to you about this because when I look at those pictures the *first* thing that I see is an inappropriately dressed employee of the firm I've spent my entire career building at a major society function. But, the second thing I see is a friend who looks a whole lot happier than I'm accustomed to seeing her."

Rachel kicked back from her desk and looked out over Central Park's thick canopy of green leaves. "I don't know, Sal. How the hell do you know?" It was meant as a rhetorical question. Rachel had been sure this morning that her relationship with Scallop had legs that were good enough for a runway. Now she wasn't. Sal answered Rachel seriously.

"I have no idea, Rachel. I'm nearing the end of my second marriage. I'm not the guy to ask about that. I wish you luck with it. I don't see that smile often. Just stay out of the papers ok?" Sal said as he picked up his folder, taking it with him to file in a cabinet where Rachel hoped it would never see the light of day again.

She stood staring out the window for a good half an hour after Sal left. Several years earlier a portfolio manager had thrown an outrageous party while at a business conference in South Beach and it made the New York Post's Page Six. That guy was immediately let go. If a member of her team, a trader or an analyst had done what she'd done, if she were sitting looking at a picture of Kendra or Lauren in the same situation, she'd have found a legit reason to fire them by the end of the day. Tallmadge had zero tolerance for negative publicity. This wasn't quite that, but it was too close for comfort.

Four hours and another meeting later she'd downed several sakes and two of her favorite sushi rolls with Dana at her favorite sushi restaurant. They hadn't seen each other since the wedding. They'd already covered Dana's honeymoon to the Greek islands, everything to do with Scallop from gritty intimate details to what his house was like, the connection Rachel felt with Lucy, and the meetings Rachel had had with both Sal and Burnham Talmadge earlier in the day. Now Rachel was energetically dredging her last remaining slices of pickled ginger through puddles of soy sauce on her plate with her chop sticks and rehashing the meeting with Tallmadge for the second time with Dana. It hadn't gone well. Rachel had gone into the meeting contrite and left feeling betrayed and self-righteous.

"I don't know *why* I'm such an idiot you know? It was foolish of me to think that I was *really* special to him. I should know better. Business is business. Tallmadge loved me because I've made him a ton of money. One step into dicey territory and it's like all of my work over the years was erased!" she hissed, stabbing at a lump of wasabi. Dana raised an eyebrow and said nothing.

"And you know what the *worst* part was? Well, besides him putting Lauren back on my team and saying I need her *"support"*? In others words she's there to *tattle on me* in case I mess up again! The worst part is that he couched everything in a fake concern for my well-being and future. He doubled down on the considerate father-figure bullshit as it was becoming obvious that his concern for me had never been anything but self-serving. I guess now I see how he managed to get where he is. He might spend the rest of his life messing with bugs and fish out on that island all by himself, but he'll always know how to sell it!"

When they'd first sat down Dana had been outraged in all the right places, just as a best friend should be when her friend has been wronged, saying "give me a break!", "he said what?", and "I always told you Lauren wasn't as great as you thought she was!", right on cue. But Rachel hadn't noticed that sometime during the miso soup Dana had stopped making emphatic exclamations of support, and become intensely interested in her plate. Now she looked up and took Rachel in.

"Rachel, you know I love you. And you know I want what's best for you, and for you to be happy. You know that, right?"

"Of course," Rachel said, knowing that Dana was about to tell it to her straight. Dana was as direct as they come, it was Rachel's favorite thing about her best friend.

"Then I'm just going to come out with this because I think maybe no one else will have the balls to say this to you. What is going *on*? When you showed up to my wedding with Scallop, we all got it. He's different, he's gorgeous, super manly, all of that - and of course, there was the added element of Tucker being there. He was a *great* wedding date. But I totally thought that when I got back, you'd have moved on. And I think if this table was turned around, and you were sitting here listening to *me whine* because my boss reprimanded me for doing something, I would have fired someone else for, you would think, "Dana is *losing it!*" You've put your relationship with this guy above everything you've worked for! The *only* way that you could possibly have spent enough time with him and his family to have gone through everything you're telling me about, is if you *completely* slacked off this summer," Dana looked at her like a fourth grade teacher would look at a student who hadn't passed in their homework in three weeks. "You're *surprised* that girl Lauren has been tasked with watching over you? I'm not. *What* are you doing? Are you serious right now?"

Rachel was dumbfounded. Dana was absolutely right. It was rare that Rachel owned up to a strong feeling. It seemed like an exposure; like she was sticking her neck out and pointing right at her jugular. But she needed Dana's help with this because she was right, she was making mistakes. She'd never been in this situation before and for the first time in her life she was making a big, fat mess. So, she told the truth.

"Dana, I guess…I'm in love with him. And I love what *my life's like* with him…how it's changed. I know there are things about it that are untenable and I suppose I've just been choosing not to address them because every single minute with him feels good, and I feel *at home* when I'm with him and his family. I've never felt anything like that. My parents sat in separate rooms each night watching television and they shipped me off to camp and then to prep school. I was always more or less on my own. I don't feel alone there. Maybe that's making me relax in a way that's really not great," Rachel said slowly, working through it in her mind.

Dana laughed a little. "You think? I saw the picture in Hamptons Magazine, and honestly, I thought you were there in costume! I'm sure he's a great guy, and interesting, and I'm sure his family is lovely. But is it all real? Is it worth risking everything you've worked for years? The world is filled with awesome guys that would fit into your life perfectly, you could probably have any of them," Dana offered kindly, thinking her friend might somehow have forgotten just how much she had to offer. When things had ended with Tucker, Rachel had spent nearly a year thinking the problem was her, maybe she'd fallen back into that.

"I know," Rachel said, and obviously, she did. "I guess I've just gotten carried away by the fun of being out there and by him. I feel like one of those dumb women who do dumb things for dumb guys! Am I dumb? I *did* something dumb, I can see that. But am I dumb?"

"It's ok Rach. I'm glad you aren't so far off the deep end you can't see that you've made a few missteps. Honestly, I was worried that you were going to get defensive. You're not dumb." Dana changed her tone to one of teasing. Rachel had seen her point. "Now, normally I'd tell you to trust your instincts. But, there are pictures of you in Hamptons magazine *dressed like a hick.* I think maybe the instincts have left the building," she said, joking.

Rachel snorted with laughter. Then said earnestly, "I do see the things that won't work. Like he's never leaving North Sea. He can't really. His whole world is out there, and he'd never change that - nor should he. I'm not going to go live out on the East End. What the hell would I do out there? But the truth is I want it to work out. I'd hate for it not to work out at this point. Not to have Scallop in my life, or Kosumi who I've fallen in love with, or Lucy... I'd be so sad. I think it would upset me more than anything has, far more than Tucker. I can't believe I'm saying that. But, I'm pretty sure it's true."

"Alright," said Dana, obviously wishing that Rachel would choose an easier path. "You just need to put a little focus back on your work and the other parts of your life. Make sure that you can find a way to walk both walks."

"Absolutely," Rachel agreed.

After Easy Eddie had dropped her at home, she'd tried to turn in early so that she could get up on Wednesday at four A.M., ready to attack the day like the barracuda everyone knew her to be. But instead she lay awake trying to build scenarios in which she and Scallop both lived happily ever after. She couldn't come up with a single happy ending in which it wasn't necessary for one of them to drastically change who and what they were.

She was headed back Out East Thursday night for Labor Day weekend, but now, for the first time since she'd been on her way to the pre-Memorial Day hunt she'd planned, she had an uneasy feeling in her gut about it. Not only was she feeling guilty about taking yet another day out of the office on Friday, even though it was a day when almost no one in New York City was working. She just didn't see how this was ever going to work.

28: Tumbleweed Tuesday

Rachel had Easy Eddie drive her out for the final weekend of the summer. She came downstairs to find him leaning against his town car smoking what must have been his fifth or sixth cigarette judging from the butts at his feet, and shooting the breeze with Larry, one of the weekend doormen. They loaded up her bags.

"Huh, not traveling light this time girlie? Am I dropping you at the shack or is there business to be done this weekend?" he teased, pointing at her dress and stilettos, the outfit she should have been wearing on the ill-fated evening in Southampton.

"Nope! I'm just walking the walk Eddie," she said with an edge she knew he would catch, "and no, I don't want to "talk it through,'" she joked. By the time Eddie's town car rumbled onto Scallop's "lawn" they'd talked it over, under, and through, and Rachel had put a dozen emphatic reminders, that she knew would be unnecessary, into her phone for Tuesday when she'd be back in the city.

When Scallop came to greet them Eddie handed her bags over then shouted "Monday night, 'Godfather' girlie!", as he drove away.

"What does he mean 'Godfather', Scallop asked.

"Should I be watching my back? Am I going to sleep with the fishes?"

"WHAT?," Rachel gasped, "You're kidding me! You actually got a pop-culture reference?"

Scallop was unfazed and unoffended. "Come on, it's 'The Godfather' for Pete's sake. I watched TV every once in a while when I was a teenager, I just don't do it now. You can't be a boy in America and not have watched 'The Godfather'. So, what did Eddie mean?", Scallop asked, easily slinging two garment bags over his shoulder.

"Oh," Rachel laughed, "we just made a pact to stick my computer up on his dashboard on the way home on Monday night and watch 'The Godfather' trilogy together since we'll surely be able to get through all of it while we sit in traffic!"

"Huh," said Scallop, looking down at one of the two weekend bags he'd just loaded on his other shoulder, "I thought you were going to leave your computer at home this weekend. It's a holiday."

"I brought my computer," she said tersely, knowing that her irritation had come out loud and clear. Scallop didn't seem to catch it though. He'd found a way to balance all her bags, and he took her hand.

"Hey, did I tell you about what happens this weekend?"

She was a little annoyed that he hadn't taken her bait, and then a little angry with herself for trying to bait him. None of what had happened with her work was his fault, it was hers.

"No," she said and when she looked up at him, he looked so good, every part of her that could tingle did. "I just assumed it was more of the same. Just another glorious Groundhog Day in North Sea. I'm happy with just doing the usual."

"We're already that boring? No way. Smell that breeze?", he asked, stopping in his tracks to give her a chance to really take a break. That's the first breath of fall. Feel that?"

Remarkably she did feel it. The air was cooler than it had ever been at his house. She was comfortable in her dress, but she would have been just as comfortable with a light sweater on. It was quiet too. No lawnmowers, no boat motors. It felt like they were out in the country.

"Alright," said Scallop, walking briskly to the door, "you go take a shower, you look like you need to wash the day off."

She stood still and watched him haul all her stuff into the house, knowing he was right. She got in the shower and stayed there for a good twenty minutes, looking up at the branches of a maple tree blowing in the breeze and letting the hot water stream over her and the steam swirl around her goose bump covered body. By the time she turned off the water she found herself in the state that she always wound up in while here, she felt both deeply relaxed and just a little wild. She expected that Scallop had left her a towel like he usually did, hanging just outside the shower where she could reach for it. But when she'd rung out her hair and brushed the water out of her eyes she reached outside and came up with nothing. Not even her clothes. She called for Scallop who didn't answer, and then she called louder. Nothing. "Great," she thought. "How much worse is being caught *streaking* around the Hamptons than being caught in frumpy clothes?" She realized that ironic as it was, in terms of optics, it would probably be better to be caught naked; naked was at least sexy.

Maybe Scallop had gone somewhere to pick up Kosumi. She called out again and there was no answer. She let out a growl of frustration and flung herself out of the shower, attempting to cover the important parts as she ran headlong across the backyard, up the back steps, and straight into the living room where she was tackled from behind by an equally naked, but considerably dryer Scallop, who must have been lying in wait in the kitchen. He picked her up and tossed her on one of his giant bean bags in the middle of the room. She sank in, her wet body spotting the bean bag's purple cover. Within seconds Scallop had taken full advantage of her position and she'd forgotten everything outside of sensation. The cool air through the windows and the decadence of being in the public part of the empty house, opened them both up. As Scallop pressed himself deep inside her she cried out from a combination of pleasure and frustration. How could something so perfect be so irritatingly inconvenient? It was infuriating. A second later she cried out louder, just for the freedom of being able to. As they lay splayed on separate bean bags at the end of a heated half an hour Scallop turned to her, "Time to get dressed my beauty. We have somewhere to go tonight."

Rachel's pieces hadn't reassembled into a whole yet. "I have to go somewhere?", she giggled, "I'm feeling really good about being right here. Right here is great for now."

Scallop chuckled and rolled towards her on his beanbag, "We have a pow-wow to go to," he said, hitting her playfully on the butt as he hopped up and headed for the bedroom. Rachel just laid there. She knew that if Scallop said they were going to a pow-wow it wasn't a euphemism for something else; they were going to an actual pow-wow. Rachel was unclear about the events that made up a pow-wow.

"Enlighten me. Where is this and why are we going there?," she asked, faking a sigh of exasperation.

"It's at the reservation. It's a yearly thing. For the first time Kosumi will be in the dance competition. He's very excited for you to see. He's been going over to the reservation every day this week and practicing for a few hours. It was a big deal to his mother. One of her cousins is a friend and he invited him. He's a natural – you'll see."

"Ok," Rachel said, with conflicting feelings. She was glad for Kosumi who loved to dance, and glad for a chance to get to see him in what she suspected would be the closest he'd ever get to his natural element. But, something about being on Kachina's territory made her apprehensive. Scallop had only mentioned her the one time. No one else mentioned her. It occurred to her that the pow-wow might be a chance to get a little more information without grilling Lucy which she felt uncomfortable doing. She wished she wasn't so interested in the one other woman that Scallop had ever had an adult long-term relationship with, but she was. "What does one wear to a pow-wow?" she joked.

"I don't know, but certainly more than you're sporting right now," said Scallop as he disappeared into his room. He stuck his head back out. "You'd be surprised how much the dancers are wearing. Everyone thinks of Indians in loin cloths and some paint. Most of the dancers are wearing enough layers to hike the Arctic."

Scallop had not been exaggerating. The pow-wow was a big deal. It reminded her of the "country" fair she'd been to in the Hudson Valley a couple of years before; real farm people and animal and vegetable competitions sitting incongruously alongside tacky swap-meet goods and Elvis paintings on velvet. Here were the vestiges of Native American culture alongside trinkets from Taiwan and modern American junk food. Parking was a nightmare and it was a long dusty walk down the unpaved reservation road to the main event. She knew if she tried to wipe away the dust that was collecting on her ankles and the beaded sandals she'd end up with dirt-streaked legs, so she let it be.

As they approached the large crowd that was gathering where Scallop said the dancing would be, she could see Lucy's blond head bobbing slightly above the others in her group as she turned from side to side talking to one and then another. Then she picked out Tim and his wife, Inga and Veronica and Scallop's mother. Everyone was there. The apprehension Rachel had been feeling disappeared. She might be on foreign territory, but she felt a warmth in her chest knowing that her people were here.

Lucy hugged her and kissed her on the cheek. "*Wait* until you see our boy! I've brought him over here a couple times while Scallop was tied up with other things," she said with a knowing leer that made Rachel blush just a little, "he's *quite* the sight."

They were standing under one of the few trees on the edge of an open area with a large raised lawn surrounded by a circular concrete wall that had been painted to represent mountains, or waves. Rachel couldn't really tell which it was supposed to be. As Lucy introduced her to some of Tim's friends, Rachel watched Scallop talking to two men, both in native dress, a little ways off. One of them, who Scallop seemed to know well, was remarkably tall and thin and bore a striking resemblance to Snoop Dog. He was introducing Scallop to the other. A short stout woman in her sixties with corn rows in her hair joined them, standing with her arms crossed and her lips pursed. Rachel waited, pretending to take in the scene, while she wondered who they were and if Scallop would invite her over to be introduced. He did not. And then, just before Scallop walked away, the little woman reached up and gathered him into an awkward hug, patting him on the back. Scallop was a popular guy on this reservation.

Scallop strode back towards the group, stopping to look up at the announcer's stand at the top of the circle where a group of drummers and singers that had just started to beat out an eight count and chant, pulling everyone's attention for a moment. On the rare occasions when Rachel had heard Native American song it always made her feel both attracted to the obvious power behind it and repelled. It was so foreign sounding. She wondered how many of the hundreds of people who had brought their lawn chairs and bug spray to watch tonight felt the same way. When Scallop returned to the crowd he attempted to launch into a conversation with Tim and one of their buddies from softball. He introduced her and they chatted for a few minutes about the weather that summer, business, and what had changed in town, but when Scallop leaned over to kiss her she caught his eye and pointed her chin towards the group of people he'd just been with, raising her eyes in question.

"Oh, that's my friend JJ. He's the one who got Kosumi involved this year. He was Kachina's second or third cousin. They just want Kosumi to feel welcome here," he stopped and stared at them over her head for a moment and Rachel knew there was something more he wanted to say. She waited. "Guilt. They feel guilty. I think they should let that go. I don't know, maybe everyone here could have been a little more supportive of Kachina when her father died.

I wasn't there. But I do know none of them were the cause of her problems," he said sadly. "I'm glad that Kosumi is here and enjoying himself. This dancing was the one thing that actually made his mother happy," Scallop said, his eyes still on the bandstand. Rachel waited for him to say more and when he didn't, she decided not to push it. He liked to talk when they were alone at the firepit in his backyard. Whatever it was he'd tell her eventually. It dawned on her that there was a chance Scallop might clam up all winter. waiting for the first spring night by the fire to unburden himself. Then she had the even more disturbing thought that he might actually *use* that firepit all winter. She didn't care how hot he was, or how much she wanted him to talk to her, she wasn't going to sit out there when it was fifteen degrees, wearing a snowsuit, and waiting for him to tell her his innermost thoughts.

Lucy came up from behind them and wrapped her arms around Rachel's shoulders.

"Are you ready for this? I kind of love this thing! When I was a kid, I used to want to be in it. I loved the things they wear on their backs that are made of feathers and look like wings. I don't exactly look the part though."

"Hmm," Scallop smiled.

"Where'd you park the chairs Luce? We'll go make sure nobody takes our spot," he said.

They found the lawn chairs that Lucy had put out and sat down, watching nothing. Scallop fished two beers out of a cooler and handed her one. The music was getting louder and an announcer was making introductions and saying thank you to the various people who had put the pow-wow together.

"So, *what* exactly are we watching here?" Rachel asked taking a giant swig of beer.

"It's basically a parade. Different groups of dancers are going to file in. They all end up on that raised patch there, and they dance. Kosumi's dancing with the Shinnecock dancers, but there are dancers from all over the country here. All different tribes. The outfits are great. Fascinating."

"Well, I've never been to anything like this, so this is kind of cool. I like the drums. They make me feel motivated."

"Well that makes sense, I think they were supposed to be kind of motivational, either to some spirit or to the people themselves."

"So, when they come out do we cheer? Like at the Olympics?"

"Nah, you just watch," he said running his hand up her neck and through her hair. And then it started. A parade of people in gorgeous Native American ceremonial clothing. "The Dancers". Many of them just shuffled along to the drums, letting their clothes be the main event. Only a few were doing anything really involved. Rachel had never seen anything like some of the outfits. Many of them had what seemed to represent wings on their backs, circles of feathers that moved as they danced. Others had rainbow colored robes with colored tassels that draped almost to the ground. Rachel craned to see down the line and caught a glimpse of Kosumi in the middle of a circle of half a dozen men who were all dressed more-or-less the same, with relatively simple clothing, compared to much of the rest of the parade. They had on natural colored cotton shirts with puffed sleeves and suede pants with a big rectangle that hung down in the front and the back. Some had necklaces of beads and shells around their necks, and on their heads they all wore a circular crown of brown and grey feathers. They were basically just shuffling along except for Kosumi who was whirling and jerking around at the center of the circle as though possessed. As the group passed, the woman Scallop had been talking with earlier, the one he had avoided introducing her to, she saw her catch sight of Kosumi for the first time. The woman gasped, then put her hands over her face forcibly, peeking out almost immediately and not taking her eyes off him as he progressed all the way around the circle and up onto the earthen platform. Scallop and family were standing and cheering Kosumi as though they were at a football game, but Rachel was transfixed by the short woman in the crowd who was having a visceral reaction to Kosumi's crazy dance. Who was she?

Rachel joined in the cheering as a segue to tugging on Lucy's shirt. "Who is that woman down there? The older lady that Scallop was talking with earlier?" Lucy didn't even glance down the line, she already knew who Rachel was talking about. "That's Jane," Lucy shouted into her ear, "she was a good friend of Kachina's father, probably more than that. I think it was her who pushed JJ to invite Kosumi to come dance. I've been told by more than one person that it was a transcendental experience, which I can't picture. But I think I maybe didn't really know her. I feel guilty about now to be perfectly honest. My guess is Jane feels guilty too."

This was the most Rachel had ever gotten out of any of them on Kachina. "Why guilty?" she asked, hoping to finally be able to figure out why Scallop had spent any of his time with a depressive drug addict.

"I think there was a time when Kachina wasn't a mess. If you talk to some of the people around here, they'll tell you what a 'sweet' girl she was. The woman I knew was *not* sweet. She was beautiful, she was as hot as you can get, but she had an edge like a switch blade. You should have seen her try to eat dinner with us. It was torture for everyone. Something happened…her dad died, she was stuck with her mother who was a piece of work, and maybe some other crappy things happened to her on top of that. I think Jane and some others, but particularly Jane, feels bad that she didn't interfere or stand up to her mother. For whatever reason, they didn't take care of her, and now they want to try to make it up with Kosumi. I think it's a nice gesture," Lucy sighed, "I don't think they should be beating themselves up. I don't know what they could have done for her that would have changed anything, but it's nice that they're including Kosumi. Obviously he's enjoying his time with them."

They both looked up to see Kosumi bouncing off one and then another of the men that encircled him, each of them redirecting his wild path back to the center of the circle. Rachel looked over at Scallop. Tears were streaming unnoticed down his cheeks, he was completely absorbed by his son, watching him with a smile that took him a million miles away.

"Tumbleweed Tuesday" marks a significant change in the pace of life in the Hamptons; traffic dwindles to nearly nothing, getting a cup of coffee takes under five minutes, and parking spaces in the villages are suddenly plentiful. Monday night of Labor Day weekend the lights of thousands of luxury cars form a string of pearls traveling westbound along Route 27 back to New York City. Many of those cars, and the people in them, won't return again until Memorial Day weekend of the following year. As the final stragglers leave on Tuesday morning, "local summer" kicks off. The summer folks are gone, the ocean, the docks, the quaint villages where generations of their families have grown, the beaches, and what's left of the farms and the woods of the East End are theirs once again.

"Tumbleweed Tuesday" is a day of celebration, a chance for those who worked more hours over the summer than they want to tally come together, breathe a collective sigh of relief, and raise a glass to a job well done.

Rachel had every intention of leaving with her own kind on Monday night, even though it meant subjecting both her and Eddie to hours stuck in traffic. When they'd made their "Godfather" pact, she had been fired-up to be in the office and going full throttle early on Tuesday. But after two beach days and two late nights around the fire pit laughing and talking about the mysteries of the universe, she found herself swayed by the inner voices that were telling her, "Just stay. It's only one more day. It's the end of the summer." She didn't want it to end. And by Sunday afternoon she had managed to convince herself it was ok that she stay for Tuesday. Even though she knew, deep down, it wasn't.

Scallop's plan for "Tumbleweed Tuesday" this year was the same as usual – follow tradition. He made "Tumbleweed Tuesday" sound like a major holiday, and she could see that he really wanted her to be there. She sensed that he was anxious. Well, as anxious as Scallop got. She noticed a barely perceptible shift away from his characteristic incorrigible optimism. "Tumbleweed Tuesday" would mark the end of *their* summer together and she knew he must be wondering how things might change for them as they moved into the fall. She was anxious too. She hadn't told him anything about Lauren's sabotage, her meetings, or why she had taken twenty extra minutes to get ready to go anywhere this weekend. But she saw him eyeing her shoes and clothes. He knew something was changing. Or had already changed.

They headed to Sag Harbor for the day. Every year the Southampton and Sag Harbor Fire Departments threw a joint keg party and barbeque at Sag Main Beach and then took over Murph's Tavern until everyone was partied out. Scallop and Rachel were on the beach by noon. Every time Rachel turned around someone was putting a fresh can of Bud Light into her hand. They swam and ate hamburgers with all Scallop's friends. Rachel tried to enjoy herself. But over and over again she found herself staring out at the water thinking about Sal sitting in his office shaking his head at her absence. By late afternoon she knew she shouldn't have stayed. They were packed into Murph's, with an exhausted but revelrous crew of pool cleaners, bartenders, landscapers and half a dozen guys who had set up and taken down party tents all season and she was wishing she had gone through with her "Godfather" pact. The tiny shack of a bar was so crowded it seemed to be moving.

Murph's was a little cape cod style house, once the home of a whaling captain, it had somehow managed to escape the modernization that had taken most of its neighbors. In 1976 Tom Murphy had opened a bar there and it had been a local staple ever since.

Scallop and Rachel were caught up in a ring game tournament. This too was a tradition. Murph's had seen a lot of ring game play. The simple game had come ashore with the whalers who sailed in and out of Sag Harbor in the 1700's, and landed in its permanent home on the wall of the little house. The ring game involves a simple brass ring tied to fishing line that's hung from the ceiling, and a hook screwed into the wall. The object is to gently swing the ring on the string so that it drops onto the hook and catches there. Rookie Rachel was holding her own even as she wished she were somewhere else. The ring had caught on her third swing and she was bragging and heckling Scallop, playing the good-time girl, as he lined up his swing. Scallop hadn't sensed Rachel's disquiet. She wondered how many times he'd had a Bud Light pressed into his hand in the past four hours. Before he swung the ring, he grabbed her around the waist pulling her against him in one smooth movement and whispered, "You my lady, are going down. And once I've had you here, we'll go home."

Rachel wished he weren't in such high spirits. Scallop took his turn, but as the ring swung towards the wall it was snatched in midair by a short, tough looking woman with scraggly blond hair. Her purple thong peeked out the back of her jeans where her well-worn Bon Jovi t-shirt hung on a pair of grizzled hips. She smiled drunkenly at Scallop waggling the ring in front of his face.

"Casey!" Scallop said enthusiastically. "How the hell are you? You work this summer?"

It was clear to Rachel why Scallop had asked. This woman looked like she lived a little rough.

"Oh yeah! What a shit-show of a summer right?" she said giving Rachel a once over. She could tell Casey was one of those locals who truly disliked city people. Rachel didn't react. This wasn't someone she needed to impress. "I worked the season at the Corner Bar. I'm going to stay on there, I think, for the fall. Nothing else to do really. How's your boy doing?" Casey asked smiling wide.

"He's good. Getting older that's for sure. Next time we're around I'll pop into the Corner and you can see him," Scallop said. With a look Scallop had included her in the "we", making it clear to Casey that Rachel was important.

Casey's care-creased face lit up at the offer. "I'd love that Scallop, really. Come in and have a beer. We've got crayons and coloring books for the kids. Tell him I'll let him sit up at the bar," she said eagerly. She took a swig of her beer and then leaned in towards Rachel. "This guy you got here lady, he's a good man," she squeezed Rachel's arm a little too hard then swung her focus back to Scallop, staring up at him. "As fucked up as it is, you did the right thing. I figured it out when I saw the news," Rachel felt the air around them fire with tension as every muscle in Scallop's arm became a hard coil. She looked up at his face, he was angry. And something else. Terrified. His eyes were wide with surprise. Casey saw it too. "Oh! Don't worry about it, Scallop," she said in a drunken whisper, trying to calm him, "No one else knew what happened to her, so no one else could know what you did. But I know, Scallop. It's ok I know. It made me proud of you."

The chord in Rachel's neck that always pulled when she was under extreme stress at work was stinging. Whatever this woman was talking about, it was upsetting Scallop in a way she hadn't thought possible. Casey moved closer to Scallop. They stood staring at one another for a second, and then it got worse. Scallop was standing still, not breathing. Casey reached out and grabbed his arm and as when she touched him Rachel felt Scallop gulp. She looked up to see a single tear running down his check. As though in slow motion Casey took her index finger and put it on top of Scallops lone tear, stopping it. Then she whispered firmly, "You've done what you could do. Just put it behind you. Bring the little guy in to see me. I mean it. He looks like her, doesn't he?" Casey smiled sadly and then turned around, a little unstable, and wove her way towards he bar.

Scallop and Rachel stood standing watching her kick someone off "her" seat at the bar, the noise of the party going on around them completely unnoticed. Rachel was the first to shake herself free of Casey's wake.

"What was that all about?" she asked looking up at Scallop.

"I have no idea," Scallop answered, shrugging himself back to life and looking elsewhere.

She knew he was lying. She was almost certain he'd never lied to her before. She was furious. This day was a disaster.

"You have no idea at all?" she said meanly glaring up at him, tugging his arm in an effort to get him to look at her.

"Nah," he said as he grabbed the ring to finally take his turn.

Rachel grabbed his hand, stopping his swing. "Scallop, you were crying. You can't tell me you don't know what was making you cry?"

Without looking at her, he peeled her hand off his and swung, it landed

225

on the catch with a clink, and then he looked Rachel in the eye. "I'll tell you why I was crying. Because this world can be a brutal place, Rachel. Awful things happen to people, and there are some people in the world who are useless and some who are evil. Those can both be contagious. I might be one of them you know. Let's go."

He strode towards the front door, not checking to see if she was behind him. As he passed the bar, he caught the eye of the bartender and gave him a wave that communicated he'd come back and settle his tab when the bar wasn't three thirsty people deep, and he wasn't in such a hurry to leave. He got a knowing nod in return. The exchange made Rachel's blood boil. What was she doing in a hick version of "Cheers"? What was she doing with a man who talked in new-age riddles? Her friends were all right. What kind of company was she keeping?

Moments later, they were in the pickup truck headed west down Noyac Road towards North Sea in a charged silence. Rachel seethed and Scallop popped in a tape, rewound it a bit, and attempted to start a new conversation.

"This song is called "When the Coast is Clear", it's about some dude in a seaside town finally getting to think and reconnect with himself after all the tourists go home. I listen to this song every year on this day. Otherwise I don't listen to it at all. This tape has sat in here for twenty plus years now. Getting thrown around getting coffee spilled on it, getting dropped, stepped on, snowed on; all of that, and it gets played only on this day. Today. I guess it could be worse for the tape. It could have been listened to and thrown out. Or sold. But instead it's gotten to live a long, but boring life. Imagine if you only did something one day a year? That'd be boring. But you'd look forward to Labor Day. When the coast is clear."

Rachel was in no mood to listen to the preposterous bullshit babble that was spewing from Scallop. She'd learned he had a habit of expressing touchy feely sentiments that showed his mind wasn't always firmly planted in reality. She'd found it so charming at the beginning of their relationship, but it had begun to wear on her. Using it as an emotional smokescreen made it utterly unbearable.

"Wow. Seriously? That's where you're going to go right now? The life cycle of a *cassette tape* in your *pickup*? Sorry. No. Whatever just happened back there. I'm stuck on that. And I'm not going to get unstuck until you tell me exactly what it was about."

"That was Casey Boyd," he said with a measured calm. He spoke as though he was giving her a history lesson on the fishing village they'd just left. To Rachel's ears it sounded condescending. "She's an old friend of Kachina's. Casey's a mess and always has been. How old do you think she is?" he paused for effect, as though this were a gossip session. "She's thirty-two!" Casey looked like she was heading towards fifty. "Her life is harder than most, that's why she and Kachina were buddies," he said with a sigh of resignation that read false. "She's too drunk most of the time, and strung out on meth the rest. Looks like she's maybe moved on to heroin. She looked fifteen years older than the last time I saw her three years ago. You know, she's *melodramatic*. She was melodramatic when she was fifteen. I don't know what the hell she was talking about. Honestly it's best to humor her."

Scallop was acting so strange Rachel almost couldn't maintain her level of fury out of shock and curiosity. Almost. "Come on Scallop! What was your comment about 'the world being a brutal place' and 'awful people' and you being one of them? Maybe she is melodramatic. I don't know her. But I do know you. You know *exactly* what she was talking about and it's something you don't want to tell me about."

"No I do not. Beats the hell out of me," he said, his voice dropping down. He was starting to get angry.

"What did she mean about the news? Been in the news lately? That has to ring a bell?"

She glared at him, waiting for him to answer. But he didn't say anything.

Scallop navigated the twists, turns and hills of Noyac Road for a while, biding time, as he considered what to do about both Rachel and Casey. He knew he was lucky Kachina had been such a private person. Most women would have half-a-dozen friends they confide in. Kachina had had one good friend. Casey. He had always assumed that their bond had revolved around drug use and partying. Now, too late, he realized that it had run deeper than that, and that after Kachina's death Casey had managed to put two and two together. His family was one thing. A strung-out bartender with a lot of ears to bend was entirely another. He'd always liked Casey. She was rough around the edges, but fiercely loyal. He thought she'd probably never talked about it before and might never talk about it again, but there was no way to be sure. She was a danger in a way that Lucy and his mother were not. He knew one thing, he wasn't going to add Rachel to the list of people who knew what he'd done.

He drove, mouth pressed shut, hoping that Kosumi and the twins would be at the cottage so he could figure out a way to sweep this under the rug, distract Rachel so that she'd drop it. But, as they pulled into the yard, there were no cars, and Rachel wasn't someone who was easily distracted.

They both sat in the truck staring at the cottage. Finally Rachel said dully, "Look, Eddie's going to be here in an hour and a half to pick me up. Can we please talk about this? I don't want to leave like *this*. You cried Scallop. I understand this is about Kachina, and that you don't talk about her much. Maybe you just don't talk about her much around me, I respect that. But you're lying to me and I don't like it. Actually, I won't have it."

Scallop felt like she'd given him an opening. It had never occurred to him that Rachel might think anything of his family's silence on the subject of Kachina. There were a bunch of reasons they didn't talk about her. But from the way Rachel was acting, she might think they kept mum because they were walking on eggshells around the new girl. Maybe he could use that to make this go away.

"Look," he said dismissively. "She was referring to something that happened to Kachina. That's all I'm going to say about it. Don't take this the wrong way but, it's none of your business."

Rachel erupted from the truck. "What the hell kind of statement is that?" she screamed as she slammed the door and hustled across the yard towards the house.

"It's a statement by someone who doesn't want to talk about something!" he grabbed her elbow and swung her around so he could make his point crystal clear, "It's Not. Your. Business," he said forcing her to look in his eyes as he said it slowly, as if he wanted to drill understanding into her.

Rachel was shaken. Scallop had never spoken to her like that. She pulled her arm from his grip and took a step back, regaining the upper hand as anger took her and every petty worry and mild annoyance that had been coalescing spilled out.

"You know what? What 'business' do I have being here at all in the first place? I must have lost my mind. I've worked *so fucking hard* to get to where I am! You have no idea how hard it is to get to where I have gotten, and now where am I? I might have just *thrown away my career* to go to a fucking beach party! Everything I worked the past decade for is hanging by a thread and I just stayed here for *"Tumbleweed Tuesday" at Murph's?* There's something wrong with me!"

Scallop just stood there, first surprised then shrunk by resignation and shame. He didn't say anything. He knew as he watched her lay into him that there was nowhere to go from here. He just let Rachel go on.

"Do you know why I dressed about twelve notches above everyone else at that party and the bar today? Because I almost got fired this week for those stupid pictures they took of us in Southampton a few weeks ago! They ended up in magazines that my clients and board members saw, and I've had to promise to be a 'good girl' from now on *and* be partially *supervised* by a girl who's been plotting to steal my job!" Rachel knew she was screeching but she didn't care. "I don't know what the hell that woman was talking about, but here's the thing, it doesn't matter! Because here's what that little exchange proved. I don't know who the hell you are. You don't know who the hell I am! You don't want to tell me what any of that was about? Fine. But I'm going to tell you something. I'll tell you who I am *not*. I am *not* someone stupid enough to destroy her life for someone who won't tell her the truth, is obviously irreparably fucked up, and is *so wrong for her* that he could destroy her life!"

Rachel glared at Scallop, daring him to say something. A part of her, a part that she wanted to punch, was hoping he'd say something to try and make it better. But, he didn't. He stood there looking sad and resigned, blank and beautiful, which made her even more angry. She spun on her heel and stormed inside. She packed up her bags with a violence the little cottage had never seen, ignoring things like her toothbrush and moisturizer, anything she felt she could live without. She balled up her beach cover-up and zipped up her weekend bag. She could feel Scallop in the doorway behind her. She could feel his heartbreak enter the room.

"Rachel, I know that all your friends have been looking at us and saying 'when is she going to stop being amused by this whole scene?' I know that's what most people are expecting. It's what *I'm expecting* for the love of God. Do you think for one second that I didn't have a pretty good idea this moment was coming? You can blame it on whatever you think you heard tonight, but that's not it. And you know it. So, go ahead, go back to your life. Make your friends happy, make your boss happy, make that crazy lady with the stupid fucking watch and insane bracelets happy. I hope it makes *you* happy," he reached around her and took her bag to carry it out. He put his hand on her back. "I was beginning to think that you could be happy here. But I was wrong."

Rachel was furious. He wasn't even going to try to get her to stay? He wasn't going to man up and explain? She really was an idiot. "Yup. You were wrong," she spat, taking back her bag, "and you know what, I *will* make them happy because they tell me the truth! Even when it costs them something! Is there even anything major behind what that woman said, or is it just all part of this absurd melodrama your family has? Your mother and sister baby you! They think you're steps from the looney bin. Do you know that they think this bullshit minimalism you espouse is the key to keeping you from going cuckoo? 'Scallop needs this. Scallop needs that. We all need to court financial ruin so that Scallop can spend his days putting up fences, fixing tractors and talking to the sun!' It's a fiction that gives all your lives *some purpose*. Here's the reality; when all is said and done, you're a really handsome, really nice, earthy *dope* who knocked up a basket case and lives in a shack at age forty. Your family will ruin themselves for you. I won't. It's time for me to get out of here."

Scallop swept up her bags with a sudden violence that pushed her backwards even though he hadn't touched her. "Don't tell me anything about my mother and my sister. Leave my family out of this. Stop talking right now. It's time for you to go." He took her bags outside and stacked them in a pile at in the middle of the yard as she followed him stunned. Without looking at her again he brushed past her. He made it to his truck in fewer steps than she thought possible, turned on the ignition and backed out, tires squealing.

"Jesus," Rachel screamed at herself internally, "how did I not realize that I was living in an episode of 'The Dukes of Hazard?'"

Ten minutes later she was in an Uber driven by a sixteen-your-old who looked like she imagined Scallop had in high school. Thinking that he'd probably be living in a spot just like this when he was forty, embroiled in a small-town family drama of his own, she yanked out her phone and used voice to text to send a message to Easy Eddie.

Meet me at the GD Starbucks in Manorville!

The next morning, Scallop sat cross-legged floating on his paddle board. Seven thirty, the time he'd promised Lucy he'd pick Kosumi up had passed unheeded an hour ago. He ran his hand absently across the marsh grasses of Conscience Point as the light dwindled. He thought of everything he'd attempted in his life that had ended in failure. A business selling fresh fish he'd caught when he was eleven, organizing a surf club when he was in high school, his brief interest in becoming a veterinarian before his Guidance Counselor had clued him in on the type of grades he'd have to have to make it happen. It was as if each time he had some enthusiasm and momentum in life, an impediment would arise and he was unable to adjust. That was the pattern. It was just repeating. The toadfish had taken a bite out of him today. His thoughts flowed backwards in time like the outgoing tide behind him.

29: In the Name of the Mother

The morning after Kachina was laid to rest, Scallop woke before dawn, packed a bag then drove to the reservation. His sister had been caring for Kosumi since he'd rushed out of the farmhouse when he'd gotten the call from the police asking him to come to Conscience Point. They thought they had found Kachina. Lucy hadn't said anything, and he hadn't said anything. They had silently agreed that it was best if she kept Kosumi. For now.

Scallop hadn't been anywhere near the reservation either. He hadn't returned to Kachina's trailer since he'd been there to help his friend John, who'd been assigned to her case, to look into signs of foul play, but they all knew there was none. Scallop knew everyone on the police force. Most of them he'd known his whole life. He was grateful that it was John who went with him. Not someone who'd grown up on the reservation. He was angry right now.

He was going to let that trailer rot. It never should have been anyone's home in the first place. June could clear it out if she wanted. He doubted anyone would do any more with it than they'd done with Kachina. Kachina's mother had made sure that everyone gave that place a wide berth, leaving it, and Kachina, alone. He imagined they were sorry now. But it was too damned late for that. He knew. He was sorry too.

It was a wet gray dawn with mist coming up off the water, and up from the hurricane-soaked ground. Scallop knelt between the graves of Kachina and her father Jonas as the sun rose over the ocean behind him, lighting the mist, but not yet chasing it away. The early November frost wet his jeans. He sat in a tense silence of his own making before he began to speak.

"Kachina, I hope your father's love can heal you. I know you are enjoying your reunion. Last night I dreamed of you and you were dancing across the sky. I guess your spirit is free now, my dancer. And even though it causes me some pain I'm happy for you. I want you to know I don't blame you for what you did. I understand the damage one human being can inflict on another. But when the life of an innocent is destroyed there should be a price to be paid. Someone should have exacted that price for you long ago."

He stood and put on his backpack.

"Kachina, my mother and Lucy are watching Kosumi. They'll do a great job with him today, as they always do. I can't be with Kosumi today but I promise you I will care for him as both a mother and a father would. Today, I have some business to take care of. I know you'll be watching me, and I want you to know that I've thought about this, and my conscience is pointing me in a clear direction. I don't know if you'd think what I'm doing is wrong. I don't know if I'd done this earlier if it would have freed you to be Kosumi's mother in the way I always believed you could be, and you never believed you could be. I'm sure you'd tell me not to do it. I don't need your approval, I'm not here to ask for it."

"Our blood is bound together. Kosumi is our bond. I don't know if there's some ritual cleansing that I could do to remove the shadow of your pain from Kosumi. I can only do what I know how to do, serve bloodshed with bloodshed, meet terror with terror. I'll be back here this evening."

The train to Penn Station left at 6:22 AM. He knew it was unlikely that he'd see anyone he knew on the train. Not many people commute from Southampton in November. But he sat by himself and kept his head down. Certainly no one would be looking for him on the train. He hadn't set foot in Manhattan since a field trip in middle school to the Museum of Natural History in 1988. At 8:30 the train pulled in and he found his way through the maze of the station, disgusted by the smell. It felt like a cesspool. The whole city felt like a sewer to him. Why would anyone do this every day? He emerged on 8th Avenue and was swept into the crowds of rushing people, who unapologetically bumped one another with their bags and coffee cups. First, he headed east and south, stopping to pick up breakfast and a coffee cup that would help him blend in at one of the several Starbucks along the way near Herald Square. Early that morning he'd tucked his hair up under a Yankees cap and grabbed a pair of sunglasses out of the cardboard box in the office that overflowed with the crap the summer people had left behind on the farm stand counter. He had on a black hooded windbreaker, jeans, gloves to warm his hands, and a maroon backpack, all of which he'd purchased the day before at Target in Bridgehampton. The gloves felt strange. No matter how dirty a task was, he never wore gloves. He liked to feel what he was doing. He guessed he was about to do the one task dirty enough to require gloves.

He ate standing at a packed counter, and when he'd finished his breakfast he continued to make his way east, stopping to buy a copy of the New York Post. He sat down to read it on a bench on East 19th Street between Park and Irving. He was watching the entry to the building across the street, 121 East 19th. It was a smaller commercial building, with no doorman. People came and went. He spotted a few sets of scrubs underneath overcoats and a few suits. Everyone else who came in or out looked like your basic New Yorker; black coats and black clothing with a little denim mixed in. At 11 AM, Scallop got up, put on his gloves, walked across the street and entered 121. He scanned the directory of occupants as he passed it. No one would have thought he'd looked that way. His training had kicked in, and his mind was working with precision. Some doctor's offices, a couple of dentists, some media and graphic design outfits – no security firms or investigators, no one who might be watching because that's what they did. He passed the elevators and opened the gray steel door to the staircase. He stopped on the 9th floor and entered the hallway. The second door read "Frears Management" in bold gold lettering. The door was open and Scallop walked right in. The office was not large, there was a reception area with modern furniture and fresh flowers and walls filled with magazine covers and blown up photos of fashion shots. Beyond that there was an office accessed through glass French doors. The doors with masked with pricey blinds on the inside.

Today the reception desk was empty, and the doors to the office were wide open. Scallop had known there would be no receptionist that day. Ted Frears had texted his receptionist Jake early in the day to say he wasn't coming in and Jake could take the day off. Jake thought nothing of it, it was a fairly frequent occurrence. One of the perks of his job. He'd never wondered why his boss didn't need him on occasion. He was there to look cute, be perky, and make the girls Ted represented comfortable with a swish and a smile. He needed to shop frequently to look that cute, and these days off allowed him to get in some quality shopping.

Ted was expecting his new client at eleven o'clock. He'd been working on her for some time. He'd made his usual reservation at The Bluewater Grill. Taryn Reilly was her name. It irked Frears that he had trouble remembering it. He might have to change it.

He hadn't taken on a new client in several months. He'd been busy representing his current stable of twenty-two models. Since he'd split with his partners a few years back, he'd been keeping his numbers down. Their business had become so large that the office needed to be manned on the weekends. There had been too much overhead, and too many eyes and ears with not enough to occupy their curiosity. He'd left. Now he had control over his space, his time, and his staff, but that also meant that his business needed his daily attention and input. It was just him and his assistant. He sent the emails, scheduled the jobs, negotiated the fees. He was good at his job and at managing wagging tongues. Despite his genteel appearance he talked tough, people thought it was his way of driving a hard bargain. His reputation was spotless.

Scallop knew all about the changes in Frears' business structure. He'd read the emails, seen the contracts, and knew the details of the schedule. Although Frears was oblivious, Scallop knew that Taryn Reilly's eleven o'clock appointment had been cancelled earlier that morning. Jake had sent an email earlier in the morning rescheduling. Frears wasn't feeling well that day.

Scallop's buddy Steve had been part of the geek squad that supported their SEAL unit in Afghanistan. They'd made an unlikely pair. Still did. Steve worked in cyber security in the city now. He'd made a special trip out to Southampton the day before to attend the funeral of Scallop's girlfriend. As he walked to the church he taken a second to toss a thick manila envelope under the bench seat of Scallop's truck. Then, first thing that morning, he'd saved Taryn Reilly from a lunch date she'd never forget. It had been too easy to get into Frears email to be any fun, but Steve felt good about it anyway. The poor girl looked like a sweetheart.

"I'm looking for Ted Frears," Scallop said, his deep voice low and controlled.

"I am Ted Frears," Ted said before looking up and taking off his glasses to give Scallop a once over. Ted Frears looked almost exactly as Kachina had described him, fit, smooth, impeccably dressed and on the short side. The glasses were new, and his hair was an attractive salt and pepper gray. There had been quite a few pictures of him in the envelope Steve had dropped. Scallop imagined the gray was the one concession Frears had made to the years. Clearly, he didn't draw the line at Botox, but he must have drawn it at hair dye. Frears took in Scallop's height, build and, as Scallop removed the sunglasses, his remarkably handsome face, and lifted his eyebrows, pleasantly surprised. He could use Scallop.

"Hunh", he said, nonchalantly. "Not too bad. You're here to leave me your photos? We don't take walk-ins, as we've posted in all the listings. But, I always need guys like you for print work, and I like that you're making the rounds. Shows initiative. If you want an appointment, leave your headshot on my assistant's desk out there, and if I'm interested, we'll call you," Frears said, as he put his glasses on and went back to his computer.

"I'm here to talk about Kachina Rodgers." Frears looked up confused. He didn't remember Kachina. Then, Scallop saw him recognize the name.

"Ah! Kachina Rodgers. She was supposed to be the next big thing, she met with me once, and then dropped off the face of the planet. Did she refer you or something?"

"You could say that," Scallop said, his eyes scanning the room. There was no surveillance system. He supposed Frears didn't want activities in his office recorded.

"Huh. She was just trashy enough to be interesting. Earthy. Great look, great lay," he said with a leer, "but dumb as a doorknob. She a *friend*?"

Frears smiled obscenely at Scallop, his teeth had begun to separate with age, his incisors pointy and predatory. Scallop knew in that moment that he needn't have gone to the trouble of researching Frears and arguing with his own conscience. This was a person without value. This man was a toadfish. There was only one thing to be done.

Scallop had hoped that the contents of the manila envelope would contain evidence that Ted Frears had turned over a new leaf. He wasn't sure what Ted could have done that would have compensated for the wrong he'd done Kachina. Donated a wing to a children's hospital? Spent every moment of his free time cooking soup at a homeless shelter? At the very least, not lured another young girl to his office and sent her on her way a shell of her former self. But the envelope had overflowed with proof that what had happened to Kachina was a regular occurrence, a hobby that had never caused Frears any trouble his lawyer and a few thousand dollars couldn't get him out of. Scallop stared down at him coldly. He wasn't going to answer Frears questions about

Kachina. He wasn't going to give this man the gift of understanding why he'd be leaving the planet momentarily.

Like a feral dog, Ted had sensed a dangerous current in the room. "Give my best to your reservation trailer trash friend and leave the headshot. If you know of any other young hotties I can fuck, let me know. If they need another Marlboro Man, you'll be my first call."

Scallop moved around the desk before Frears realized what was happening. He grabbed, him, spun him around, and with great precision and force snapped his neck. He'd been trained to do this. He had enough experience to know Frears was dead without having to check. He dragged him across the room, opened the window, and tossed him out with such force that the body arced out over 19th street before it landed on the roof of a parked car.

Scallop stepped back from the window, and turned and left the office, putting his sunglasses on as he left. On the landing between the sixth and seventh floors, he opened his backpack. Inside the backpack was another, this one black, and a change of clothes. He took off everything he was wearing, putting his hat, gloves and coat, in the red backpack, and changed into the other set of equally unremarkable clothes. He left the building, and glanced at the growing crowd of horrified people circling the car where Frears body lay. One woman was on the phone with the police. He didn't stop to look. He'd watched an episode of some cop show once while keeping his dad company. He made his way uptown.

He zigzagged his way up to the Metropolitan Museum of art, the one and only place in Manhattan he'd ever been interested in seeing. He stared blindly at the Dutch masters for a couple of hours and then caught a 6:40 train back to Southampton.

That evening back at North Sea Farms, Lucy had never been so relieved to hear her brother's crumby old truck pull into the gravel driveway at the farm. For the past hour she'd been reading the same page of the battered copy of "Anne of Green Gables" she used to read to the girls, hoping it would calm her. She'd put little Kosumi to bed an hour ago. Earlier that week, when it had become clear that Scallop was in no condition to be his primary caretaker, she and her mom had resurrected a crib from the attic and set up in her room. They had been taking turns caring for the little guy, carrying Kosumi around with them in a baby backpack as they did their chores, buttoning up the farm for the winter.

Scallop had barely spoken since he'd gone to the beach to identify Kachina. He had fallen back into the morose rhythm he'd lived by when he'd come home from the service. But this time there was an undercurrent of fury to his disengagement. And this time he was not living at home, where they could keep an eye on him. He hadn't taken Kosumi back to his cottage with him once since it had happened.

Lucy could understand the sadness, but Scallop was so furious, that when he walked into a room she felt compelled to move away from him. Where was the anger coming from? Was it directed at Kachina? Although Lucy felt bad about it, she knew in her heart that Kosumi and Scallop would be far better off in the long run without the instability and drama that Kachina had inflicted on those who were foolish enough to let her into their lives. Hurricane Kachina.

Her mother said Scallop just needed a little bit of time. But she didn't believe it, and she didn't think her mother did either. Scallop had been gone all day and she knew he hadn't been at home either. She'd swung by his cottage with Kosumi earlier hoping to catch him. He hadn't been there and though she felt like she was being the worst kind of big sister she walked around to the back of the cottage to check the position of his stuff. His boards, boats and bikes were all in the same place they'd been for days. He wasn't using the things he needed to cope.

She threw on her robe, hoping that Scallop would come up to see Kosumi. But as she knotted it she heard the big door to the barn roll open. What was he doing in there? She decided to go down and make him a cup of tea. She'd catch him on his way out and try to get him to sit down and talk, ask him to make a plan for how he was going to care for his son. She put the kettle on by the stove light, not wanting to turn on all the lights and scare Scallop away. As she waited for it to boil, she kept a steady eye on the door to the barn. Like her, Scallop hadn't turned on the large fluorescent lights. Just the small lamp on the inside of the door. At first Lucy wasn't sure, it could have been Scallop's breath, or maybe he'd pulled his truck into the barn. But then the smoke drifting past the light became thick enough, and persistent enough for Lucy to be sure it was caused by fire. She turned off the stove and ran for the barn.

She didn't know what she expected to find when she got there, but Scallop feeding a pair of pants into a smoking metal barrel was not it.

"Scallop!", she shouted, surprising herself by clapping her hands loudly to get his attention. "What the hell are you doing?"

Scallop stared blankly at her then peeled his shirt off and tossed it in the barrel.

"What the *hell* are you *doing*?" she repeated. There was a terrible plastic smell in the smoke. She walked around beside Scallop to get upwind, and peered into the barrel covering her mouth and nose with her hand. Through the flames, she could see the remnants of two backpacks. She looked up at Scallop. He was a blank. The anger was gone. A wave of panic washed over Lucy. Whose clothes was Scallop burning? It hadn't occurred to her before that Scallop might have played any other part in Kachina's death than the lover left behind after a suicide. But now she was terrified he'd played a very different part. People burned clothes because they'd killed someone, she'd watched

236

enough "Law and Order" to know that.

"Scallop, you need to tell me what the hell this is. Right now. Whose clothes are those?"

"They're my clothes," Scallop said.

"*Those* are your clothes," she said pointing at his regular fall gear sitting on a tractor seat behind him; a long sleeve t-shirt, a faded navy chamois, and a down vest that was probably from the 80's. "Did you go shopping today and then decide to burn everything you bought because it wasn't 'you'? *Those* are *not* your clothes," she said, staring him down.

"Well, I wore them," he said.

"Why?"

"I needed to go into the city."

That surprised her. As far as she knew Scallop had never voluntarily gone into New York City. And what could that possibly have to do with Kachina? Maybe nothing. Kachina had died during a hurricane, and Scallop was burning some completely pristine clothing and what looked like brand new backpacks. He didn't kill *her* in those. She felt like she was going to vomit. Something was desperately wrong with her brother.

"What for? Why did you go into the city?"

"To go to the Met. I needed to look at something beautiful and I thought I'd look nice doing it."

"And then you'd burn it all down?" She realized she was starting to get a little hysterical. "Scallop, there's only one reason people like you burn clothing."

She'd seen every side of Scallop. Her brother had dark parts that she didn't understand. She didn't think he understood them either. She didn't want to think it, but there was a chance he had gone completely off the deep end and this was chapter one of his serial killer saga. She had to help him, and for her to help, she had to know what he'd done.

"Scallop, tell me where you were and what you've done or so help me God, I will call John and tell him to drive his squad car over here and take a look in our barn. Tell me. Right now."

"I killed the man who raped Kachina. It happened a long time ago. She was a beautiful young girl, a teenager, not much younger than Olga and Veronica. She was a good girl like them too. But she didn't have anyone. She didn't have you or us. She wasn't always the way you saw her. She was fierce, and free, and *clean*. A scumbag modeling agent raped her and first she ruined herself because of it, and then she killed herself because of it. I paid him back today. I broke his neck and tossed him out the window."

Lucy fainted.

"Luce, Luce!" Scallop's voice was an annoying protrusion on the heavy buzzing in her brain as she came to in the flatbed of Scallop's truck behind the barn, the cold of the metal burning through her robe. She could feel him leaning over her. She opened her eyes and sat up pushing him to the side, gulping the clean cold air. She reassembled her brain. She could fix this. She turned to him and pulled his face close to hers.

"Walter Kozlowski, you listen to me. Here's what you're going to do. You are going to be *happy* now. Do you understand me? You're going to give that little boy so much love that he won't know what to do with himself. You're going to leave her, and everything else you've been through behind, and you're going to be one hundred percent a part of this family. That's it. That's *all* you're going to do. You will do everything you need to do every day to live a happy healthy life. I will help you. I will help you until the time anything you've done today puts my children or your child in danger. Then I will turn you in."

Scallop nodded down at her, looking suddenly sad.

"Are you satisfied now?" she asked quietly "Can you let this go?"

Scallop was sitting with legs crossed silently watching the smoke blow out across their field. He didn't answer.

"Tell me you don't have some bullshit plan to go spread the ashes of those clothes all over the grave?"

Scallop nodded speechlessly. How had her beautiful little brother become so warped? "Of course, that's what you were going to do. You were going to sprinkle evidence all over her grave! What's your plan for that barrel? Make sure you leave it right where Pedro will find it, so he'll have the mystery of a bunch of melted plastic to solve. I'm taking that to the dump tomorrow. Did you do any of this smart? I thought you were trained for this kind of thing, but it doesn't look like it to me. Are they going to find you?"

"No," Scallop said with certainty. He looked at her, annoyed she though he was foolish enough to get caught. "Kachina told almost no one what happened. It's been years since they had any contact. No one will ever make the connection. There were no cameras, no witnesses, there will be no fingerprints. I didn't research from here or anywhere near here. A friend who's an expert did it. I don't think it will come back to our family. I know you don't believe me, but I want nothing more than to take care of Kosumi now. To be a good Dad. To take his special spirit and make sure that it's safe."

Lucy could see that he meant it. She wasn't sure he'd be able to do it though. "That's what you're going to do then. Let everything else go and just be here with your boy. If I ever think you might do something like this again, I won't hesitate to call someone Scallop. You need to do what you need to do to be well. There are people who need you to be put together. You need you to be put together."

The trouble was she believed that even when you did a terrible thing for a terribly good reason, the net was still terrible. Her brother had killed someone. Not because he was defending himself, not because he was defending his country, but for revenge. He was unbalanced. Could daily workouts and a measured life keep him on an even keel?

30: Uptown Girl Stops by Woods on a Not So Snowy Evening

Rachel woke up the next morning with a clanging headache. Nevertheless, she launched herself out of her bed, took two Tylenol and showered, it was time to move past yesterday.

The kid in the Uber had dropped her at Starbucks. Rather than have another colossal meltdown buying a latte, she walked across the street to the shopping plaza and bought herself two bottles of pinot noir, a cork screw, and a plastic cup at the liquor store. Easy Eddie found her fuming at a picnic table by the burger truck permanently parked next to Starbucks. She was two thirds of the way through the first bottle of wine and using the bottle opener to stab a pattern into the picnic table.

"Woah, I don't know which is worse Darlin', the slobbery crying the last time I got you here, or *this shit show.* Get in the car before anyone sees you."

She'd insisted on watching "The Godfather" as planned and sat intermittently sipping and grinding her teeth all the way home. When Eddie tried to get a conversation going she shut him down, telling him to pay attention to the road. Once at her apartment he'd taken her bags out of the trunk and stacked them on the curb, then patted her on the shoulder, "Goodnight Princess. Don't let that pea grind away at your beauty sleep. You're back in the palace now. Be happy! That freaking shack never suited you. And the guy? A new-age dope!"

"Thanks for coming to get me Eddie, but that does not help," she'd said in her most formal voice, knowing and not caring that it would piss him off. The night doorman had helped her upstairs with all her bags, and as soon as she'd closed the door behind him she pulled off her clothes angrily and threw herself on the bed in her underwear. She didn't want anything touching her, not even clothes.

She was livid with herself for being so hurt. She rubbed at the lump in her throat as she listened to the hum of the central air conditioning and the distant sounds of the street twenty-seven floors below. Her hand was itching to pick up her phone and call Lucy and tell her about the argument. But she knew Lucy would try to present some perfectly rational reason why Scallop had acted the way he had. Or she'd tell her some sob story that would convince Rachel to let the whole thing go. She didn't want to. She didn't want to be distracted from the fact that he was lying to her. She didn't want to be distracted from the way he'd treated her. That, and she had a niggling feeling that Lucy hadn't been honest with her about Kachina. She couldn't think why she felt that way, but it was there. Everyone had been so tight lipped about her. No one had ever told her anything more substantial than "she was a beautiful mess". Why was she so rarely mentioned to Kosumi? No, she wasn't going to call Lucy. She was going figure out what that woman had been talking about on her own. First though she was going to drink some more wine and cry. But tears didn't come. Every part of her insides ached, from the lump in her throat, to her chest exhausted from holding her breath the whole ride home, to other parts of her that were already missing Scallop.

Spurred by the ache, she jumped off the bed and started flipping through the suits in her closet. She knew that whatever she might discover about what Scallop was hiding it wasn't going to make any difference. She was going to put her career back together. She was going to get back to what she should have been doing the whole summer. She was going to go into Tallmadge and assess the damage she'd done with this escapade, and find her way back to the pinnacle of her career. She picked out a killer suit and blouse, pulled out a pair of Jimmy Choo's, washed her face and took half a sleeping pill.

When Easy Eddie arrived in the morning, he took her and her resting bitch face in as he opened the car door for her. "That's my girl", he said, "time to go kick some ass and take some names! Good for you! That schmuck in the shack was sapping your mojo. I sure am glad to see you in your Jimmy Choo's looking hot as a hammer. Let's go get 'em."

Despite herself she blushed.

At Tallmadge, she made a show of stopping as she crossed the floor, batting banter with her guys as they inappropriately ogled her, and scanning the room for Lauren, hoping she was somewhere taking notice before she bee-lined for her office and shut the door. She grabbed the coffee that was waiting for her on the desk and downed it as she sat down to work. How many coffees had gone in the garbage this summer when she hadn't made it into the office?

She heard her office door swing open. Lauren, dressed perfectly in an impossibly tight black pencil skirt and matching blouse, strode in and put her hand on her hip. "Rachel! Management meeting upstairs, I told Tallmadge I'd come down and get you, since you're in today," she said with a beautiful smile and a sneer in her voice that she couldn't mask. Rachel just starred at her, holding Lauren's gaze long enough to convey that she knew exactly who and what Lauren was.

"I'll be up in a minute, Lauren. Nice to see you, can you grab me a fresh coffee on your way up?" Lauren looked like she'd swallowed a mosquito. It was the only time Rachel had ever seen her look unattractive. She dug in harder, "Oh! And I saw your notes on the Illinois Teacher's Association passing on us. I think I can take care of that. I actually know the President, we played soccer together in fifth grade. Why don't we give her a call together after the meeting?"

Rachel watched as Lauren tried to control herself. She even felt a little sorry for her knowing what was coming for her. She'd crush her in the meeting. She'd put it all together before she came in. Smaller accounts Lauren hadn't gotten over the summer that Rachel knew she could easily get with a phone call, emails to clients in which Lauren had meant to undermine Rachel but also succeeded in undermining the company, and a screenshot of a social media post that could have been construed as an SEC violation. That was all it would take. By the end of the day Lauren would be making her unsteady way out of the building under a pile of shopping bags that held the contents of her office and a cloud of SEC induced anxiety.

Rachel watched her close the door to her office and then hopped on the chat application of the Bloomberg terminal and found her friend, Heddy Lesslaw the Headhunter.

RACHEL JONES (TALLMADGE CAPITAL): Bill's?

Rachel knew she'd be quick to respond. Heddy had been trying to convince her to make a move for a year now. Why not? Rachel was a sure thing for Heddy. She was top of her field and infinitely employable. Heddy could have Rachel at a different hedge fund in a few weeks at the same or better draw, and she stood to make a decent chunk for herself in the process.

HEDDY LESSLAW (OPPORTUNITIES GROUP): When?
RACHEL JONES: Tomorrow? Late lunch or early drinks? I don't care.

Three floors up, the glass-walled conference room was already filled with the senior level employees of Tallmadge. Everyone was already in their seats. A few of Rachel's colleagues were staring at their cell phones pretending to send one last urgent text or email before the meeting officially began. Her chair was waiting for her. Rachel was unsurprised to find that the coffee she'd asked Lauren for was not. She could see they were waiting for her to begin, but she took a moment to lean over a nearby cubicle that belonged to an analyst she knew had a propensity for gossip and ask him to bring her a coffee in a few minutes. She breezed in to the conference room and took a seat, smiling at Lauren who had been invited to the meeting for the first time, her betrayal had earned her a seat at the table. When she opened the door, Rachel hit a wall of tension. She knew exactly why it was there.

She looked across the table at Tallmadge. He looked sunken. It had been years since he'd been at one of these meetings in the summer. He'd limited his presence to the February and January meetings when it was too cold for him to be outside, and the rest of the year he let Rachel and Sal run the meetings. He'd trusted them. Both he and the tension that pervaded the room were here because they'd lost over eleven percent of their clients over the summer. Rachel knew this was largely her fault. Looking around the room she felt sick to her stomach. She had let Tallmadge down. She had let everyone else in the room down too. She hadn't been herself all summer. That, and the mess Lauren had made had led to the biggest single quarter decline in Tallmadge's business in a decade.

She settled herself in her chair, placing her elbows on the stack of bound reports she'd picked up in the copy room on her way upstairs. She caught Sal's attention and subtly pointed at herself, silently asking him to let her take the lead. Then she smiled around the table until she locked eyes with Tallmadge.

Irritated, at her apparent cluelessness the old man cleared his throat and pulled himself towards the front of his chair.

"Well, I guess we'd better get started," he said awkwardly, not quite knowing how to take charge after so long away from the reigns.

Rachel took advantage of the open air and jumped in.

"Yes, I think we'd better. I'm sorry I did not get you all my agenda earlier, but I had a last-minute change of plan," she said, all confidence. She stood and with repeated rapid-fire movements slid a copy of the bound reports across the table towards each of her colleagues.

"Before we move into our regularly scheduled program, I want to say something; I owe you all an apology," she said, looking pointedly at Tallmadge, and pausing long enough for it to land on everyone. "I have not been at my best this summer. I want to start by saying, I'm sorry for that. I haven't been eating it up like I usually do, and I see now that I can't allow that to happen. I don't have a good excuse, other than to say that everyone has ebbs and flows. I guess *this* was my first ebb. Let's all hope it's my last, because it seems that my ebbs translate to an ebb for the company."

As she looked around, guilt, blame and anger looked back at her in equal parts. She knew everyone had noticed her disengagement. She also knew that in many cases her colleagues had used her disengagement to justify taking a step back themselves while others had actively used it to try to gain an advantage for themselves.

"So, let's take a good look at what happened this summer. Open those packets I just gave you please. I kept it simple, no spreadsheets today, just simple lists. The first page and a half is a list of clients that we lost this summer, and who was handling them." Rachel paused for effect, and for everyone around the table to read through the list. She knew what they'd find, their own names, next to accounts they'd lost. Her name was there twice, most people's names were there more than that, and Lauren's name was there most often. She'd made sure to arrange the list so that Lauren's name was next to every client on the second page. It was a page comprised entirely of Lauren's treachery and incompetence. A ripple of dismay flowed through the room as people read that second page.

"So, what the hell happened?!", Rachel asked emphatically. "I'll tell you how I lost those two accounts; my clients felt ignored. That's all. And it looks a bit to me like you all ignored your clients too. Just to be clear, it's not my job to nurture the clients that I hand over to all of you – it's yours. But I usually do it. This list is what happens when I don't."

She paused and waited for someone to argue with her. No one did.

Tallmadge had stopped looking exhausted, and was sitting back in his chair, enjoying the show. His girl was back.

"Page one," she said, making it sound like a question, "will all be back as of this afternoon, I can guarantee it." She nodded at Tallmadge, so he knew it was a promise.

"Page two is different. I can't promise we can get those clients back because we lost them for a different reason. Lauren," she said, half looking at Lauren as she pretended to scrutinize the list for effect, "why do you think you lost all these clients?", she asked plainly.

Lauren gripped the report, her fingernails turning bright red beneath her French manicure. She glared at Rachel and replied in the same measured manner she'd learned from the mentor she'd just spent the summer trying to marginalize. "I don't know," she said, haughtily, "and anyway I think you want to tell me."

"You're right. I do," Rachel said, allowing her own anger to come through so that Lauren would know, without a doubt, that she was coming for her.

"At the top of that list is Stewart Campbell. You *all* know who Stewart is," she said as amused murmurs and snide looks passed around the table. Stewart Campbell's status as one of the company's top clients coupled with his awkwardness, and his ability to make others feel awkward made him a Tallmadge legend. Rachel nodded around the table in conference with her colleagues and then glared at Lauren, leaning backwards slightly like a cobra about to strike. "*They* know not only who he is, but they know *how* he is," she said at Lauren. "All of these people know how to handle themselves with Stewart. In fact, I'm certain that you remember the coaching I gave you in May, specifically addressing how to walk the line with Stewart? What were my three Stewart rules? Be kind, ask *him* questions, and don't tell him anything personal. Remember, discussing this? Do you remember why I told you not to tell him anything personal?" Lauren gave a slight, sullen nod.

"MmmHm!" Rachel said. "I told you that because if you give Stewart personal details, he misinterprets your relationship. I knew you remembered. That's why I was so surprised when I heard through the grapevine last week that Stewart had been seen at the office of Risearch Capital. He was shopping around our competition! Stewart *looooves* us," Rachel said dramatically, her anger beginning to break through her veneer of professionalism. "There's only one reason Stewart would be there. Someone here compromised our relationship with him."

At the end of the table Tallmadge's wrinkled hands rubbed his face in frustration. He could see what he'd done. Lauren had taken him in. He'd been the one to hand Stewart to Lauren. Rachel barreled on, "I could only imagine it was you Lauren, since you'd been tasked to be his account manager, as a reward I suppose. I called him. Lauren, did you really accept a social dinner invitation from Stewart? Did you actually *do that?* How did you imagine that was going to end? Not only did you break the cardinal rule of not dating clients, or people in the industry, you decided to break protocol with *Stewart?*" Lauren was turning red; she clearly knew better than to answer Rachel who seemed to be taking up every molecule of available space in the conference room. "You," Rachel said slowly, "knew perfectly well, that I had already gone down that road with Stewart. That I had repaired an awkward moment in our relationship with Stewart after he had gotten the wrong end of the stick and asked me out. Were you just trying to take it a step further by actually going out with him to see if you could do it better than me? That would be sick. Were you using your position as a gold-digging platform? Or were you just entrusted with a client who was above your paygrade and you weren't skilled enough to handle him?" Rachel let the questions hang in the air for a moment, knowing she wouldn't get an answer. Tallmadge shifted uncomfortably in his chair knowing the last question had been, in part, directed at him.

"Regardless of why you did it, it didn't end well, Lauren. You went out with Stewart and it became immediately clear to him that you had an ulterior motive, because despite being socially awkward, he's remarkably insightful. You hurt his feelings. You hurt Stewart's feelings and you made a lot of the other clients on this list unnecessarily uncomfortable. In some cases, it was because you tried to throw me under the bus. In some cases, you tried to make yourself so important in the client's eyes that you made it seem like you were the only operator at Tallmadge. Our clients want to feel as if a qualified team of experts are handling their billions. You know that. But you tossed everything I taught you in the garbage because you thought you knew better. You lost these clients by degrading the value of this company in our client's eyes with your behavior."

Rachel took a deep breath and looked around the table. There was an air of discomfort that she needed to reign in before she finished. She needed everyone to be on her side when she finished this.

"So, everyone," she said, pulling back her intensity for a second, "what is this business about?" Everyone at the table knew the answer to that question, and they knew that when asked, you said it out loud. "Trust." They all said firmly.

"Yup," said Rachel. "This business is one hundred percent about trust. I trusted *you,*" she said turning back to Lauren, "and I handed you some of my clients. Somehow you must have gotten confused about where "trust" fits in here. You wanted those clients to stop trusting *me* and *trust you instead*. That's not what it's about by the way. You told them pretty little stories about my little incompetencies, hoping that a shared laugh over what I wore to a social event would create a bond. Here's the thing about a framework of trust, you can't "reconfigure" it; if you pick at trust, it simply breaks down. *You broke our clients trust in us,*" she said, her hard gaze never leaving Lauren. Lauren's eyes roamed the table, hoping to find a friendly glimmer in return, before they dropped to the table.

"Stewart won't be leaving us; I spoke with him this morning. We had a lovely chat. In fact, Burnham Tallmadge, he'll be out to look at the Fall flora on your island next weekend. I've also spoken to several of the other clients on this second, who are clients once again, and relieved to have each and everyone one of you *besides* Lauren helping them. Hopefully the bulk will be back with us by the end of the week." Rachel said, to Tallmadge who looked angry as a hornet willing to sacrifice his life for a well-deserved sting. He flipped the report closed and gathered himself to speak. She knew exactly what he was going to say, she'd heard him say it a hundred times, and in a hundred different ways. This time he stood when he said it, his blue shirt crisp, his thin grey hair slicked back and perfectly in place despite his agitation.

"Integrity. Discretion. Service. THAT is who we are. THAT is what we do. Our clients can go many places for a return on their investment. They come to us for integrity, discretion and service, and when they don't find it, they go elsewhere." He looked at Rachel, then at Sal, both of them nodded sharply in agreement with his motto. It was what he expected, what everyone around the table knew he expected. Lauren kept her head bowed.

"Miss," his voice dropping as he went in for the sting, "you do *not* have integrity, nor do you have discretion, and it seems that you serve only your own ambition. Trevor will go with you to your desk while you pack. Best of luck to you finding a position at a firm where loyalty isn't a prerequisite for employment."

Trevor popped out of his chair and practically frolicked to hold the glass door open for Lauren. Lauren stood slowly, cold eyes pulsing with a hate Rachel didn't think she deserved, before she turned and stared straight ahead as Trevor smiled sarcastically at her, motioning her through the doorway. Rachel didn't think she would ever forget watching Trevor skip down the hallway behind Lauren as she haughtily hauled ass to pack up her desk. It was priceless.

At seven pm, Aaron brought her the dinner she had ordered and she told him he could go home. His job had been pretty cushy so far. Poor kid, he didn't know what long hours he was in for. As she ate her salmon and green beans she Googled "Kachina Rogers Obit", then "Kachina Rogers Death", and "Kachina Rogers Drown" and finally "Kachina Rogers Scallop Koslowski". The only formal obituary was written by the funeral home in Southampton. There were several articles that mentioned her death in local publications - The Southampton Press, Easthampton Star and the Sag Harbor Express. After nearly an hour searching she didn't know any more than she had last night. Kachina's death had been ruled suicide by intentional heroin overdose. She'd been found at Conscience Point after Hurricane Sandy. There were no details about how the police reached their conclusion. There was also no hint there was any uncertainty about the cause of death, the articles were very matter-of-fact.

Now that the office had cleared out, the bravado Rachel had felt when she'd jumped out of bed at five am and dressed to slay had disappeared. It had been replaced by nausea.

"As fucked up as it is, you did the right thing. I figured it out when I saw the news…"

When Scallop had told her about Kachina that first night next to the firepit, when he'd been so open and honest, he hadn't said *how* Kachina had committed suicide. Good god. *Had he killed her?* Is that what Casey had been saying?

"No one else knew what happened to her, so no one else could know what you did. But I know, Scallop. I know."

Had Scallop killed Kosumi's mother to expunge her from their lives? He'd been a Navy Seal and he'd been in a war. He'd killed before and he'd know how to do it. He was uncommonly gentle. But this was a man who physically punished himself to the point of exhaustion on a daily basis. He had a core of steel and he'd shown her its sharp edge yesterday. When faced with a lifetime of sharing his beautiful boy with a woman who was certain to destroy his happiness and spirit had he taken advantage of the opportunity presented by a natural disaster? Had he let the hurricane wash away evidence? She vaulted from her seat and ran to the bathroom, throwing up what remained of two and a half bottles of wine and the little she'd eaten during the day.

By ten am the next day, Rachel had picked up three clients that Lauren had failed to sign and she and Heddy were sitting at a table at Bill's Townhouse on East 54th Street. A century-long fixture in Midtown, Bill's was a three-story historic townhouse restaurant known for its staying power and killer burgers. Rachel felt her heart thump walking in. This was a better place for her than Murph's .

Heddy and Rachel had worked together at Goldman Sachs in Fixed Income Sales before Heddy had moved to a new career in Head Hunting. Rachel dove into her summer, Scallop, and what happened the day before. It felt good to talk about it to someone. Rachel knew she could trust Heddy not only to keep their conversation confidential but also to push her to make the change she knew she needed, since it was in Heddy's best interest.

"What do you *think* she was referring to?," Heddy asked. "Do you think he had a part in Kachina dying?"

"I don't know. I don't want to think that, but I don't know. How screwed up is that? Maybe I'm just being melodramatic. Making up some grand story when the reality is it just wasn't going to work. Maybe I'm romanticizing something simple. I totally blew my top on him. I just spent my entire summer messing up my life, and messing around with this guy, and I couldn't tell you if he did something like that or not. I don't know! Have I lost my mind? Am I stupid? Or am I just lost and lonely. I have no idea, Heddy." And she didn't. By the time she got home the night before she had convinced herself that their breakup was just that. A breakup, not some murder mystery she needed to solve. She had never considered herself to be a dramatic person. But she had a suspicion that she might be becoming one. Any other explanation was too outrageous.

Heddy shoved a bite of Cobb salad in her mouth and examined Rachel carefully, thinking about what she was going to say. This was one of the things Rachel appreciated about Heddy; she never just told you what she thought you wanted to hear.

"I don't know, Rachel. I don't know him. I've seen the pictures, everyone did, and now I've heard your stories. He's gorgeous. He's interesting. That's all true. But I think you may have gone there in the first place because you just want something different, something new. He represented that to you. But it sounds like all drama aside (and if any of that's real, that's some serious drama), it's too much of a stretch. Maybe you were using him, *unconsciously of course,* for a bit of adventure. There are other ways to rock the boat if that's what you want." Heddy said, clearly planting a seed. Like any great salesperson, Heddy knew how to use everything she was given.

Rachel rolled her eyes, only half pretending this hadn't been why she called Heddy in the first place. "Alright, what do you have?"

"Head of Investor Relations for Tantallon. A Partner level role. They've been asking me about you for a year now."

"London?", Rachel asked, surprised.

"How's that for a change? You want an adventure? You want to sever whatever was happening in Southampton? You want to not run into people from Tallmadge every day once you've left? This is a way to do that."

Tantallon Capital was a hedge fund based in London. They were just behind Tallmadge in terms of assets under management but closing the gap quickly. Several portfolio managers had left Tallmadge and other funds for Tantallon over the last few years, and they was a buzz about them. Their performance had been stellar across a period when other funds were down.

"Yeah. We've pitched against them a few times over the past year for new money and won. Not their fault, really."

"Well, they are sick of being beat. They've discussed offering a $2.5 million floor, a huge chunk of equity, and the freedom to structure the department as you see fit. I'm betting that's better than what you've got now. But the job is in London."

"Tell them $3 million and I'll talk to them."

"Seriously?"

"And I want my moving expenses paid. All of that. Three is the magic number."

"Ok. I can ask them what they think. That's steep."

"No, it's not. Not for me. And not for what I bring in," she smiled pointedly at Heddy. Friends or not, now they were down to business. Then she flipped the switch. "Heddy, maybe you are right. Maybe I just need a change of scenery. A new challenge. A new city. Some new faces. See what they say," Rachel said, feeling an unexpected tingle of excitement as she finished her salad.

In late September, Rachel called the farm. She had left behind small things in the office in the farm stand, and in her haste to leave the cottage she had left a garment bag of clothes she knew she'd regret not retrieving. She also had an ache for Scallop's family that she hoped would lessen if she had to the chance to speak to Lucy and at least say something. She wasn't quite sure what that something would be.

Rachel was relieved when it was Lucy who picked up the phone, not her mother and not Scallop. "Hi Luce, it's me," she said more meekly than she wanted to.

"Rachel?" Lucy asked. Rachel couldn't tell anything from her tone.

"Yes, it's me. I've been wanting to call you. I just don't know what to say. But I didn't want to never speak to you again. That seems ridiculous."

"Yeah," Lucy said calmly, "it would be ridiculous. But I have to tell you, I'm really bummed about you and Scallop. Scallop told me that there was some nonsense with Casey. She's nuts you know, right? She's drunk most of the time and high the other part of it. Whatever she said shouldn't have caused all this trouble."

"Oh Luce, you know that wasn't all there was to it. We were always going to have problems. I can't come live out there and Scallop's life is there with you guys. And, it wasn't about what Casey said. It was about Scallop's reaction to it. He scared me a little."

"Really?" Lucy said, neutral. "What do you mean?"

"Well, he was rude and angry in a way I hadn't seen him be before." Rachel knew she wouldn't be comfortable being this frank with almost anyone else. But she knew she could just lay it all out to Lucy. "I know you all look after him, which is nice. But now, I've seen a hint of why you do that. I don't really know if I can sign up for that. Would you? With everything else?"

"I know you were making him happy. I know he was making you happy. I don't really pay attention to anything other than that which is probably why I spend half my days with pieces of corn husk in my hair," she said giving Rachel a dose of her self-effacing humor like a gift that cleared away the cloud between them.

Rachel laughed out loud. "It's the perfect look for you Luce."

How could she not be honest with Lucy? "I'm sad. I'm really sad about it."

"Well…" Lucy was waiting for her to say something more. Talking to Lucy wasn't making the ache go away. The opposite in fact. Rachel found herself feeling dizzy and sorting through scenarios in which she forgave Scallop and everything went back to the way it was a month ago. She shook her head and cleared her throat to snap herself out of it.

"Well, it doesn't really matter because I took a job in London. If it was hard before, it would be impossible now. And, you know what? I do need to know what that woman was talking about and why Scallop got so angry with me. Any insight?"

"You took a job in London?" Lucy asked so smoothly, that Rachel wasn't sure if she had dodged the question or if Lucy was just curious about her job.

"Yes, I'm going in a week. There are some things I need to get from the cottage and from the farm before I go. I'm going to come out on Tuesday to pick it all up. Is it ok if I come by around ten?"

"Yes, but why don't we do this? I'll get the stuff from the office and get it over to the cottage. Why don't I have Kosumi with me and you and Scallop can at least say a goodbye that doesn't suck. You could go to the cottage. I'll make sure he's there. Is that ok?"

Rachel knew Lucy was right. Finishing what they'd had in a shouting match and a cloud of pickup truck dust was not what she wanted, it was overdramatic.

"Ok Lucy, as long as you're sure that will be ok with Scallop. I could just send Eddie."

"No, don't do that," Rachel could hear a tinge of disapproval in Lucy's voice, along with something she thought might be desperation. "Scallop will want to say goodbye properly. Even if it's over, you were the best thing to happen to him since Kosumi. You made him happy like he was when we were young." Again, the hint of desperation in her voice.

"So, what about what that Casey woman said Luce?"

"Rachel," Lucy said, suddenly firm. "I don't know what that could be about… nothing with Kachina made any sense, it was all just drama, and Casey can't find her way out of a paper bag most afternoons…"

Rachel waited for Lucy to say more, to make excuses for Scallop, give some explanation for his behavior that would soften her feelings. Instead she could sense that Lucy wanted to get off the phone. Annoyed, she decided to do her a favor and end the call.

"Ok…" Rachel didn't want to hang up with Lucy, "If you find yourself in London come and find me. I know it's a stretch, but if a few months go by and you find yourself with a little freedom, bring the girls over and I'll show you all around."

"That would be a really great trip," Lucy said, clearly relieved that Rachel wasn't going to press the issue.

After Rachel hung up the phone she sighed at the futility of it all. She'd decided to leave, Scallop wouldn't apologize, he obviously didn't think he'd done anything wrong, this visit was going to create a new moment of pain to remember. It was just going to add another few hours on to the colossal amount of time she'd wasted becoming a part of a family she wasn't going to be a part of. And the little seed of hope that kept trying to implant itself in her heart despite her constant attempts to toss it out was pissing her off.

It was unseasonably cold when Easy Eddie dropped Rachel at the cottage. She hesitated to get out of the car. She'd already decided to make this quick. She'd say she was sorry it didn't work out, grab her stuff, and go back to her life. She would not go into the backyard, that firepit was like the Bermuda triangle, and she wasn't going anywhere near it. As she examined her lipstick in a compact mirror, telling herself she wasn't nervous, Eddie adjusted his rearview mirror; the better to glare at her.

"Sweet baby Jesus, what the hell are you doing Girlie? That lipstick hasn't changed color on any of the days you've worn it for the last three years. I've seen you put it on perfectly while I hit every pothole on the FDR. Go get your crap! You're on to bigger and better things. You're leaving me for a new life in London, la-de-da, and you're not going to ever think about this shit-shack again. Do you want me just sit out here and honk so you can move it along or do you need "closure" or something stupid like that? I can just go in there if you want."

Rachel snapped her lipstick closed and gave Eddie a shove from behind. "Eddie, this isn't that easy. I was an asshole, he was an asshole, I'd like to not have *that* be what I remember. OK? Why don't you go down the street to The Country Deli and have a coffee and then come back and bring me one. I'll be done by then."

She tugged on her down coat and walked stalwartly up to the door without looking back at Eddie. When she didn't hear him leaving she turned around and motioned for him to go and then knocked at the door. There was no answer. Reluctantly she walked around the back, already breaking promises she'd made to herself, and he was there, sitting cross-legged on top of an overturned canoe down by the water looking out at the bay. There was a dying fire in the pit, leaves covered his boards and rowboat as thickly as they covered the backyard. The hammock was blanketed. It wouldn't have surprised her if Scallop had been covered in leaves. She could sense his pain from there, and every part of her ached to just let whatever had happened a few weeks ago go. She realized she'd been propping herself up these past few weeks, and she just wanted to sit down next to him. She should have known all of her self-talk was bravado. What was real was the magnetic pull she felt between them.

She started towards him and he heard the leaves beneath her feet and turned. He unfurled himself and came towards her. He looked terrible and heart-breakingly beautiful at the same time. What the hell had he been doing with himself? Without saying anything he enveloped her, holding her to him, taking her head between his hands and kissing her forehead, then her lips when she let him.

She looked into his eyes and waves of sadness washed through her.

"I'm sorry I lost my mind and said those things that night," she said. "I don't believe most of what I said."

Scallop looked at her, showing her his hurt. "Oh, I think you meant some of what you said... I know I regret what happened. The way I acted. You offered me a different path, one that involved you, and I don't know what happened." He kissed her again. She clung on to him, feeling powerful and like she was losing her power all at once.

She pulled away. "Scallop, you don't look good. What have you been doing?"

He laughed. "Things have been a little rough around here the last couple of weeks. But I have to concentrate on Kosumi. Always. That's what I've been doing." He stepped away from her, forcing himself to be separate, and poked the fire.

"How about you? What's been new, Betty Lou?" he struggled to utter.

The wind went out of her. "I'm moving to London," she said looking across at Robins Island instead of at him.

"What?"

"A competitor based in London made me an offer, and I took it. They are paying me more than double, and they got me a townhouse in Notting Hill. I thought it was good timing. I'd been stuck in one place for a while there, and I know that a change of scenery, and a new challenge, would be a great thing for me right now. I start next week, this week I'm just tying up a few loose ends and, well, saying goodbye I guess."

"Double huh? Congratulations," Scallop said, letting a slight edge creep into his voice as his heart dropped. He'd had visions of a reconciliation, visions of Rachel spending weekends with them at the cottage as the wood burning stove blazed and snow piled up outside. He threw another log on the fire.

Rachel sat down on one of the Adirondack chairs, looking up at him with the water behind. There was no help for it now. She was leaving. "I want you to know, Scallop, that you opened my eyes. To what could be. To the magic that's out there, and how there can be surprises around any corner. You reminded what love is, and you reminded me that the world is wonderful," Rachel said.

"Then why..." Scallop trialed off. "I know we had an argument...you're frustrating me. I gotta tell you."

"Scallop I've thought a lot about this. If we were two people deserted on a desert island, we'd be perfect. We'd have a great life and make some babies. But, we are very different. Do you disagree?"

"I do. I think that we were made for each other. I think that you need me and I need you. You never had a family life, or a community, or any kind of connection to a place, or a way of life. I shared mine with you. And you challenge me. As you've pointed out, since I've been in the service I haven't been pushed. I haven't been challenged. And you called that out, and it's true. But beyond that we have a pure connection that doesn't happen often. That's what I think."

Rachel thought about what he said, but it was all the same things she had been turning over and over in her own head over the past few weeks.

"All of that is true. But that doesn't mean that we would work in the long run."

"I guess." Scallop rubbed his face. He was feeling the futility of it now too. She'd decided to go to London. So he changed the subject.

"I have some news too. We are going to sell the farm. Lucy has looked into all the options the bank has laid out for us, and I guess none of them make any sense for us. Tim wants to move to St. John and is all set to sell his house."

"I'm sorry to hear that but, hey, look at the bright side; you will all make some great money." Scallop scrunched up his face as though in pain. The last thing he cared about was 'great money'. Now it was Rachel's turn to feel frustrated. He didn't understand. They were too different. This was exactly what she was trying to tell him.

"When?" she asked.

"Pretty soon. Wallace Construction wants to get going, they need permits and all that, so I'd say next season will be the final for North Sea Farms. It's breaking my heart. It's hard for me to think of any other kind of life. We are all a part of that farm. That's who we are."

"Scallop, you can't stop change," she said lamely, for lack of anything better to say. But her platitude angered Scallop and it turned the conversation.

"Maybe. But you seem pretty good at changing, if you count running from things as change."

Rachel could feel where this was going.

"Wait a minute, before you examine my whole emotional and intellectual landscape, let's talk about what started our argument in the first place, shall we? For weeks I've been wondering what that woman Casey was talking about in Murph's that night that sent you reeling?"

Scallop looked into the fire once again, balling his hands up on top of the arms of his Adirondack chair. For a long moment he sat there, a log in the fire popped like a firecracker, but he didn't flinch. Once he crossed this line, there was no going back. Scallop looked to the sky. He let out an unexpected roar of frustration that sent Rachel's heart into her throat.

"I told you, I'm going to tell you the truth," he said, looking at her. "You're gonna wonder if I'm full of regret. And I am sort of! But I'm also glad the son of a bitch is dead."

Quickly he told her, leaving out no detail. He outlined his troubled relationship with Kachina, the details of her encounter with Frears as they'd been told to him and coldly, clinically, he described how he'd killed him.

"I snapped his neck like a twig, and I would have left it at that, but it was what he said. The way he looked at me with no regret in his eyes, and the words he used when talking about Kachina. Like he was making a point to tell me he had no conscience at all, he was just a predator. And he raped the mother of my son, so I threw him out the window. I wish now that I hadn't done it. Not because he didn't deserve it. But because I crossed a line. I crossed a line I can never uncross. My sister knows I crossed it. I endangered my family and I put a black mark on my soul."

Rachel looked at the bay in silence. After a few minutes of the wind, waves, seagulls and the fire providing the only noise, she stood up. She looked at him. She didn't know if she saw a murderer, or someone who couldn't control himself, or a white night. The one thing she did know was that she'd made the right decision.

"I remember reading about that in the papers. I'd like to say goodbye to Lucy and the girls."

"They are going straight from pumpkin picking to a kids play in Sag Harbor, so they won't be back until tonight."

"Ok." She could hear Easy Eddie's car idling in the front yard.

"This is goodbye then, Scallop. This is where it ends for us. I'm glad it happened. I'm glad I met you. But this is goodbye."

As she walked to the car she cried for Scallop. She cried for herself. She cried for Kachina, and she cried for little Kosumi who she hoped would never know the sort of sacrifices his parents had made for his happiness.

"Just go Eddie. And please I'm going to just sleep for a while. Just listen to Francesa and don't bother me for a while." Rachel hid behind her unnecessary sunglasses, looked out the window, and cried until the Midtown Tunnel.

Scallop's crying outlasted the fire and the moon. Another summer person gone. And just like he was a kid and his friends from The Shores had gone home for the winter, he was left in North Sea by himself. Left to contend with the memories of the Toadfish he'd done in.

At seven o'clock in the morning, he heard his sister's car out front. So he gathered himself and walked inside. The funny pretend playtime was over. Rachel was gone and it was time to be a father again.

32: Fall Back

When Rachel arrived in London, she had time on her hands – more time than she wanted. Her contract with Tallmadge had included a six month non-compete clause which barred her from working for a competitor within six months of leaving, and from trying to steal any of Tallmadge's clients. It was standard practice in the industry, and Tantallon's lawyers insisted she honor it. She couldn't take any new client meetings or do any fundraising. She found herself wishing she weren't quite so well informed. It would have been a relief to bury herself in research and internet snooping. But she already knew most of the players in London and Europe, and there were only minor differences between the way Tantallon and Tallmadge operated. She needed to find other ways to fill her mind, and time.

She visited all the tourist spots that she'd never had the time for on past trips. As she toured The Tower and The National Gallery her mind drifted over and over to that final afternoon with Scallop. She window shopped and walked her way through the conversation hundreds of different ways, each time finding a different path through, a path that led somewhere besides Scallop telling her what had happened with Ted Frears. More than anything, she wished she didn't know. Had he done the moral thing? Maybe. She couldn't imagine taking a man's head in her hands and ending his life. She tried to imagine it. But, she had never done many of the things Scallop had done.

She reminded herself again and again, that he hadn't done the legal thing. And that was terrifying. She tried not to worry about him, worry about Kosumi and Lucy too. How safe were they? Would anyone ever put two and two together? Would that Casey woman get slobbering drunk and tell a crowd one night at Murph's? More than once in the weeks that followed Scallop's confession, she found herself stopped in her tracks by visions of Scallop and Lucy being arrested by some of the local cops she'd met on Tumbleweed Tuesday. She was angry too. As angry as Rachel was at Scallop, she was just as angry at Lucy. She'd made her love her. She knew Lucy only wanted the best for Scallop, but part of Rachel felt she'd been trapped in a web of Lucy's design, constructed to catch Scallop some happiness. It was absurd to expect that Lucy would have told her about Kachina. Lucy was in an impossible position. But Rachel still felt betrayed. Lucy hadn't reached out to her before she'd left for London.

And there was guilt. Guilt because Rachel understood why Scallop had murdered the man. She didn't even know that she could blame him. In the moments when she found herself justifying his actions to herself she felt as though she felt guilty herself. She knew that in some ways she was in fact guilty, she knew about a cold-blooded murder and was choosing not to report it.

Amidst all of this, there was a kernel of relief. She was relieved to be on another continent. She'd wisely given herself no other choice than to move on. She was determined that she would make an actual life here.

When the attempt to quiet her mind with tourism failed, she created her own obsession. She threw herself into decorating the townhouse that had come to her as part of her contract with Tantallon, trying to make it feel like her home. She scoured antique shops for furnishings that made her feel comfortable and made the space special. For the first time in her life she completely ignored the voice of her mother that played inside her head as she made her choices and arranged her rooms. She didn't care about color schemes, a consistent style or whether or not pieces would work if and when she moved them elsewhere. She wanted them to work now. She didn't realize she was creating an elevated version of the farmhouse at North Sea Farm.

She ran in Hyde Park on weekends and joined a book club with two women from work. She accepted dinner invitations from colleagues, and was charmed when she found that they were inviting her into their homes rather than meeting up at a restaurant. She got to know their families a little. She forced herself to become a joiner.

She joined a yoga class, and while inverted, in an obnoxiously long downward dog, she decided to invite her family to visit her for Thanksgiving. She desperately wanted them to be part of her life. Thanksgiving plans would give her a deadline for finishing her apartment, and she thought being on neutral territory, in an exciting place, might give them an opportunity to connect.

She had talked to her sister Meri the week before. Meri was in the midst of a divorce. Her husband Ben had been a source of division in Rachel's family for years (as though they needed another one.) He was tall, dark and handsome, and argued to hear himself make a point. He was rude to her sister, her mother, her father and her stepmother. Rachel had always wondered why his equal-opportunity rudeness hadn't galvanized the rest of the family against him - he was a common enemy. But Ben had a unique talent, he was able to make everyone hate him, and everyone hate one another all at once. He was skilled at creating a cacophony of hate. Rachel hoped that his exit from the family might give the Joneses a chance. She longed for the family closeness she'd felt with the Koslowski's. She didn't know if she'd ever find it again. Surprisingly, being a joiner had helped a little, but it wasn't the same. She logically reasoned with herself that her best bet was to cultivate family within her own family.

She was encouraged when everyone aside from her stepmother had agreed to come. Jeanette was perhaps the most absurd addend in the complex equation that was Rachel's family. For years she had refused to talk to Rachel, or her sister, because of a perceived slight. Jeanette had been Rachel's father's secretary who had, by all accounts, pursued him with the headlong aggressiveness of a woman with no self-awareness and nothing to lose. Once she had caught him, she had expected Rachel and her sister, even, absurdly their mother, to include her in the family. When they didn't count their lucky stars that she had seduced their father, she was petulant, rude and catty. Rachel knew it was too much to expect her to come. It was better if she didn't. But her father was coming without her, which Rachel tried not to interpret as his first step back into the light.

She planned a slate of activities for their visit: dinners at well-known restaurants in London for her sister - the biggest food snob Rachel knew, a private guided tour of Chartwell, Churchill's home, for her Dad the history buff, two West End shows, and shopping at some private boutiques for her mom.

Their first day was a success. They visited Chartwell, chatting with one another and pointing out interesting information as they were absorbed in a place and a history they weren't familiar with. As they drove back into the city to change for dinner Rachel realized she had enjoyed the day and allowed herself to feel optimistic about the evening. She pointed out some of the spots she'd been frequenting since she'd been there as they drove past, and they asked her for details, and her dad even joked. They seemed like a family.

But, during dinner at City Social the fireworks began. As the wine was served, Rachel's mother reached across the table and awkwardly patted her on the hand. "Rachel, I think this is the place for you! I'm glad you made the decision to move here. It got you out of whatever rut you were in with that farmer out there in the Hamptons," she said rolling her eyes towards the windows. From their perch at City Social, they had a close-up view of the Gherkin, and her mother gestured to it, giving the pickle-shaped monstrosity the opportunity to agree with her: her daughter had dodged a bullet.

Rachel felt like she'd been punched in the gut. She hadn't told her mother a thing about Scallop. She hadn't told her father either. She'd told Meri about the summer, leaving out everything that had happened after Tumbleweed Tuesday. They'd had the first good sisterly talk they'd had in years. Meri had been sympathetic and open to hearing about Scallop and his different kind of intelligence and life. As she looked around the table she knew instantly that Meri hadn't kept a word of their conversation to herself; both her parents had been read in. Their waiter watched as she turned crimson and lightly laid his hand on the back of her chair as he passed behind her to pour for her father. Under normal circumstances she would have been touched by his sympathy. Right then she thought she might deck all of them. "Jesus," she thought. "Even this stupid waiter can see what jerks they are!"

Her father did try to come to her aid. "There you go again, Ruth," Stanley said. "You have to be critical, don't you? You never met the man. Did you ever ask Rachel about him?"

Rachel's mother ripped a piece of bread in half and buttered it dramatically, punctuating her response with each shmear. "Oh! (spread) I'm sorry. (shmear) No I did not. Thank (shmear) you (shmear) for that timely parenting tip, Stanley! What would I have done, raising two teenage daughters without your expert guidance?" she finished off by emphatically embedding the butter knife in the butter dish.

"Can both of you please relax," Meri demanded. "Please? Can we all just enjoy this great place, these wonderful views and Rachel's new life here in London?", she said eyeing Rachel cagily. She knew she'd been caught in the act of breaking Rachel's confidence, and was trying to reign in the mess she'd made. Rachel looked at her plate and closed her eyes, wishing them away.

When it was clear that Rachel wasn't going to engage, her mother swung her attention in Meri's direction. Once her motor was running it was hard for Ruth to shut it down.

"Meri, I'm so sorry to see that Benjamin isn't here. Have things improved? Is he still sleeping in the pool house?" she asked pointedly. Meri wasn't going to be allowed to play peacemaker. Ruth knew full-well the state of things between Meri and her husband, but she wanted to be certain her ex-husband knew the state of their daughter's marriage. Somehow, this was his fault.

"He is still in the pool house," Meri said quietly. "Things have improved in that the divorce is nearly final. The lawyers are drawing up the paperwork with the terms we've agreed on," Meri spoke to her father, ignoring her mother's glare.

"Tell me you took him to the cleaners?" Ruth said, butting in.

"I got half. Which is the best I could do."

"Half!? With all you've been through? I'd think with all the lawyers you know out there, someone could be able to get you more," Stanley cried, rubbing his face in disgust.

"*Thanks* for asking the most important questions. Really! In case you were wondering, I've gotten custody of Robin," Meri snipped, referring to her fifteen year old daughter. Everyone picked at their bread for a moment.

Then Meri went in for the kill. Deflecting her parent's attention from herself onto Rachel had worked for her for so long, she didn't know how to do anything else, even though she'd vowed to be a better sister. "Maybe there's a handsome surfing farmer in Malibu who I can have a lusty fling with to clear my mind. Tell mom and dad about ending things with the Crab man! Wait…Lobster? Crawfish? He's some kind of crustacean, right?" she said nastily.

"Scallop," Rachel said staring Meri down. She knew Meri knew perfectly well what Scallop's name was.

"*Scallop,*" her mother said, "I'm sure you're much better off without him. Too rough around the edges, I imagine."

"Something like that," Rachel said, making it clear that this was the end of the conversation. She was furious, but she had to consider it a lucky break that their snobbery made it easy for them to dismiss Scallop. Under the circumstances, having a family who was disengaged was better than having to give a lengthy explanation of their breakup to a family who cared too deeply.

"Rachel, you did the right thing," her father said, attempting to be kind, "You had to cut that chord. Next thing you know, you might be out there living with them. Operating a farm. Watching the seasons of your life go by. I don't know, doing whatever people like that do."

They were impossible.

The waiter arrived to take their order. Rachel ordered, although she felt sick to her stomach. She regretted inviting them. She would have much preferred watching the seasons go by from Scallop's back yard with Lucy and Keith Hernandez around the picnic table than spend another night out with these people. She begged off dessert and coffee and sent them off to their hotel, taking her own cab home.

When she got home, she put on her pajamas and curled up on the big easy chair in what had become her favorite corner and read the papers that had been sitting there since that morning. This felt like a better way to spend the next few days than following through with the plans she made for her family that she was now dreading. Then her phone rang. The caller ID said "Lucy Koslowski". For a second Rachel considered not answering it. She was already emotionally exhausted. But her curiosity wouldn't allow that. She answered.

"Rachel Jones."

"Rachel, it's Lucy." She sounded unsure. Rachel couldn't stop her heart from warming at the sound of Lucy's voice.

"Lucy! What time is it there? It must be one in the morning. What are you doing?"

"Smoking on the back porch. Taking a break from making the half-a-dozen pumpkin pies I need for tomorrow. Half a hundred hungry Koslowskis are on their way for Thanksgiving, and they want pie."

Lucy was joking, but she did sound a little tired.

"You don't smoke."

"No… I don't let anyone *see me smoke*. There's a difference. It takes me about three weeks to get through a pack of cigarettes. I just do it when I'm super stressed. Like when I've got to bake things for way too many people."

Rachel laughed. She guessed Lucy would always be able to make her laugh.

"I've been thinking about you. Thinking about what you must think of me," Lucy said. "What you must think of Scallop. He told me he told you the truth. Rachel, I'm sorry I couldn't tell you. You must think I'm a horrible person for helping him. Sometimes I think I'm a terrible person."

"I don't think you're a terrible person Lucy," Rachel said. Suddenly exhausted. "I think you love your brother."

"I do," she said quietly. "But also, every time I start to feel guilty about

260

it, I think of that man. I imagine him like a rabid coyote with short man's disease. He was evil, and he couldn't control himself, and he kept getting away with it. He had done what he did to Kachina maybe a hundred times! I've always thanked my stars that my girls were just ordinary looking, so that they wouldn't attract the kind of attention that Kachina did. That's messed up, I know."

Rachel sighed.

"Luce, I don't know what you should have done. Every time you like someone Scallop's interested in, you can't pull them aside and say, 'Hey, full disclosure, my brother kills rapists, so…there's that.' I guess you could just try to stay out of it when it happens again. I don't know…" Rachel doubted that Lucy would ever be able to stay out of anything that had to do with Scallop.

Rachel could hear Lucy exhaling her secret cigarette.

"I don't know Rachel. Maybe you were the last one there will be. Scallop's doing well. Really. He's putting on a happy face for Kosumi about you, about the farm. But, like you said, he can't be telling every girl he dates what he did. You just walked out…I mean, you could have done anything…"

Rachel understood now that at least part of the reason for this call was that Lucy was afraid she might say something to the authorities. She rushed to ease Lucy's mind.

"Yes, I just walked out. That's all I'll ever do about it. And maybe Scallop learned something from that. Maybe the next 'me' won't get the whole story. To be honest, I wish I didn't have it."

"I wish that too," Lucy said sadly. "Well anyway, I was thinking of you, over there in London. This summer, I really thought you'd be one of us, around the table. It's going to be a tough Thanksgiving here. The closer we get to selling this place, the tighter we hold to it."

"Oh!" Rachel felt a wave of guilt that she hadn't reached out to Lucy about this before. Just before she'd left the states, Dana had insisted that they go on an apple picking outing in the Hudson Valley. The farm they had visited had been an absolute mad house. Five thousand people lined up to pick apples, buy cider doughnuts and pies, climb on jungle gyms made of hay bales, and taste wines. It had been surreal, and anything but bucolic. But none of the families from the city, dressed in their apple picking costumes of plaid shirts and seven-hundred-dollar leather work boots, seemed to notice. One thing was certain, it was a money maker.

"Lucy, if you're really want to find a way out of that, go to the website I'm going to text you. I went to a farm in the Hudson Valley that could be a model for you to completely changing the way you use your farm. It would mean turning it into a crazy tourist attraction. I don't know how much that would interest you or your family. It would change how you use and experience your land. I know Scallop won't like it…" she trailed off. Spending his days pushing cider doughnuts instead of coaxing green beans would not be Scallop's thing.

"Send it to me Rachel," Lucy said enthusiastically, "The closer it the sale gets, the tighter we hold. Maybe if there's a way to stay here, Scallop would take it."

Rachel could hear a tinge of skepticism in Lucy's voice. "Alright. Well, if you think it might work, go up and take a look at the place. Maybe you can talk to the owners about how they get those crowds there," she said firmly, making it clear that she was willing to provide the idea, but not willing to consult with Lucy about it on an ongoing basis. She loved Lucy, but she could already feel that nothing good would come of maintaining their friendship. Lucy's voice made her long to be sitting on Scallop's lap in front of that Bermuda Triangle of a fire pit. It would always be that way.

"Thanks Rachel, I appreciate you thinking of us," Lucy said. Of course, she understood exactly what Rachel was saying. "Well, I'd better go back in and finish up those pies."

Rachel couldn't let her go without saying one last thing. "Luce, I don't think you're a terrible person. I think you're a good person who was put in a terrible position. Scallop too. Now I'm in a similar spot. But I think it's best if I just walk away."

They said their goodbyes and Rachel returned to her papers and glass of wine, dreading the next day with her family.

The rest of their visit was the same. The Jones's argued, they bickered, and they fought the same old battles against the backdrop of The Old Smoke. Rachel's role of keeping the peace was arduous and exhausting. She was looking for family, but it was clear that she was going to have to look beyond the obvious.

33: Davis Creek Duck Hunting

On Black Friday, as many souls across the land brainlessly flocked to strip malls to spend hard earned money things they don't need, Scallop and Keith upheld their annual tradition of duck hunting on Davis Creek, not far from Towd Point. It was a bitterly cold day, but the water hadn't frozen. The duck blind provided refuge from the wind, which was quite cold as it blew across the marsh. They'd started at dawn, and each of them were one duck short of their allotted limit of three. It was now nearing eleven, and Keith had begun taking down his bottle of Wild Turkey just after nine. Scallop was quieter than usual today, his eyes peeled across the grass looking to any sign of waterfowl.

Kosumi had headed to the Children's Museum of the East End with his cousins. The museum holds an annual day after Thanksgiving play day that focuses on the Native American perspective of the first Thanksgiving. The tradition for Scallop and Keith started six years ago. They both catch their limit, and whoever wants to can join at Keith's for a great early dinner of duck, pasta and some wine from Keith's extensive cellar. Lucy and Tim especially liked this tradition, and Keith is not only a charming host with a world class wine cellar, but a great cook.

It had been a while since either of them had discharged their shotgun. The last duck went to Keith, and after Scallop retrieved it the flow had slowed down. Keith had sensed Scallop's tone and was rather quiet for the majority of the morning. He also knew that Scallop had strict rules against talking or moving when they were hunting.
Keith took a swig of his Wild Turkey, and handed the bottle to Scallop once again. This was the fifth attempt, and Scallop relented.

"One for five. That's just about my batting average the last year. Welcome to whiskey land my crustacean monikered friend," Keith said as Scallop swigged, somehow without grimacing.

"Good to be here. Was that really your batting average the last year?"

"Ballpark. Couldn't have been much higher than last year with the Indians. Career average was .296 though. Let's focus on the positive, shall we? That last year in Cleveland was a shitty time. A royally shitty time."

"How so?"

"After all the excitement of the 80s of the Mets, and New York overall, being out in Cleveland just didn't work for me. From a lot of angles. Not much to do. Not much excitement. I lasted like fifty games and called it quits. I think back about that time quite a bit. I was somewhat relieved when it was over, believe it or not. I felt free. I didn't have to do it anymore, and it felt good."

"Interesting," Scallop said as he checked his gun.

"Speaking of tough times. I knew the last few months have been really hard for you, man. I do. I see you going through it, and I want you to know I've been thinking about you. A lot."

Scallop didn't look over at Keith. They both stared straight out through the slot in the blind. Keith took another swig.

"I've learned so much from being friends with you. I tell people about it all the time. They make fun of me. But the people I'm on the road with, my family members, friends from the playing days, they all mock me. 'Oh great another story about Scallop' and I guess they have every right to. And it's fine by me. The truth is...you've really taught me to enjoy the day. And appreciate it. And you've shown me the value of nature, ritual, and have really redefined for me what adult friendship can be. I used to think that developing genuine new friendships as a fully formed adult is impossible. Being friends with you has shown me that's not the case. I thank you for it. And I really want you to know that."

"I'm glad you think that Keith. You know I've learned from you also. Sorry if I haven't been myself recently. I really feel like I made an ass of myself. Opening myself up like that, and exposing Kosumi's emotions, I just feel like I was an idiot for being vulnerable and letting that happen. Anyone could see it wasn't going to happen. Myself included. I was selfish."

"Bullshit. Sorry. Anyone would have done what you've done. That woman dropped in here and fell head over heels for you, and for good reason. We all watched it happen. There was nothing you could do but go with it. And you did. And it didn't work out. Well you know what? You of all people know that this too will pass. The sun will rise and you remain an unbreakable man. You're a tremendous father, brother, son and friend. You can grieve for a while, that's fine, but fuck you for calling yourself selfish for putting yourself out there and falling in love. Most people don't have the guts to ever really put themselves out there in life. At all. In terms of anything. As Thoreau said, 'the mass of men lead lives of quiet desperation' which is the sad truth. You? You lay yourself out there man. It's what you do. Leaving home at eighteen. Traveling from Alaska to Patagonia. Your courageous service. Your way of life. You show your beautiful colors, and proudly fly your freak flag off of a truly unique pirate ship, and it's what makes you the greatest. I love you pal. Don't stay sad for long. The world needs you."

His point made; Keith knew he'd said enough.

"Let's bag one more each and get out of here. The 1979 MVP is freezing his balls off and there is football to be watched this day. In a few hours I'm keen on watching the Oregon State Beavers battle the Oregon Ducks in the Civil War, and the Washington Huskies take on the Washington State Cougars in the Apple Cup. A fine Pinot Noir from the Pacific Northwest in front of the fire beckons this day."

Scallop shook his head and laughed at the wonder that is his friend, the one and only Keith Hernandez. They spent another hour in the blind, and Scallop took down one more duck, before taking the Zodiac to Scallop's through lightly falling snow.

34: Blizzards of Winters Discontent

Scallop was very conscious that he needed to keep up a display of robust good cheer for his son. All fall he'd concealed his broken heart as best he could. He knew Kosumi was only going to be four once, and someday Scallop would look back and miss these days. Lucy put a fine point on it when she very gently reminded him that once she'd had two young daughters and a far bigger loss to contend with. He owed it to his son not to lose himself in a murky sea of depression and regret. Just like everything else, the sadness would pass.

October had been spectacularly beautiful, the trees ablaze with autumn color, the water a brighter, cooler blue than in the summer. Kosumi was alight with the world and the two were inseparable, doing all the things Scallop felt like a boy of four should do with his autumn. They surfed, fished for bluefish, carved pumpkins, split wood for the winter, played football, made apple cider at a friend's orchard, and Kosumi donned a "Jake and the Neverland Pirates" costume for the Sag Harbor Halloween parade. Scallop marched beside him as Captain Hook.

Scallop had another issue on his mind; he wanted to give Kosumi the best life possible. An unexpected consequence of having spent time with Rachel, had been that he'd come realize he might not be doing that. He wondered how he got to age forty with so little to show for it. He'd seen more adventure than anyone he knew, and had thrilling experiences, but when he returned, he'd become a member of an endangered species: the northeastern farmer. His farm was his bedrock and now it was going. He failed at "staying in the now" more and more these days. The uncertainty and the loss were pulling him into a vortex of circular thoughts. He knew some money would come out of the sale of the farm, but he really didn't feel confident about how much it would be. Lucy, who was still hoping for a white night, was vague about it. After loans and mortgages were paid off would there be enough money to live on for several years? Maybe. But not enough to live both their lives on, and likely not enough to live on and put Kosumi through college if that was something that he wanted to do. What would Scallop do for work once the farm was gone? Could he turn his odd carpentry jobs into something more? He wrestled with it, and worried about it, all the while showing a happy face to his boy.

On Thanksgiving morning, he and Kosumi had arrived at the farm extra early to help with the preparations. Scallop had been carrying a bushel basket full of potatoes in from where they were curing in the barn for his mother to peel. Lucy had come at him the moment he'd walked through the door, and dragged him out to the office to look at the webpage of a farm up in Northern Westchester. It looked insane, like a farm-a-palooza. He didn't want to sell their home either, but Lucy was grasping at invisible straws. Even if they wanted to, North Sea Farms wasn't large enough to handle the number of people that were at that farm. They didn't have nearly enough land. In the background of many of the pictures on the farm-a-palooza's prolific Instagram feed was a parking lot that would have taken up three quarters of their land. There was an aerial photo from Columbus Day weekend that showed every inch of the place crawling with people, packed in, should to shoulder. It looked like a nightmare.

He'd simply said, "We can't do that Luce," holding her head in his hands so that she'd look him in the eyes and calm down. When he could see that she understood, he kissed her on the head, said, "Stop smoking cigarettes would ya? Those things will kill you,", and went back to the house. Lucy followed him a quarter of an hour later, having put on her own mask of holiday happiness.

They had their typical homegrown Thanksgiving, made up of offerings from the farm. This Thanksgiving would be their last at North Sea Farms. There were more silences at the table this year, punctuated by forks against plates and requests to pass the green bean casserole. Normally they would have discussed next season, and plans for improvements or changes. No one mentioned those. The only reference to the impending sale of the farm was when Captain Koslowski raised his glass at the end of the table, struggling to speak clearly.

"To this farm," he said with all the gusto he could muster.

The table echoed him with the sound of sadness and regret. "To this farm.'

After dinner, when his father insisted on watching Fox News, Scallop sat by him and wished Rachel was there with him. He could wink at her when he asked his Dad leading questions to set him ranting about the state of the world and the "communist pacifist left" that he so voraciously abhorred. Of course, Scallop didn't agree with him on anything political, but the rant brought a faint sparkle to his dad's eyes that he liked to see.

He missed her again on New Years, when they sang Auld Lang Syne at the Coast Grill with all the locals and Kosumi clanged his kazoo with a spoon as they toasted the coming year. He felt divided between two times, remembering the night he met her at the bar. He missed her almost all the time.

It was a true winter on Long Island. That January had seen more snow than the previous three combined and it had been colder than Scallop could remember. In February, the hits kept coming. Snowbanks were chest-high, ice floes the size of small islands floated on the bay, and there was a hush over the residential neighborhoods of Southampton that would have been nice. had it not been so persistent that it had become eerie. It was too cold in the cottage. Scallop had spent the last three days feeding the fire in his woodstove, trying to keep the temperature in the cottage high enough that he and Kosumi wouldn't have to wear their coats, as a blizzard raged outside. The view through their windows was obscured by ice crystals, and they played near the stove with blankets wrapped around them. The weather report on the radio predicted a break in the storms for a day and then another blizzard. When the skies cleared, Scallop told Kosumi to pack up his pajamas and toothbrush in his backpack while he shoveled them out to the road then drained down the plumbing. They'd have to go up to the farm for the next storm. He was afraid if it got any colder he wouldn't be able to keep the pipes from freezing, no matter how vigilant he was about keeping the fire fed. They also needed some company, and Scallop knew Kosumi would love to be with his cousins to eat junk food and watch the Super Bowl later that weekend.

As soon as they got to the farm he knew he'd done the right thing. Inga and Veronica were taking turns choosing which of his mother's albums from the 60's to put on the record player while they put together a puzzle. Kosumi immediately ran to the kitchen to help his Grandma make a batch of cookies and his father was asleep in front of his television. For the first time in months it felt like it normally did at the farm. This is exactly what would have been going on during a snowy February afternoon at North Sea Farms anytime across the past fifty years.

They decided Saturday would be pizza and game night. Lucy saw with relief that Scallop was in good spirits, teasing Inga and Veronica and singing along with a Monkees songs. He'd been so up and down the last few months, she was happy to see him genuinely enjoying himself, not just faking it for Kosumi. She took the opportunity to run out and do some errands in the Village before picking up the pizza. She stopped at the pharmacy for her father's medications and got some poster board for Inga who had a school project due soon. She ran into the toy store and picked up a science kit for Kosumi, thinking the girls might enjoy doing the simple chemistry experiments with him when they finished their puzzle. She spent a few minutes browsing the book store, coming away with a couple of romance novels for her and her mother to trade off, and a non-fiction bestseller she thought Scallop might like – it was always a little tough to tell what he'd dive into and what he'd discard. Then she went into La Parmigiana, the local staple that had been run by the Gambino family since the seventies, to pick up the pizza for everyone. When she walked in she took a deep breath, filling her lungs with the smell of her childhood. "La Parm's" pizza was the first pizza she ever had as a kid, and she hoped it would be the last pizza she ever had. As a teenager she'd been here two nights out of three, meeting friends after school to do homework, getting pizza after a movie, or having a "romantic dinner" with some boy she was dating. This was her pizza place. Lucy knew every member of the family, all seven Gambino kids. She sat on the same stool she always chose whenever she came in now and had a glass of red wine at the bar, chatting with Gambino's as they passed by seating guests or carrying pies, and catching up with the bartender, Joey, whose mother had gone to high school with Lucy. Joey was young enough to be completely self-absorbed. He gossiped about his girlfriend and their plan to go to Mexico in a few weeks and he didn't ask her a single question about herself, her family, or her farm. It was a refreshing change for Lucy.

Everywhere she'd gone in the past few weeks, concerned friends and neighbors had asked her how she was doing as the sale of the farm loomed. They were signing papers next week. Wallace had conceded to let the Koslowski's stay in their house until early April, when they would have to vacate so it could be renovated. Lucy was grateful to Joe Wallace for agreeing not to knock their house down. She knew he'd rip out the insides to make it "fresh" and "farmhouse-modern", so that some city family could spend six weekends of the year there in magazine-worthy comfort. But, when she drove by, she would still see her childhood home standing amidst the five or six other monstrosities he'd build around it. It was a small comfort.

Bills were piling up; vendors that the family had longstanding relationships with were growing impatient for payment, nervous that the sale was taking place because the Koslowskis had reached a level of debt that meant they might never be paid. She would be happy when that part of the nightmare was over. The warmth of "La Parm" and smell of fresh dough baking calmed her nerves. She would have loved to stay and listen to Joey's chat and have three more glasses of wine and some pasta at the bar. But the pizza was ready and the family was waiting for her back at the farm. Plus, it had started to snow heavily again. As she left, Karla Gambino shouted to her to take care in the snow. She was glad she'd brought Scallop's truck, which had four-wheel drive.

Lucy took the back roads home, Seven Ponds to Water Mill. It was the most direct route. Normally in bad weather she would have taken Majors Path, the larger road that was plowed more often, but she wanted to enjoy a few more moments of peace before she got home and she loved driving through snow with the lights of the few occupied homes twinkling through the woods every now and again. WEHM was playing "Closer to Fine" by the Indigo Girls and she sang along cheerfully, feeling more relaxed than she had in months.

She realized too late that she hadn't been watching her speed. A family of deer came right at her; she hit the brakes and swerved into a wide drive that had been cleared of snow at some point, but never used. It was a sheet of ice. The truck spun wildly, skating down the steeply sloping drive and slamming into a tree, leading with the driver's side. After the clang and crunch of the truck hitting the tree there was no sound and no movement. There were no airbags to deploy in the truck, there was no emergency call system. There was silence and a quiet country road. It was nearly half an hour before another car passed and called the police. Scallop and Tim received the call via the North Sea Fire Department and drove to the scene, which was only two miles from the farm. When they arrived, they had no idea Lucy was the victim.

35: Scallop's Prayer

Three weeks later, Scallop picked up Kosumi from Keith's house. Keith had been nothing but a godsend over the last few weeks to the whole Koslowski clan.

"Keith told me that Aunt Lucy was asleep after her car broke, did she wake up yet Daddy?" Kosumi asked as Scallop helped him buckle his belt in the back seat of his sister's car. He had picked him up from Tommy's house where he'd been for two days while the rest of the family was spending every minute at the hospital.

"No, buddy, she didn't wake up yet...soon I hope. She has bleeding near her brain, the doctors call it an intracerebral hemorrhage. She needs to sleep so that her body can heal up, and then she'll wake up and we'll bring Lucy her favorite ice cream and read her stories until she feels all better," Scallop answered, he didn't want Kosumi to be scared by the big words people were using. His sister was sleeping. That was the nice way of saying she was in a coma.

He'd just dropped his mother and Lucy's girls at home. Kay had insisted the girls go home and go to sleep. She said that he should do the same, that everyone should try to get rest in their own beds tonight. Scallop agreed since it was just warm enough for the cottage to be livable.

Scallop tucked Kosumi into bed as the wind whipped off the bay, fueling the near constant thundering whistle they'd grown accustomed to that winter. He'd had to dig logs out of the snowbank that the woodpile had become in order to get the cottage warmed up again.

He refilled the stove and plopped down into one of the beanbag chairs. The thought of Lucy being gone was incomprehensible. Without her, Scallop simply didn't know which way was up. He could not reconcile the sister who bustled around the farm, taking care of everything and everyone, with the person laying in the hospital bed with half a dozen tubes flowing in and out of her body. He thought of the girls, and how they'd just recovered from losing their father, and how this might be too much for them to bear. Lucy acted as a mother to Kosumi; she picked him up from school, bought his clothes, organized his trips to the doctor, hugged him and bandaged his boo-boos. He'd already lost one mother, now he might lose another. Nothing was fair or right about this.

A few days ago he'd overheard the checkout girl at the hardware store saying to another customer who was dealing with a plumbing catastrophe, "Everything happens for a reason." At the time he had been waiting in line thinking about Rachel and it had rankled him. *What a ridiculous thing to think, let alone say.* The idea that each and every experience someone has is a step along the way towards their destiny, or a teaching moment, was absurd. As if the cosmos is setting up an obstacle course for each us. He thought, "If I punch someone in the face for no reason at the Country Deli one morning while I'm getting coffee, what 'reason' was there for that?" There was no 'reason' his sister was in a coma, she just was. There was no reason he'd met Rachel and now she was gone. There was no 'reason' Kachina had been one of Ted Frears's victims, she just was. Trying to attach reason to random occurrences in life was a waste of time. God wasn't trying to teach Scallop and his family some lesson on their way to enlightenment. But that didn't mean he didn't exist. Scallop saw God every day in the sky and the waves and in his son. Just because God wasn't manufacturing the plot of their lives didn't mean he wasn't there. He was just absorbed in manufacturing goodness.

Without thinking about it, Scallop got down on his knees. It was almost involuntary; an innate reflex which prompted him to combine his old boyhood prayers with a grownup plea,

"God bless Lucy – please God bless her. God bless Kosumi, Tim, Mom, Dad, Inga, Veronica, Rachel, Me and everyone we know and love, especially all the people who have let me know they are praying for Lucy too. God bless them."

"God, this is truly it. This must be bottom for me. I've seen awful things; I've been ordered to kill people, and I've chosen to kill people. I've had to hold my brothers as they passed. And I've withstood it all and remained sane, alright, sane to a point. But this one will break me. It will break all of us. Lucy keeps us together, she makes us be our best selves. Please God, be with Lucy. And guide us. Keep us strong and together, as Lucy would. I don't care if we lose the farm. I don't care if we lose everything, just let us keep Lucy. I know I haven't been a perfect person, Lord. I've stepped over the line more than once, but not Lucy. Thank you for the blessing of such a wonderful sister. Please let me keep her."

36: Red Solo Cups

Rachel was in Oslo Norway. She had spent the week introducing herself to the Government Pension Fund of Norway. There had been meetings, lunches and dinners back-to-back since Monday morning, leaving Rachel exhausted on Thursday evening as she strolled back from yet another business dinner. It was nine thirty at night, and it had been dark since four thirty, which made it seem even later. She had hoped Oslo would be a nice break from London. The dark skies and cramped streets there had been getting to her. She had realized with annoyance a few months back that her body had become accustomed to the unplugged outdoor lifestyle she'd lived in North Sea over the summer. She was not enjoying city life. She felt confined and unhealthier than she could ever remember feeling. She ran outdoors daily and tried to limit her time on her phone and computer, but the truth was, she didn't really enjoy her lifestyle as she once had. She'd been spoiled. The escape to Oslo had helped. Beautiful scenery, wide open streets and a very chilly boat ride had lifted her spirits up a bit.

She was walking back to her hotel from her final commitment of the workweek futilely trying to come up with new tactics to achieve some happiness in her current situation. She and Dana had talked about it on the phone the night before but that hadn't helped. Dana couldn't understand how she had become disenchanted. As she walked down a street called Hegdehaugsveien, a yellow neon sign, and classic rock leaking from a bar called "Horgan's", caught her attention. It sounded like a party. An American party. She crossed the street and opened the door. Crowds of Norwegians dressed in American athleisure were belting out a Journey song without bothering to curb their accents. Rachel laughed out loud and decided to go in. Why not?

"How-die and welcome to Horgan's. It's red solo cup Thursday," the blonde hostess said with a thick Norwegian accent. Taking a red solo cup from a stack at her podium and holding it out for Rachel.

"Ten euros gets you a red solo cup that gets you free Budweiser, Coors Lite and Miller for the night. Well drinks are half price with the cup too."

"Red solo cup Thursday?", Rachel asked, baffled as she looked around at the
walls adorned with all things pop Americana; posters from the NFL, NBA, MLB, NASCAR, rock bands and presidential campaigns and the clumps of young professional Norwegians pretending they were American.

"Yes. In America, when they have a party, everyone has a plastic red cup. They call it a solo cup. At Horgan's, we make like every day is the 4th of July keg party, we have red solo cup Thursday's. Tonight, we are showing a recording of the American Super Bowl, which was last Sunday. Would you like to buy a cup?"

"Sure. Why not?" Rachel said, paying for the cup and heading to the bar. She had to laugh watching all the Norwegians doing their best American. There was a buffet along the back wall with fried chicken, collard greens, macaroni and cheese, onion dip and apple sauce. Just as a stocky Norwegian bartender dressed as Patrick Swayze in "Dirty Dancing" handed her back her solo cup full of Bud Light, "Chicken Fried" started to play. To a man, the crowd all cheered. Rachel felt as though she was part of an elaborate, transatlantic, practical joke. This silly song had chased her from North Sea, Long Island to the North Sea.

Rachel watched a few plays of the Super Bowl and finished her beer as the crowd launched into "The Devil Went Down to Georgia."

She thought of Inga and Veronica, who shared in her disdain for "Chicken Fried". Rachel hadn't contacted them. Just like Kosumi, she knew she had to let them be. But she did check in on their Facebook profiles every once in a while, using her alias profile. Inga's profile picture was a shot of her and Veronica wearing cutoffs, t-shirts, and huge smiles with their arms wrapped around each other on the back of Scallop's pickup. Rachel was tempted to go show it around at the bar. The Norwegians would love it. She scrolled down the page. There were posts for "thoughts and prayers" for her mom from a dozen of Inga's schoolmates. There were "virtual candlelight vigils" there as well. Something had happened. Rachel Googled "Lucy Crowley, Southampton, New York" and "news". The story in the Southampton Press detailed the circumstances of the accident, right down to the errands Lucy had run before she'd spun out of control. She was in a coma. Rachel put her red solo cup down and walked out the door of Horgan's, dialing her assistant as she made her way back to her hotel.

Scallop stood on the stage of the North Sea Community Association House looking out at the sad faces of over three hundred people who'd come to the interfaith service for Lucy. The Catholic, Presbyterian, Lutheran, Greek Orthodox, Dune Methodist, and Baptist Gospel churches had all sent parishioners and clergy to the candlelight vigil. The synagogue from Easthampton sent its Rabbi and a bus filled with ten well-wishers. The immediate family, minus Kay who wanted to stay at the hospital, occupied the front row, and every spot was filled, with the overflow spilling onto the porch. Scallop had already seen many of the same faces at the hospital over the past week. The Kozlowskis had had so many visitors that the hospital staff had begun to turn people away. Lucy, conscious or not, needed rest. When Scallop's friend Jenna and some other members of the rescue squad were turned away, they decided to put together the vigil to give people a place to talk about Lucy and let the Kozlowskis know that the community was there for them.

Father Vinny from Our Lady of Poland began the service with a call to prayer. He introduced Cousin Joe who sang "Bridge Over Troubled Water", one of Lucy's favorites. Father Vinny then spoke about the power of prayer, and how each and every good thought for Lucy helped. Every prayer "went someplace", as he put it. Each minister and the Rabbi in attendance offered up their own prayer for Lucy, leading the community group to offer their own as well. Then it was time for Scallop to speak, to represent the family and thank everyone for coming. He'd worn the suit Lucy had bought him that summer. He knew she would have wanted him to wear the darn suit even though no one outside the clergymen was dressed up. He didn't mind being overdressed. If everyone had worn a suit it would have made it feel too much like a funeral.

"Hello everyone," he said, doing his best to smile out at them all. "On behalf of my family and I, I want to thank everyone for being here. All of us, being here together, shows just how special Lucy is, and how many of us love her. It shows that she has had a profound effect on all of us. I'm pretty confident that Lucy is going to pull through this, and I say that because of karma. She put so much good out into the universe. Some of it has got to be on its way back to her, and to us. Lucy experienced the loss of her beloved husband, Sam, just a few years ago, and she didn't get angry. She could have, but she didn't. Instead she became the keystone of our family. When I came home from the service, she didn't allow me to put anger and sadness out into the universe. She *insisted* I put good out. She insisted loudly," he joked, "and then, she showed me how to do it. Her absence now leaves me…and all of us…with a void. And we don't know which way to turn, because we always turn to Lucy. And it's tough."

Scallop lowered the microphone. His lip quivered and he felt he was going to completely lose his composure. He was blanking on what to say next, even though when he'd gotten up to speak, he'd known what he wanted to say. He looked around for something to remind him where he was. He could see Father Vinny standing, coming to help him finish and then to end the service. The moment got very long and awkward for everyone present.

The front door of the community house flew open breaking the silence, and there was a rustling in the back of the space as a newcomer wedged their way in. As the mass of humanity in the entryway shuffled to make way, Rachel stumbled into the aisle from the crowd, losing her footing in the process. She then popped up, righted herself and confidently moved forward, directly towards Scallop. When she reached him, she grabbed his hand, turned, and faced the crowd with him. Scallop looked down at her, half of him still lost in his speech, and the other half trying to process the fact that Rachel has just emerged from nowhere and joined him in front of this crowd.

"Hi." Rachel said, looking up at Scallop.

"Hi." Scallop replied, into the microphone, which made everyone laugh.

"I'm back," Rachel said to Scallop. "Finish your speech." Scallop looked at Rachel, and suddenly he regained his composure.

"So, everyone, please know that every prayer, every thought, every intention, they all go somewhere. They go right to Lucy. Keep them all coming. We're so lucky to call this town home. Thanks for all of you! God bless!"

Only a few people knew the context of what they just witnessed, but those who did found it to be quite powerful. The vigil came to an end after a closing prayer, sending everyone carefully driving home into the night. Scallop said goodbye and thank you to as many people as he could, and then made his way to Rachel, who was catching up with the rest of the family. She pulled Scallop aside, addressing him separately.

"I missed you. So much. I thought about you all the time. I had to fight every inch of everyday to not think about you, and then I realized that I wanted to think about you; because against all odds, I'm madly in love with you. And if you'll have me, I want to come back. We were off to a good start, I think, and I'd like to keep it going if you'll have me," Rachel said as she looked up into Scallop's eyes.

When she touched his arm, it was as if he swallowed her whole. She found herself against the building inside the shelter of his arms and hair as he kissed her until she was light headed from lack of breath. Finally, when he seemed satisfied that she wasn't going to escape he pressed his face against hers and cried.

"I came as soon as I heard," she said quietly. "I missed you. So much. I thought about you all the time. I fight through every inch of everyday trying not think about you, and it's not working. I want to think about you and I want to come back. Tell me, tell me what's happening," she said, detaching his face from hers so she could look in his eyes.

"Oh God," he said, kissing her until she was breathless again.

"She's in a coma still. Rachel, I don't know what we'll do if she doesn't wake up. She was so worried and stressed all winter. I hate that I was part of the cause of that stress. The girls are devastated. They feel the same as I do, as though they could have been less of a burden to her."

"Where's Kosumi?"

"On his way here right about now. He's been spending a lot of time with Keith since I've been going back and forth to the hospital and trying to help my mom with my dad. I think he might be getting more of an education than I'd like him to have." Scallop wasn't joking. She could see that this had been hard for him to handle.

"Alright. I'm here now. I'll help. Will they let me see Lucy?" Rachel had begun to head back to her rental car, expecting Scallop to follow.

"They will…", he said, not moving. He didn't look at her. "Rachel, how long are you staying? What did you tell them at work?"

"I told them there was a family emergency back home, and that I'd be back when I could. But I don't think I'm going back."

"What do you mean?" Scallop asked with an intensity that made her feel deeply guilty for causing him pain at this moment. "Rachel, as horrible as all of this is, as much as I need you here, and want you here, and want your help, I can't go through this again. Neither can you."

"Stop. We don't need to be talking about this right now. I'm *supposed* to be here. This is where I'm supposed to be. This is supposed to be my home and I am supposed to share it with you, forever. I get that now. I don't know what I'm going to tell work; I haven't gotten there yet. Scallop, I put an ocean between us, I buried myself with work and some pretty stupid hobbies, and I couldn't stop thinking about you. The one tiny moment when I felt at home while I was over there, was when I talked to your sister on the phone. This is where I belong. You are who I belong with. I don't care how either one of us got here. That's the way it is and it won't change," she said, watching to see if he believed her, waiting for him to come to her. He stared at her for so long she thought he might be working up the nerve to tell her to leave before he finally choked back something he couldn't say and nodded his head yes. She could hear Kosumi enter, she stepped back, winked and yelled loudly.

"And where oh where is my little boy? Where is he? Where is my Dinosaur boy?"

Rachel yelled as she moved to her knees, arms extended. Kosumi ran across the room into Rachel's arms; smashing into her so hard she fell back onto the hardwood floor upon impact. They hugged, laughed tickled one another and wrestled on the floor.

Rachel stood up. She looked tired and not as put together as she normally did. she hadn't slept since her last night in Oslo. Her assistant had found her flights home, but she'd had to make some odd connections to get here. She'd been wearing the same clothes for days.

Half an hour later, they were in the waiting room outside in the hospital. Kosumi whispered, "Rachel, Aunt Lucy has cebral hem-hoarage, and she doesn't wake up," into her hair as she hugged him.

"I know sweetie," Rachel said smiling at him and tapping him on the nose with her finger. "But I believe she will wake up. She wants to see us. I'm going to go in right now and tell her how much we love her ok? You stay out here with Grandma and Daddy, and then you and I will go home and make some dinner for everyone. We'll be good helpers. How does that sound?"

"Spaghetti and meatballs?" Kosumi asked excited.

"Spaghetti and meatballs sounds perfect," she said hugging him and smiling at Kay. She couldn't tell whether Kay was glad to see her or not. Her best guess was that she was resigned and a bit relieved.

Rachel sat next to the bed and had a good look at the woman she had felt a connection to since the moment they'd met. The tubes and the beeping from the machines that were helping her stay fed and hydrated were tough to take. They weren't Lucy's style.

She took Lucy's hand and gave it a few tight squeezes. "Lucy? I'm so sorry. I think you can hear me. I know you are going to come out of this. And I'll tell you what I'm going to do until you come back. I'm going to fill in for you. I'm going to take care of your family the way that you would. I'll make sure your daughters, brothers, parents and nephew are taken care of and making the best decisions they can. I won't fall down. I promise. I'll start with your daughter's outfits. I don't know *what* they think they're wearing. You take as long as you need, but come back."

Rachel wished real life was like the movies. She wished that her silly joke would lead to the moment when Lucy would wake up. It didn't, which meant she had a lot of work to do.

278

38: Monday Morning Kitchen Table Summit

Before the accident, Lucy was moving through the process of selling the farm, working with a lawyer and an accountant. They had met several times over the course of the fall, and drafts of a contract had been drawn up. It was a complicated undertaking. The farm had state subsidies and tax credits, and there were centuries-old rights-of-way the Kozlowskis had been using via handshake agreements that needed to be formalized in order for Wallace to use the land the way they intended. Lucy viewed all the back and forth as progress, albeit progress that broke her heart. While Joe Wallace was an understanding guy, he was also on a tight timeline and needed the keep the train on the track. He had left the Kozlowskis alone for more than a week, but he needed things to move forward.

On a cold Monday morning, the family gathered in the kitchen with a lawyer and an acquisition representative for Wallace Construction. Nothing had been signed, but the draft of the contract for sale said that Wallace construction would pay the Koslowski's nearly twenty-two million dollars for North Sea Farms. Initially this had sounded to Scallop like an outrageous amount of money. But Lucy had explained that large chunks of it would go towards capital gains taxes and paying off mortgages on the property and loans for equipment. Once all was said and done, each of the three Koslowski kids would walk away with around nine hundred thousand dollars and their parents just over a million, much of which the kids assumed would get eaten once one of their parents needed serious medical care. For the siblings, it was enough to live for a while. Live quite well, somewhere. But it was not enough for them to buy even a small home in Southampton, where tiny houses sold for nearly a million dollars. Scallop had his cottage so he would stay, but the others would move elsewhere.

Rachel and Scallop had spent the weekend sifting through the papers on Lucy's desk. It was so cold in the office that Rachel wore gloves with open ended fingers, and several layers of down clothing borrowed from the girls, and still needed to take frequent breaks to do jumping jacks out in the farm stand. They warmed her up and cleared her head before she dove back in. She skimmed each bill, statement, and contract while Scallop stood ready to put them in a pile based on their importance and pertinence to the sale of the property. On the morning of the second day Tim brought them mugs of coffee and stayed a while, leaning quietly against the chipped door jam, intermittently watching them, and starring at the floor.

When he left, Rachel paused long enough to ask Scallop, "What's he thinking do you think?"

"I don't know," said Scallop, watching out the window as Tim stopped in the driveway to look up at the farmhouse before he climbed the steps the porch. "He hasn't said much. He never does. I'm sure he feels like I do, guilty about leaving Lucy all of *this* to deal with for so long," he spread his arms wide to encompass the piles of paper held in place by small rocks and tractor parts. "He always wanted to sell. But now he might feel differently. It's impossible for me to imagine Mom and Dad living somewhere else. Going and living in another town. I don't want to think of Lucy coming home, and then having to turn around and find a new one. Maybe he's feeling that way now too."

"Maybe you should ask him. Mortgage pile," Rachel said, touching his leg as she handed him up another pile of papers.

"Yeah, I probably should. Just to talk, I guess. But I think it doesn't matter what we *feel*, don't you? Look at all of this! This is literally a pile of debt. Lucy kept this farm running on borrowed money. We can't do that forever."

They took the piles home with them in the evening and poured over them after they put Kosumi to bed. When they'd finally neatly filed everything from tractor manuals to the deed of the property in the three cardboard file boxes they'd sent Inga and Veronica into town for earlier, they collapsed facing each other on two beanbags drinking wine in front of the fire.

While Lucy wasn't the most organized person, she was right on the money about how the sale would play out for the family.

"We don't have any choice but to sell. Do we?", Scallop asked Rachel.

"Well, first off, I think that Wallace is giving you a *fair* price, but not a good one. I think we could probably negotiate for more, based on what other pieces of land are selling for. I understand why Lucy didn't get a real estate agent involved in this, you would have had to pay them a lot of money, but they would have negotiated on your behalf. I was looking at land prices around here when I was on the plane, and I think they offered low. Lucy's so nice, she probably didn't drive much of a bargain, and maybe she felt them letting you stay in the house until the spring was a big concession. It's not. I think you ought to let me negotiate with them for a higher price. If they don't pay it, someone else will. You don't *have* to sell to Wallace. I think you're only selling to them because they approached you. You know him and you like him."

"Yeah, all of that's true," Scallop said. She could see that the details of the sale didn't interest him. Getting more money didn't matter. Selling the farm was a catastrophe for Scallop. What she wondered was how much he would be willing to give to keep it.

She reached her foot across the space between them and pressed it against Scallop's, rubbing her borrowed wool socks against his.

"Can you ask Tim to let me do the talking tomorrow at this meeting? Just ask him to let me negotiate? I know he probably doesn't trust me right now. He might think I'm about to hop the next flight to London. But just convince him that you shouldn't negotiate on your own. You shouldn't. You're all tired, and sad, and confused and that's a bad place to be coming from. Let me do it."

"Yes. Ok, I'll talk to him," he said, looking into the fire. "You're not about to hop the next flight to London, are you?", he asked, leaning forward. "Rachel, you left for a good reason. What I told you, is that going to come back and bother you again? Once we're not in crisis anymore are you going to be sitting here with me like this? Or is that going to come back again."

Rachel got up and nestled into Scallop's beanbag next to him, making sure that some part of her from top to toe was touching some part of him.

"I'm going to sit here with you," she said, wiggling against him, "I'm going to sit here with you despite that. Maybe even a little because of it. I want to be here. With you."

They sat like that until the air became chilly, and the fire needed another log. Rachel finally broke the silence.

"I want to be here with you, but I would like to request some insulation. Can we agree on properly insulating this place do you think?"

"If that's what it will take, then that's what it will take," Scallop joked, rolling over her on his way to feed the stove.

Kay and Tim had flipped through the mortgage and loan files over omelets and pancakes the next morning. While both agreed that Rachel could take the lead at the meeting with Wallace's representative that morning, it was because Scallop insisted that she should. They were cold and uncomfortable and too polite to ask why they should allow the woman who had left in a big hurry a few months ago settle the terms of their future.

Kay had barely looked at the files, before closing their covers and burying herself in a sink full of dirty dishes. She already knew what was in them. She'd seen this coming for a long time.

"Scallop, take those back out to the office, will you please? I don't want them cluttering up the kitchen," she said as she scrubbed down the griddle.

Rachel cleared her throat. "I'll help you take them out. I need to run out and get some clothes. I don't have much with me and I feel I need something better than teenage hand-me-downs for this meeting."

This was true, but Rachel also wanted to give them some time as a family, without her. She was sensitive to the fact that she'd shown up out of nowhere and stuck her nose in. When they were alone in the office, she pushed Scallop against the wall and kissed him.

"Would you go back in there and tell your family I'm your girl? And while you're at it tell them what a barracuda of a business woman I am. I'll be back in time to kick ass and take names on their behalf. Make them understand. Also, I might want to make an entrance, so don't get worried if I get here right on the money."

The simple kitchen was gleaming clean when Dale Johnston, Wallace

Construction's CFO arrived. They sat around the table with fresh cups of coffee that were untouched by the family.

"This is obviously hard for all of us given that Lucy isn't here," Dale said. "However, we need to proceed since it's in the best interest of all parties, and the wheels have been in motion now for some time. I think we'll all feel a lot less stress once this is buttoned up," he said, smiling kindly at them.

"In just a few years, ten beautiful homes will sit on this site, including this farmhouse, as we've agreed. We'd like to call the development "North Sea Farms", if that would suit everyone?" The door to the porch flew open, and a cold gust of wind accompanied it. In from the porch walked Rachel, her Wall Street Journal in hand. It was a prop.

"Sorry I'm late."

"Hello," Dale said, flustered at the interruption. He looked around the table waiting for an introduction. Dale was young and handsome. He looked like a J. Crew marketer's reimagining of a carpenter, in a cashmere sweater over a shirt and tie, with jeans that were cut for the country but tight fitting, and high-end work boots. He had managed to strike the perfect balance; he both fit in the kitchen and didn't. Rachel began to think this might be just a little bit fun. He was a worthy adversary.

"And you are?" he asked, rising from his seat when no introduction was forthcoming.

"I'm Rachel Jones. Tantallon Capital, London. The Kozlowski's invited me, they've asked for my counsel."

"Ok then, Dale Johnston, Wallace Construction," he said, making an effort to take her in stride. "We were just going over the details of our offer to purchase North Sea Farms. Please join us."

"Dale, this is a difficult time for this family, I think it's best if we suspend the discussions until I've had a chance to read through the proposal, and have my lawyers look it over. I can't in good conscience offer them my advice without doing some due diligence. Lucy has been handling this for the Kozlowskis, and she's not here. I think it's wise for the whole family to take a fresh look at this, to educate themselves," she said, leaning against the sink casually.

"Sorry, but I'm a bit lost. Does anyone here grant this woman the right to speak on behalf of your family?"

Scallop and Kay raised their hands, Tim's followed, and Kim followed him. Dale looked around the table dismayed. Rachel felt sorry for him. She knew he'd have to go back to his boss and describe the scene.

"Dale, I know Joe Wallace is a family friend, and I'm sure this is a fair deal, but I haven't had the chance to talk to everyone here about what they want out of this deal, or if they want it all. I'll read every word of your proposal. Once we've sorted through things I'll be in touch. I know Lucy would appreciate it if you would grant us a little extra time, under the circumstances."

Dale began to gather his papers, defeated. It was hard to argue with what a woman in a coma would want. If he pushed, he would make Wallace Construction look like the big bad wolf trying to blow down the house of Southampton's favorite family. He said his goodbyes and showed himself out. When the door closed behind him Tim's eyebrows were in his hairline.

"You certainly can show someone the door. I hope you know what you're doing," he grumbled.

"I do. I know business. And real estate is just like any other business. You can't let them dictate the pace, tone, or format of something like this. You have something they want. I think Lucy didn't fully understand its value. We'll set the tone, and we'll get you all we can for it."

39: The New Sheriff Brings a Spring Awakening

Rachel tackled everything at once. She'd decided the Kozlowskis were her family. Likewise, she'd decided that her new family would not survive the loss of their farm, and she liked them just the way they were. She wanted to be able to tell Lucy they'd found a way to save the farm as soon as she woke up. She began her quest to create a viable business plan for the farm the next morning at dawn, and she didn't come up for air.

She'd already seen the books from two years ago, and Lucy had almost completed the books for the previous year. She met with the representatives of the two banks that held mortgages on the farm and negotiated better terms. She looked at every lease, arrangement, and relationship the farm maintained. She examined exactly how much they were selling of each product, and whether it was profitable. She met with the owners of all the restaurants in North Sea, first individually and then collectively. She met with the owners of the local wineries, and with local shellfish farmers and fishermen. She also met with realtors. Then she took Scallop, Kosumi, Inga and Veronica on a trip. She told them to dress warmly and wear heavy socks. They stopped to see Lucy in the Hospital, each taking a turn talking to her quietly on their own before they piled in Rachel's car and drove up into the Hudson Valley.

They stopped in one of the towns along the Hudson at a taco restaurant where everyone started to relax a little, loosening their grip on their troubles. Then Rachel drove them to the farm that she'd told Lucy about in the fall. She pulled the car up a long winding drive behind a few other cars packed with children, the pom-poms of their winter hats sticking up over their seats. They drove past a farmhouse that was about the same size as their own, but nearly a century older. and then on into a huge parking lot with an orchard behind it. The lot huge lot was dotted with at least a hundred and fifty cars. In front of them was a barn with a front porch that Scallop recognized. A line of people stretched out the front of the barn, while others exited a side door carrying steaming to-go cups and baggies of cookies and doughnuts. This was the farm from the website that Lucy had shown him in the fall.

"Daddy!" Kosumi shouted tugging at the seam of his coat, and pointing off to the other side of the barn. "Is that for skating?"

Sure enough next to the barn was a waist high enclosure. More than a hundred people were on the rink, some gliding along, some clinging to the sides laughing. On the other side of the rink were two open sided sheds where dozens of people sat on rustic benches resting and warming their feet at fire pits.

"I thought we could use a little outing," Rachel said to Kosumi. She pulled several twenty dollar bills out of her wallet and handed them to Inga. "Girls why don't you take Kosumi over and rent some skates? Scallop and I are going to take a look around, and then we'll come skate too."

"Yay!" yelled Kosumi, taking his cousins hands. The girls seemed excited too. It was nice to see them having some fun. When they walked away Scallop took Rachel's hand.

"I know why we're here. You think we can do this at our farm. Lucy's showed me their website last fall. I guess that was your idea, huh? You think we can turn it into a kind of agricultural theme park? But I think there are some things you don't understand about farming Rachel. Look at that orchard," he said, gently turning her around, "that orchard alone is three times bigger than our land. Look at this parking lot. It's huge. We don't have the room to do any of this. We wouldn't have any room to grow anything. It would be a farm that wasn't a farm."

"Is that your only objection?", she asked. "If there was a possibility of doing something like this at North Sea Farm would you do it? In order to stay there and have the farm remain in your family, have it remain your family business?"

"I guess," he said reluctantly. "I mean, all these people. Heck, this is nothing! I saw the pictures of how many people come here in the summer and fall. Running an entertainment doesn't really interest me. But losing our home doesn't either." He rubbed his face in frustration.

"Ok. Good. That fits into my plan," she said, grabbing his arm to bring him back. "I think there's a way for us to do this, for you to keep the farm, and for you to keep doing what you do every day. The farm would change, it would have to, but your life wouldn't. If your only objection is the lack of land, I have a solution for that."

"You do?" He didn't know how she could. Could she make land? Did she want to build a hydroponic plant next to his mother's house? Maybe she hadn't gone country enough to realize that wouldn't be the same for him. There were no large tracts of land available anywhere near the farm, certainly not any that they could even begin to afford.

"Scallop," she said firmly, "this is a business proposal I'm about to make. Because, I'm about to offer you a lot. But if you accept it means you'll be stuck with me. Forever. Not just as your partner in life, but as your business partner. Do you want to go there?", she asked. She said it with a smile, as though she were joking, but she knew it was no joking matter. If he said yes, that was it. If he said no, she knew that would be the end too.

He took her chin in his hand and stopped her joking. "Rachel, I want nothing more than for you to be my partner in every way there is. Please tell me what the hell you're talking about."

They called a family meeting the next afternoon. Rachel was relieved that she could conduct this most important meeting in the Koslowski kitchen, in her jeans and a ponytail. She was exhausted from running all over the east and north forks for meetings, pouring over family papers, and from the apprehension she'd felt about asking Scallop to stand with her in asking the rest of the family to take her on.

This time Scallop and Rachel invited Inga and Veronica to sit at the kitchen table with the older members of the family. Their plan involved the girls and they'd both agreed that they should be able to voice their opinions. This time Scallop took charge. He started with a sigh.

"I don't want to leave here. Inga and Veronica, I want this to be your home. I want it to be Kosumi's home. Maybe I'm a coward, but I can't imagine us scattered to the winds, or our fields becoming people's pools. I don't want to do it," he said. He looked around the table and with the exception of Rachel, everyone's eyes had dropped to the quilted placemats in front of them. They all knew this, and they were stealing themselves to have to argue with him that selling was a necessary evil.

"I also want our kids to have a future here. A *real* future where they're running a real business, not sinking deeper and deeper into debt. I don't want Inga being the one dealing with piles of papers filled with bad news like Lucy was. We need to get away from that. Rachel has a plan for us to stay here, and turn this into a different kind of business. It would still be a farm, but a different kind of farm, and I don't mean potatoes instead of carrots. It would mean a few things. First, we'd have to make a lot of changes, second, we'd have to work pretty hard. I know we work hard already, but this would be different, and third, we'd have to give over some control to Rachel. Personally, I'm willing to do that. I think Lucy would be too. She asked Rachel for advice before the accident, and Lucy tried to share her ideas with me, and I dismissed them. I feel bad about that. Rachel's willing to invest a lot of her own money to make the plan work. Anyone object to hearing her thoughts?"

He looked around. The girls looked optimistic. He sensed that his mother was cautiously optimistic too. Tim and Kim seemed concerned, but he went on when they didn't object outright.

"Alright Rachel, why don't you explain the idea. When she's done, I want everyone to say what they really think, ok? Don't hold back. This is the time when we decide we can do this, or we call that guy Dale back, and ask him to give us a little more money."

Tim nodded. Rachel felt a little sorry for Tim and Kim. She could tell that this was exhausting for them. They just wanted out.

"Ok, first, Tim and Kim, I know you're looking forward to your retirement, and I don't see why you can't go forward with that. There are a couple options for you. First, we could subdivide your house from the farm and sell it. I've met with the banks who hold the mortgages and they feel like there's plenty of value in the remaining property to cover the mortgages. You would walk away with all the proceeds after taxes. I had a market analysis done on it and three different real estate agents gave me a ballpark of one and a half million to one million seven hundred fifty. You wouldn't need to contribute anything to the farm in the future or have any responsibilities." She smiled at them when she finished. They both looked shocked. Kim lost ten years in an instant.

"The other option is for you to allow us to buy you out slowly. We would be able to do that within five years. We'd put it in a contract. There's an upside for you if we go that route, you wouldn't have to pay realtor fees, or capital gains taxes, and most importantly your house would remain part of the farm for whichever member of the younger generation wants it,"

She looked at Scallop for some help here, they'd discussed this. "That kid of yours, Richard is pretty attached to this place," Scallop said, "Who knows, he might decide to come back here and be part of the farm. He would get first dibs on your house with Veronica and Inga behind him," Scallop smiled at his brother who quietly shook his head that he understood. Tim turned to his wife and a conversation took place with a look.

"Yup. We'll do that. We already own the house down in St. John, we don't need to walk out of here with a pile of money tomorrow," he snorted, a combination of laughter and resignation, "and you're right about Richard. I've tried to convince him that there are hundreds of other things he could do and hundreds of better places to be than here, but it doesn't seem to be sinking in. If there's a way for us all to be happy, I say we do that."

Rachel smiled at Scallop. They'd had long discussions about the possibility of the change in plans upsetting Kim and Tim. She knew he'd be relieved that this part had gone so smoothly.

"Great. So, the next big part of this plan is my involvement. One of the obstacles to increasing the profitability of this farm is a simple lack of space. I have a solution for that. If we all agree, I'm going to buy two large parcels on the North Fork. It would triple our land. All the vegetables will be grown over there, Scallop will be in charge of that with Pedro and Louis. Part of that business will be a summer school for college kids who are interested in farming. We'll give them glamping quarters, and they'll work the farm while they learn, and their parents will pay us piles of money while their kids work for us." Inga and Veronica both giggled and raised their eyebrows at one another. They knew it would work; their summer friends' parents were always paying for them to do those sorts of things.

"One of the parcels is already an apple orchard with some unused acreage. The best use of that acreage is a Christmas tree farm. It will take a few years to have a harvest obviously, but that orchard will become a destination spot. We'll buy a big boat that leaves from the Peconic Marina, and takes people over there for apple tree picking and Christmas tree cutting."

"Oh, that's awesome! Just like that farm we went to, but with a boat," said Inga enthusiastically. "I'll help with that!"

"Great. I want everyone to understand that the land purchase and the purchase of the boat are my investment in the business. That investment will total just over five million dollars."

Scallop looked around the room to catch the shock on each of his family's faces. He knew they had no idea how much money someone like Rachel made. He hadn't known either. He could see in their looks of incredulity a seed of doubt. Why was she doing this? He turned to her quickly, before she could launch into the next part of her plan and said, "Tell them about the Norwegian bar."

"Oh," said Rachel, caught off guard. She was in the zone. She cleared her throat, "Ok…. so, Thursday night, I'm in Oslo, and I wandered into this ridiculous American-themed bar. It was full of giant Norwegian guys singing that stupid song 'Chicken Fried' at the top of their lungs, and of course I thought of all of you." She winked at Inga. "I looked at your Facebook page, and I saw all the prayers for Lucy, and it was perfectly clear what I had to do; come here. I'm not someone who talks about their feelings, but I'm going to tell you this because I don't want you to think I have any ulterior motives for making you this offer. I don't really have a family, not like this one. In fact, I apologize in advance for the way my family will act when they come here someday. And I don't have a place that feels like home to me. And each day that goes by in my life, I can't help but think that I'm filling my days with activity; I'm staying really busy. But I'm not living really. Not like I want to. Last summer, I met Scallop and I think it was something larger than that silly watch that brought us together. I love this farm. I love spending time with all of you, and spending my days being part of the work around here. So, if you will all have me, I'll have you. We'll be partners. I think we need one another." She looked at Kay, who had been quiet, watching Scallop as Rachel's talked. When she realized Rachel was waiting on her, she closed her eyes and nodded silently. She was passing the care of her son off to Rachel. Rachel felt honored. She hadn't expected that to be so easy. Lucy had told her that her mother thought she was the best thing that had ever happened to Scallop. Now she believed her.

"But you should know, I don't do things half-assed. If you want to let me in here, I'll be in full tilt. I'll run this business as a *business* with Lucy's help, but you'll have to trust me, and you'll have to let me make decisions. How does everyone feel about that?"

"Ok by me!", Inga and Veronica both said at once.

Scallop had walked around behind his mother. He put his hands down gently on her shoulders. "Mom, you would know what Lucy would want. You get two votes."

She reached behind her and took his hand. "I think this is the best of all possible worlds, and I'm sure Lucy would feel exactly the same. We're happy to have you Rachel," she said patting the empty chair next to her at the table for Rachel to sit. When she did, she took Rachel's hand.

"It was something more than a lost watch that brought you here, for sure.

This feels like your home because it is. We're blessed that you're willing to be here with us, and blessed that you're willing to make it possible for all of us to stay here."

Scallop put his other hand on her shoulder, and she knew she'd done the right thing. These people made it easy to forget Scallop's admission. She knew that if she stayed here, it wouldn't be a part of her mental landscape. It would fade in importance as it was replaced with all the good things she knew would come. The parts of Scallop that had attracted her that first night – his humor, his bravery, his connection to this place, and his appreciation for the beauty of life, were his substance. Not something brutal he'd done in anger and sadness. Any niggling doubts she'd had were banished around that kitchen table. She held Kay's hand, hoping that she'd feel the same once she told her the next part of her plan.

"Well, the third part of the plan is the part that you all might not find quite so savory. The use of this property would change. Your house would stay just as it is Kay. You and the Captain would live here with Lucy, Inga and Veronica, just as you do now. But other than that, this farm will be a Disney-meets-hipster attraction for people from the city. We won't grow much here besides pick-your-own flowers, berries, watermelons, pumpkins. There will be a petting zoo and the old barn will be used for weddings and parties. For Halloween, we'll have pumpkin picking, a haunted house, hayrides, a Halloween dance, and anything else that we can think of. Every holiday will be an opportunity for us to make money. We can still close down the farm from New Years until Easter, I'm fine with that. When we get back here, everyone will be focused, recharged, and ready to rock."

"We'll partner with a few of the best local wineries, too - sell their wine in the stand and when we have gatherings here and concerts here. Yes, we'll have concerts. On top of that, I've talked to the local restaurants, and already quadrupled our partnerships with them. And right now, that's where we're at. What's everyone think?"

For a moment no one answered. Then Inga smiled and said, "I think my mom would really like it. She'll be excited when she wakes up."

Veronica reached over and hugged her and nodded her head at Scallop and Rachel.

"Ok then," said Scallop. "We're doing it. Tim, beers all around. Even for the girls."

A month later, Rachel was in the office going over the books. She'd had it spruced up by the contractors who were working on turning the old barn into an event venue, adding a stage and a bar and two rows of rustic chandeliers. Gone were the cardboard boxes full of old tools and tractor parts. She'd had the famous Kozlowski photos rehung on a corkboard wall. She'd bought two matching office chairs for Lucy and herself and she kept Lucy's desk clean, waiting for her return.

It was unseasonably warm, and she'd had a productive morning of visiting the sign shop in town to approve some changes to the sign for the orchard on the North Fork. She'd brought the carpenters who were working on the barn back some muffins and coffee, and spent some time looking over their work. Now she was reviewing the accounting system she'd set up. They'd done a lot in a short time, but in order to have the barn, the boat, and the other farm ready to plant by the spring was going to take every second she had. The office phone, the one that hung next to the doorjamb, rang. It was a call from the hospital. Rachel hung up and ran to the house, her new Danner boots slipping a little on the icy driveway, and then to the new petting zoo building where Scallop was working on stalls. Rachel, Kay and Scallop piled into her car and rushed to Southampton High School to pick up the girls. Within the hour they were peering through the window of the room each of them had visited daily for the last month and a half.

When they entered, the doctor was sitting calmly next to Lucy. Lucy was still hooked up to some of the equipment that had been keeping her alive while she slept, but the feeding tube had been removed and she was propped up and smiling at the four of them as they entered. The twins descended on their mother, sitting on either side of her and hugging her middle. They were curbed by the doctor, who was quick to tell them to be gentle and sent them out to visit with her one by one.

Rachel let the rest of the family go before her in case Lucy tired quickly. But she was still sitting up when Scallop opened the door for Rachel to come in. Lucy patted the bed next to her and Rachel sat down close.

"So," Lucy said, lifting her eyebrow. "I hear we're partners?"

"Partners," Rachel said, mimicking Lucy's look. "Wait until you see our office. It's spiffy."

Lucy smiled. She needed sun, but Rachel could still see the same things she'd seen in Lucy's eyes when they had first met on the beach that first time – fun, love, beaches and fields. "I knew you'd be here."

It was the first day that autumn had a chill in the air. There had been frost on the grass that morning, and leaves tossed in the wind as Christa pulled into the parking lot at Southampton train station in her battered maroon pickup truck, her surfboard rattling around in the back. Late day sunlight pierced through the trees temporarily blinding her as she backed into a parking space.

Christa's twin sister, Shasta, was arriving on the LIRR from New York City. Christa sat on the hood of the truck and listened to the sound of the train in the distance. It always made her imagine a giant mechanical bee barreling into the country, to deposit city detritus everywhere. It was the Thursday before Columbus Day weekend, and as the train doors opened, Shasta was one of the few people who stepped off the train. Tomorrow afternoon there would be pumpkin pickers and concert goers on the same train, many of them would find their way to one or the other of the farms Christa's family owned over the course of the long weekend. But in the fall, Thursday was a quiet night. Shasta smiled and waved to her sister from the platform.

"Christa vista!" Shasta yelled, extending her arm in the air.

"Shasta vasta!" Christa hollered back from the parking lot. They'd found this routine unendingly amusing since they'd been in Kindergarten.

As they hugged, the autumn light exposed their differences. Christa a brunette; Shasta a blonde. Where Christa's skin was dark, Shasta's was light. Their contrasts even extended to their styles. Christa, ever casual, in her fall standard - a lamb colored Patagonia jacket, flip-flops and a denim skirt, and Shasta wearing a chic power suit and carrying a sharp briefcase.

"Love ya sister," Christa said.

"Love you too. How was the ride?"

"Not bad. Any word on the whack job's ETA?"

"Are you kidding? No way. I sent him a text five days ago trying to get some kind of idea when he'd be here and I got back two words, 'by sundown'", she said, tossing her sister's briefcase into the back of the pickup, her long hair blowing in the wind, while Shasta watched in mock disbelief.

"That briefcase cost close to a bazillion dollars you realize?", Shasta said good-naturedly. Christa shrugged and tossed Shasta's suitcase, which she assumed cost two bazillion dollars, into the pickup as well, smiling at her sister.

"Great," said Shasta, "We've got some time to kill. Shall we grab a drink?"

"As usual, I'm one step ahead of you," Christa said. They wove their way through town using the streets only the locals know, streets named after residents from long ago; David White's Lane and Halsey Farm Road. As they drove south towards the ocean, the sight of Mecox Bay made Shasta's mind and body relax. She could feel the stress leaving her like someone had just turned on her bilge pump. The familiar scent of salt air reminded her she was home. They pulled into the empty parking lot at Flying Point Beach and drove straight onto the beach.

Christa parked facing east, got out of the truck, opened the flat bed, and set up two sturdy beach chairs facing west, into the sun. She had a small cooler filled with a six-pack of Blue Point for her, and an open bottle of white for Shasta. She went back to the cab and pulled two blankets, a pair of jeans and a sweatshirt, and some flip flops out from under the seats. Without speaking they did a little ballet, Christa holding up the blankets for Shasta while she changed into the casual clothes her sister had brought her without a grain of sand touching her work clothes.

When she was finished, they wrapped themselves in the blankets and plunked down onto the same mobile Happy Hour lounge set they'd been using since they were seventeen.

"You are always thinking sister," Shasta said, her eyes on a crashing wave.

"Cheers!", Christa said, taking a swig of her beer.

They gazed down the beach, waiting, comfy under their blankets as the sun played with the wind.

They'd spent countless days here growing up, learning to swim and surf. As teenagers they'd been Flying Point lifeguards for six summers. Their lifeguard stand was up the beach, on its side, resting for the off-season. Their names were carved into its northern-most post. They came here whenever they had time.

Everyone in town always said that their parents had gotten their names backwards: Shasta had been the serious one, the competitive athlete who went into business, yet her dad had given her a name that sounded like she'd always be first in line for the next Woodstock revival concert. Christa, whose name had been selected by her mom, was the "free-spirited" art teacher who was known for building giant sculptures of all sorts of leftovers she found after local events, concerts, and beach weekends. But that was just people's way of putting them each in a box. Really, they were both practical, and they were both free spirits, in their own unique ways.

They talked to one another several times a day, in one long, never ending conversation. They were talked out for the moment. They'd spent the last few weeks planning for this weekend, and waiting for their brother. For the first time in three years Tristan was coming home.

A quarter century ago in the middle of an ice storm, Christa and Shasta were born a minute apart at Southampton Hospital. Just under a year later, Tristan was born in the same hospital during a hurricane. Their grandmother had always joked that it was a fitting circumstance for such a boy to be born.

Tristan was a wild one. He was a creature of the sea. He'd howled like a hyena when he'd had to go to kindergarten rather than "help" his dad on their boat. He'd made it through high school and gone to Cal State to study Agriculture, but structure chaffed him, and he'd dropped out to take odd jobs and travel the world. He'd worked as a shepherd in Australia, a day laborer at a quarry in South Africa, a deck hand on fishing boats, and at a Youth Hostel as a jack-of-all-trades in the Greek Islands.

He was finally coming home, finishing his circumnavigation of the globe by walking the south shore of Long Island, from Coney Island, Brooklyn, to Flying Point Beach in Southampton.

He'd only been in touch a few times a year, which drove everyone in the family, aside from his father, mad. They'd spent three years wondering if he was okay, if he was sane, if he was healthy, or hungry, or bewitched by some sorceress on an undiscovered island. He'd been walking the beach on the South Shore for the better part of three weeks.

Christa saw something in the distance and grabbed the binoculars she'd brought. In the distance a solitary person walked the beach carrying a large backpack and a walking stick. He was taking his time.

"I have a visual," Christa said in a deep, mocking voice that she thought sounded military. Half an hour later, almost exactly at dusk, Tristan made it to Flying Point Beach.

"Shall we?", Shasta asked.

"Oh, definitely," her sister answered. They rocketed out of their chairs and down the beach, tackling their brother and throwing him backwards onto his pack. They rolled around hugging and wrestling until Christa climbed off him.

"Oh my God Tristan! You smell like a sweat sock that's had been left in a salty port-a-potty for a decade. *When* was the last time you had a shower, or touched soap?"

"No idea. I'm home," Tristan said. As soon as they stood back to look at him, they could see his profound exhaustion. He looked thin and dehydrated, and his coloring wasn't quite right. The sisters exchanged their concern via a look.

"Yes, you are," Christa said. "Mom will probably make you bathe with the pigs. Let's get you home. You look like you could use a decent meal."

"You did it, you nut job," Shasta said, touching him gently on the shoulder and taking his bag.

They helped him into the truck. They'd have to get him cleaned up and fed before their mother saw him. It was important that he not cause a scene this weekend.

41: Saturday, October 12th, 2041

Two hundred and fifty guests sat beneath the wedding tent at North Sea Farms. Smaller wedding receptions were held inside the barn, but this was not a small wedding.

"Good evening everyone, and welcome," Rachel said into the microphone in the center of the dance floor. Her hair was gray, but at fifty-nine she was tan, fit, and still stylish.

"For those of you who I haven't had the chance to meet yet, my name is Rachel Kozlowski, and I'm Kosumi's mother…well, technically, his stepmother, but I never thought of it that way. I want to welcome you and thank you all for being here tonight. A special thanks to everyone from California and Hawaii who came so far to be with us today. Welcome to North Sea. And thanks to all our local friends for coming too. Since none of you ever want to leave this place, we figured we might as well have the wedding right here; we're set up for it. As you meet people tonight, here's a helpful shortcut, if there's a "ski" at the end of someone's name, they're one of Kosumi's relatives - a cousin, an aunt, an uncle - and they all live within five miles of this very spot. I kid you not people, most of them haven't been over the canal in months…years even," she laughed along with the crowd.

"For those of you that are here visiting, I was once a visitor here also. A city girl who came out here for a work event. The next thing I knew I'd married a local farmer and was running a farm and mothering four kids. So be careful, this place might be gorgeous, but it will suck you in," she joked drifting over to the short table at the head of the dance floor where the bride and groom sat.

"Kosumi, I love you my Dinosaur boy. I've loved you since I first saw you on the beach at Flying Point twenty-five years ago. You brought joy to my life that I didn't know to look for. Your dad and I are so proud of you - your career, your decisions, and you. Everything," Rachel reached down to kiss Kosumi on the cheek and then turned to his bride, "Teagan, we've loved you since the moment we met you. Welcome, darling. We are so glad to have you. But I must warn you…get out while you can! Run! Run fast and keep going! If you don't, the next thing you know, you just might turn out to be me; happy as a pig in the mud, and sometimes as muddy as one, and surrounded by the best family on earth."

Kosumi stood up from the bridal table and hugged his mother. He looked like a darker echo of his father. Tall, with hair that just brushed his square shoulders. He wore his suit with ease, and his eyes sparkled as he bent down to kiss Rachel on the cheek. Rachel held his face between her hands, just for a second, to look at him. He would always be a treasure to her. She knew now that she would have always had children of her own, but Kosumi was hers because he was meant to be, and because she'd been brave. She patted his cheek.

"I'm going to pass over the mic to my husband, now which I'm sure will be entertaining for all of you. If he starts talking about how the Earth needs us, or how the trees can see and feel, or how we should all eat dirt and grass to feel closer to the creator…just sit back and enjoy. Like my marriage to him, it might get weird, but it will be interesting," she joked as the crowd, most of whom were familiar with Scallop's quirks, roared with laughter.

At sixty-five, he still had long hair, with some blonde. As the years passed, it had become streaked with grey, and now there was some white here and there. Deep laugh lines, freckles and permanent dark spots from a life spent in the sun marked his face. He wore a blue suit, still the only one he owned.

"Hello everyone, welcome! My name is Walter Kozlowski, but most folks call me Scallop." He paused for a moment, stopping to do what Rachel called "his setup". He did it whenever he was going to speak from the heart. First he looked at his foot and took a breath and a moment that was just long enough for the people waiting for him to say something to get uncomfortable. Rachel had seen him do it more times than she wanted to count. As people started to look at one another bewildered, he launched in.

"In life, you never know what's going to happen. You really don't. That can be a blessing; it can be a curse; and sometimes what seems like a blessing becomes a curse, and the curses switch spots with the blessings. That's life." Scallop looked at Kosumi and Rachel, standing together.

"In 2012, I was two years out of the military, and really still adjusting to being back here in North Sea after having been gone for a while. Kosumi's mother and I, weren't in particularly great shape at the time, and becoming a father wasn't something I was particularly excited about, or ready for. Then, I was suddenly a single father raising a boy by myself. I couldn't have done it alone. I had my parents, my sister Lucy, her daughters, my brother Tim and his wife and their son Richard. They all helped me out. I know it is a cliché, but it really does 'take a village' to raise a happy healthy little kid. When Kosumi was four, I met Rachel, which was the best thing that ever happened to me. For most women, a guy with a kid would have been a nonstarter. Rachel became Kosumi's mother, and she did it just as well as she does everything else. My wife walked away from a life of privilege to be with me and Kosumi. I think Kosumi might have been the main attraction. Rachel and I got married and had the twins and Tristan, but Kosumi has the special, first place in my heart; because for a while there, it was just the two of us, living in the tiny cottage down on the beach, with a wood burning stove to get us through the winter, and some bean bags that were our forts, and our furniture. Over the years as Kosumi grew, we all got to see the special person he was becoming. A kind, smart, loving young man who loved the Earth he is so happy to be living on. Kosumi and I have climbed Denali, hiked the Appalachian Trail and the Pacific Crest Trail, and shared some truly special moments while doing it.

I know his mom is so proud that he's parlayed his love of Wind Surfing into a successful company. While I'm just glad he's outside. But we are most proud of Kosumi's decision to marry Teagan. Your marriage will be wonderful, if you choose to make it so. My best to both of you as you set off on this journey. Kosumi, my boy, I can't imagine my life without you in it. You are the greatest blessing I've had. I love you, my son." Scallop hugged both Kosumi and Teagan with tears in his eyes.

Lucy was looking on from her table nearest the house. She could see Scallop winding up to launch in again and she made a bee line for the DJ and prompted him to start the couple's first dance. It was time to get the party started. She and her husband Craig had been looking forward to this night for months. Lucy planned to dance herself right out of her dress.

As the night wore on, Scallop and Rachel passed from table to table together, saying hello to the new in-laws and their other guests. Normally with such a large wedding at the farm, Rachel would have been weaving through the crowd, supervising staff and anticipating snags - never allowing a hiccup. But, by now the farm's staff was so experienced at serving large weddings that she had decided she would just let them do their thing. She knew they would all want to make Kosumi's wedding perfect for his own sake.

Kosumi had been very particular with the DJ, and the music was a mix of classic wedding songs, "Put a Ring on It", "Chicken Dance" and the like, seventies nature rock, and country. Scallop and Rachel were out on the dance floor for "Just a Little Louder" when the DJ got around to Stevie Wonder's "Superstitious", which was a very particular joke between Tim and Rachel. Neither one of them knew how it had come about, but over the years they'd somehow developed a full-blown dance routine for it and they did it with spirit.

On the final chord everyone's laughter was interrupted by the Kozlowski kids standing at the microphone.

Shasta thumped the microphone to ensure it was on, and cleared her throat as her siblings tittered behind her. "Hello everyone! We have a special surprise for all of you. Would you all take a little field trip across the street? There are glow sticks at your places. Crack them open and head for the fire trucks! Our daddy's buddies from the fire department have volunteered to make sure we all get across the street safely. We'll lead the way."

Noyac Road lit up with wedding guests wrapped in pink and yellow glow sticks. Diners at the Coast Grill craned to see what was happening, as floating colors passed the windows. The guests filed onto the dock trying not to snag their heels between the dock's boards, or fall off the edges into the water. Most of the guests were game for the little adventure. Rachel's stepmother, was complaining to those in front and behind her that she was cold in the ocean air. Someone had taken great pains to set up a microphone at the end of the dock. Guests lined the dock and the bulkhead as the Kozlowski children gathered around the microphone.

"Ok," said Christa into the microphone, "We promise, this will be worth it."

Then Kosumi stepped in.

"If you don't know, today is my parents' twenty-fifth wedding anniversary. They met right up there at the Coast Grill," he said. Congratulations and whoops went up from the crowd.

"My mother was here for a work event, and one of her guests, a batty rich lady with too much jewelry on her wrists, if you believe my dad's description, dropped her watch into this water behind us. Mom went looking for a hero, and she found dad inside the Coast Grill. He volunteered to find it. Mom was doubtful he could do it, particularly once she saw the wild getup he uses for diving," she laughed.

It was Tristan's turn at the mic. They'd all planned to do just a bit of the story. "But mom didn't know that dad is the master of these waters. He got his nickname diving for Scallops out in the middle of the bay. I've been around the world and I've never seen someone dive like my dad, even when it's their job," he said handing the mic off to Shasta.

"So tonight, to celebrate our parents' anniversary and marriage, we have a special treat for all of you. Behind us, twenty feet deep in the water, is a well-lit target, and behind that is a special present from all of us to our parents. Dad, do you think you have it in you? If not, I guess *I* could give it a try. The water is cold; you might just want me to do it."

Scallop begrudgingly walked to the end of the dock. They threw him his bathing suit and a towel, which is all any lifelong surfer needs to get changed. Kosumi stood by, taking the pieces of Scallop's suit as he wiggled out of them beneath the towel. Shasta ran over to the farm's boat, docked where it was waiting to take apple pickers across the bay in the morning, and grabbed up a jumble of tubes. Rachel laughed hysterically as she saw her hand the mess over to her father. She didn't know where the kids had found Scallop's old gear. Scallop must have stashed it somewhere she could never find it. because after twenty-five years she definitely would have thrown that mess out if she could. He put his getup on, being careful not to pull too hard on the goggles, lest the old strap snap.

Scallop dove into the water with a liquid smoothness that belied his years and quickly made his way to the shining yellow light that marked his target. His children had managed to find the deepest spot off the marina. He was proud that they knew their stuff. He was slower than he once was, that was certain, but he made the dive easily, breaking out of the water forty seconds later holding a small box. He held it up in the air as he surfaced, just like he had Swizzle Hooper's watch.

Scallop handed the box to Kosumi, and pulled himself onto the dock, where the girls wrapped him in towels.

All the guests clapped. Some were impressed with the dive but everyone was impressed with his ability to withstand the cold waters, many of them looking to Rachel to see if she echoed their concern. She was unfazed, Scallop still maintained his daily fitness routine. An early fall dip was nothing.

"Thanks Dad. Now for what's inside! We contacted the family of the late Swizzle Hooper, the owner of the watch that was dropped in the water here so long ago. We told her daughter our story, and asked about buying the watch from her. She thought the story was so cool, she just gave it to us," Kosumi said, as he presented the open box to his parents. "We love you Mom and Dad," the kids all said together as Scallop and Rachel held up the framed Rolex.

The party made its way back across the street, where a band made up of some of Kosumi's high school buddies was set up for a long set to close out the evening.

Three songs in, the band dedicated one to Rachel, who was pushed to the center of the dance circle. She would recognize the first few chords of "Chicken Fried" to her dying day. She tried to make an escape but Scallop caught her and escorted her back to the center of the circle so that she could do his favorite dance. Secretly, she didn't mind the song anymore. In fact, she liked it. When she was done, Scallop walked over, picked her up by her waist, and held her like a child, which he was surprised he could still do. He lowered his wife down slowly, and gave her a kiss as he placed her gently on the ground in the middle of the circle, and they hugged one another as hard as they could. They both knew what the other was thinking, they were lucky, they were safe, they were meant to be together in this place.

THE END

Acknowledgments

I'd like to thank my wife, Kristi, and my children Declan, Rosie, Lucy and Teagan. When I began writing this book, I was sitting in my car on a snowy morning in the parking lot of the New York Aquarium in Coney Island. Declan was asleep in the back as I waited for the aquarium to open. Rose and Lucy were a few months old and Teagan wasn't born yet. Kristi has stood by me as I worked on, talked about and obsessed over this story. She has shown tremendous support and encouragement and that is one of the many reasons I'm lucky to be married to her. Love you!

Thank you to my parents, family and close friends who've encouraged me with this project; especially those from Southampton Shores, who all played little parts in this novel. I hope to see you all soon.

I'd also like to thank my good friend, college classmate and relative by marriage, the superbly talented, insanely committed, otherworldly focused and tremendously gifted Amy Wallace, who edited this book. Without Amy, this book doesn't exist. She saw potential in the idea, and was willing to lend a huge amount of time to help make this book into a reality. A special thanks to her husband, "My Cousin Vinny" Wallace, and their daughter Lily, who had to endure many nights where Amy was in her office working on what you just read. Thank you, Amy! You never oscillated!

Thank you to The Shinnecock Indian Nation for giving me a tour and educating me on their rich, interesting history. I'd also like to that thank the farmers, local merchants, first responders and residents of North Sea, Southampton, New York for inspiring this tale. It's a special place that's loved by many. Including me, in case that wasn't obvious.

And lastly, thank you. God Bless, be well and don't be a stranger.